LYDIA HARTE

BY

TED KOZAK

Who needs justice when you carry a big gun?

This is a work of fiction, and the places, persons, events, and organizations depicted in this novel are creatures of the author's mind. Any resemblance to any person, living or deceased, is entirely coincidental. However, it must be kept in mind that the author is highly familiar with the City of Los Angeles and its institutions so that it almost impossible to write about such a city without some reference to them.

Published 2019 by Midnight Star Press

MIDNIGHT
STAR PRESS.

ISBN-13: 978-1-7339231-1-8

ALSO BY TED KOZAK

Alex and Christina—Saving Lumenaria
The Messiah's Spy
Teresa—The Snake Witch
Charlie Wolf's Revenge
Charlie Wolf's Justice

Special thanks to Michelle Van Hoof, Jim Kerr, and Virginia Kozak who made suggestions for improvement of the manuscript that led to this book.

Any errors in the manuscript, unfortunately, are mine alone.

CHAPTER ONE

Summer 2005

LYDIA HARTE lied about why she wanted to be a police officer on her employment application; she lied during the employment interview to a panel consisting of two LAPD sergeants and a Personnel Department human resources specialist; and she lied to Sergeant Hector Maldonado from LAPD's Intelligence Division about her knowledge of her stepfather's ties with organized crime.

The only person who knew she lied was Maldonado. He cleared Lydia for employment as a police officer because he wanted to find out what she knew about her mother's supposedly accidental death and what she intended to do if she learned it wasn't accidental. He was not about to tell any of the people who interviewed Lydia why she wanted to join the police department, because if he had, they would have never recommended her for employment.

Lydia Harte was hired by the City of Los Angeles because no one else knew she lied about her reasons for wanting to be a Los Angeles police officer. She excelled at the Police Academy, becoming the first woman to reach the top of her class in the Physical Fitness Test. She outran everyone in her class, leaving in the dust an ex-professional football player on the Academy training staff who had never been beaten in a foot race by a recruit.

Stung by defeat at the hands of the young woman, the former athlete reviewed her personnel file and was astonished at what he found. Three months prior to entering the Police Academy, Lydia Harte was on the

UCLA's women's track team beating everyone she ran against in the 440-meter and 440-meter hurdle events. Her coach at UCLA told the Personnel background investigator that Lydia could easily qualify in both events for the 2008 Summer Olympics in Beijing.

The former athlete found that Lydia's academic grades at the Police Academy were near the top, but she was a so-so marksman. He didn't know Lydia had never touched a gun before she joined the Police Department, although she had once lived in her stepfather's mansion with an underground vault holding a collection of nearly every handgun made in the last 100 years.

Following graduation from the Police Academy on November 5, 2005, Lydia reported for work at LAPD's Century Division in West Los Angeles with four of her Academy classmates, none of whom she knew well. She didn't want to know them. She didn't join LAPD to make friends.

The new recruits were greeted by the Captain, a dark-featured man with squinty eyes named Tomas Kemper. He welcomed them to the division, preached a very short but obligatory sermon about community relations, and told them to report to Lieutenant Morton on P.M. Watch.

When Lydia got up to leave Kemper's office, he stopped her, saying he wanted to have a private word with her.

"I understand you're related to Milo Benedict."

Kemper stared at her with those squinty eyes as if he didn't quite believe what he was seeing. It was understandable. Milo was grossly ugly. Lydia was not.

"He's my stepbrother, sir."

Kemper nodded as if that explained everything. "He's a good man."

"Yes, sir," replied Lydia in neutral tone, not wanting Kemper to know how much she detested the little creep.

"He's one of our best reserve officers," Kemper continued. "I've been trying to convince him to go regular. We could use a man like him."

"Yes," Lydia replied, thinking it would be a cold day in hell before Milo became a regular police officer. He was making too much money working for his father, Jonathan Benedict.

"Haven't seen him for a while. When you do, tell him to drop in for a chat."

"I will," Lydia said, hoping Kemper would stop talking about her stepbrother and let her go.

On her first day of work in uniform, Lydia and her four classmates made the mistake of taking seats in the back row of the roll call room. The officers filing in looked at the newcomers in amusement as they walked by. They took their seats, shaking their heads, saying nothing.

A tall officer, who Lydia later discovered was named Jim Searles, entered the roll call room. He stopped and looked down at the five rookies.

"Why are these assholes sitting in my row?" Searles asked in a booming voice.

Searles was a tall man with a thin face and narrow shoulders. He smelled of stale tobacco smoke, and his crumpled uniform hadn't seen the inside of a dry cleaners for more than a week.

"They don't know any better," said one of the officers from up front.

"I think you people need to move," Searles said, glaring down on the rookies.

The five rookies got up and took a seat in the next row.

"Rookies sit up front," Searles said, "and stay there until they pass probation."

The five rookies got up again and took seats in the front row. There were three other probationers already seated there. One of them, a woman with ash blonde hair and the face of a teenager barely out of high school leaned over to the newcomers and whispered, "You need to stay away from those guys in back."

Lydia nodded her thanks even though she had already figured that out.

Lieutenant Morton, a tall man with ginger hair, strikingly handsome, entered the roll call room with his assistant, an elderly sergeant with a dead face named Cooley.

The first thing Morton did after Cooley read off the assignments for that evening was to have the five rookies stand up and introduce themselves. The result was one mean-spirited insult after another hurled at the newcomers.

When Lydia's turn came to introduce herself, there were a few wolf whistles, which Morton put to a stop by rising to his feet and glaring menacingly at the miscreants.

Lydia was surprised that no one in the roll call room seemed aware she had a stepbrother who worked in the same division as a reserve officer. This was fine by her because Milo was not someone she liked to be associated with.

Lydia was assigned to work a patrol car with two street coppers named Robbie Cruz and Rick Mosby. Whenever Mosby was off, she would work with Cruz and vice versa when Cruz was off. She quickly discovered that even though Cruz and Mosby received extra pay as training officers, neither of them liked having to work with probationers. They made it clear at the outset that working with a rookie slowed down their style. The irony was they were lazy as all hell, which caused Lydia to wonder why they were selected to be training officers in the first place.

Once in roll call, Lydia overheard Cruz loudly telling another officer that he thought the only place a woman belonged in a police car was in the back seat with her legs spread open. Lydia wondered if Cruz had ever heard of sexual harassment or even knew that female police officers were told that anytime they were subjected to harassment while on duty, they should bypass their supervisors and report the incident directly to the Woman's Coordinator in the Chief's office.

But Lydia didn't care. She had more important things to worry about. Like how to gain access to the computers in the detective squad room without being seen. She quickly found out that it was nearly impossible to do so. There was always someone in the detective squad room, even late at night.

CHAPTER TWO

LYDIA FOUND most police work to be tedious and boring. But she would not find out until much later when assigned to a more proactive partner by the name of Dick Hagerty that the reason police work seemed boring was because Cruz and Mosby carefully avoided doing anything requiring initiative.

The area where she worked with her two uninspiring partners was an eclectic neighborhood of residential homes, apartments, and retail businesses located in the southern end of Century Division, a far cry from the large area at the northern end of the Division that included some of the wealthiest residents and most successful businesses in the City as well as a major university and the headquarters of the Los Angeles field office of the FBI.

Her shifts on patrol typically included handling calls for service that involved helping people in crisis, taking crime reports, defusing family disputes that couldn't be defused, and writing traffic citations to pissed-off motorists. In between calls, she and her indifferent partners patrolled their assigned area for hours on end in the hope of catching a criminal in the act of committing a crime. Her chances of doing the latter were minimal with Cruz and Mosby as partners.

Friday and Saturday nights were the busiest. The shift would start off slowly, but by 8:00 p.m., it would get busy with units sometimes getting as many as five or six calls at a time. When it got busy, Cruz would try to find a drunk driver to arrest so they could get out of the field and into the station for an hour or two where Cruz would have a cup of coffee and relax while watching Lydia write up the arrest and vehicle impound reports.

In her first two weeks on the job, the only excitement Lydia experienced was catching a "211 in progress" call at a bank on Wilshire Boulevard. The adrenaline she experienced by the wild ride to the bank where a reported robbery was in progress quickly abated when she and Cruz entered the bank with guns drawn and learned that the teller had accidentally hit the alarm button.

Lydia Harte made no friends with the other officers who were serving their probationary periods in Century Division. She didn't need any more friends than she already had, and more importantly, she didn't join the Los Angeles Police Department to expand her social life. She had her boyfriend, Jake Nilsson, and plenty of other friends from UCLA.

One Friday night, she unexpectedly found herself without a partner. Mosby was on a day off and Cruz had called in sick, and Lydia didn't find out until Lieutenant Morton began reading off the assignments at roll call. She was assigned to her regular car, but the name of the officer assigned to partner with her was totally unexpected.

It was Jim Searles, the bastard who kicked her and her classmates out of their seats in the back row of the roll call room on their first day of work.

Searles loudly protested being assigned to work with Lydia. "Goddammit, Lieutenant, I don't work with fucking boots!"

The Lieutenant looked up. "Calm down, Searles. It's just for one night."

"I don't get paid to work with recruits."

"Too fucking bad. You work where I say you work."

"I don't like it."

The Lieutenant turned his attention back to the assignment sheet.

Searles persisted. "What about my regular partner?"

Morton looked up. "Jackson will be working the front desk."

Someone from the back of the room said, "Shit."

Lydia assumed the comment came from Jackson.

"Why can't *she* work the front desk?" Searles asked.

"Why don't you just fucking shut up?" Morton said.

Most of the experienced officers who worked in the Century Patrol Division were training officers who regularly worked with probationary officers and held an advance paygrade position for their efforts. But the six officers who sat in the back row on P.M. Watch held a lesser paygrade and didn't work with recruits as a matter of choice. They considered themselves to be an elite group and called themselves the Wrecking Crew. They sat in the last row during roll call, making wisecracks and farting on command whenever the Watch Commander said something they didn't like.

Since they were not assigned to a specific district, they worked special problems, such as patrolling an area that had an identifiable crime pattern. They were not assigned radio calls unless the patrol cars assigned to specific districts were overwhelmed by the sheer volume of calls and unable to handle the workload.

But occasionally, the six officers in the back row were assigned to work with a rookie when the rookie's partners were off duty. And working with a raw recruit pissed them off no end as Lydia discovered when she heard the exchange between Lieutenant Morton and Searles.

Lydia was not in a happy mood either as she carried a shotgun and two riot helmets out to the parking lot to find her assigned car. Searles had stayed inside the station presumably because he wanted to talk to Lieutenant Morton about being assigned to a fucking probationer or boot as he called a police officer fresh out of the Academy.

She found her assigned car and threw Searles' helmet violently into the back of the trunk, creating a loud *thunk* that caused other officers to turn and look at her. Ignoring them, she noisily racked back the slide of the shotgun and loaded it with five rounds of double-aught buckshot.

The officers who saw her in the parking lot as she loaded the shotgun would later tell Lieutenant Grayson of the Officer-Involved-Shooting Team that Officer Harte seemed to be in an awfully angry mood that Friday evening.

CHAPTER THREE

LYDIA WAITED in the police car for five minutes and Searles still hadn't come out of the station. She decided to go back inside and see what was keeping him.

The first place she looked for Searles was the Watch Commander's office. Lieutenant Morton was sitting at his desk with his head down over several watch assignment sheets scattered in front of him. Sergeant Cooley was seated at a desk opposite Morton writing something with a pencil on a yellow legal tablet.

Searles wasn't there, so Lydia turned and walked down the hall to the detective squad room where an area had been reserved for patrol officers to write reports. She saw Searles in one of the soundproofed, prisoner holding cells with glass windows. The door was shut. He was pacing the floor, his head down, talking to someone on a cell phone, and animatedly throwing his free hand from side to side as if trying to make a point.

Lydia watched him for a while and then went back out to the police car to wait.

Searles hardly spoke to Lydia during the first three hours of the watch. At one point, he turned to her and asked if there were any specific crime problems in her district. Even though Lydia was certain that Searles was trying to humiliate her, she tried to answer by saying she had been told the biggest problem in the area was business burglaries.

Searles seemed interested. "What kind of burglaries?"

"Business."

"You already said that. What kind of businesses?"

"Retail stores. They've been hitting stores with big box items like televisions and sound systems. We had one store where most of the inventory in the back room had been taken."

"Where was that?"

"It was a box store in the Evergreen Mall."

Searles grunted.

"We also have a few residential burglaries," Lydia added.

Searles didn't respond. He didn't seem interested, so Lydia kept her mouth shut.

As the evening set in, Lydia noticed they had not once entered their assigned patrol area. Searles followed a random pattern, driving through the area between Wilshire and Santa Monica Boulevards but never going farther than Sepulveda to the west.

By 8:30 p.m., it got busy and they were assigned five calls simultaneously. The calls were scattered across the division, ranging from a report of a stolen car in a high rise on Wilshire Boulevard near Westwood to a drunk pestering pedestrians for money in Century City. When a unit received multiple calls that didn't require an emergency response, it was up to the officer's discretion which call to handle first.

Lydia picked up the mike and acknowledged the calls. After a few moments, she turned to Searles. "Which one are we going to handle first?"

"Which what?"

"The calls we were assigned."

Searles drove for a few moments before responding. "They'll keep."

This answer puzzled the hell out of Lydia. One of the reasons they were out on the streets in a patrol car in the first place was to respond to calls for assistance made by the public, yet Searles made no effort to respond to any of them.

A few minutes later, Lydia decided she needed to say something. "I don't understand. What do you mean they'll keep?"

"Just that! Not one of these calls have any legs to them. Whatever problems these people have will go away. Why waste our time when we're doing real police work?"

"But what about the stolen vehicle report?" Lydia asked.

"What about it?"

"It's not going to go away."

"They'll get tired of waiting and either go to the station or call it in again. Then we'll handle it." He looked at Lydia with a weird smile on his face. "I take it that you prefer handling calls than doing real police work."

Lydia resisted telling him they had not been doing real police work for the past four hours. They hadn't done a fucking thing since they left the station except drive around in lazy circles.

"Part of our job is handling radio calls," Lydia said. "That's what we get paid for."

The weird smile never left Searles' face. "Alright," he said. "Let's go and see if we can catch this dangerous drunk. It's not far from here."

The drunk was gone when they got there, and Searles looked at Lydia with that unsettling smile. "See what I mean. The drunk is gone. Problem solved. So, we answered the call and what the fuck did we accomplish?"

Lydia didn't answer.

Searles made no effort to handle any of the other assigned calls until the person who reported the stolen vehicle called back and demanded an esti- mated time of arrival for the police unit. Then and only then did Searles head in the direction of the call.

Lydia took the report in less than fifteen minutes, and after broadcast- ing a description of the stolen car, they were back on patrol.

At around ten o'clock, they had handled just three of their assigned ra- dio calls and had made no traffic stops. Lydia began wondering what the hell was going on. Were there many police officers on the force like Searles who didn't give a shit? And what was he looking for? He continued to drive the same pattern aimlessly. Was he looking for someone or for some- thing about to happen?

Shortly after ten o'clock, the radio crackled to life and the dispatcher, a woman in a calm and measured tone of voice, announced, "Any unit in the vicinity, a 459 alarm at 1455 South Gardiner."

To Lydia's surprise, Searles picked up the mike and acknowledged the call. She stared at him as he stepped on the accelerator.

Searles looked at her and said. "This is the kind of break I've been hop- ing for. Gardiner is only two blocks away."

The warehouse at 1455 Gardiner was a monolithic brick structure occupying most of an entire block. From the street, it looked abandoned, the front door boarded up, the windows high enough that kids could not break them—unless they had a slingshot or b.b. gun.

A sign above the front door read, AKHEISER STORAGE FACILITY.

"I know this building," Searles mumbled. "It used to be a supply house for the construction trade."

Searles turned into a wide alley alongside the south side of the building and then into a huge parking lot located in the back.

A loading dock ran along the rear of the building. It was divided in the middle by a ramp leading to a door large enough for a big rig to pass through. Searles confidently drove up the ramp into the cavernous building as if he had been there before and knew what was inside. He stopped the police car just inside the building.

Directly in front of the police car were two rows of shipping containers creating a long aisle that led to the front of the building. Parked halfway down the aisle was a large box truck that was facing them. The driver's side door was open, but there was no one in or around the truck.

Lydia stepped out of the car, letting her hand fall on the butt of her Beretta FS.

It was dark inside the cavernous building, the only light coming through the high windows was from street lamps outside the building. Lydia reached into the back seat of the police car and retrieved her flashlight.

"Put out a Code Four," Searles said.

"What?"

"A Code Four. Don't they teach shit like that at the Academy anymore?"

Astonished, Lydia stared at him for a moment. A Code Four meant that the police unit had things under control and didn't need back up.

Searles threw her an angry shrug that meant for her to get on with it.

Why, Lydia thought, *would he want to put out a Code Four when we haven't even checked out the place?*

Lydia reached into the car, picked up the mike, and broadcasted a Code Four. When Lydia finished making the call, she looked up and saw Searles staring doubtfully at the truck.

"It's probably a customer who doesn't know how to turn on the lights," Searles said. "Let's check it out."

Lydia walked cautiously toward the truck with Searles to the left of her. When she got there, she flashed her light up into the front window of the cab and confirmed no one was inside.

She looked at Searles.

He signaled her to move toward the back of the truck. He took the left side of the truck, Lydia the right side.

Lydia shifted the flashlight to her left hand and tugged lightly on the butt of the Beretta to make sure it was loose in the holster. When she passed the cab, she flashed her light up onto the side of truck. A sign indicated it was a rental.

When she got to the rear of the truck, she found that Searles was already there. The rollup door was open and Searles was playing his flashlight into the interior of the cargo bay. Except for a few shipping blankets, it was empty. Lydia turned her flashlight on the locks of the shipping containers on either side of her. They were secure.

She looked at Searles. It occurred to Lydia that he seemed far too casual for this type of call. He had not even unfastened the clasp of his holster.

Searles headed back toward the police car.

Lydia followed.

Searles unexpectedly darted off to the left and down a wide aisle that ran across the back of the warehouse.

Lydia paused for a second, wondering what he was doing and why he was not communicating with her. She shrugged and followed him.

As it turned out, there were several more rows of shipping containers on the north side of the building with aisles wide enough to let a small truck through. When they got to the last row of containers, Searles stopped and shone his flashlight down the aisle.

Halfway down the aisle was a container with an opened door.

No one was around.

"You go down and check it out," Searles said. "I'll check out the offices."

Lydia stared at Searles as he walked into the gloom.

Didn't they teach at the Academy that the worst thing you could do was to split up from your partner?

Lydia had by now resigned herself to the fact that there was a disconnect between what was taught at the Academy and what was actually practiced by officers in the field.

When she got to the shipping container with the open door, she shone her flashlight inside.

It was empty.

She looked around and paused for a moment thinking. What was this place? If this was a typical storage place where you could rent a locker or shipping container and wanted to access it at your convenience, why would it have an alarm on it? Customers couldn't be relied on to turn the alarm off every time they entered.

Retracing her steps to the end of the aisle, Lydia looked off to the left where Searles had disappeared.

Beyond the last row of containers was an open door to an office. It was dark inside and Searles was nowhere in sight.

She cautiously approached the door and looked inside.

The office was large and backlit by light coming from the high windows at the front of the building. Two long rows of desks, dusty and dirty, stretched across the room, paper and pieces of fallen ceiling were strewn everywhere. It looked like a sales room that had been hastily abandoned.

Hadn't Searles said he would check out the offices?

How did he know there were offices back there? Had he been here before?

And where in hell did he go?

Lydia saw another door across the room. It was partly open, but she couldn't see what was on the other side because it was dark. She heard voices, low and indistinct, coming from the room on the other side of the door. Lydia paused trying to hear what was being said but couldn't make out the words. The first thought that came to her mind was that Searles might be in trouble.

"Searles!"

No answer.

Lydia removed the Beretta FS from her holster and slowly moved toward the door. "Searles, are you in there?"

The voices stopped.

Lydia stopped and listened. She could not hear anything. She began moving toward the half-open door again when it was suddenly and violently flung open.

The silhouetted form of a large man with narrow shoulders materialized in the doorway.

Lydia brought up her flashlight. She saw gloved hands holding a dark object that was pointing at her.

Before she could react, a flash of orange flame, nearly two feet long, jumped out at her, accompanied by a deafening roar that rattled the windows.

A massive force hit Lydia in the stomach like a sledgehammer. She stumbled backwards and fell, smacking the back of her head on the concrete floor.

She tried to sit up but was overcome by dizziness. A sharp pain roiled in her stomach like boiling water, causing her eyes to water. She blinked her eyes and tried to clear her mind, but her thoughts seemed to be drifting away.

A shadowy figure appeared above her. Lydia could make out a hand holding a gun. It was being extended toward her face.

Lydia called up barely enough strength to raise her Beretta. She pulled the trigger and the blast echoed through the building.

A few seconds later, Lydia heard another shot and then blacked out.

CHAPTER FOUR

LYDIA DIDN'T know how long she had been in the hospital when the fog finally lifted, and she could think. For days, she was half-conscious, aware only of the feeling that she was floating, her mind drifting as if it didn't want to be engaged in the real world. Occasionally, she felt a stabbing pain in her abdomen and cried out. A blurred figure in white would come, do something next to her bed, and the pain would go away.

Slowly, Lydia became aware she was in a hospital bed in a room all by herself. She felt uncomfortable and tried to turn on her side. A bell started ringing in some far-off place.

A nurse came in, looked at her, and said, "Lie still, honey. I'll be right back."

Lydia tried to ask where she was, but no words would come out of her mouth. She tried to sit up. A shooting pain ripped through her stomach, and she screamed.

The nurse came quickly back to her side and looked at the drip line. "You shouldn't move, honey. You don't want to tear out the stitches."

Through watery eyes, Lydia saw the nurse was doing something to a drip line hooked to her right arm.

"There," the nurse said in a soothing voice. "This will make you feel better in a few seconds." The nurse looked down at her, concern in her eyes. "You're perspiring."

The nurse took her temperature and then disappeared for a few seconds. When she came back, she wiped Lydia's forehead with a wet towel.

"Go to sleep, honey. You're going to be alright, but you need to rest. Go to sleep."

Two days later, Lydia woke and found she was no longer in a fog. Someone touched her arm, and she turned to look. A doctor was standing alongside her bed. He asked Lydia what her name was, and she told him, her voice slurred, her tongue feeling as if it were coated with peanut butter. When he asked if she remembered what happened to her, she paused for moment and then told him that she thought someone had shot her.

She paused for a moment, thinking.

That can't be right!

She was wearing a bullet resistant vest.

Why didn't it protect her?

It took her a few moments to work out that the vest covered her upper torso and didn't cover the abdomen.

The doctor told her she was doing well and might be well enough to be discharged from the hospital in a week or so. She had been in the operating room for six hours. They would remove the colostomy bag in two days and put her on a special diet.

What colostomy bag? Lydia wasn't even aware she had a colostomy bag.

When the doctor asked if she felt any pain, Lydia answered yes. When she was asked if she wanted something to relieve the pain, she said no. She wanted to remember what happened to her. The pain would make sure of that.

When the doctor began to explain what had been done to her since her arrival in the hospital, Lydia interrupted him. "Do you know what happened to my partner?"

The doctor sat down in a chair next to the bed and said nothing.

Lydia shifted in the bed, so she could see him. She grimaced when she felt a ripple of pain in her lower abdomen.

"You need pain medication," the doctor said, gently.

Lydia shook her head and stared at him.

The doctor was young, in his early thirties, movie star handsome, deeply tanned with a look of friendly concern on his face. His name tag said he was Doctor Garrett.

"No more pain medicine," Lydia said.

"Alright, it's up to you. But if you need it, just ask."

"You didn't answer my question, doctor."

"What question?"

"What happened to my partner?"

"There are some detectives who want to talk to you. They will tell you what happened."

Lydia frowned. "Did I shoot someone?"

"All I know is what I read in the papers."

"I haven't been able to read a newspaper. What do they say?"

"The papers say that you and your partner were shot while investigating a burglary. They don't know who did the shooting."

"What happened to Searles?"

"Who is Searles?"

"My partner."

"He died."

Lydia held a hand to her face.

"I'm sorry," the doctor said. "Were you friends?"

Lydia remembered she had fired one shot at a silhouetted form after she had been shot. Did she manage to shoot her own partner? If so, she was going to need an attorney. She turned toward the doctor.

"Can you keep them from seeing me until I get an attorney."

"I can," the doctor said. "What about visitors? Your father and a young man named Jake Nilsson have been wanting to see you. He says he's your fiancé."

Lydia bit her lip. "He's not my father."

The doctor looked away. "Your stepfather then? Do you want to see them?"

Lydia hesitated and then said yes.

The doctor smiled. After a moment, his face became serious. "Miss Harte, I need to talk to you about your injuries and what you can expect in the future."

It was quiet for a moment while Lydia stared at him. She shifted a little and felt another stab of pain in her abdomen. Finally, she said, "I think I know what you're going to tell me."

He nodded slightly.

"I will never be able to have any children," Lydia said.

"I'm sorry. There was a lot of interior damage we couldn't repair."

Lydia didn't say anything. She bit her lip and looked up at the ceiling. After a moment, she looked at the doctor, a tear running down her cheek. "You were my surgeon?"

"I was one of them." The doctor stood up and looked away. "I'm sorry Miss Harte. I wish I…" He turned and looked down at her. "If you need anything, just ask."

What I need, Lydia thought, *is a fucking gun!*

"Well, I…" The doctor turned to go. "I'm sorry," he said abruptly.

Lydia stopped him as he was about to leave the room. "Doctor, I've changed my mind about visitors. I don't want to see anyone. And I don't want to talk to the police until I'm ready to go back to work. Can you make that happen?"

"You really should see your father and your beau. They're worried about you."

Lydia frowned. *Who in hell ever used the word 'beau' anymore?*

"You just said to ask if I wanted anything, doctor."

"I did."

"Then issue an order saying I can't see anyone until I'm cleared to go back to work."

The doctor stepped forward, started to say something, but then stopped. Lydia stared at him. The doctor was hesitating.

Was there more bad news?

After a moment, the doctor said, "Miss Harte, I will do what you ask, but I'm afraid you will not be able to do any work that requires physical effort for a long time. People are very different when it comes to recovering from the kind of trauma you have experienced. Some people do very well. Others don't. But in my opinion, it is unlikely you'll ever work as a police officer again."

A few days later, Jake Nilsson showed up in her room, a benign smile on his face, a dozen yellow roses in his hand. Lydia grimaced when she saw him. The yellow roses didn't help either. Lydia detested yellow. She thought Jake knew that.

"How are you?" Jake asked.

Lydia stared at him for a moment before answering. "How did you get in here?"

Jake offered the flowers to Lydia.

She didn't take them.

"What's wrong?"

Lydia looked out the window. It was a beautiful day outside.

"What's wrong?" Jake repeated.

Lydia turned toward him so suddenly that the pain caused her to grimace. "Didn't you get my message?"

"I did." Jake looked away nervously.

"I meant what I said, Jake. I don't want to see you again. I thought I made myself clear."

"But, Lydia, maybe..."

Lydia picked up the call button and pressed it.

"Lydia..."

A minute later, a nurse came into the room.

"I left instructions I didn't want visitors."

"But this man said he was your fiancé."

"He's not. Please show him the way out."

Lydia thought a lot about what had happened in the warehouse on the night she was shot as she lay in her hospital bed. A lot of things didn't make any sense. It bothered her that Searles ordered her to put out a Code Four before they even had a chance to look inside the warehouse. How in hell did he know everything was all right before they made sure it was not being burglarized?

And once they were inside the warehouse, what was it Searles said about the office? About checking it out? It was dark in the back of the warehouse, and Lydia couldn't see the door to the office until she got close to it. How did Searles know there was an office there when she couldn't see it from where they were standing?

Then one night, Lydia had a dream about the shooting that was so intense that it startled her awake. She sat up in bed and began remembering what had happened in vivid detail; her cautious entry into the half-lit office, voices coming from somewhere she couldn't see, a door suddenly flung open, and the sudden flash of orange fire accompanying the bullet that maimed her for life.

The thoughts bothered her so much she couldn't get back to sleep. And they didn't go away even when she remembered why she joined the Police Department in the first place. She had joined the Department for a specific reason...to find out something very important to her...and to figure out what she was going to do about it when she found out what she had long suspected.

And it never occurred to her that the reason she joined the Police Department might have also been the reason why she had been shot in the first place.

CHAPTER FIVE

ON THE day before she was to be released from the hospital, Lydia Harte was sitting in a wheelchair in a hospital conference room with her attorney, Michael Hoshino. She had received an order signed by the Chief of Police directing her to submit to an interview with Lieutenant Peter Grayson from the Officer-Involved-Shooting Team and Sergeant Hector Maldonado from Intelligence Division.

When Lydia received the order, she immediately called Eric Milburn, her mother's attorney, who had an office in Santa Monica. Milburn did estate and trust work and didn't have the experience or expertise to represent her in a case that might involve disciplinary action, or worse yet, a criminal prosecution, but he agreed to help her find an attorney. It didn't take him long to find one who had built a reputation representing police officers in trouble with the Department. His name was Michael Honshino, and he had offices in Little Tokyo not more than two blocks from Police Headquarters.

Once Lydia hired Honshino, he moved fast. He had her surgeon certify in an affidavit that the stress of an interview in her current condition would be detrimental to her health. Once Honshino had the affidavit, he filed a motion in court for a restraining order preventing the Department from questioning Lydia until her doctor gave his approval. The judge agreed and ordered that Lydia should only be required to submit to an interview when it was determined by her doctor that she was well enough to be released from the hospital.

After the court issued the order, Honshino came to Lydia's bedside and spend two hours with her, asking questions about what happened in Akheiser's warehouse and then briefing her on what to expect during the interview. Lydia was impressed by the thoroughness of his preparation and felt very comfortable about being interviewed with him at her side.

"Okay, here's the deal," Honshino said to Lydia as they awaited the arrival of Lieutenant Grayson and Sergeant Maldonado. "I have been assured by Lieutenant Grayson that all they want to ask you about is the events that led up to the shooting and what you remember about the shooting itself. I have a written agreement, signed by Grayson, that this interview is for administrative purposes only, and that you will not be criminally charged, nor will you be charged with any misconduct based on what you say in the interview."

Lydia nodded. "What about the rumors I killed Searles?"

"What rumors?"

"The papers quoted some anonymous officers who said I shot Searles."

"Grayson wouldn't tell me if you shot Searles. If he thought so, I don't think he would have wanted to interview you. He would have referred the case to the District Attorney."

"Why does the guy from Intelligence Division need to be present?"

"I don't know. They wouldn't tell me, so I did a little investigating on my own. My sources tell me that your stepfather is closely associated with an organized crime family on the West Coast."

"The only thing I know for certain is that he owns an arms manufacturing plant in South Carolina and a car conversion business in Culver City. I don't have any knowledge of his involvement with organized crime, so I can't say anything that would be of interest to Maldonado. He's wasting his time if he thinks I can."

"No problem. Your stepfather and his business interests are outside the scope of the interview. You will not be required to answer any questions about him."

Lydia had shaded the truth when she denied knowing the extent of her stepfather's business activities. In the short time Lydia had lived at Oceania Manor before she was packed off to prep school, she was certain her stepfather was involved in business activities that were frowned upon by law enforcement.

Jonathan went to great lengths to keep his business affairs secret, and Lydia had been warned by her mother not to ask questions. Jonathan met frequently with men wearing expensive suits behind closed doors in his library, and his visitors were always accompanied by burly men who remained outside while business was being discussed inside.

And then, there was Jonathan's obsession with security. He had a bodyguard named Carlos Aldana who always travelled with him, and he also employed four men in the gatehouse who took turns watching the dozen or so monitors covering nearly every inch of his estate on the coast just south of Malibu.

When Lydia had once asked her stepfather about the reason for the extensive security system, he told her that it was because of the collection of handguns he kept in a large vault in the basement. But that didn't seem to make much sense. The costs of maintaining a security force far exceeded the value of the guns.

"One more thing," Hoshino said just before Grayson and Maldonado entered the conference room. "Do you see this box of paperclips?"

Lydia frowned.

What the hell was he talking about?

"Keep one eye on my hands during the interview. If you see me take a paperclip out of the box and push it to the side, that means you've been asked a dangerous question. Think about the question before you answer. If you have some doubt about how to answer, ask to stop the interview so you can have a private conference with me."

Lieutenant Peter Grayson was a big man, clean shaven, buzz haircut, who looked like a Marine First Sergeant trying desperately to look like a business professional in a tailored grey suit. Sergeant Hector Maldonado was a short, dark-featured man who Lydia had met when she was applying to become a police officer. Maldonado smiled when he saw her, but the smile was quickly replaced by a look of alarm that flooded his face when he saw how much weight she had lost.

After being introduced, Grayson sat down and stared at her for a moment, his head slightly tilted to one side, but it was Maldonado who asked the first question.

"Are you all right, Officer Harte?"

"I'm fine," Lydia said.

"You've lost a lot of weight."

"Getting shot in the stomach does that to you."

"Do you feel up to this interview?"

Lydia shrugged and looked at Grayson.

"Has your attorney explained the reason for this interview?" Grayson asked.

"He has."

"Do I have your permission to record this interview?"

Lydia looked at her attorney and he nodded.

Grayson reached down and pulled a small tape recorder out of his briefcase and set it on the table. To Lydia's amazement, Hoshino also removed a tape recorder from his briefcase and set it on the table next to the box of paperclips.

"Are you ready?" Grayson asked Lydia, eyeing the paperclips.

Before Lydia could respond, Hoshino held up a hand and waited until the tape recorders began playing. "This interview, of course, is subject to the agreement you and I signed yesterday evening in my office."

"Of course, Mike."

Grayson looked at Lydia and again asked if she was ready.

"I am ready to answer any question you have about the shooting on one condition."

Grayson looked at Honshino. "I thought we had an agreement, Mike."

"So, did I," Honshino said, turning to Lydia. "What kind of condition are you talking about, Lydia?"

Lydia replied evenly. "I'm not going to say a damn thing about the shooting until they tell me what happened to Searles."

"I think that's reasonable," Honshino said to Grayson.

Grayson glanced sideways at Maldonado. When Grayson's response came, it was slow and hesitant. "Searles got shot."

"Who shot him?"

Grayson looked at Honshino and then at Maldonado. He leaned back in his chair. "I'm afraid that part of the investigation is confidential."

Lydia turned to Honshino. "Could you ask one of the nurses to take me back to my room?"

Grayson leaned forward. "Officer Harte, you have been served with an order by the Chief of Police to submit to an interview about the shooting that occurred on the night of November 19, 2005. If you do not answer my questions, I am duty bound to inform you that you may face disciplinary action and may be terminated from employment with the City of Los Angeles. You are required to answer my questions."

"I also happen to know the law, Lieutenant." She turned toward Honshino. "Did Lieutenant Grayson turn any of his reports over to you?"

"He has not. That was part of the agreement. The Department wants to keep the investigation into the death of Officer Searles confidential."

Lydia stared at Honshino for a moment finding it hard to believe that he may not have done his job. She turned back to Grayson. "I didn't sign that agreement, Lieutenant. I have a legal right under the Peace Officer's Bill of Rights to see any documents involving the Department's investigation into the shooting before being interviewed. I never gave up those rights." She paused for a moment, enjoying the look of frustration on Grayson's face. "When it gets down to it, Lieutenant, I *really* don't want to see your reports. All I really want to know is if I shot Searles."

Lydia noticed that Maldonado put a hand to his face to cover a smile.

After a moment, Grayson nodded his head. "All right, Officer Harte. I will tell you what we know on one condition. You can't discuss any of this with anyone other than your attorney. The investigation into what happened is confidential."

Honshino held up a hand to keep Lydia from saying anything. "I agree that we will not disclose anything you may tell us, provided that you will not be prosecuting Officer Harte for any crime or misconduct."

"Mike, we already talked about that, and I told you that Officer Harte didn't shoot anyone."

"Then who shot Searles?" Lydia asked.

"I don't know, Officer Harte," Grayson replied. "That is what I'm trying to find out. What I do know is that whoever shot you also shot Searles. The bullets were fired from the same gun. As far as I can tell, your shot didn't hit anyone. We found your bullet in the header above the door, and for reasons I can't discuss I don't want anyone knowing that."

CHAPTER SIX

Three months later
February 26, 2006.

LYDIA WISHED she had a camera to record the looks of surprise on the faces of the officers when she entered the roll call room at Century Division. She sauntered nonchalantly past the back row where members of the so-called Wrecking Crew looked up when they got a whiff of her perfume. They stared at her in stunned silence, and then feverishly began whispering to each other after she passed.

Most of the officers were already in the roll call room. When they heard the hurried murmuring coming from the back row, they turned to look at what was causing the fuss.

Lydia heard someone say, "Jesus Christ, the walking dead is here!" and then "You gotta be fucking kidding me!" She walked down the aisle, ignoring them with a look of mild amusement on her face.

Captain Kemper and Lieutenant Morton were already in the room. They were standing on the platform in front of the desk, watching Lydia as she took a seat in the front row.

Neither of them was smiling.

One of Lydia's classmates nudged her in greeting, but she ignored him. She looked up at Kemper and Morton.

Kemper held up a hand and waited until the room had quieted down. "The reason, I'm here," Captain Kemper said, looking out with squinty eyes at the officers in the roll call room, "is to welcome Officer Harte back to work. I was truly amazed when I got a call from Personnel yesterday telling me that she was returning to work. Officer Harte had been told by her doctors that she would never be able to work as a police officer again. She could have taken a disability pension, but she didn't. Instead, she has made a determined effort to return to work. I think we need to applaud her for her courage."

Lydia didn't expect much in the way of applause, and she wasn't disappointed. It was light and mostly came from her Academy classmates.

"Who shot Searles?" came a gruff voice from the back of the room.

"We don't know who shot Officer Searles," Kemper said. "But we do know it wasn't Officer Harte."

"How do you know that?"

Kemper didn't answer.

"Who shot Officer Harte, Captain?" This came from a voice that was so deep that Lydia turned to see who said it.

She saw an officer three rows back she had never seen before. He had sharp features with dark eyes set in a thin face with hollowed cheeks. He was the only officer in the roll call room wearing the official service cap.

"We don't know that either, Officer Hagerty," Kemper replied. "I can assure everyone in this room that Robbery-Homicide is actively working this case."

"What about ballistics?" said a voice from the back row. "They can do matches on bullets, you know. Or has Forensics been cut out of the budget by the fucking mayor?"

Kemper sighed. "The investigation is confidential and is ongoing and Lieutenant Grayson wants to keep it that way. All I can say is if Officer Harte did something wrong, she wouldn't have been allowed to return to work."

"But why is Grayson handling this if it wasn't an officer-involved shooting?" another officer asked.

"Lieutenant Grayson also handles shootings where an officer has been killed while on the job," Kemper said, sounding really irritated. He paused for a second. "I have talked to several officers who have been shot while on duty. It is a demoralizing experience. It makes a person question why they became a police officer in the first place. Officer Harte was the most seriously injured officer I have ever talked to. Her doctors said she would never be able to return to work. But she has…and she should be respected for that."

Lydia Harte didn't give a damn about the lack of enthusiasm for her return to work. It wasn't until later that she realized what happened next at roll call was the best possible thing that could have ever happened to her.

When Lieutenant Morton read off the assignments and announced she would be assigned to her old car with Mosby and Cruz, Mosby immediately objected.

"I don't want to work with her, and I know Cruz sure as hell wouldn't either."

Morton's reply was brittle. "I make the assignments, Officer Mosby. You're working with Officer Harte tonight whether you like it or not."

"I don't want to work with anyone who gets their partner shot."

Lydia angrily turned to look back at him and was about to say something but stopped when she saw the inhuman look on his face. Mosby looked like a snarling cat ready to engage in a street fight.

"You *will* work with her, Mosby!" Morton said. "That's an order!"

"I'll go off sick if you assign her to me."

"You're not sick, Mosby. Now sit your ass down!"

"Wait a fucking minute," interjected another officer.

Lydia recognized the voice as belonging to the officer that Kemper had called Hagerty.

"Assign Harte to my car, Lieutenant. I will work with anyone who has the guts to come back to work the streets after being shot. She shouldn't have to face the humiliation of working with a fucking weasel."

"You better watch your fucking mouth, Hagerty," Mosby shot back.

"Shut the fuck up!" Morton yelled as his face turned red. "That means all of you! This is my roll call, so shut the fuck up!"

It was silent in the roll call room for a good minute before Morton took up a pencil, scratched out the Harte/Mosby assignment, and assigned Lydia to work with Officer Richard Hagerty.

Roll call finished, Morton stood up and dismissed the watch. His last words on leaving the roll call room were, "Mosby, come upstairs with me. We're going to see the Captain."

Lydia stood up and was startled to find Hagerty standing in the aisle next to her. She was surprised at how tall he was. He was at least six foot-six, and the hollows in his cheeks reminded Lydia of the actor who played the bad guy in *Shane*.

Hagerty surprised the hell out of her by offering to shake her hand. She took it, expecting to find a crushing grip. His hand was rough and cal-loused, but he shook her hand as if he were shaking the paw of a puppy.

"Welcome back to work, Harte. Are you ready to do some police work?"

"Yes, sir."

The officers in the back row were huddled together in deep conversation when Lydia followed Hagerty out the back door of the roll call room. One of them made eye contact with her and said something to the others. They all turned and glared at her as she walked out of the room.

Lydia was fastening her seatbelt when she became aware that Hagerty was staring at her.

"What's wrong?" Lydia asked.

"I have to ask you something personal."

Lydia paused for a moment. "I can't talk about the shooting."

"I know that. I heard you're related to Milo Benedict. Is that true?"

"He's my stepbrother. Why do you want to know?"

"What does he do for a living?"

"He works for my stepfather."

Hagerty's eyebrows raised. "Doing what?"

"If you're going to ask me if he's a crook, I don't know for sure. Some people think he is. I happen to think he's too fucking dumb to be a crook."

"If he was a crook, they wouldn't have let him into the reserve program. What does he do for your stepfather?"

"He works at his car conversion shop."

"Doing what?"

Linda shrugged. "It's sort of complicated. When a customer imports a luxury car from Europe or Asia that hasn't been approved for import into the U.S., they have to convert it to meet EPA standards." Lydia said this, realizing for the first time that the car conversion business would also be a good place to switch out vehicle identification numbers on stolen cars.

"Is he good at it?"

Lydia was getting irritated. "Why do you want to know all of this?"

"Because I've worked with him and I know him. I hope he's good at the car conversion business because he sure as hell sucks as a police officer."

Lydia smiled. "He sucks as a brother, too."

"I didn't mean to pry," Hagerty said as he started the car. "Let's go to work."

Lydia picked up the radio and cleared their unit for calls. They were the first unit out of the station and immediately received three calls for service. The first one they handled was the report of an aggressive drunk outside a liquor store.

The drunk was gone when they arrived. Problem solved.

The second call was a report of a stolen vehicle. Lydia wrote the report under Hagerty's watchful eyes and then called it in to Communications. She would turn in the report the next time they went to the station.

The third call was a family dispute. A woman who answered the door said everything was all right now, she didn't need the police. Hagerty insisted that her husband come to the door. He did so.

Lydia smiled when she saw the man holding a towel with ice in it to his forehead. He said he had tripped over a coffee table, but he was all right.

Five minutes later, they were out on the streets again when Hagerty saw something that caused him to turn on the emergency lights and pull the car sharply to the curb.

"Did you see it?" Hagerty asked.

"What?"

"That man in the blue jersey walking away from us. He has a gun tucked inside the belt on the right hip."

Lydia saw the man in the hooded blue jersey. She didn't see the gun.

Hagerty jumped out of the car before Lydia could react. He pulled out his revolver and ordered the man to stop and put his hands over his head.

The man, a Caucasian in his early thirties, turned to face him. When he saw Hagerty's .357 Magnum pointing at him, he mumbled something under his breath and slowly raised his hands.

To Lydia's amazement, Hagerty was right. The man did have a gun, a small Polish semi-automatic concealed under his jersey. It was cocked with a round in the chamber, and he didn't have a concealed carry permit. He refused to say why he had it or what he intended to do with it. It turned out he had a criminal record for armed robbery and was on parole.

They booked the man into the West Los Angeles jail, and Lydia wrote up the arrest and evidence report.

Later, they ate at an upscale restaurant on Wilshire Boulevard. After they ordered, Hagerty asked Lydia a question that surprised her.

"Do you have a fireplace?"

"I live in a condo."

Hagerty looked at her. His eyes seemed to be smiling. Lydia noticed they were dark blue.

"I do have a fireplace," Lydia continued. "I never use it. Why do you ask?" She glanced down at his left hand. He was holding a coffee cup and was wearing a wedding ring.

"In my spare time," Hagerty said. "I do two things. I cut down trees the Forest Service wants removed up near Gorman, and I sell good quality firewood for a good price. I also do a lot of target practice. A hundred rounds, once a week." He stared at her and said in a low voice that seemed almost threatening, "If you are going to be my partner, you'll do the same."

"Cut firewood?"

"No. Firing a hundred rounds a week."

Lydia frowned but didn't say anything.

"Look here, Harte. My number one job is police work. My number two job is to train recruits to do good police work. And to do that, we need to survive. Both of us. I have been involved in two shootings. The first one involved me and my partner running across a guy who had just robbed a bank and opened fire on us without warning. My partner fired six rounds at him and missed. I fired one and killed the suspect. So, if you're going to work with me, you will go to the range with me once a week, and we will work on different firing positions—at least a half dozen of them the Department doesn't teach."

Lydia stared at the coffee cup for a moment or two. Finally, she looked up and asked, "Did you make your partner…the one who missed all of his shots…did you make him go to the range with you?"

"I didn't."

"Then why do you want me to go to the range with you?"

"Because you're alive and he isn't."

Lydia stared blankly at him, not saying anything in response.

"Did you hear what I said?" Hagerty asked.

"I did."

"Do you understand what I said?"

"I do. I'll go to the range with you."

"A piece of advice."

"Another war story coming on?" Lydia asked.

Hagerty shook his head vigorously. "Have you noticed what kind of gun I'm carrying?"

Lydia tried to answer without being too smug. "A .357 Magnum."

"That's right. You carry a Beretta FS. I've got nothing against Beretta. They make a fine gun. But I don't like semi-automatics. Too many moving parts, too many things that can go wrong. They give a body too much of a sense of security. Coppers like the fact they have a gun with fifteen rounds in it. In my opinion, it creates a feeling of false security. I prefer the .357 Magnum with a six-and-half-inch barrel. It's a lot more accurate than a semi-automatic and a lot more powerful. I can get more done with one bullet than most officers can with ten or twelve."

"But you're not allowed to load it with a magnum round on duty. You have to use the .38 Special."

"I load my gun with a .38 Special for roll call—just in case we have an inspection. Before I get into the car, I reload it with magnum rounds."

"But that's against…"

"I know. It's against Department policy! But when it comes to my life and my family, I say fuck Department policy!" Hagerty said this so loud that several people in the restaurant turned to look at him. He looked around, nodded in apology at the people he had offended, and turned to Lydia. "Sorry about the language."

Lydia waved him off. "Are you suggesting I get a .357 Magnum?"

"I think it'd be a good idea. They're expensive. But I think you should get one. Preferably, the Model 37. It's a fine weapon."

Lydia thought about the collection of firearms her stepfather had in his basement. He had several thousand revolvers in a vault, many of them duplicates.

She had been out to the mansion only once since she was shot and that was to see her grandmother, Sofia Benedetto, who was living in a bedroom on the first floor. Sofia was her stepfather's mother and not really her grand-mother, but that was what Lydia called her ever since she was a teenager.

When Lydia drove up to Oceania Manor on that one occasion, she did not want to see or talk to Jonathan Benedict, so she walked quietly by the library where he conducted his business and was surprised to see who else was there.

Jonathan was talking to her ex-fiancé, Jake Nilsson. The two men were leaning forward on easy chairs, talking quietly, drinks in their hands. Milo Benedict, her fucking stepbrother, was standing over them, a glass of scotch in his hand, listening intently to what they were saying.

Her stepfather knew she was coming and had probably arranged for Jake to be there in the hope of Lydia getting back together with him. But Lydia had moved quietly down the hall, taking care not to disturb them. She spent ten minutes with Sofia and then quietly slipped out of the man-sion without being noticed.

"So," Hagerty said, "do you agree?"

"What?"

"Will you buy a .357? And practice with me? A hundred rounds a week?"

"Yes," Lydia said.

Later that night, Lydia got into bed and pulled the duvet over her head, burying herself like a cocoon, letting her breath warm the air under the cover. It was warm outside her condo, a luxurious high rise on Pico Boule-vard near Century City that was purchased for Lydia by her mother. Lydia had set the temperature down low in her apartment an hour before she went to bed because she liked to sleep under the covers when it was cold.

She thought about her experience with Hagerty that evening. Together, they had done more police work in one shift than she did when working almost two weeks with Mosby and Cruz.

While at UCLA, Lydia had majored in computer engineering and found her studies to be stimulating, but that stimulation only energized the brain. Proactive police work was different. It energized the entire body. And there was the thrill of working with a professional police officer who viewed his job as something a helluva lot more important than driving around looking at women with tanned legs.

Hagerty had asked her if she would buy a .357 Magnum, a big gun that was built to withstand the pressure of a high-powered round, and she had said yes. As a matter of fact, she knew where she could get several of them.

CHAPTER SEVEN

TWO DAYS later, Lydia showed up for roll call and learned she had been assigned to the front desk by Captain Kemper. When she cornered Lieutenant Morton in the hallway and asked why, Morton simply said it was the Captain's orders. When Lydia began angrily walking away, he told her to meet him in the roll call room in a few minutes.

Lydia waited in the roll call room for a good ten minutes before Morton showed up.

"Okay," he said, "I had a talk with Kemper. He told me that a number of officers were unhappy with you, and he thought you needed to be pulled out of the field until things simmered down."

Lydia felt heat rising in her face. "I get along with Hagerty. Why do I have to be quarantined because somebody doesn't like me?"

"You're not being quarantined."

"I'm being sent to the front desk just because a bunch of jerks don't like me? Come on, Lieutenant, that's ridiculous!"

"Officer Harte, there are some people in the Division who think you killed Searles."

"I…" Lydia stopped, remembering what Grayson had said about not talking about the shooting.

"Harte, I know you didn't shoot Searles. If you did, you wouldn't have been cleared to come back to work. Work the front desk for a few weeks. You don't even need to report to roll call. I'll try and get you back in the field with Hagerty and Ferris in a few weeks."

"Who's Ferris?"

"Ferris is the third man assigned to your car. You'll work with him when Hagerty is off."

The front desk was not really a desk at all, but a long counter in the lobby of the police station. Lydia hated working there from the moment she stepped behind the counter. She had two partners. One of them was an overweight officer, last name Lewis, who smelled badly and made no attempt to conceal the fact that he hated the police brass and didn't want to work the streets under the 'current conditions', whatever they were.

The other officer was a tall, good-looking black officer named Boudrie who was on light duty recovering from a concussion he sustained in a fight. Boudrie spoke very little but did his job politely and efficiently. When not busy with customers, he stared at the wall containing photographs of three Century Division officers who had been killed while on duty.

A loaded shotgun was kept on a rack under the counter, and Lydia noticed that every time Boudrie walked past it, he let his fingers lightly touch it. After making a few attempts at talking to the two officers who worked with her and not getting an encouraging response, Lydia gave up trying to get to know them.

The work was boring. It consisted of taking reports from people who had walked into the station to report a crime or talking with citizens who felt they had been wronged by a police officer and wanted to make a personnel complaint. Occasionally, there were a few people who came in and had an appointment to see a detective about an active case.

The one favorable thing about the job, in Lydia's view, was that the Watch Commander's office was in a room directly behind the front counter, and there was a computer sitting on a corner of Sergeant Cooley's desk. Lydia wondered if Grayson's reports about the death of Searles were computerized. If they were, they would probably be protected by a password, and she would need a significant amount of time trying to get past it. And time, she didn't have. The Watch Commander's office was always busy, and if Morton or Cooley did happen to leave, they would return less than a minute later.

So, the computer sat there on Sergeant Cooley's desk, inviting her to come in for a look, but saying you can't come in.

On the third day Lydia was assigned to the front desk, a frail black woman entered the lobby, stopped halfway in, and studied each of the officers behind the counter. Having made up her mind whom she wished to speak to, she approached Lydia and in a shaky voice asked to speak to Sergeant Vernor.

Lydia quickly found Vernor's name on the Division roster. He was a detective assigned to the Burglary Unit. She asked the lady to take a seat on the bench and rang up the secretary in the detective squad room to let her know that Sergeant Vernor had a visitor.

A few minutes later, a man who Lydia assumed was a detective from the way he dressed emerged from the Watch Commander's office and looked around the lobby. He looked at Lydia and stared at her for a surprised beat before asking who wanted to see him. Lydia pointed at the woman seated on the bench. Vernor slipped around the counter, sat down next to the woman, and began talking to her.

Lydia wasn't sure why, but Sergeant Billy Vernor made an impression on her. He was probably thirty pounds overweight, but he was dressed neatly, wearing a tailored light gray suit, white shirt, and maroon tie, and he smelled and looked as if he had just shaved even though it was late in the afternoon. The impression he generated by the way he sat next to the woman and listened carefully to what she was saying was that he was a person who cared a lot about people.

When Vernor had finished with the woman, he helped her out the door. When he came back inside, he approached Lydia and looked at the nameplate on her shirt.

"Harte, is it?"

"Yes, sir."

"Do you like working the front desk, Officer Harte?"

Lydia did a sideways glance at Lewis who was glaring at her. Boudrie was not paying attention to the conversation. His eyes were fixed on the pictures of the dead officers on the wall.

"I just love it here," Lydia replied.

"Sarcasm," Vernor said. "I like that. Did they say how long you have to work the desk?"

"Why?"

"My partner is off long term sick. I could use some help on the Burglary desk."

"Are you offering me a job?"

"A temporary one."

"Doing paperwork?"

"Lady, you'd be surprised at how much detective work is paperwork."

"I don't like being called 'lady'."

"Sorry. An old habit."

"What do burglary detectives do?"

"Are you kidding me?"

"No, I'm not. What do burglary detectives do?"

"A lot of burglary detectives spend their time doing paperwork. I do paperwork when it's necessary to put some asshole in jail. When I'm done with that, I go out into the field and find more assholes to put in jail."

Lydia thought about it for a moment. There were several computers in the detective squad room. Maybe, she could get access to one of them when nobody was around. Finally, she said, "They tell me I have to spend a few weeks on the front desk."

"Say only the word, and I'll see what I can do about having you loaned back to me."

"Okay. I think I'd like working with you, Sergeant Vernor."

"Good," Vernor said. "I'll be in touch."

After Vernor left, Lydia felt her skin crawling. It felt as if someone had invaded her space. She turned to see Lewis staring maliciously at her. "What's your problem, Lewis?"

Lewis' reply was succinct. "Suckass!"

Lydia smiled and said, "Lardass," as she turned to go to the restroom.

Chapter Eight

LYDIA DROVE her silver BMW convertible up to the front gate of Oceania Manor. She had lived here with her mother and stepfather before being unceremoniously shipped off to boarding school when she was sixteen.
She waited for at least a minute before the wrought iron gate slowly slid
open on a creaky rail.

A black Pontiac Firebird Trans Am was parked on the apron next to the
gatehouse. Lydia got out of her car and looked up at a window on the second floor.

The window opened and a man with a face that could only have its
genesis in the Mediterranean poked out his head. He was smiling broadly.

"I knew it would be you on duty, Carlos," Lydia said.

"Want a popsicle, little girl?"

"Not the kind you're offering, *cabron*."

"Come on up for a while, Lolita."

"Can't," Lydia said, not meaning it. She really did want to come up and
see Carlos, if nothing more than for old time sakes. But she knew she
could not do what Carlos would like her to do.

"I have your favorite bourbon. Maker's Mark."

"I don't drink anymore, Carlos. Do you have orange juice?"

"I've got water. The best you can get. Right out of Owens Valley. Fla-
vored with duck shit."

Lydia decided she wanted to check out the CCTV system that Carlos
was monitoring in the gatehouse, so she accepted his offer to come inside.

"So," Carlos said as he opened a bottle of water he had taken from the refrigerator, "I've been hearing some bad things about you. I heard you joined the local gestapo and got shot."

Lydia didn't say anything. She took the bottle of water he offered and wandered over to the bank of monitors. There were fourteen CCTV monitors covering various parts of the estate, two more than Lydia remembered. The estate was large, twenty-two acres, with a wrought iron fence in front and a chain link fence facing the hills in back. Lydia had spent time here in her early teens, and she knew there were places the monitors didn't cover.

"Bet you can't wear a bikini anymore," Carlos said suddenly.

If anyone other than Carlos had said this, it might have set Lydia's nerves on fire, but the word 'bikini' conjured up a memory that she would never forget. When she was sixteen, she had put on a bikini and sunbathed on the lawn, not more than fifty feet from the gatehouse where Carlos was on duty.

She did it every day until she got what she wanted and more.

One afternoon, Carlos came storming out of the gatehouse, ripped off her bikini bottoms, and raped her. Lydia let Carlos rape her fourteen times that summer until her mother learned what was happening. She insisted that Carlos be immediately fired, but Jonathan refused, so Lydia was packed off to a preparatory school in the Napa Valley where she flourished under a renowned track coach.

Lydia turned from the monitors after closely examining the areas of the estate they covered and smiled at Carlos. "You were never much interested in bikinis, Carlos. How many of mine did you destroy?"

He shrugged and smiled.

"If I remember rightly," Lydia added, "the only reason my mother found out what we were doing was because she caught me sneaking into my bedroom while I was trying to cover myself with a shredded bikini bottom."

Carlos laughed so loud that his face looked like a gargoyle.

When Lydia was sixteen, she thought he was the most handsome man she had ever seen. Now, the dark circles around his eyes and the rough skin on his face made him look creepy.

"Can I ask you something, Carlos?"

"If you're lookin' to get laid, pussycat, you know what the answer is."

"It would be nice" Lydia lied, "but the doctors said I would have a problem with that kind of recreation for some time."

Carlos snorted and then said, "Too bad."

Lydia looked at the bank of monitors. "Why does Jonathan need all this security, Carlos? I mean, you're not the only one who works here. How many guys are taking turns in the guardhouse?"

She already knew what the answer to that question was, but she asked it to find out how clever Carlos could be in coming up with an answer that evaded the question.

"It's not a guardhouse, Lydia. It's a gatehouse."

"But why all this, Carlos? Why? You even have two new cameras installed."

"Some boys cut a hole in the fence and were stealing oranges."

Lydia laughed. "So, all of this," she said, waving her water bottle at the monitors, "is to keep little boys from stealing oranges."

Carlos shrugged.

"Why have you stayed on so long, Carlos? Watching this"—Lydia pointed to the monitors—"must be boring as all hell."

Your dad pays me well, Lydia. And I get to travel with him. And boy, does he ever travel."

"How much does this cost him?"

"The monitors?"

"No, the number of men he has watching his back."

Carlos looked at her suspiciously. "I would say close to a million a year."

"And you get a big chunk of that." Lydia paused for a beat. "Does he have a lot of enemies?"

"He does." Carlos looked at the monitors. "You know what's going on here, Lydia. I don't have to tell you."

"I have no idea what goes on here, Carlos. Maybe, you could clue me in."

Carlos responded with an enigmatic smile. "He has made a lot of enemies, little girl. You keep prying like that, and they might come after you. And you don't have a bodyguard."

On her way back to her car, Lydia looked up at the window of the gatehouse. Carlos was leaning over the window sill, looking down at her, the lecherous smile still on his ferret-like face.

He really did look like a gargoyle, Lydia thought, and he didn't have a clue as to what kind of enemy her stepfather really had.

The long drive up to the mansion was lined with Italian cypress. The property that Jonathan pretentiously called Oceania Manor was situated on a hillside near Pepperdine University on the Pacific Coast Highway and was surrounded by similar estates, all heavily watered to keep them green in a state with persistent water shortages.

The house, a three-story, gray structure that looked like a medieval castle, was situated on a small knoll with a partial view of the ocean. Behind it were the arid hills of the Santa Monica Mountains interspersed with fire trails that Lydia knew all too well from her early teens when she raced with her friends across the rugged trails on mini-motor bikes.

Lydia drove her car into the circular drive and parked behind a blue BMW convertible that she recognized as belonging to Victoria, her stepfather's girlfriend. The car was brand new, a 2006 model that was identical to Lydia's except for the color. It still had a temporary tag pasted to the left rear window.

Directly in front of Victoria's car was a four-door Maserati that Lydia thought could only belonged to her stepfather. When Lydia got out of her car, she paused to admire the car. It was a fifth generation Maserati Quattroporte, a five-seater saloon car, that had only become available that year. The car cost over 100,000 dollars new and Lydia wondered why her stepfather decided to go out that night with the cheapest car in his personal fleet.

The front door was already open. Carlos had probably called the house, and her stepfather was expecting her.

Lydia found her stepfather in the massive wood-paneled and bookless library having martinis with her stepbrother, Milo. Jonathan's girlfriend, Victoria Ravesies, was seated demurely on a sofa, legs crossed, a large glass of white wine in her hand.

Jonathan and Milo were wearing suits, the older man's a Navy blue and the younger man's a charcoal gray. Jonathan was tall, blond hair thinning at the top, athletic in appearance, except for an incipient beer belly that looked like the beginning of a baby bump.

Milo Benedict, her stepbrother, was the product of his father's first wife who was a transplanted beauty from Italy. He had a shockingly weird appearance, having inherited none of his deceased mother's good looks. He was five feet six, two inches shorter than Lydia, with a horse-like face that appeared larger than it was because he kept his long hair combed back with the sidewalls cut incongruously short. Lydia had never known Milo to have a relationship with a woman that lasted longer than three months.

Jonathan set his drink down on a side table and moved forward at less than enthusiastic speed to greet her. He didn't hug her. Instead, he held her out by the arms and looked her up and down.

"You look well," he said, "considering what you've been through."

"I'm fine," Lydia said, wanting to push him and his martini-laced breath away from her.

"Can I get you a drink? A martini, perhaps."

"A water would be fine."

"Please sit, down. Next to Victoria. I'll get you a water."

Victoria, smiling, held out a hand to Lydia as she approached. Lydia not knowing what to do lightly patted the back of Victoria's hand and sat next to her.

Milo Benedict didn't move. He had a smile on his ugly face that would have frozen his martini.

"How are you?" Victoria asked.

"I'm fine," Lydia said for the second time, wondering if Victoria was deaf or just didn't pay attention to what she said a few moments ago. "Where are you going, dressed so nice?"

Victoria was wearing a tight cocktail dress in black with a string of pearls around her neck. She was a beautiful woman, svelte, long black hair set in a ponytail, and closer in age to her stepbrother than her stepfather. She worked in an advertising firm that handled Jonathan's gun manufacturing business.

Lydia had long suspected that Victoria and her stepfather had a relationship even while her mother was alive.

"We're going down to Malibu Creek for dinner," Victoria said. "We were hoping you could join us."

"Cook's day off?" Lydia asked.

Victoria shrugged. "We wanted Italian for a change. Maria doesn't know how to make anything that doesn't taste like it came from the south of Tijuana."

"Martin can cook, can't he?" Lydia was referring to Jonathan Benedict's personal assistant.

"He works banker's hours," Milo interjected.

"He threatened to quit when I asked if he could work until six," Jonathan said as he handed Lydia a tumbler of water filled with ice.

Milo sat down. He leaned forward, his elbows on his knees, looking at the floor, his martini dripping over the rim.

God, how she hated that smug bastard.

"So, how do you like being a policewoman?" Victoria asked cheerfully.

"I like it well enough," Lydia said, not wanting to correct her by pointing out that all officers, even women, had the civil service designation of police officer.

Milo looked up, smiling maliciously. "Even after?"

"After what?" Lydia asked, tension in her voice.

"After being shot."

"Even after that," Lydia replied. *You fucking bastard,* was what she wanted to add.

"I heard you're working with the Cowboy," Milo said.

Lydia stared at him but didn't say anything. She didn't want to get into a discussion with him about why she had just been assigned to the front desk.

"What are you talking about?" Jonathan Benedict asked Milo.

"They got this guy at Century who thinks he's Wyatt Earp. He carries a .357 Magnum with a six-inch barrel. The guys call him Gunsmoke behind his back."

"Why don't they call him that to his face?" Lydia asked, her voice raspy with irritation.

Milo bit his lip and stared into his drink.

"Who do you work with when you do your two days a month?" Lydia asked.

Milo looked up at her as if he had been asked a trick question. "Usually Clay Jackson," he said hesitantly.

Lydia recognized the name. Jackson was one of the six assholes, now five of them after the death of Searles, who sat in the back row at roll call.

"This guy," Jonathan said, "this guy you're working with. What's his name?"

"Dick Hagerty."

"Is he a good man?"

"I've learned a lot from him already. As a matter of fact, that was the reason I came up to see you. I need a .357 Magnum and I can't get the one

I want because they're on back order. I wonder if I could borrow one of yours for a few weeks?"

Jonathan hesitated for a few seconds.

"Those guns are collector items," Milo Benedict said. "For display only."

"They are collector items," Jonathan said. "But if Lydia wants to borrow one for a few weeks, I see no reason why she can't have one. Chances are she'll never have to use it."

"You never know if you're going to have to use a gun when you hit the streets," Milo said.

"So, how many shootings have you been involved in?" Victoria asked sweetly.

Lydia wondered if there was a subtle dig in the question.

Milo got that impression too. He shrugged but didn't say anything.

"Sort of hard to get into a shooting when you only work two days a month," Lydia observed. "Tough life being a reserve officer who works with a drone."

Jonathan stood up, holding out a hand to keep Milo from responding. "Lydia, we have to get going. Would you care to join us for dinner? I can take you down to the vault after we get back."

"I need to talk to grandma."

"She's not here. Visiting a friend. She'll be gone for several days."

"I thought she couldn't drive anymore."

"Marlene hired a special van for her. They picked her up yesterday."

"When will she be back?"

"Sunday."

"I suppose," Lydia said, "I can come back tomorrow if you have to leave."

"I'll give you the combination to the vault," Jonathan said. "The .357's are in middle of the left row. I think the Model 66 with a 4.25-inch barrel would be just right for you." He went to a desk and wrote something on a note pad. He tore off the page and handed it to Lydia. It was the combination to the vault.

"How many .357's do you have?" Victoria asked.

"I have every single model ever made," Jonathan responded. "Not only the ones made by Smith and Wesson, but also by Kimber, Colt, Taurus, and Ruger. If a single model has optional barrel lengths, I have one of each. I also have the stainless steel model of each if it comes in that style.

Several of the models are pink, for God's sake. I don't know if it was meant for women or fags."

"Why?" Victoria asked, her eyebrows raised.

"Why what?"

"Why so many guns?"

"I like to keep track of the competition."

"Do you have a Smith and Wesson Model 27?" Lydia asked.

"Of course, I do," Jonathan said. "That's a heavy gun, Lydia. Why don't you try the Model 66 with the K frame? It's about a dozen ounces lighter than the 27."

"I'd like a heavier gun. It stays down when fired," Lydia said, repeating what Hagerty had told her.

"I can understand that—if you use a magnum round. But LAPD only allows you to use .38 Special cartridges. Have they changed their policy?"

How does he know that? Lydia thought.

"It's because the Cowboy carries the bigger gun," Milo interjected.

Jonathan looked at him sharply. He turned back to Lydia. "Well, if you want the Model 27, help yourself. You might have a problem finding the right kind of holster for it."

"I've already bought one."

"But not the gun?"

"The store didn't have a Model 27 in stock. They should have one for me in a few weeks."

"Good, I see you've thought of everything. Are you sure you can't come with us? How about coming down for a drink?"

"Dad, I really have to go." Lydia paused for a second. "Is it all right if I look for something in my old room? I'm missing a necklace Mom gave me."

"Honey, this has always been your home. I have left instructions that nothing is to be removed from your room. Same with your mother. You are always welcome to come here. And stay permanently if you like."

Fat chance of that, thought Lydia as she watched them leave.

Chapter Nine

LYDIA DIDN'T find the necklace in her old room, but when she entered her old closet, she found three nice sweaters she had left behind. She folded them carefully and placed them in a black carryall bag that was lying on the floor.

She looked around before leaving. The room was the same as she remembered it. The bed was made up and the carpet showed signs of having been recently vacuumed.

The photographs that had been in her room were now in her condo. After her mother's funeral almost three years ago, Lydia removed most of her belongings, never intending to come back.

But being in her room once more caused Lydia to remember that funeral with some degree of sadness. Vivienne was a warm and generous woman who suffered greatly when she had to send Lydia away to a prep school to keep her away from Carlos.

Lydia decided to look around her mother's bedroom before she went down to the basement and took what she needed from the gun vault. Her mother's bedroom was a few doors down the hallway from Lydia's and was twice as large. Lydia entered the bedroom and turned on the lights.

Her mother's perfume still filled the air, the pleasant fragrance of orange blossoms. One of her mother's dressing gowns was laid neatly on top of the bed, giving the appearance she had just stepped out for a moment.

Lydia moved slowly through the room, letting her fingers run across an armoire as she passed. She stopped, went back, and opened the door of the armoire. It was empty.

Didn't Jonathan say nothing had been removed from her mother's room?

Lydia looked at the bed and the dressing gown. She wanted to touch and feel the gown, but she didn't. Tears rolled onto her cheeks when she saw a nightstand where her mother kept a studio portrait of herself with Lydia sitting on her lap when she was just five-years old. Lydia took the portrait and placed it gently into the carryall.

Another photograph was lying face down on the nightstand on the opposite side of the bed. Lydia walked around the bed and picked it up. It was the wedding photo of her mother and Jonathan taken almost eight years ago. They were smiling happily.

Lydia opened the top drawer of the nightstand. Something rattled inside. She pulled the drawer farther out and found a cartridge at the back. She picked it up. It was a .40 caliber cartridge. There was a stain of some sort on the bottom of the drawer. Lydia bent over and sniffed it. It smelled of solvent—the kind of solvent used to clean guns.

She remembered her mother hated guns. If her mother had known that Lydia intended to become a police officer, she would have done her best to convince her not to do it.

But why was her mother keeping a gun in a house that had so many security measures in place?

Lydia looked at the set of closed double doors that led to Jonathan's bedroom. There was no lock on the doors.

Was her mother frightened of Jonathan for some reason?

She studied the cartridge for a moment or two before putting it back where she found it. She then began searching the rest of the room. Two minutes later, Lydia entered her mother's walk-in closet.

Later, when Lydia thought about it, she could not understand why it took her more than a minute before she realized that half of her mother's clothes were missing. Vivienne Benedict was a fastidious woman whose insistence on perfection had sometimes annoyed Lydia, and there was no more proof of this than the way she organized her closet. Normally, the clothes she wore around the house or to lunch or to run errands were on hangars on the left side of the closet. The clothes she wore whenever she went out to dinner or to see a play or to attend a social event were on hangars on the right side of the closet. Even then, there were degrees of separation in the way they were arranged that only Vivienne understood.

But there were large gaps in the rows of clothing on either side of the closet. Over half of them were missing.

The discovery caused Lydia to think back to the days before her mother died.

Was Vivienne planning on taking a trip?

Lydia couldn't remember if she was.

She wondered if the police had also noticed the missing clothes and asked Jonathan about it. But why would they? Her mother was killed in a traffic accident. There would be no reason for the police to come out to the house except to make a death notification, and there was no way Jonathan would even let them come onto the property without a search warrant.

At the far end of the closet was a built-in shoe rack. Underneath the rack was a large space where her mother stored her suitcases. There was only a single suitcase on the floor. It was a small one, a carry-on size.

Lydia knelt and opened it. Inside was a folded sheet of white paper. Lydia unfolded the paper and discovered it was a color copy of her mother's passport. She closed the suitcase and shoved it back against the wall, exposing a folded sheet of stationary underneath it. Lydia picked it up and opened it. It was a note hastily scribbled in her mother's handwriting.

All it said was, *"God, please help me."*

Lydia had been in the gun vault once before when her stepfather was entertaining some guests with dinner and decided to show them his storied collection of semi-automatic pistols and revolvers. All the weapons in the vault were modern weapons manufactured in the past 100 years. Not one of them was a bona fide collector's item from the Western frontier or had a history that would have made it particularly valuable.

The vault was protected by a steel door covered in green baize. Lydia punched in the code Jonathan had given her and opened the door. A string of fluorescent lights came on as she entered a long narrow room that looked like the gallery of an opulent museum.

Rows of glass-covered cabinets lined either side of the room. The metallic smell of gun oil and solvent permeated the room, even though an air conditioner and humidifier were working to purify the air.

From her previous visit to the vault, Lydia knew that revolvers were stored in the cabinets on the left side of room and semi-automatics on the right. Each gun was displayed in a felt-backed niche with a brass plate that showed its make, model, serial number, and date of manufacture. The guns were organized in the cabinets by manufacturer, and each of the cabinets had open spaces at the bottom for additions.

Lydia decided to look at the cabinets displaying the semi-automatics. She walked down the long room until she came to two cabinets with guns manufactured by Beretta.

She found what she was looking for—an empty space with a label showing it had once been occupied by a Beretta 96F. The gun used the .40 caliber cartridge, the same caliber of cartridge that Lydia found in the drawer of her mother's nightstand.

Lydia looked around to make sure no ammo was kept in the vault. There was none. Her mother would have gone out to buy it unless Jonathan had a stash of ammo kept in the house.

When she turned to face the cabinets containing the revolvers something caught her eye at the far end of the room, something she had not noticed when she had been down here before.

It was another door. It was made of heavy steel and painted to match the color of the back wall. She opened it and found a long tunnel stretching out into the darkness. Dank cold air flowed onto her face bringing with it the stale odor of decay. Stepping inside the tunnel, she found a keypad alongside the door, the same kind of keypad that was on the main door to the vault

The tunnel ran west to east, and Lydia tried to picture in her mind what was on the property between the house and the fence line to the east. She remembered there was a tool shed about 100 yards behind the house. That had to be where the tunnel terminated. She had no doubt that Jonathan's hidden business dealings made the addition of an escape tunnel a necessity. Security personnel and fourteen monitors were not enough to protect him.

Lydia turned her attention to the keypad and checked to make sure the combination was the same combination as for the main door. It was. There might be an occasion in the future to get into the house without letting Jonathan know she was there. She also checked the door to see if it was wired for a security alarm. It wasn't.

She went back inside the vault and shut the tunnel door. She walked along the row of cabinets until she came to the cabinet containing a large assortment of Smith and Wesson Magnum revolvers. There were different models, different sizes, different finishes, some blued, others in stainless steel, and several in pink. She found the model she was looking for and put it into the carryall.

And then a sudden thought struck her. She had no idea what danger she might face if she discovered the truth about her mother's death. Lydia was certain that someone had killed her, and whoever did it might come after her as well if they found out what she was doing.

She needed to be prepared for any eventuality. Once she had made up her mind, she moved fast. She took several guns from the magnum display case and placed them in the carry-all. When she realized that the empty spaces would be noticed, she moved several revolvers from the bottom row and placed them into the vacant spaces. She left one space open, the one for the Model 27 she told Jonathan she wanted to borrow. And just to make sure that nobody noticed that some of the guns in the bottom row were missing, she removed the labels and put them into her bag.

She turned toward the cabinets that held the semi-automatics. There was a nice selection of pistols that fired the .45 ACP cartridge. She helped herself to several small semi-automatics and took one large one as well, a 1911 Springfield that was originally designed for the armed forces.

When she walked out of the vault, she was carrying over twenty pounds of guns.

Chapter Ten

Lydia met Dick Hagerty at six a.m. on Saturday morning at a private gun range along a creek near Santa Clarita. The entrance sign identified itself as the RIVERCREEK RANGE. She was amazed at what she saw when she drove over cobbled concrete pavement through the creek and onto the property that was once an off-road motorcycle park.

There were eight ranges, all of them backing up against a hill scoured with motorcycle trails. None of the ranges were alike. The first one was neatly maintained with covered wooden cubicles and concrete paths leading to human-shaped targets at the twenty-five-yard line. Next to it was a combat range, with mechanically-operated targets on swivels.

But the six other ranges shared none of the orderliness of the other two. They were separated from each other by tall concrete walls covered with rough lumber and contained a wide variety of targets. Shooting positions consisted of ordinary wooden posts, window frames, fences, wooden walls, barrels, concrete culverts, fireplugs, telephone poles, a mailbox, and even an abandoned car shot full of holes.

Dick Hagerty was already there when she arrived. He was standing near a dark blue Mustang outside a double-wide trailer talking to a man wearing an Army Ranger baseball cap, an olive green T-shirt, and khaki shorts.

Lydia parked her BMW next to the two men and got out. She looked up at the large sign over the door to the double-wide. It read, HOME OF THE GUNFIGHTER'S COMBAT COURSE. And underneath it was another sign in smaller print that read, ONE SHOT, ONE KILL.

Hagerty introduced the man standing next to him as Jeremy Morgan, the owner of the range.

Lydia could not help but notice that Morgan had a below-the-knee prosthetic leg. He was young, probably around thirty, and his green eyes had a look of amusement in them when he caught Lydia looking at his leg.

"Jeremy runs a combat shooting course," Hagerty said. "I highly recommend it. He offers a discount for my friends."

"Is something like that really necessary?" Lydia asked. When she noticed that Hagerty and Morgan exchanged quick glances, she added, "We are already required to qualify on a combat course every other month."

Morgan smiled. "That combat course that you shoot at the Police Academy is not like anything you'd ever encounter in the field. You fire at paper targets while both you and your target are stationary. You qualify every month with an unobstructed line of fire, and you don't fire under stress. But what would happen if you got into a gunfight out in the field? Either you or your target are moving. Officers often get involved in a shooting after a foot pursuit when they cannot control their breathing and hold a gun steady. How do you cope with something like that without proper training? And then what happens at night when your only target is the flash of a gun being fired at you."

The last scenario laid out by Morgan was identical to what Lydia had experienced in Akheiser's warehouse. A silhouetted form that popped up in a door unexpectedly, a blinding flash of fire out of the darkness, and trying to shoot back while on the ground with a bullet in the stomach.

The first order of business was to sight in the .357 Magnum that Lydia borrowed from Jonathan's gun vault. One problem. She hadn't expected the recoil from the gun to be as powerful as it was. It rocked back like a wild animal squirming to get out of her hands, and she had problems bringing it down quickly for a second shot. That problem was partially alleviated by Hagerty's coaching on how to hold the gun when firing. Even so, the recoil from the gun was awesome. Lydia couldn't imagine the kind of damage the .357 magnum bullet would do to a human body.

Lydia wondered if Jonathan would have allowed her to borrow the gun if he knew she would actually fire it. She had heard him say once to a visitor that none of the guns he had in the vault, except for the older guns whose provenance he didn't know, had been fired. If she cleaned the weapon thoroughly, would you still be able to tell it had been fired? She wasn't sure.

Within an hour's time, Lydia had fired 100 rounds through the .357, and her shoulders ached as if she had done a hundred bench presses.

"Now you know what it's like to fire one of these with a full load," Hagerty said as Lydia cleaned her revolver at a work bench. "Magnum rounds are expensive. When you practice, I'd recommend you fire at least six magnum rounds before switching over to a .38 Special."

"I can afford magnum rounds," Lydia said.

"Yeah, I heard something like that," Hagerty said.

"Something like what?"

"That you can afford magnum rounds."

After she finished cleaning her weapon, Lydia sat on a spectator's bench and watched Hagerty practice with his revolver. Morgan came up and sat alongside her.

"He's really good, you know," Morgan said.

"I can see that."

Hagerty had fired nearly fifty rounds on the target range and had now moved to the combat range. At first, Lydia was puzzled by what she saw. Hagerty didn't fire from a standing position. He moved from barricade to barricade with his gun holstered and the clasp snapped shut. Then he would unexpectedly stop, draw his revolver while dropping to a knee, and fire at a target.

At first, Lydia thought this routine was overly dramatic, but then she realized that he never missed. His routine was Rivercreek's philosophy, one shot, one kill. Anybody running across Hagerty with a gun in his hand would be on the losing end of a gunfight.

Morgan echoed her thoughts. "He is really good, but you don't get to be good without the hours he puts into it." Morgan looked at Lydia. "But I happen to think he's got it wrong. He'd be better off with a semi-automatic. You don't have to reload after firing six rounds."

He started laughing unexpectedly. Puzzled, Lydia looked to see what he was laughing about.

Morgan shook his head. "Sometimes I talk in circles and don't realize how much bullshit my mouth is capable of producing. The point of my training program is one shot, one kill. The point of the semi-automatic is that if you miss, you have a lot more rounds left to bring your suspect down. In the meantime, the sonovabitch might be shooting at you with a weapon that is a lot more lethal."

He looked at Lydia. For a moment, his eyes lingered on her face a bit too long. Then he turned away and said, "You know what is wrong with the way your Department runs the combat course, don't you?"

Lydia shook her head.

"Of course, you don't. It's this whole business of firing two shots into the body mass and then one in the head. Christ, have you ever heard of anything so stupid? Why would anyone be dumb enough to fire at the head after missing two shots at the body? And if the suspect doesn't go down after you fire two shots, do you think he'll be standing there to let you get a shot at his fucking head. Hell no! He's going to be shooting back, and he might not miss."

Customers were beginning to drift onto the property when Lydia left the range two hours later. Watching Hagerty practice and listening to what Morgan had said convinced Lydia that his combat course had merit. Even though she hadn't planned on staying with the Department, she liked the idea of making one shot count. She signed up for the combat course. It consisted of six-half days, and the first round was scheduled for next Saturday. She thought it was the right decision. One day, she might find it necessary to use some of the things that Morgan was planning to teach her.

CHAPTER ELEVEN

EARLY MONDAY morning, Lydia wearing her service uniform and the .357 Magnum she borrowed from Jonathan entered the detective squad room. It was a large room, cluttered with table-desks that could accommodate four detectives with each member of a team sitting across from each other. Five or six detectives were already in the room. One of them was Sergeant Billy Vernor who was sifting through a stack of crime reports.

Lydia could not help but sneak a look at a door at the end of a short hallway on the left side of the squad room. It had a sign above it that read, HOMICIDE. The door was usually closed as it was now, but when Lydia had been in the detective squad room on several other occasions, it was open, and she could hear people working in the small office.

Vernor looked up as she approached. Frowning, he looked at Lydia, his eyes roving over Lydia's body from the top of her head to her gun belt.

"Did we bring civvies to work with us today?" Vernor asked.

Lydia stared at him for a moment and then nodded.

Vernor looked at her holster. "Is that a .357 Magnum? A fucking six-inch?"

"Yes, sir."

"Hagerty's idea of fun and games?"

Lydia nodded.

"I carry one, too. With a four-inch barrel. Not the cannon you got there. Do you have an off-duty holster for it?"

"Not yet, sir."

"Is your Beretta or whatever piece of crap the Department issued you in your locker?"

"Yes, sir."

"Do you have an off-duty holster that goes with it?"

"Yes, sir."

"Then get it! And get into your street clothes."

"Yes, sir." Lydia turned to go but was stopped by Vernor's gruff voice.

"Harte!"

When she turned, she saw he was smiling.

"Don't call me sir. Never been knighted by any queen or king. Never will be. Call me Billy."

"Yes, sir…I mean, yes, Billy."

She left the squad room wondering why the word 'goat' came to mind when she heard him say his first name.

Lydia returned to the squad room fifteen minutes later wearing a blue pullover sweater and jeans. She wore her Beretta on her belt under a charcoal gray blazer she borrowed from one of the female officers in the locker room.

She sat down across the desk from Vernor. He shoved a stack of reports toward her.

"These are the weekend's 459s in my patch. I'm responsible for everything that happens south of Santa Monica. Look them over to get a feel for what's going on, and then pin the locations on the map."

Lydia nodded. She quickly reviewed the reports. They were crime reports, all burglaries, some residential, some commercial.

Vernor was on the phone, and Lydia listened to what he was saying while she sifted through the reports. He was talking to some of the victims of burglaries committed over the weekend, trying to glean further information about what had happened and making sure that Latent Prints had already come out to lift prints and to take photos of the point of entry.

Lydia stood up, and taking the reports with her, walked over to the large map of Century Division that occupied a good part of one wall. Colored pins marked the location of serious crimes; murders, rapes, robberies, burglaries, vehicle thefts, and the like. The pin designated for burglary was bright green. The area that Vernor was responsible for was about one fifth the size of the area north of Santa Monica Boulevard, yet Vernor's area had twice as many burglaries.

She noticed that the green pins were spread uniformly across the map except for one anomaly. There was a concentration of about thirty pins centered in an area about five blocks south of Santa Monica Avenue. Most of them were green, but there were also blue ones, marking the locations where cars were stolen.

"Do you know why there's so many pins in that spot?"

Lydia turned to find Billy Vernor standing behind her. She turned back to the map and after a moment said, "There's a high school there. Jefferson High, I believe."

"That's right. What does that tell you?"

"It's a no-brainer. Students are responsible for this."

"And guess what?" Billy said. "Nearly all of these capers are pulled off by just three boys." He paused for a moment. "Do you know what that map looks like during summer break?"

Lydia shook her head.

"The green pins fly out all over the place…like a bunch of ants after someone kicks open their mound." He paused for a moment and then mumbled. "There are only two discernible burglary patterns in this Division, and that is one of them."

Without saying anything more, Vernor went back to his desk, leaving Lydia to wonder what the other pattern was.

Lydia set about the task of putting new pins onto the map for each of the burglary reports that had been reported over the weekend. Behind her, she heard other detectives coming into work. She overheard some wiseass comments when they noticed her working on the map, but none of them were serious enough to piss her off.

When she was done, Lydia rejoined Vernor at the desk. Seated at the other two chairs at their table was the other team of detectives who Vernor introduced as Finlayson and Gordon. Both detectives were excessively polite, both warmly welcoming her to the burglary table, causing Lydia to wonder if they had been talked to by Vernor.

Gordan sat in the chair next to Lydia and Finlayson next to Vernor. Both men were overweight, a physical condition that seemed to plague the detective squad room, even among the few women who worked there. Finlayson and Gordon immediately got to work and began making follow-up phone calls to the victims of burglaries that had occurred over the weekend in their part of Century Division north of Santa Monica Boulevard.

A few minutes later, Vernor looked across the table at Lydia. "As soon as I get done with my paperwork, we'll head down to the D.A.'s office to see if we can get a filing on these two assholes."

"What two assholes?" Lydia asked.

Vernor slid two folders across the desk and Lydia picked them up. The first one contained the rap sheet of a man named Frankie Stoudemire, a white male, age thirty-one. Most of his arrests were for petty crimes, but three of them were for burglary. He was convicted of burglary twice and spent three years in prison on the last charge.

Also, inside the folder was an arrest report. Stoudemire had been arrested over the weekend by officers who caught him coming out of a closed business in the early morning hours.

The second folder contained an arrest report for an eighteen-year-old named Danny Murdock who had never been arrested before. There was a picture attached to the arrest report. He had a look of shock in his eyes.

Lydia felt the detective named Gordon nudge her arm with his elbow. Irritated at the unwelcomed contact, she glared at him.

"Sorry," he said. "Are you doing okay?"

She smelled a hint of whiskey on his breath that was masked by after shave.

Vernor with hooded eyes glared at Gordon.

"I'm fine. And you?" Lydia said.

"I just wanted to tell you that if you took out Searles, you did all right by me."

"I didn't take out Searles," Lydia said without thinking.

"She's been instructed not to talk about the shooting," Vernor interjected.

"I wasn't asking her anything about the shooting. I was just making a fucking statement."

"It was a statement likely to elicit a response about the shooting."

Gordon laughed. "I'm not as subtle as you, Vernor."

"Nor as good looking," his partner added.

Vernor got up from his chair. "Let's go, Lydia, before Gordon unleashes one of his famous farts."

Lydia found the trip to the D.A.'s office to be interesting. If what had subsequently happened with the filing deputy was the norm, the criminal justice system was wobbling and just short of being fucked up.

The filing deputy was a red-headed kid a half year out of law school who had an attitude that anyone who didn't have a law degree was from the inferior social classes. He approved a burglary filing on Murdock, but only after reading the burglary, arrest, and follow-up reports two times. When he got to the materials on Frankie Stoudemire, he became truculent and began acting like the ass he was.

"How come they didn't get Mr. Stoudemire to sign a waiver of his Miranda rights?"

"Because," Vernor said patiently, "the officers didn't give the asshole his Miranda warnings."

"They didn't give Mr. Stoudemire the Miranda warning?" the kid asked, emphasizing the word 'mister'.

Vernor looked at Lydia. "Didn't I just say that?"

Lydia nodded.

"Isn't it your Department's policy to give the Miranda warning to all arrestees?"

"It is the policy if you intend to question the fucking suspect."

"They didn't question him?"

Vernor shook his head. "They didn't need to question him, counsel. The officers saw his pickup parked next to the back entrance of an electronics store at three in the morning. They waited until he came out. When he did, he was dragging a box containing a big screen TV. They caught him in the act of committing a burglary. Why would they want to fuck up their case by asking him questions?"

The kid stared blankly at Vernor for a few seconds and then suddenly and without warning got up and walked out of the room.

Lydia looked at Vernor. "What's going on?"

"Probably going to see his supervisor," Vernor explained. "For advice on what to do. Did you see his graduation certificate?"

Lydia had. The kid had graduated from the USC law school.

"If he's working here," Vernor added, "he doesn't have a daddy rich enough to place him in a major law firm."

A few minutes later, the kid from the USC law school came back and approved a filing for burglary on Stoudemire.

After lunch at a deli on Sepulveda, Vernor surprised Lydia by not going back to the station. Instead, he drove east on Olympic and then turned south into a residential neighborhood. A few minutes later, he slowed the car as they approached Jefferson High School.

The school was a huge monstrosity that had an ornate entrance made of buff-colored brick. Most of the windows were open, evidence of an in-operative air conditioning system. No one was on the steps or sidewalks in front of the school and it was strangely quiet.

"No one's in school today," Vernor said. He spoke so quietly that Lydia had to lean over to hear what he was saying. "I keep in touch with the at-tendance counsellor. She told me it's teacher's conference day or something like that. We'll come back tomorrow at three when the kid gets out of school. Maybe, he'll still have the goods on him—if he hasn't sold them al-ready."

Lydia had no idea what Vernor was talking about and told him so.

"Three of the burglaries reported last Friday afternoon were from houses on the same block not far from here," Vernor said. "Two of them reported nothing was stolen other than credit cards and loose change. The third victim reported a .38 caliber Smith and Wesson Airweight and a Springfield 1911 were stolen. A kid by the name of Jimmy Spahn likes to steal guns. He goes to Jefferson."

"Spahn?"

"His uncle is the infamous Willie Spahn. Busted a half dozen times for burglary. The entire family is fucked up. Father currently in prison for rob-bery. Mother arrested several times for shoplifting. Not very bright, but a fine looking woman for someone in her forties. Believe it or not, she keeps a nice home on Maple within walking distance of the high school."

They drove by the Spahn home on Maple. It was a freshly painted, pre-World War I, Cape Cod. A woman, wearing a T and tight shorts, was on her knees digging crabgrass out of the lawn and showing off a neatly sculptured butt.

"Don't look," Billy said as he glided the car smoothly past the house. "That's the Missus. She keeps herself in shape when she isn't busy scoping out Macy's for freebies."

After they had passed the house, Lydia leaned over to get a view of the woman in the sideview mirror. The lady was standing up, trowel in hand, staring at their car.

"She spotted us," Lydia said.

"Got eyes out the back of her ass," Vernor said. "Comes in handy for a professional shoplifter." He made a right turn at the corner, and as he did so, Lydia took one more look up the street. Mrs. Spahn was back to picking crabgrass.

"Why does the boy go for guns?" Lydia asked.

"Think about it. A kid with no car—unless he steals one—which he frequently does. You can't steal a plasma screen television without a car. Stealing an iPad or cell phone is next to worthless if you don't know the password. A gun and credit cards are the easiest things for a kid to steal because they can be easily hidden."

"What does the kid do with the guns?"

"He sells them."

"Why would someone want to buy a stolen gun?"

Vernor looked at Lydia as if he didn't quite believe what she said. After a minute, he said, "I seem to forget you've only been out in the field for just a couple of weeks. A lot of people want a gun that can't be traced just in case they have to shoot someone. Bank robbers, liquor store bandits. Maybe a hit man, although I seriously doubt that. Maybe even a husband who wants to kill his wife."

"Or," Lydia said, "maybe a wife who wants to kill her husband."

Vernor smiled. "That's also true."

It appeared to Lydia that Vernor was driving randomly through the neighborhoods, occasionally driving onto a street with commercial buildings and retail stores, but then turning suddenly into a residential neighborhood. He was always paying attention to who was walking on the sidewalks and would frequently look back in the rearview mirror if he saw something he thought worth a second look.

Lydia remembered one of the things Hagerty had told her about police work. Knowing what to look for is a matter of experience and being able to recognize when someone is doing something that just doesn't look right. Lydia had no intention of staying on the job long enough to learn how to do that, but she was so impressed by how Hagerty and Vernor managed to stay so focused on police work that she found herself trying to imitate what they did. Watching people on the sidewalk, people going into stores, people in parking lots, and people in cars next to them.

She didn't realize where they were until Vernor suddenly slowed the car down. In front of them on the left side of the street was the large brick warehouse where she had been shot and Searles had been killed.

Chapter Twelve

"Do you mind if we go in and have a word with the owner?" Vernor asked when he noticed Lydia had pressed a fist to her mouth and seemed to be trying to suppress a cough.

She looked at him. "What?"

A car behind them honked the horn.

Vernor pulled the car to the side of the road and turned off the engine.

"Maybe, we should go back to the station…"

"I'm all right," Lydia said, a little too loudly.

"I'm going back to the station."

"No, you're not. Not because of me."

Vernor started the car and began driving down the street past the warehouse.

When Lydia saw what he was doing, she turned to him. "Billy, you're not going back to the station because of me. If you need to go in there for some reason, let's go back and do it."

Vernor sighed and made a U-turn.

Lydia was unconsciously rippling the fingers of her left hand across her belly as if she was playing a piano when Vernor drove into the parking lot behind the warehouse.

Several cars were parked in spaces next to the dock and Vernor pulled alongside one of them.

Lydia got out of the car and paused to look up at the open door at the top of the ramp. She noticed for the first time that a video camera was installed above the roll-up door.

"Are you coming in?" Vernor asked. He was already halfway up the ramp and looking down at Lydia.

"Yes," Lydia said, feeling an odd sensation in her stomach.

Once inside the warehouse, Lydia looked off to the right towards the doorway that led to darkened offices at the far end of the dusty aisle. The odd feeling she had in her stomach was gone. The only feeling she now had was curiosity—curiosity about what had happened in that dark place and why.

But now, Billy Vernor was walking in the opposite direction toward a small well-lit office with glass windows that looked as if it had been built as a hasty afterthought.

Lydia had not seen the office the night her stomach was ripped apart by a bullet. She followed Billy toward the office.

A short man with a stubby build came out of the office to greet them.

"When did the shipment come in?" Vernor asked.

"Like I said over the phone. It came in over the weekend." He motioned toward the front of the building. "The crates are stacked over there."

Lydia looked to her right where there was a large space with hundreds of crates stacked on top of each other. Next to them was an industrial grade forklift.

The man looked at Lydia. "Who's the young lady?"

"This is Officer Lydia Harte." Vernor turned to Lydia. "Officer Harte, this relic standing before you is Bernie Akheiser. He owns this hellhole and is too goddamn cheap to hire anyone to help him out."

Lydia couldn't help thinking the man's last name sounded like someone sneezing.

"That's not strictly true," Akheiser said, grinning. "My wife helps with the books."

He stared at Lydia and Lydia stared back.

Akheiser wasn't just short; he was excessively short and built like an overweight penguin. His odd choice of clothing marked the appearance of an eccentric who didn't care about style. He wore a striped blue and yellow T shirt stained with coffee, camouflage grey and white cargo pants, and old-fashioned black and white tennis shoes that squeaked when he walked.

"Is this the young lady who…"

"The person who got shot," Lydia interrupted. "That's me."

"Are you all right?"

By now, the question was becoming routine if not annoying, but Lydia did not show her irritation. "I'm fine, thank you."

"So, who owns the crates?" Vernor asked.

"Robert's Club and Warehouse. They store their goods here when they don't have room in their stores. I'm amazed they're still with us."

"Why do you say that?" Lydia asked.

"What?"

"That they're still with you."

"We got hit for a half million of their product three months back. If I didn't have insurance, Robert's would have found some other place to store their goods."

"What's in the crates they brought in over the weekend?" Lydia said.

"Big screen televisions, high-quality sound systems, computers, stoves, refrigerators, and the like." Akheiser threw a sideways glance at Vernor and his voice dropped a scale. "They also had a lot of goods in here on the night of the shooting. Maybe even more than now."

"I noticed you have a video camera above the loading ramp," Lydia said. "Was anything recorded on the night of the shooting?"

Akheiser looked from Lydia to Vernor. "Don't you guys talk to each other?"

"We do," Vernor said, "but we haven't talked about what happened here."

Akheiser looked at him in disbelief and then turned to Lydia. "That camera sends a feed to a recorder in my office. It was turned off the night that happened."

"Who turned it off?" Lydia asked.

"I don't know. I didn't do it, and my wife didn't do it. We found the plug had been pulled out of the electrical outlet. Not all the way. Just enough to break the connection."

"Was anything taken that night?"

"Not that I know of. Robert's shipment wasn't touched. None of the containers had been broken into. Look, I told all of this to Sergeant Vernor."

"I'd like her to hear it from you," Vernor said.

"Okay, I get it. You're just checking to see if the answers are the same, aren't you, Billy?" Akheiser said, looking very amused. "I see that on a lot of cop shows."

Lydia noticed the informal use of 'Billy' when Akheiser spoke to Vernor.

"Do you two know each other," Lydia asked.

Vernor shrugged. "I interviewed Mr. Akheiser one night at his home. His wife invited me to dinner. I think I might have stayed too long."

"And drank too much," Akheiser said. "I had to call a taxi for him."

"Okay," Lydia said, wondering if there was more to it than that. "I have one more question, Mr. Akheiser. Is that back door at the ramp always open?"

"As a matter of fact, it isn't."

Lydia said nothing, hoping that silence would keep the man talking. It worked.

"Okay, here's the deal. I open the door at seven when I get here and lock it at night when I leave. Usually around six. It shouldn't have been open that night unless a customer left it open."

"How do the customers get in if the place is locked up? Do they have a passcode?"

"They do, and they don't. If they need to get in after hours, they call my answering service and get the code for the day. It changes every night."

"Did anybody call in and get the passcode the night of the shooting?"

"Two people. Bill Samuels who collects junk that he sells at flea markets and Anita Covell from Jay's Tire Emporium."

Vernor answered her unspoken question. "The lady from the Tire Emporium verified she made the call, but Samuels said he didn't."

Lydia nodded. "So, someone who knows how this place works made the call and got the code. Does anyone work here besides you and your wife?"

"I have a service that comes in once a week with a sweeper." Akheiser looked around in disgust. "Not that you'd notice it. It looks like we store coal dust in here."

"Do you have an accountant or someone who comes in and handles the books?"

"My wife does the books and handles the receipts and bills. I handle the customers. I have no employees. I don't need the headaches."

"What about vacations? What happens when you want to take some time off?"

"I live in Beverly Hills. Who needs a fucking vacation when you live in Beverly Hills?"

Before they left, Vernor suggested they look at the office where the shooting took place.

Lydia didn't mind. The initial feeling of dread she experienced when she first entered the warehouse was now replaced by curiosity.

Akheiser led them to the darkened office Lydia had entered on the evening she had been shot. He found the light switch and turned it on. The area where Lydia had fallen had been swept clean. There was no trace of dried blood anywhere, but there were traces of chalk marks still on the floor not far from where she went down.

The rest of the room was just as dirty as Lydia remembered it.

"What's in the next room?" Vernor asked, pointing to the door where Lydia had seen a silhouetted figure suddenly emerge on the night she got shot.

"It's a hallway," Akheiser answered. "And a lot of offices for the honchos who ran this place. Some of them are quite nice. I don't use them. I prefer to be out on the floor where I can see who is entering my building."

"What was this building used for?" Lydia asked.

"They sold steel products for the construction industry. The room here was where the sales people took orders."

Lydia walked over to the door on the other side of the room. She looked up and saw a jagged hole in the header where a bullet had been lodged and then removed by forensics.

"Never did understand how a bullet hit that header," Akheiser said. "Whoever fired that shot needs a lot of practice."

Lydia saw Vernor staring at her, expecting her to react to what Akheiser had just said. She remembered Vernor's comment earlier that morning about Gordon making a statement that was likely to elicit a response.

Is that why Vernor brought her? To get her to say something about the shooting?

Before, they left, Vernor told Akheiser he should hire an on-site security officer for Friday and Saturday night just in case someone decided to break in and steal the crates belonging to Robert's Club and Warehouse.

Akheiser replied he would think about it.

Once they were back inside the car, Lydia turned toward Billy. "I hope you didn't mind me asking all of those questions."

"I didn't. I already asked him the same questions."

"Did he say anything different."

"He didn't. But I did learn something new." He looked at her and smiled. "I learned a lot about you."

CHAPTER THIRTEEN

LATER, WHEN Lydia entered the squad room, she saw two boys in Eagle Scout uniforms adding and removing green marker pins from the wall map. She turned to Vernor. "Why did you have me working on the pin map when we have volunteers who do that?"

"Because I want you to get a sense of the crime patterns in this division," Vernor said. "I would like you to think about what we can do better to track crime in this Division by computer."

"Why do you think I can do something like that?"

"I've been told you have a degree in computers."

Lydia slowly sat down on her side of the desk, wondering what else Vernor knew about her.

"My major was computer engineering, not computer programming. And it was in hardware design not software."

"There's a difference?"

"About twenty thousand a year." Lydia looked at the crime map. "I did take one or two courses in programming. But from what I've seen, it would not be an easy thing to do. You would either have to redesign the crime reports to set the parameters you want or have someone doing data entry who is savvy enough to understand what you need."

"What do you mean by someone savvy enough?"

"That person would have to be trained on what to look for in the body of the report and then make a judgment about what needs to be entered into the computer." Lydia thought for a moment and then said, "I have a friend who's a programmer. I can have her look at it if you let me take a few reports home. But I really don't think she can help us."

"Who in hell came up with this idea," Jenny Hamilton said as she slid the burglary reports across the table toward Lydia, but then took them back and started flipping through them again. "Right now, the only fucking thing you can do with these is on a macro scale, like how many crimes were committed in an R.D….whatever the fuck an R.D. is, and…"

"An R.D. is a reporting district," Lydia interrupted.

"Whatever! You got a serious problem here, sweetie. You can't make a computer do what you want it to do without making major formatting changes to the reports, and I'm pretty sure that neither you or that guy you work with is in a high enough position to do that."

They were sitting outside on the patio of a small restaurant called Jason's in Westwood just a few blocks south of the UCLA campus.

"What about crimes with large outcomes?"

"Outcomes?"

"Yes. There's a storage facility not far from here that had a half million dollars of merchandise stolen. How could you track burglaries for example that had a loss like that?"

Jenny Hamilton was a beautiful woman whose black hair was the same as Lydia's but kept shorter. She differed from Lydia in that she had skin so pale she had to stay out of the sun. The contrast between her black hair and pale skin made applying morning makeup a challenge. When Jenny went out in the evening with Rod, her fiancé, and needed to dress up, she had to work hard on her face to avoid looking like one of Dracula's wives.

There was another thing that made Jenny different from Lydia.

Jenny was bisexual.

Lydia wasn't…or didn't want to be.

One night, after the track season had wound down, Jenny had lured Lydia to her apartment after she got Lydia so drunk she could hardly walk. Lydia couldn't remember much about that evening, but she did remember that Jenny had licked her private parts like a little kid lapping up an ice cream cone and the outcome was explosive.

The experience had Lydia shaking like a caffeine high the next day and had the effect of disrupting her post-season practice routine for at least two weeks. She didn't know why she had been so shaken by the experience, but she resolved she would not let Jenny do that to her again.

Jenny worked as a computer programmer in a large investment firm in Century City where she helped financial analysts by designing programs that would allow them to look at financial data in new and different ways. She was good at it even though she had graduated from UCLA less than two years ago. If anybody could figure out a way to do what Vernor had suggested with mapping crime trends, Jenny would be that person.

Lydia watched Jenny flip quickly through the reports. After a moment, Jenny looked up, her eyes began rapidly blinking, a nervous habit that Lydia had seen before when Jenny was in deep thought.

"You work in Century Division?" Jenny asked.

"Yes."

"How does a detective in your division know if someone in another division pulls off the same kind of robbery?"

"They brief us in roll call on serious crimes in other divisions. I suppose burglary detectives get the same kind of information."

"Sounds primitive to me."

Lydia shrugged. "It's the government, Jenny. No one in City Hall is raising hell about getting a better crime tracking system."

Jenny leaned across the table. "Why are you doing this, Lydia? You could be making three times as much money as you are now."

"I don't need the money."

"I know that, sweetie! But you could be on the Riviera right now... soaking up the sun." She smiled mischievously. "Or whatever."

"I live in California, Jenny, and I have all the sun I need. What's in that portfolio you brought with you?"

Jenny picked up a leather folio that was on the floor next to her purse and opened it. She pulled out three files and then looked across the table at Lydia with a look that made Lydia think of the devil. "He's very rich, Lydia. Maybe even richer than you."

"Okay."

The waitress approached, and Jenny quickly slid the files back into the portfolio and deftly grabbed both checks.

After the waitress left with Jenny's credit card, she smiled. "It might not be a good idea to let anyone see what's in here."

"I suppose not. Are there any surprises?"

"Yes. Your dad has too much money. He should give some to me."

Lydia grimaced. "I already know that. And he's not my dad!"

"I estimate he's worth more than 500 million dollars, but then again, so are you."

"Not quite. I only get an allowance."

Jenny snorted. "Until you're twenty-six and then you get the corpse."

"The corpus," Lydia corrected. She looked around to make sure no one was listening.

"If you live long enough." Jenny saw the look on Lydia's face, so she quickly added, "Sorry to say, my dear, but you *are* in a dangerous profession."

"No more dangerous than coal mining."

"Your dad…excuse me, what do we call him?"

"Jonathan."

"Okay," Jenny said, reaching across the table and tapping the portfolio she slid across the table to Lydia. "Jonathan is a crook."

"He's not a crook," Lydia said. "I would consider the word 'crook' to be a euphemism for what he really is."

"Okay then. He's a mobster."

"Does your research tend to prove that?" Lydia asked, nodding her head at the portfolio

"Do you know his real name?"

"It's Benedict."

Jenny shook her head. "It's Benedetto."

"I didn't know that." Lydia frowned and paused for a moment, bringing her hand to her face.

"What's wrong, Lydia?"

"I should have known that, Jenny. He's Italian. His mother's last name is Benedetto."

Jenny smiled. "Well, duh!"

"I hate that, Jenny."

"What?"

"The 'well, duh'."

"People say it all the time."

"That's why I hate it. Why do you suppose Jonathan would take an elegant name like Benedetto and shorten it to Benedict?"

"Because Benny was already taken by a comedian?"

"Very funny." Lydia leaned forward. "So, are you going to let me look at those files?"

"Shall we go up to my apartment where I can lay them out for you in private?"

"No." Lydia said sharply. She looked away for a moment and then said very quietly. "Jenny, you know I don't want to do that anymore. Besides, what would Rod say if he found out." Lydia looked away and said softly. "Even if I wanted to, I can't have sex anymore."

"You don't need a uterus to have sex."

"Damn, you can be so insensitive at times!" Lydia said, tears forming in her eyes.

Jenny reached across the table and laid a hand on Lydia's. "Sorry, hon. I didn't mean to upset you."

Lydia stood up and picked up the portfolio. "Jenny, thank you for everything. I owe you."

She wiped the tears from her eyes. She wanted to tell Jenny that it wasn't the gunshot wound that was causing the problem with her sex drive. It was the loss of any desire to have sex.

That evening Lydia went out to the small balcony on the third floor of her condo. It overlooked a small park directly below and a golf course farther out that had a few stragglers trying to get a game in before it got too dark. To the northwest, the sun was making a blazing exit over the towers of Century City.

She laid the portfolio on a small wrought iron table and opened it. It contained three files documenting businesses owned or managed by Jonathan Benedict.

The first two businesses she already knew about. Her stepfather was the sole proprietor of The Benedict Armory, a specialty small-arms manufacturing plant located in South Carolina. What she didn't know was the financials, but they didn't surprise her when she saw them. The total assets of the company exceeded several million dollars and was valued at two hundred and fifty million dollars.

The second company was Pacific Coast Conversions, a foreign car conversion plant located in Culver City. She already knew that her stepbrother, Milo, managed the business, but she was surprised to learn that he and Jonathan were also partners in the enterprise.

The third file caused Lydia to stop breathing for a moment.

Jonathan also had a partnership interest in a trucking company that she didn't know about. It was also in Culver City, not more than seven miles from where she lived. There were two limited partners. One of them was her stepfather, and the other was Milo. But the big surprise was that the general and managing partner was her ex-fiancé, Jake Nilsson.

Lydia's hands began shaking as she sifted through the file. She got up, went to the kitchen, opened a bottle of wine, and poured herself a glass. She drank it down and then poured another glass and took it out to the balcony.

Jake Nilsson! Her former fiancé?

What the hell?

Why had he lied to her about what he did for a living?

She picked up the file again. How could Jake be managing a trucking company when he worked as an attorney?

He was an attorney, wasn't he?

Lydia remembered that Jake had taken her to his offices in Santa Monica on several occasions and had even introduced her to his secretary and to several other lawyers. She had even seen his office. He had a desk with a nameplate on it. A picture of them together at a restaurant in Malibu was on a credenza.

She sat for a long time that evening on the balcony, slowly sipping the wine, not tasting its bitter flavor, not realizing it had gone bad. It wasn't until the sliver of the moon had set over Century City that she got up and went to bed.

CHAPTER FOURTEEN

ON HER way to work, Lydia stopped and checked out the trucking company that was managed by Jake Nilsson. She was surprised at what she saw.

Strictly speaking, the facility wasn't just a trucking company. It was a modern warehouse facility occupying an entire block and ringed by a tall chain link fence. Two uniformed security guards manned the guard station at the front gate.

The warehouse, painted chalky white, was at least a hundred yards long and had a loading dock running across its entire length. Attached to the east side of the warehouse was a smaller building shingled in rustic wood that housed the office and next to it were two banks of fueling stations. Strangely enough, there was no name anywhere on the warehouse. Just a wide red band painted above the rollup doors that ran the length of the building.

It was busy this time of day with trucks pulling into the lot and backing onto the dock. Lydia counted over two dozen eighteen-wheelers on the lot.

Lydia made a U-turn and took one more pass across the front of the property. A red Corvette was parked next to the guard shack. Lydia couldn't see who was inside because her view was blocked by a security guard leaning over the driver's side window. Jake Nilsson owned a red Corvette.

Lydia arrived at the detective squad room at 7:30 a.m. to find Billy Vernor already at his desk. When he saw her, he immediately shut a black three-ring binder he had been examining and placed one hand on top of it.

"Sorry, I'm late," Lydia said.

Vernor looked into her eyes. "What happened to you? Your eyes are a little bloodshot. Are you a drinker?"

Lydia shrugged. "Didn't get much sleep last night." She glanced at the door to the Homicide room. It was closed.

Vernor noticed. "Would you rather be working Homicide than Burglary?"

Lydia stared at him for a moment before she realized he was joking. "I find working with you entertaining enough."

Vernor smiled. Lydia could not ever remember him smiling before.

"Okay, here's what you're going to be doing today." Vernor slid a stack of burglary reports across the desk towards her. "We didn't have many burglaries last night, so it should take you less than fifteen minutes to pin them up on the map. After that, I want you to take some of these reports and begin making follow-up calls to the victims. Did you hear what I was doing yesterday when I was calling victims?"

"You were asking for additional information. Isn't it a bit early to be making phone calls?"

"Makes people think we're on the ball when we're not," Vernor said dryly. "Plus, you'd be amazed at how many people south of Santa Monica have to get up early to go to work. You'll also have to ask if Latent Prints has been out, and if not, find out why not."

They finished the paperwork and the phone calls by 10:00 a.m. and went out onto the streets. This time Vernor didn't drive the neighborhood around Jefferson High School. He drove into a residential neighborhood just south of the I-10 Freeway. He had a stack of burglary reports on the seat between him and Lydia, and every so often, he would pick one up and look at it.

"What are we looking for?" Lydia asked.

"A daylight burglar operates this area," Vernor said. "He appears to be very selective. Hits about once a week, usually just before the lunch hour."

Lydia remembered seeing on the map a small pattern of about eight or nine green pins in the area Vernor was cruising.

"How do you know he hits just before the noon hour?" Lydia knew she had made a mistake asking that question from the way Vernor made a funny noise in his throat and shifted in his seat.

"I read," Vernor said. "I study my burglary reports carefully every day. The other team doesn't. They prefer to schmooze with their victims who tend to be a lot richer than the victims we have down here. They get a lot of perks doing that."

It occurred to Lydia that Vernor really didn't need a computer to track crime patterns. His memory did just as good a job as any computer ever could.

Vernor made another turn onto another residential street and pulled the car immediately to the curb.

Lydia saw a street sign that indicated that today was a street-sweeping day and no parking was allowed in the morning. The street had no vehicles parked on it, but in a driveway about four houses down was a black, mega-SUV, its nose pointing out to the street. No one was around the SUV, but its rear door was open.

"It takes balls to do that in broad daylight," Vernor said.

Lydia felt her heart beating rapidly. She believed they were about to catch a burglar committing a crime in progress.

But she was wrong.

A tall man came down the driveway and reached into the back of the SUV.

Vernor pulled his car forward and parked it at the curb, one driveway away from the SUV. He flipped through the reports until he found what he was looking for. After looking at it for a few seconds, he got out of the car and began walking across the lawn toward the SUV.

Lydia quickly followed.

The man pulled an oversized box from the back of the SUV and sat it down on the ground. He was out of shape and the effort caused him to bend over and begin wheezing.

"Mr. Driskell?" Vernor asked.

The man looked up. He looked at Vernor, then at Lydia, and then at their car parked at the curb.

"You can't park there," the man said, trying to catch his breath. "It's street-cleaning day."

"Are you, Mr. Driskell?" Vernor asked.

The man nodded. "What do you want?"

Vernor held up his badge. "Sergeant Vernor, LAPD. I talked to you this morning. I have a few more questions about the burglary you reported yesterday evening."

The man paused for a few seconds. "Oh," he said. "Prints have already come out. Thank you for your call this morning."

"What do you have in the back of the SUV?"

The man nervously shot a look inside the vehicle.

Lydia had no idea what was going on, but she sensed something was wrong. She pulled back her blazer and put a hand on her revolver.

"Oh," the man said. "I was going to call you. I already found my stolen property and was taking it back into the house."

"Really," Vernor said. "How fortuitous. Where did you find your stolen property?"

"In an alley."

"What alley?"

"I don't know. A few blocks away. I can take you there…if you want."

"Were they hidden or lying in the open."

"They were behind a dumpster."

"Really?"

The man nodded.

"Did you get an address?"

"There was no address. It was in an alley."

"May I see what you got in the truck?"

"It's an SUV."

"May I see what you got in the SUV?"

"I see no reason why not. Everything in there belongs to me."

Vernor stepped forward and the man backed slightly away. Vernor glanced back at Lydia and mouthed, "Watch him."

Lydia nodded.

Vernor began checking the contents of the SUV against the burglary report he held in his hand.

Vernor turned to Driskell. "What have you already taken into the house?"

"A flat screen TV and a handgun."

"Do you have any weapons on you?"

"No, sir."

My partner is going to search you, Mr. Driskell. Turn around and place your hands on your head."

"Am I under arrest?"

"Yep."

"What for?"

"Well for one thing, falsifying a police report. If you reported the stolen property to your insurance company, they are going to insist you be prosecuted for fraud. They take a dim view of people who steal from them."

Driskell began slowly backing up toward the house.

Vernor held up a hand. "You better stop right there, Mr. Driskell! Now, turn around!"

Driskell stopped moving.

"Now, put your hands behind your head. My partner is going to search you for weapons."

"She better not touch my balls," Driskell whined.

"I wouldn't dream of it," Lydia said.

Before they left, Lydia canvassed the neighbors in the area and found a frail old lady across the street who claimed she was on her porch drinking coffee and smoking a cigarette at 6:00 a.m. the day before and saw Driskell removing the items from his house and placing them into the back of the SUV.

When Lydia later asked Vernor how he knew Driskell was lying about finding the property in an alley, he explained that if the stolen items had been in an alley all night, there would have been a coat of dust on them and there wasn't.

It didn't occur to her until later to ask Vernor how he knew what Driskell had done in the first place.

CHAPTER FIFTEEN

WHEN THEY finished the paperwork on Driskell, it was already 2:40 p.m. and Lydia expected they would go out for a sandwich. But Vernor wasn't done, yet. He stood up from his desk, put on his coat, and said, "Let's go."

Lydia was thinking lunch, but when they had passed at least a half dozen cafes and sandwich shops, she asked where they were going.

She stared at Vernor expecting to get an answer, but he didn't. He was stonily concentrating on driving, hurrying to get somewhere.

Minutes later, Vernor drove his car into an alley and parked next to a freshly-painted two-car garage. He got out of the car and told Lydia to follow.

"What are we doing?" Lydia asked.

Vernor didn't answer. He was already entering the backyard of a house through a wooden gate.

Lydia followed, hurrying to catch up with Vernor who was moving fast. When she got past the garage, she found herself in a pleasant garden with pink and red azaleas under small shade trees and a virgin lawn without a weed in it. The house was a two-story affair painted in white with blue trim that looked unimpressive from the rear but probably was designed to look like a simple Queen Anne from the front.

By the time Lydia caught up with Vernor, he was already using a key on the back door.

"What are you doing?" Lydia hissed.

"Will you shut up?" Vernor said as he opened the door. "And get inside."

"Not until you tell me what you're doing."

Vernor turned to look at her. "This house is across the street from Jefferson High School. We're going to try and catch that sneaky little bastard in the act of selling the guns he stole last week. I want to find out who he's selling them to."

"Spahn?"

Billy nodded.

"How did you get the key to this place?"

"The real estate agent gave it to me. We're going upstairs. Follow me and quit flapping your mouth."

Lydia followed Vernor through the kitchen and down a hallway to the front entrance where a wooden stairway stained in walnut ran in a reverse direction to the second floor. To the left of the entrance was the front room. All the furniture had been removed and an overwhelming odor of varnish dominated the air.

On the second floor, they entered a carpeted and freshly painted room that overlooked the front entrance of the high school. The room had large double windows with drapes drawn partially back to reveal gauze curtain panels. A folding chair was placed a few feet back from the window.

Vernor went up to a window and cautiously peered out the side of a gauze panel. He looked at his watch and then back at Lydia. "Come in a little closer so you can see. He'll come out the main entrance."

Lydia nodded. "So, what do we do when he comes out."

"Good question. You run around to the front and follow him. I'll get the car."

"How will you know where I am?"

"You have a cell phone, don't you?" Vernor turned back to the window and muttered something about college kids.

They waited for a few more minutes, Vernor at the window, Lydia just far enough back to see the front entrance of the school.

Cars began pulling up to the curb in front of the school, and shortly afterwards, kids began streaming out of the building.

"How can you spot him in this crowd?" Lydia said.

"He always wears a black T or a black hoodie, sometimes with a Raiders logo on it." Vernor turned to look at Lydia. "You're going to stand out like a peacock on the street wearing that blazer."

"I can't take it off without anyone seeing I'm carrying a gun."

"Well, he knows me, but he doesn't know you. So, stay at least a half a block behind him. He has a habit of looking back when he's carrying stolen goods, but he doesn't check the opposite side of the street. That's where you want to be." Vernor moved forward and pulled open one of the gauze panels a wee bit. "Okay," Vernor said, "he's on the front steps now, talking to some girls."

Lydia stood on her toes and saw him. Jimmie Spahn was smaller than the two girls. He had a thick head of black hair, his face stark white in contrast to the hooded black sweatshirt he was wearing. The girls were avidly listening to what he was saying.

Finally, Spahn waved his hand at the girls, pulled the hood up over his head, and started walking east on Ohio Street.

Lydia noticed for the first time that Spahn was carrying a large camo-green backpack on his back.

"Let's go!" Vernor said as he turned from the window and headed for the door. "And watch out. Chances are, he's got a gun on him."

Lydia followed Vernor down the stairs. When they got outside, Vernor headed for the alley where the car was parked, and Lydia turned the corner toward the front of the house.

Once on the sidewalk, she looked east and saw a black hoodie in the crosswalk, a half block down. She hurried to catch up. Within two blocks, she was forty yards behind Jimmie Spahn on the opposite side of the street. She called Vernor on her cell phone and told him where she was.

"He's heading for a shopping center, two blocks down and then two blocks left," Vernor said.

How in hell does he know that? Lydia thought.

Vernor was right. There was a large shopping center on the northwest corner of the intersection of Illinois and Marquette. While waiting for the light to turn green in his favor, Jimmie Spahn turned and looked down the sidewalk. His eyes never made contact with Lydia who was walking with her head down on the other side of the street. When she looked up, Spahn was in the crosswalk, moving fast, the hoodie of his sweatshirt over his head.

Lydia continued across the intersection, keeping an eye on Spahn who turned suddenly across a raised landscape berm and then stepped off a low wall onto the parking lot of the shopping center. Lydia kept walking north on Marquette and then realized she had made a mistake.

Spahn had disappeared among the cars.

"I lost him in the parking lot," Lydia said into the cell phone.

"Find him, dammit," Vernor hissed.

Lydia crossed the street, stepped up onto the berm, and looked around. The parking lot was massive. The store nearest Marquette was a drugstore and the next in line was a supermarket called Mason's.

If Spahn went into one of the stores, he would be difficult to find.

Then she saw him, a black hoodie two rows of cars over, walking toward Mason's. Lydia heard the tinny voice of Vernor coming from the cell phone she was carrying at her side. She brought up the cell phone and said, "I've got him. He's in the parking lot in front of Mason's."

Spahn was now approaching the driveway in front of the supermarket, but he didn't go inside. Instead, he turned left and came back down the next row of cars.

"What in hell is he doing?" Lydia muttered to herself. She held her position on top of the berm, watching the bobbing hoodie swiveling from side to side as it made its way down the row. It wasn't until Spahn reached the end of the row and turned up another row that Lydia realized what he was doing.

He was looking for a car to steal, one of the newer luxury models with a keyless entry and ignition system. She remembered a lecture at the Police Academy by a detective from Burglary-Auto Theft Division who said that the new keyless systems were great for people who liked the convenience of getting into their car without fumbling around for a key. But the really lazy ones took it one step further. They never took their key fob with them. They left it in the car, so they would not have to go hunting for it before leaving their house. The problem was that it also made life easier for people who liked to steal cars.

Lydia watched Spahn as he suddenly ducked between the cars and stooped down. She got on the cell phone to Vernor. "I think he's trying to steal a car."

"Get a license number."

Lydia stepped down from the berm and jogged across the driveway and two rows of cars. She could no longer see where Spahn had gone. She moved slowly through another row of cars and looked up and down the driveway.

No Spahn.

Where in hell was he?

Then she heard a car start up to her left. She slowly began walking in the direction of the sound. A tail end of a silver car began backing out of a parking spot. It was a new Mercedes coupe and Spahn was behind the wheel.

Lydia lowered her head, pretending to look at her cell phone. She looked up when she heard the car stop moving.

The car was in the middle of the row facing her, but Spahn was looking down, apparently trying to find out how the gear shift lever worked. It took him a few seconds to get the car going again.

Lydia kept walking as he drove by, aware out of the corner of her eye that Spahn was looking at her. She slipped in between two cars and looked over the roof of a car as the Mercedes slowly drove up the lane toward Mason's, like a silver fish cruising a stream.

She brought the cell phone to her ear and heard Vernor yelling.

"Where in the hell are you, Harte?"

"He's in a silver Mercedes CLK with temporary tags. He's making a right turn in front of Mason's."

"Toward Marquette?"

"Roger that!" Lydia was already running, hoping to see what direction the Mercedes would turn when it got to Marquette. When she got to the driveway in front of Mason's, she looked to the right. The car was stopped at the Marquette exit, its left turn blinker on.

"He's turning left."

"I see him," came back Vernor. "Get out here!"

Lydia began jogging toward the Mercedes.

"You got a plate number?" Vernor asked.

"Negative. It has a temporary. New car."

"I see him. What's he waiting for? There's no traffic."

Lydia slowed when she realized the reason why Spahn had paused before entering the street. He was staring at her in the rearview mirror. Before she could bring the cell phone up, the car accelerated out of the driveway, its wheels spinning, laying down a trail of vaporized rubber.

She heard Vernor yelling on her cell phone, "Get out here now! He's made us."

When she got to the curb, she saw Vernor driving north on Marquette on the wrong side of the road, his horn blaring to warn oncoming traffic.

He pulled to the curb allowing Lydia time to jump into the car and then took off before Lydia got the door closed.

Up ahead, Spahn turned right onto a side street.

"Did they teach you how to run a pursuit at the goddamn Academy?"

Lydia didn't respond. She was trying to fasten her seatbelt.

"Give me the goddamn mike!" Vernor yelled.

Lydia gave up on the seatbelt and grabbed the mike. "What's our call sign?"

"Five-Delta-Sixteen."

Lydia keyed the mike. "Five-Delta-Sixteen is in pursuit of a 2006 Mercedes Coupe northbound on Marquette from Illinois."

Spahn suddenly turned the car to the east.

"Make that eastbound on Indiana," Vernor yelled.

Lydia repeated the command into the mike and put on her seatbelt seconds before Vernor threw the car into a four-wheel slide rounding the corner at Indiana.

"Do we have a siren?" Lydia yelled over the whine of the motor as Vernor gunned the accelerator.

"No," Vernor yelled back. "He's now southbound on Joliet."

Lydia repeated the command over the radio, and it was then and only then that a male dispatcher came on the frequency and asked, "All units, standby. Unit in pursuit, you're breaking up. Identify yourself."

She picked up the mike. "Five-Delta-Sixteen is in pursuit of a stolen Mercedes CLK southbound on Joliet from Indiana."

The dispatcher repeated what Lydia said and then asked if they had emergency equipment.

Lydia looked at Vernor for guidance. They were in a plainclothes car and it had no emergency equipment. No siren or emergency lights.

"Tell him that's an affirmative," Vernor yelled as the car bounced off a drainage channel running across the road at the next intersection.

"What?" Lydia yelled.

"Tell him we have emergency equipment. If you don't, we'll be ordered to shut down."

Lydia did what Vernor told her to do, knowing it was a violation of Department policy to go into a pursuit in a car without emergency equipment.

Vernor drove the car like devil was after him. He had cut the distance between them and the Mercedes down to fifty yards.

Up ahead the Mercedes hit the first of two drainage channels on either side of the intersection at Joliet Avenue sending up a shower of sparks as the rear of the car bottomed out.

Lydia braced herself for the impact of the first drainage channel. The car hit it hard and bounced Lydia out of her seat belt, striking her head on the roof of the car. She quickly recovered and braced herself for the second impact by forcing her feet up against the dash. The impact shook her insides, but it was not as bad as the first.

Vernor had narrowed the distance to thirty yards behind the Mercedes when it turned south at the next intersection and avoided a spin-out by bouncing off the side of a parked Cadillac.

Lydia picked up the mike. "Suspect is now southbound on Lasalle approaching Illinois."

The dispatcher repeated her broadcast.

Vernor turned onto Lasalle in a neat four-wheel drift that only a Hollywood stuntman could have executed. He was now ten yards behind Spahn as they approached busy Illinois Avenue.

Spahn busted the red light at the intersection, bringing heavy traffic in both directions to a screeching halt.

Vernor slammed on the brakes and looked both ways before crossing Illinois.

And then a voice over the radio, "Five-Delta-Sixteen, Air Two has a five-minute E.T.A. He'll take over the pursuit when he sees you."

Air Two was the LAPD helicopter that covered the San Fernando Valley area.

"Like hell, he will," Vernor shouted at Lydia. "I'm not about to let that little shit ditch his fucking guns."

One minute later, the pursuit was over. Spahn drove a few blocks down LaSalle and then turned west into a residential neighborhood. Halfway down the block, he pulled over to the curb and bailed out of the car. He ran around the front of the Mercedes, crossed the sidewalk, and ran down the driveway of the nearest house.

Vernor pulled up alongside the Mercedes. "Go after him! I'll try to head him off."

Lydia jumped out of the police car and ran down the driveway where she had last seen Spahn. She arrived in the backyard just in time to see

Spahn using his hands to vault over a four-foot chain link fence. The boy cried out as the bare metal at the top of the fence scraped his hands.

Lydia didn't need to climb over the fence. She lofted over it cleanly as if she had been running hurdles in a track meet.

The boy ran through another backyard, down the driveway, and onto the next street without looking for traffic.

Lydia was not so lucky. She had to slow down when a speeding car nearly hit her. She heard a helicopter coming in her direction from the east.

Was it Air Two?

If she thought about it, she would have realized it wasn't. Air Two would have been coming from the Valley, from the north, not from the east.

She chased Spahn into the next yard. He ran down the driveway alongside the house and reached a heavy wooden gate at least six feet high. He opened the gate and disappeared into the backyard.

When Lydia arrived in the backyard, the helicopter was almost overhead.

The boy, his backpack bouncing up and down on his scrawny back, was running like hell toward a six-foot board fence at the rear of the yard. He stopped, looked around, saw Lydia coming, and then spotted a dog shed backed up against the fence next to the garage. He ditched the backpack and used the shed's roof to loft himself over the wall.

Lydia sprinted at full speed toward the dog house and the wooden fence. In retrospect, she should not have been surprised at what happened next.

A six-foot gate, a six-foot wall surrounding the backyard, a fucking doghouse!

Too late to do anything about it, she saw a Doberman come out of the doghouse and start running toward her. She was not going to be able to make it to the fence in time to escape a mauling, so she cut right, then left, then changed direction again, heading straight for the confused dog who threw out his front legs to stop his momentum.

Lydia vaulted cleanly over the dog's head, changed course, and using the technique she learned for jumping the obstacle course at the Police Academy, planted her foot on the fence and lofted herself cleanly over it, landing in the soft grass of the neighboring yard.

Spahn was no longer in sight.

Lydia ran toward the driveway and saw the boy already crossing the street and entering the driveway of the next house over. She knew she could catch the little bastard. He would tire out a lot faster that she would.

Once she got to the street, she glanced both ways but not for traffic. *Where in hell was Vernor?*

She continued running and looked up to get a glimpse of the helicopter. It was somewhere behind her and she couldn't see it. She entered the next yard and ran down the driveway, only to find the little bastard already climbing over the next fence, this one five-feet high with a row of tall viburnum bushes on the other side that acted as a screen. She jumped the fence and landed into a dry, dusty space between the bushes and had to push her way through the dense underbrush to get into the backyard of another house.

But when Lydia arrived in the backyard, Spahn was no longer running. He was trying to open a wrought iron gate alongside the house. Lydia was on top of him in seconds.

Spahn heard her coming and turned to see Lydia reaching out to grab him by the collar. He tried to escape by ducking under her arm, but it didn't work.

Lydia grabbed Spahn by the hood and flung him around so hard that he landed in the lawn nearly ten feet away.

When Spahn got to his feet, Lydia tackled him and knocked him to the ground. She turned him over and put a knee to his back. Spahn continued to struggle, wriggling his body, making it difficult for Lydia to control him.

Frustrated, Lydia pulled out her cell phone and smacked him alongside the head. He yelped like an injured puppy and stopped resisting.

Lydia took out her handcuffs.

Spahn turned his head, trying to see Lydia. "You're in big trouble, lady. Wait until mother gets here."

"I'm already here," said a voice behind Lydia.

Lydia looked up and saw a woman standing about five feet away. She was dressed nicely in a black polo and white shorts, looking as if she had just returned from lunch with her girlfriends at a chic Beverly Hills restaurant.

She was also pointing a semi-automatic pistol at Lydia's head.

Lydia rose slowly to her feet. "I'm a police officer, lady. Put that gun down."

"I don't give a shit who you are. I'm going to teach you a lesson for fucking with my boy. Get on the fucking ground, bitch! Face down!"

"Teach her a lesson, Mommy," the boy said, rising from the ground. He was crying. "She hit me for no reason."

"You know, of course, there's a helicopter up there watching us?" Lydia said to the woman.

The woman looked up. The gun wavered and Lydia saw her chance. She charged the woman and plunged her head into her midsection.

They both went down, and the gun went off.

Lydia rolled off the woman, got to one knee, and looked around for the semi-automatic. It was on the ground about three feet away, but there was no way the woman was going to retrieve it. She was flat on the ground, staring at the sky in agony, making noises as if she was having an orgasm while trying to catch the wind that had been knocked out of her.

Lydia checked the boy to make sure he hadn't been shot. He was standing up, hands handcuffed behind his back. He was bawling like a baby. "Mommy, Mommy, please get up."

"Your Mommy's going to be okay," said a voice off to Lydia's right. "So, stop crying."

Lydia turned to see Billy Vernor standing about ten feet away, his gun hanging loosely in his hand.

"About fucking time you got here," Lydia said drily.

"Well, I got stuck in traffic," Vernor replied, bending down to pick up the gun the woman had pointed at Lydia. He looked at the woman who was now sitting, her head between her knees, breathing heavily.

"Mrs. Spahn, I'd like you to meet my new partner, Officer Lydia Harte. She's really something, ain't she?"

It was the first time Lydia realized that they were in the Spahn family's backyard.

Vernor waved Lydia over. "You alright?"

Lydia nodded.

"Where's the backpack?"

"A Doberman a few yards back is guarding it for us."

Vernor smiled. "Did you use any force on the boy?"

"I tackled him. Why?"

"Smile, Lydia. You're going to be on the six o'clock news."

Lydia looked up. The helicopter hovering overhead was from a local television station.

CHAPTER SIXTEEN

ONE OF the first things they did after taking the Spahns into custody was to retrieve the backpack Jimmie Spahn had dropped in someone's back yard. The Doberman wasn't about to give it up so easily. He sat in the backyard with his front paws around the backpack like he was the Sphinx guarding an ancient treasure and growled every time Vernor tried the latch on the gate.

Lydia went around the front and knocked on the door. The owner was an elderly man who listened in disbelief as Lydia explained the situation. He finally agreed to help retrieve the backpack after looking up and down the street to make sure he wasn't a victim of a prank that was being televised. He went out to the back yard and managed to divert the dog's attention with a treat while Lydia entered the yard, grabbed the backpack, and ran like hell for the gate.

When Vernor opened the shredded backpack, he found the Springfield 1911 and .38 Smith and Wesson Airweight that had been taken in a burglary a few days ago.

Both guns were loaded.

Lydia was writing the arrest report on Emily Spahn in the detective squad room when a tall black man in his early thirties approached the burglary desk.

He glanced at Lydia, smiled, then turned his attention to Vernor. "I heard the Spahns finally hit into a double play."

"Two more are in jail, this time for a long time," Vernor replied.

"And this young lady helped you do it?"

Lydia stared at him, wondering who he was. He was better dressed than anyone in the squad room, wearing a neatly-pressed white shirt with maroon tie and gray dress slacks. He was a big man who looked like he had spent a lot of time in the weightlifting room at the Police Academy.

"Lydia," Vernor said, "this is our boss, Lieutenant Hardemann. He's just come back from a month at the FBI Academy where they stuffed his head so full of shit that his bald head swelled twice its size."

Lydia suppressed an urge to rise, but then had to do so when the big man offered his hand. She shook hands with him, surprised how gentle the handshake was for a man with a hand that was twice the size of her own.

"Good to have you on board," Hardemann said, and then to Vernor, "How long will she be staying with us?"

"I think to the end of this week, but I'd like to keep her."

"Not possible," Hardemann said. "Congratulations on a job well down, Officer Harte. Billy has been trying to take down the Spahn family for years, and he finally got a partner that helped him get there."

Vernor looked across the desk to Lydia. "Do you see this big jerk, Lydia? He's going to be promoted to Captain in a couple of weeks, and the Department, in a stunning display of absurd theater, will probably assign him to a specialized detective division where he doesn't know his ass from a knot hole."

Surprisingly, Hardemann smiled. "If I had a better partner when I worked Burglary, I might have learned something."

Vernor looked at Lydia. "That's an insult, Lydia. I'm the partner he's talking about. But this guy is so dumb he couldn't teach a dog how to beg."

"How do you get away with talking to a lieutenant like that?" Lydia asked Vernor. They were on their way to serve a search warrant on the Spahn residence.

"He introduced me to my first wife." Vernor chuckled a moment. "Actually, my only wife."

When Lydia didn't respond, he continued. "Actually, she was married to Hardemann at the time."

"You're kidding."

"I'm not. She was a real bitch, one of those broads..." Vernor paused, looking to see if he offended Lydia "...one of those women who can project themselves as being the nicest person on earth when she is in public, but who becomes the vilest bitch that ever walked this earth in private. Hardemann never once hinted what she was like. He dumped her, and I started seeing her. When I married her, he bought me a case of beer." Vernor paused again. "Every once in a while, we get together and toast her memory."

"What happened to her?"

"She died. About two months after we married."

"What happened? An accident?"

When Vernor answered, his voice was soft. "Home invasion. Someone shot her when I was working late at night."

"How awful."

It was quiet for a moment and then Vernor said, "You know. I kid Hardemann quite a bit. I shouldn't get on him when people are around. He's a real classy guy and doesn't deserve to be treated like that."

But Lydia wasn't thinking about Vernor's self-recrimination. She was thinking about how convenient it was to get rid of a bothersome wife so quickly. She was also thinking about her mother and how she had been found dead in a place where she had little reason to be.

The search of the Spahn home proved to be very fruitful. One disused bedroom was loaded with a treasure trove of stolen goods. Most of them had price tags from major department stores still on them, but a lot of them were small items like jewelry and watches that showed signs of use. The latter had probably been stolen by Jimmie Spahn from homes he had burglarized. They even found several devices used by Department stores to remove security tags from clothing in Mrs. Spahn's jewelry box.

During the search, Vernor removed an expensive mink coat from the closet. He looked at Lydia and said, "Do you know what surprises me about this? This is a big haul for a shoplifter. I think maybe the boy stole this from one of the houses he burglarized." Vernor had paused for a moment and looked around "Actually, this is small time shit. There's bigger fish out there we don't even know about. And they're running fucking circles around us."

Lydia thought about that for a moment. "If we don't know who they are, how do we catch them?"

"We know what they do." Vernor paused for a moment. "One example is that warehouse where you were shot." He paused when he saw the corner of Lydia's mouth twitch.

"What about the warehouse?"

"That place has only been hit once, but I know of at least five other jobs where a whole shitload of big-ticket items have been stolen. Three in this division, two not far away in Pacific Division."

"So, how do we go about catching them?"

Vernor shrugged. "Hope we get a break. I have a few informants that have their ears to the ground. But all they managed to do so far is to get their ears dirty."

Later, they were in the detective squad room working on the report itemizing the 331 items of property they had recovered from the Spahn home.

"What do we do with all this?" Lydia asked.

"First things first," Vernor said. "We take care of booking this shit into evidence."

Tomorrow, he wanted Lydia to go through the residential burglary reports for the past three months that occurred within a two-mile radius of Jefferson High School and try to identify which of the stolen items belonged to which victims. Vernor hoped they would be able to establish additional charges against Jimmie Spahn if they could identify where they were stolen.

Meanwhile, Vernor would concentrate on building a tighter case against Mrs. Spahn. They already had enough evidence to charge her with theft and receiving stolen property, but Vernor wanted more. If they could prove she entered a store with intent to commit larceny, that was a different matter altogether. It was no longer theft; it was burglary, a felony that could draw serious jail time. The presence of department store security devices in Mrs. Spahn's jewelry case just might be enough to prove the requisite intent.

Lydia had noticed that throughout the evening Hardemann was working in his glass-walled office, his head down, apparently busy reading or writing something. When Lydia had finished the evidence report, she got up and put on her blazer.

Vernor looked at her with a weird smile on his face. "You're not done, yet. The boss wants to see you before you leave."

Lydia hesitantly approached Hardemann's office, throwing a sideways glance at the open door to the Homicide Unit's office. Hardemann looked up when she knocked and motioned her to come in and sit down.

"So, how do you like working with Billy Vernor?"

"It's interesting," Lydia said noncommittally.

"Just interesting?"

"I'm learning a lot from him, sir."

Hardemann leaned forward and rested his arms on his desk. "You're a real puzzle, aren't you?"

Lydia waited to see if Hardemann had anything further to say before responding. When he didn't, she asked, "Did I do something wrong, sir?"

Hardemann smiled. "Nothing wrong, Officer Harte. I'm just curious." He paused. "I ask myself why someone with your education would join the Police Department. You go to college and get a degree in computer engineering. I'm told you were so fast in the hurdles that you would have a shot at making the next Olympics, but instead, you join the Police Department. Do you know what my father said when I told him I was turning down an offer for a job with a law firm to join the Department?"

"No, sir."

"He asked if I lost my mind." Hardemann sat back in his chair. "Maybe, he was right. A day didn't go by on my first year on the job when I didn't ask myself if this was the day I was going to get shot."

Lydia shifted in her chair but said nothing.

"So, why are you here…doing something you don't need to do?"

Lydia thought of the lie she told the three board members during her employment interview. "Because I wanted to help people."

"Everyone says that." Hardemann smiled. "Maybe, what you really want to do is to find out who murdered your mother."

Lydia was so astonished at Hardemann's provocative comment that she didn't respond even though he obviously wanted her to do so. It was the first time that she heard someone from the Department use the word 'murder' in connection with her mother's death.

Hardemann continued. "You see, I know all about you, Officer Harte. I know you're not happy with how the Department stonewalled you when you asked for the details of your mother's death. I know your father's a crook. I know…"

"He's not my father," Lydia blurted out.

"Your stepfather, then. But then, there's your stepbrother who is a reserve officer with us. I have a feeling he is up to no good with that phony car conversion business of his, but the Captain for some reason thinks he's a straight-shooter. I also know you're upset with the investigation into your mother's death and that you want to find out what happened."

Lydia took a deep breath before replying. "If you were me and you believed your mother had been murdered, wouldn't you want to know who killed her? I tried talking to your people in Homicide, and they wouldn't tell me a goddamn thing about how she was killed."

"When did you talk to my people in Homicide?"

"A month or two after my mother was killed."

"Well, I wasn't here then, but I can tell you this. They were told not to discuss the case with anybody."

"Why?"

"I have no idea why, but I want to warn you that you are to stay out of the Homicide squad room."

Lydia stood up quickly, trying to keep the anger contained inside her.

"The reason why I don't want you going in there, Officer Harte, is there is nothing in my Homicide Unit about the investigation into your mother's death. One of the detectives who handled that case is retired. The other transferred out to a Homicide Unit in the Valley. I know very little about this case, Officer Harte. But I do know that the detectives who handled the call-out were able to identify your mother by the driver's license. found in her purse. They ran your mother's name through the system. Fifteen minutes later, they got a call from Detective Headquarters to stand down. An hour later, they were relieved by a team of detectives from Robbery-Homicide Division.

"Our people wrote up a report about what they saw and did and handed it over to the detectives from Robbery-Homicide. We don't have a copy of the report, and I have never seen it. The only thing I know about the investigation was second hand information I got from my Homicide Coordinator."

"And that's it? There's nothing here about my mother's death?"

Hardemann shook his head. "Nothing. Not even the detectives who handled it."

Lydia bit her lip and looked through the window at Billy Vernor who was still at his desk. Vernor was watching her. Lydia turned her attention back to Hardemann. "I've been told, Lieutenant, that my mother's death was an accident and that she had been drinking. If that's true, why was the case transferred to Robbery-Homicide?"

"That's a good question, and I don't know the answer to that either. It might have something to do with the fact that your stepfather is involved with organized crime." Hardemann paused and when he spoke again his voice was a lot softer. "Let the professionals handle this case, Officer Harte. Stay out of it. For your own good."

"It's been almost three years since my mother's death, Lieutenant. The professionals haven't done a damn thing since she died."

"Goodnight, Officer Harte."

"Goodnight, sir."

Sergeant Billy Vernor stopped Lydia as she was walking out to her car in the parking lot. "Did he tell you what happened to the investigation into your mother's death?"

"How do you know about my mother death if it's such a goddamn secret?"

"Hardemann told me."

Lydia thought about it for a moment. "Let me guess. He wants you to keep an eye on me."

Vernor nodded his head. "So, are you going to listen to what he told you?"

"If you are going to keep an eye on me, Billy, why do you expect I would answer that question?"

"Why are you so feisty, Lydia?"

"Because when the subject of my mother comes up, it pisses me off."

"Have you considered the position he is in?"

"Who?"

"Hardemann."

Lydia shook her head.

"That man will go far in this Department. He can't afford to make any mistakes."

"Well, fuck him and his ambition."

Even in the half light of the sodium vapor lamps, Lydia could see Vernor's face changing color.

"You don't understand a goddamn thing, Lydia," he said angrily. "Maybe, you should just keep your damn mouth shut and see what turns up."

CHAPTER SEVENTEEN

THE NEXT day, a Wednesday, was a busy one for Lydia. Vernor had gone downtown to the D.A.'s office to get a filing on a burglary suspect that uniformed officers arrested the previous evening, but he left Lydia in the station to do the tasks he had set out for her. She had pulled all the residential burglary reports that occurred in the entire Division for the past three months and was comparing the items reported stolen with the items recovered from the Spahn residence.

She liked the work she was doing. It might become tedious over time, but for right now it required a lot of concentration and Lydia liked doing things that were challenging.

By half past nine, Finlayson and Gordon began to annoy Lydia. The other burglary team rarely left the station, and the two men spent a good deal of time trading barbs with other detectives in the office when they weren't shoveling through their burglary reports. The banter became so annoying that Lydia got up and took her paperwork to the breakroom.

By noon, she had matched twenty-one different pieces of jewelry found in the Spahn house with nine different residential burglaries. Better yet, she learned that the technician from Latent Prints had recovered fingerprints from three of the items.

Lydia went back to the squad room that was nearly empty except for Hardemann and his secretary. Lydia set the stack of paperwork on the desk and noticed that Vernor had left his briefcase on his side of the desk. Inside she saw the spine of the black binder that Vernor hastily closed when she approached the desk the other day. She looked around to see if anyone was watching.

No one was.

She hesitated for a moment before deciding to look at what was inside the binder. It was a good thing she did, because just at that moment, Billy Vernor walked into the squad room.

Vernor didn't sit down. He merely motioned Lydia to follow him. She followed him out to the parking lot.

When Lydia got into the car, Vernor turned to her. "We're going to meet someone you might want to talk to."

"About what?"

"About your mother."

They stopped in a strip mall on Olympic in front of a Chinese restaurant whose front was a nightmarish design of maroon and gold dragons. Vernor led her to a stall at the back of the gloomy restaurant where an overweight man wearing a western style shirt with snap button pockets was having a beer. He got up when he saw them enter the restaurant, but his eyes were fixed on Lydia as they approached his table.

"Gawd," he said with a big smile on his round face. "Billy, how the fuck did you land a partner that looks like this?"

Vernor looked at Lydia. "This cowboy is Roger Prentiss, Lydia. They made him retire because he couldn't understand why the Department made such a fuss about sexual harassment."

"I knew what sexual harassment was, Billy. I just couldn't understand what was wrong with it." He turned his attention to Lydia. "You don't remember me, do you?"

Lydia shook her head. She tried to remember if she had seen him before. His round head was closely shaven and stone white in contrast to his sunburnt face. He was clean shaven except for a small goatee. She tried to picture him with a full head of hair, but it didn't work.

"Give it a few minutes and you'll remember," Prentiss said.

They sat down. A waitress immediately appeared and insisted on standing by their table until they found what they wanted on the menu. They ordered and got rid of her.

Prentiss began asking Vernor a few questions about what was going on at Century Division.

Lydia tuned out their banter while she continued to stare at Prentiss. He did look familiar, but she couldn't place him.

Prentiss suddenly turned to her. "You really don't remember me, darling, do you?"

Lydia shook her head.

"We met only once, but we talked on the phone several times."

It suddenly dawned on Lydia. "You were at my mother's funeral."

"I was."

Prentiss began tapping his fingers on a large manila envelope Lydia had not noticed when she came in.

"My partner, Taylor, and I were the first detectives to arrive at the scene of your mother's *accident*," Prentiss continued, emphasizing the word 'accident' in a sarcastic tone. "Afterwards, we were ordered not to discuss anything about the case with anyone, including you. But dammit, you were *so* persistent. Kept calling me and my partner every day until I got a little upset and said a thing or two I regret."

"I remember now," Lydia said thoughtfully. "You were not very pleasant."

"Neither were you. You really pissed me off, little girl."

Lydia nodded her head in agreement. "All I wanted to know was what happened to my mother. I couldn't get a straight answer from anyone."

"I already told you the answer to that. We were ordered not to discuss the case with anyone."

"Who told you that? Was it Hardemann?"

"Hardemann wasn't there three years ago. It was that idiot, Michaelson. Got killed in a traffic accident a year ago."

"Why were you ordered not to talk to me?"

"They didn't trust you. They knew you were Jonathan Benedict's daughter."

Vernor cut in. "She's his stepdaughter. There's a difference."

"But you lived with him, didn't you?" Prentiss asked Lydia.

The glare that Lydia threw at him could have melted steel. "I didn't live with him. I lived with my mother and she lived with him. And it's been more than seven years since I lived in that house."

Prentiss's eyes danced away from Lydia to Vernor and back to Lydia again.

"I didn't know that." He looked at the manila envelope on the table. "I always believed there was something fishy about what happened to your mother. I don't mean about how your mother died. I mean about how quickly Robbery-Homicide took over the case and asked for the original and all copies of our reports. The more I thought about it, the more it bothered me. It's not unusual for Robbery-Homicide to step in and take over a case, but it is unusual for them to ask for all copies of our reports. So, I made an extra copy for my own records and did a little investigating on my own. That's when I found out who your mother was married to. I showed up to the funeral because I was curious about who else was going to be there. I got my ass chewed out for doing that. That's when I found out that Robbery-Homicide didn't have the case anymore. It was transferred to Intelligence."

"To Sergeant Maldonado?"

"How do you know that?" Prentiss asked, surprised.

"I've been interviewed by him."

"Can I ask a question?" Vernor asked.

Prentiss nodded.

"Why was this a Homicide call-out? This sounded like a traffic accident to me."

"Because it was a suspicious death. Taylor and I got called out with the understanding we were investigating a suicide."

"It wasn't a suicide," Lydia protested vehemently. "I know my mother. She would never have taken her own life."

"I reached that conclusion a few minutes after I got there," Prentiss said.

"How did you determine it wasn't a suicide?" Vernor asked Prentiss.

"When I got there, one of the patrol officers was climbing up the hill. The first thing he said was that it looked like her car had been pushed off the road by another car. I went down for a look, and I saw what he meant. There was fresh damage to the rear of the car. I took a good look at the tracks the car left going down the incline. The car went straight down the hill until it hit a boulder. There was no way that car could have incurred damage to the rear bumper rolling down the hill.

"When I got back up the hill, I told Taylor what I saw, and he pointed out something very interesting. The place where your mother went off the road has a dirt shoulder. There were two distinct sets of tire marks in the dirt. I could see the tire marks left by your mother's car right up to the edge of the cliff. A second set of tire marks partially covered the tracks of your mother's car but stopped four feet before the edge of the cliff and then backed up. We concluded that someone in another car pushed her car off the hill."

Vernor looked at Lydia. "Did you know this?"

Lydia shook her head.

Prentiss slid the manila envelope across the table to Lydia. "This is my report. You can have it."

"Did you see any suitcases in the car?" Lydia asked as she took a report out of the envelope.

"I didn't see any suitcases."

The waitress brought the food. Vernor and Prentiss ate while Lydia read the report.

After a moment, Lydia looked up. "Do you have any idea where my mother was going?"

"I don't. But it appeared that the car was going in a westerly direction. It was about two miles east of the 405."

Lydia remembered that her mom had a friend in Bel Air just off Mulholland Drive, but she couldn't remember her name. But there was a problem. If her mother was going to Bel Air from Malibu, she was coming from the wrong direction.

When they were ready to leave the restaurant, Prentiss slid a business card across the table. Lydia looked at it. It listed Prentiss as the sole proprietor of the Prentiss Ranch.

Prentiss stood up. "Listen, I've got to be going. If you have any questions, call me on the cell phone. Anytime."

"I've got one more question before you go, Mr. Prentiss," Lydia said. "Why did they assign a homicide case to Intelligence? Does Maldonado have any experience working homicides?"

"He does. He worked Robbery-Homicide for ten years before he transferred to Intelligence." Prentiss laughed. "That is a story all by itself. The next time you see Maldonado, ask him about it. You'd be surprised how much you and he have in common."

After Prentiss left, Lydia turned to Vernor. "Do you know what he meant when he said I had something in common with Maldonado?"

"He lost a brother who was killed while trying to develop an informant who had connections with the underworld. About a year after that, Maldonado transferred to Intelligence. The story is that he is obsessed with finding out who killed his brother."

On their way back to the station, Vernor looked at Lydia who was in deep thought. "Do you have any idea how involved your stepfather is with organized crime?"

Lydia paused for a few moments, looking out the window of the police car. "Maldonado interviewed me several times. Once when I was applying for a job with the Department. Back then, I thought it was part of the employment process. But later, when he interviewed me again at the Police Academy, all he asked me about was my stepfather's business interests, and I couldn't tell him what he wanted because I didn't know everything."

"What about your mom? Was she involved?"

"My mother didn't work. She never needed to. She had money of her own."

There was an embarrassing pause when Vernor didn't say anything.

"If you're thinking that my mother's death was connected to her involvement in organized crime, I don't think that was the case," Lydia continued. "She inherited money from her grandfather who was an industrialist in Europe. She also inherited a majority interest in a small shipping company from her father. It's headquartered in San Pedro. The one thing she did do was to attend board meetings, but she didn't even like doing that. It took too much of her time, reading all that stuff they gave her. She lived the kind of life you see in those romantic comedies from the forties. She was very carefree, had a lot of friends, and played tennis very well. No one could beat her at tennis."

Lydia looked at the manila envelope in her lap.

"Sounds like an interesting woman," Vernor said.

"She was," Lydia said in a soft voice. "A good woman and a good mother."

Billy nodded. "You said she had a majority interest in a shipping company. Do you mean overseas shipping?"

"Yes."

"She owned ships?"

"Yes. About a dozen or so. I'm really not sure how many."

"So, who owns them now?"

"It's managed by the trustee."

"In your favor?"

"I am the beneficiary."

"So, when do you get the trust property?"

"When I'm twenty-six." Lydia glanced at Vernor. "You're not paying attention to what you're doing, Billy. You nearly hit the curb."

"I've got a question, Lydia," Vernor said as he slowed for a red light. "What the fuck were you thinking when you joined the Department? If you really want to know what happened to your mother, you could have hired a dozen private detectives to do the work for you."

Lydia didn't answer. After a moment, she looked over at Vernor. "Billy, I want to thank you for arranging the meeting with Prentiss. I learned a lot of things I didn't know."

"I didn't arrange the interview."

"Who did?"

"The baldheaded guy you talked to last night."

"Hardemann?"

"Yes. Hardemann."

CHAPTER EIGHTEEN

THAT EVENING after dinner, Lydia took the manila envelope Prentiss had given her into the den. She had spent hours in this room, studying while she attended UCLA. It was a pleasant but functional room, neatly ordered with not a scrap of paper out of place. There were two matching bookshelves on one wall, one containing books she had acquired while studying at UCLA, the other containing books she read for pleasure.

The den had a large desk with a computer on the left side and a printer on the right. In between was a row of reference books held in place by bookends depicting two snarling bears pushing the books toward each other. Above the bears was a small life-like portrait of her mother on a tennis court. She was smiling and looking very happy.

Lydia sat down at the desk and opened the manila envelope.

The report was six pages long and neatly typed. Lydia was amazed at what Prentiss and his partner, Taylor, had accomplished in the two hours they were at the scene of the alleged accident. Lydia's initial impression of Prentiss was that he was an amiable buffoon who pretended he was a cowboy, but the report showed that he and his partner had done a thorough job investigating the incident during what little time they spent at the scene.

Prentiss arrived at the scene of the incident at 11:30 p.m. and Taylor, five minutes later. They called for a photographer, forensics, and the Coroner's office, but none had arrived during the two hours they were there.

The precise time that Prentiss had run her mother's name through NCIS was noted, and the precise time they were informed that a team from Robbery-Homicide would be taking over the investigation was also noted, the interval between the two being eleven minutes.

Despite being informed they were being relieved, Prentiss and Taylor continued to work the scene until the team from Robbery-Homicide arrived.

The report indicated that her mother's car, a Mercedes sedan, went straight down an incline of forty-five degrees for eighty-two feet without tumbling over. It stopped only when it plowed through loose shale at the bottom of the hill and hit a rocky ledge. The car was mired in loose dirt up to its front grill.

The noise and lights of the car careening down the hill attracted the attention of an elderly couple who were entertaining another couple in their backyard about fifty yards below where the car ended up. They called the police to report what they believed to be a traffic accident.

The road where the car went off was curved to the left and the tire tracks went off the road at an angle of thirty degrees. The distance from the road to the edge of the cliff using the left side tire tracks as a marker was twenty-one feet, three inches.

The tire tracks from the car that pushed her mother's car off the road showed that the driver stopped a few feet from the drop off, then backed up and turned to the left to get back onto the road. There were no signs of any recent footprints in the area.

There were no houses at the top of a barren hill on the opposite side of the road, so there were no known witnesses other than the elderly couple and their guests.

One of the officers who initially responded to the scene had gone down the hill to determine if there were any survivors. He came back up when he saw that the driver was dead.

Prentiss went down the hill to make sure. He shone his flashlight through the closed passenger window of the car and saw the body of a female Caucasian in her late forties or early fifties, no seat belt, slumped over the wheel of the car, her neck obviously broken. Prentiss tried to open the car door, but it was jammed shut in the shale.

Lydia thought about this for a moment. Her mother always wore a seat belt. She was an absolute fanatic about it, demanding that all passengers in her car be seat belted before she even started it.

She remembered looking into her mother's closet and seeing that some of the clothing and suitcases were missing. None were mentioned in the report. She had asked Prentiss about it, and he said he saw no suitcases in the car. But, did he check the trunk? The report didn't say.

Lydia picked up her phone and dialed the number for Oceania Manor, hoping that neither Jonathan or Milo would pick up the phone. She was surprised when a maid answered since Jonathan insisted that most of the help had to be out of the house by seven.

Lydia identified herself and asked to speak to Sofia Benedetto.

The voice that answered the phone was bright and cheerful. "Hello, who is this?"

"It's Lydia, grandma."

"Lydia? I don't know any Lydia. Wait a minute. Lydia? Are you the young lady that used to come around years ago and pretend like she was my granddaughter?"

Sofia Benedetto always played the 'who are you, game' when Lydia called, and Lydia played along with it until she got bored.

"So, how are you doing, Lydia?"

This was a question that Lydia had grown tired of answering, but she answered it patiently. "I'm doing fine, grandma. And you?"

"I'm not talking about your health, Lydia. I'm talking about the game you're playing?"

The question gave Lydia pause. Even though the question sounded ominous, Sofia's voice was lighthearted.

"I'm sorry, Lydia. I didn't mean to sound so catty." Sofia's voice had softened. "How are you? Really?"

"I'm doing okay, grandma. No pain. Still in good physical shape."

"Are you back to jogging, yet?"

"Actually, I've been running a lot lately." She was thinking about having to run down that little bastard named Spahn. She had no problem catching him, but she needed to get back to a daily work-out schedule again that included a lot of wind sprints and some long-distance running.

"Why is the maid working so late?"

"Actually, the cook is here too. Jonathan has a few of his friends in for dinner. I'm excluded. I shouldn't be. After all, I built this place."

Lydia heard her sigh.

"Anyway, I'm glad you called. Jonathan told me you came over to pick up a gun. Didn't they give you a gun when you joined the police?"

"Listen grandma, I need to ask you a question. Were you around on the day my mother died?"

Sofia paused for a long while, and for a long moment Lydia thought she had hung up.

"Grandma?"

"I'm here, Lydia. I heard you. It's just that I miss her. She was such a wonderful woman."

"I miss her, too, grandma."

"I was here when she left, Lydia. Jonathan was out somewhere. He never tells me where he's going anymore. But I know for sure he didn't know Vivienne was leaving him. Or at least, I don't think he knew. You never know with him."

Lydia was surprised. "You knew she was leaving Jonathan?"

"She never told me a thing about it. I saw her loading suitcases in her Mercedes. After she left, I checked her closet. She took a lot of her clothes with her."

"Did she put the suitcases in the trunk?"

"Some of them in the trunk. Some in the back seat. Why do you ask?"

"I don't know," Lydia lied. "I guess I'm just trying to find out what happened to her."

"She ran off a cliff."

"That I know," Lydia said.

"And you think that someone killed her?"

"I don't know," Lydia lied. "What time did she leave the house?"

"Listen, Lydia. Can we meet somewhere for lunch? I've got something to give you."

"Do I have to pick you up? I mean at Oceania Manor?"

"You don't want to come here?"

"I don't want to go to that house unless I have to."

"I don't blame you. Are you still in that apartment that your mama gave you?"

"I am."

"How about if I come down to West L.A?"

Lydia thought about what Sofia Benedetto had said early in the conversation. Was there some hidden meaning in her comment about the little game she was playing? Did she or Jonathan know the real reason why she joined the Police Department?

Sofia Benedetto was close to eighty-years old, but still sharp as a tack even though she had three minor strokes. It was a known fact that Jonathan didn't take over the family businesses from his father. The wealth, illicit or not, but more likely illicit, came from businesses on Sofia's side of the family, and Sofia ran them until she decided to turn them over to Jonathan.

Lydia's mother had told her that Michael Benedetto, Sofia's second husband and Jonathan's father, was found drowned in his bathtub by his valet...in one foot of water. Sofia's first husband, Wilbur Cromwell, had mysteriously disappeared while on a clandestine trip with another woman to Las Vegas.

Coincidence, losing two husbands like that?

Probably not.

Did Sofia have anything to do with what happened to them?

Maybe.

Yet, Sofia Benedetto displayed an innocence that was disarming. Lydia liked her,...in fact, called her grandma when she really wasn't. But Lydia had no illusions about who she was or who she had been.

After a moment, Lydia continued reading the report. The detectives meticulously went about their job, taking measurements, interviewing the first responders, and making sure that everything was done by the book.

When she got to the last page, she noticed something was stapled to the back. It was a small buff-colored envelope, the kind whose flap was shut by a string and button. She found eight photographs inside that appeared to be have been taken with a cell phone.

She examined them closely. The first two showed the turnout and the tire tracks leading to the edge of the cliff. The others showed her mother's car at various angles. Lydia examined them carefully, looking at each part of the car, hoping to find some answer as to what happened by some anomaly in the bodywork.

And then she came to the last picture. It was of her mother, the side of her head resting on the steering wheel, her face looking toward the camera, her mouth open, her eyes clouded over like glassy marbles, and a terror-stricken look on the face of someone who knew she was about to die.

Lydia got up quickly, ran to the bathroom, but didn't make it. She fell to the floor in the hallway and vomited.

Chapter Nineteen

LYDIA DROVE to work the next morning, tired and bleary-eyed, and deeply despondent. She was up most of the night, trying to shake the memory of that ghastly picture of her mother staring out into nothingness. At one point during the night, she got out of bed and went back into the den and stared at the manila envelope. The pictures were back in the envelope, the string tied around the little button. She didn't remember putting them back in the envelope.

At work, she sat down on her side of the desk and looked down at the blotter without acknowledging Vernor.

"I said, good morning," Vernor said, looking concerned.

Lydia looked up at Vernor. "Sorry. I didn't hear you."

Vernor stared at her for a moment. "What happened to you? You look like you've been up all night. Have you been drinking?"

Lydia didn't say anything.

Vernor stood up. "Get up. We're going outside for a little talk."

Lydia looked around. The squad room was empty. "Why?"

He grabbed her by the arm and pulled her to her feet.

"Listen to me. I don't know what you've been doing, but you're in no condition to work. If you don't come with me, I'll pick you up and carry you out of here over my shoulder."

Lydia got up and followed Vernor out to the parking lot.

He opened the door to a plainclothes police car. "Get in."

"Where are we going?"

"I'm going to take you home before somebody sees you."

Fifteen minutes later, Vernor pulled the car into the circular drive of the condo where Lydia lived. Pedersen, the on-duty security officer, came out of the lobby and opened the door for her.

Lydia stumbled out of the car.

"Are you all right, Miss Harte?" Pedersen asked.

"She's fine," Vernor said. He followed Lydia to the door.

"Sir, may I ask who you are?"

"No."

"You can't leave your car parked in the drive, sir."

"It's a police car, buster. I'll be right back." Vernor followed Lydia who was already through the revolving glass doors.

He looked around at the immense lobby and then up at the enormous chandelier. Before he knew it, Lydia was getting into an elevator. He got there just before the doors closed.

They rode up in silence, Lydia huddled in the corner, her face to the wall.

The bell pinged and Lydia got off on the third floor. Vernor followed her down the hall. Lydia fumbled for the keys in her purse and tried to open the door. She couldn't. Her hands were shaking too much.

Vernor took the keys from her and unlocked the door. Lydia went inside. Vernor stepped into the apartment and into a very large and plush living room.

He saw Lydia walking toward a long hallway to the right. He looked around. Expensive furniture. Berber carpeting. A fireplace. Large screen television.

Vernor walked over to the patio window and looked out. There was a balcony with two chairs and a small wrought-iron, glass-topped table. A park stretched out below and fifty-yards beyond was a golf course. Off to the northwest was Century City perched on a hill, pretending like it was a modern Camelot.

The place smelled like roses. Vernor looked around but didn't see any flowers. An open kitchen was on the left side of the room, neat and clean, dishes put away. A pass-through window to what was probably a dining room beyond. On the opposite wall next to the fireplace was huge entertainment center with a plush sofa and matching easy chair.

Everything in the damn place looked expensive.

"Where's the fucking maid?" Vernor muttered to himself.

To the right of the entertainment center was the entrance to the long hallway where he last saw Lydia. Light was spilling out onto the carpet from two rooms down the hall.

He called out. "Shall I make coffee?"

No answer.

"Lydia?"

Still no answer. The air conditioning came on, which was strange because it was already cold in the apartment.

He walked down the hallway, past a den, and then arrived at an open door. He saw Lydia in bra and panties getting into bed and pulling the covers over her.

"Jesus Christ," he muttered under his breath. "She should have been a model for Victoria Secret."

He walked back down the hall and noticed the lights were on in the den. When he went inside to turn off the lights, he saw the manila envelope that Prentiss had given Lydia on the desk. He stared at it a few seconds before deciding to see what was inside. The first thing he saw when he shook out the contents was the picture of Lydia's mother.

He immediately understood what was wrong with Lydia. It wasn't drugs. It wasn't alcohol. It was the shock of seeing the photo of her dead mother.

Lydia was confused when she woke up because it was dark outside. She rolled over, turned on the lights, and looked at the clock. It was 9:33 p.m. She had slept the entire day. The air conditioning was on, blowing cold air into the room. Shivering, she put on her robe and walked over to the thermostat. It was set for sixty-five degrees. She turned on the heat.

On her way to the kitchen, she stopped at the doorway to the den. The lights were off. She didn't remember turning them off. She turned them on. The manila envelope that had been on her desk was gone.

CHAPTER TWENTY

WHEN LYDIA woke up the next morning, she felt great. The anxiety that had plagued her the day before was gone, her mind restored by hours of sleep. She took a shower and dressed, stopped to look at herself in the full length mirror that was in her bedroom. She remembered how terrible she felt last night. But that was all gone today...except for the anger. That she could control. She had to control it, because there was work to be done.

Vernor was at his desk when she got in. He looked up and stared at her, curiosity in his eyes.

Lydia sat down and stared back, wondering how, if ever, she was going to approach the issue of why he removed the Prentiss file from her apartment.

"Are you okay, Victoria?" Vernor asked.

"What?"

"Just a joke. Answer my question."

"I'm okay. Thanks for taking me home."

Vernor picked up what appeared to be a telephone message from his desk. "We got work to do. I got a guy that's going to hit a house right after nine this morning."

Lydia frowned. "How do you know that?"

Vernor smiled but didn't answer.

"Okay," Lydia said, "so, you got an informant who tells you these things."

"Do I get a feeling you disapprove?"

"If an informant knows what a crook is going to do, he has to be a crook himself."

"What's wrong with that? Have you ever fished?"

Lydia shook her head.

"Sometimes, the best bait to catch a fish is a smaller fish."

Lydia thought about it for a while and then said, "Fish stink, don't they?"

"Most do."

"Aren't you afraid the smell will rub off on you?"

Vernor blinked his eyes for a moment and then burst out laughing. He stopped laughing when he saw Lydia was serious.

"Billy, I've got to ask you something."

"Go ahead."

"Why did you take the report that Prentiss gave me from my condo?"

"I wanted to read it."

Vernor picked up his briefcase and began rifling through it. He removed the black three-ring binder and placed it in on the desk in front of Lydia. She resisted the urge to open it.

Vernor grunted when he found the manila envelope Prentiss had given her. He slid it across the desk toward Lydia.

"Have you read what's in there?" Lydia asked, her eyes fixed on the binder as Vernor put it back in his briefcase.

"I did," Vernor said. "I don't know what to say, Lydia. I can't imagine what went through your mind when you saw what was in there."

"What do you think?"

"About the report?"

"Yes."

"Do you really want to know?"

"Of course, I do."

"I think your mother was dead before the car went over the cliff."

"Okay. So, tell me how you figured that out."

Vernor shrugged. "The way her head was positioned against the steering wheel. It looked like her neck was broken. The fact that the airbag didn't deploy. It was either defective or someone had disabled it. Prentiss told me the same thing."

"You talked to Prentiss?"

"Last night."

"What did he say?"

"Someone killed her. Prentiss is sure of that. But you already knew that before you even looked at that report, didn't you?"

Lydia nodded. "Can I see what you got in that black binder?"

"No."

"Why not?"

"It's private!"

"How can I get a copy of the Coroner's report on my mother's death?"

Vernor stared at her for a moment, and then shook his head. "You make my head spin, Lydia. Your mind shifts faster than a race car driver going through the gears."

"Can you answer my question? How can I get a hold of the Coroner's report?"

"There's no way you're ever going to see that report."

"Why not?"

"If the investigation's confidential, so is the Coroner's report."

"Do you think bribery would work?"

Vernor looked around the squad room. It was still early. No one else was in the room.

"You'd bribe someone to get that report?" he asked.

"What good is money if you can't use it?"

Later, Lydia and Vernor were sitting on camp stools in the back of a dilapidated Ford Econoline van that had been stripped down and dressed up with a stained carpet to deaden the noise. They were peering out through smoke-colored ports at a house across the street in an upscale residential neighborhood. A team of patrol officers in civilian clothes were backing them up by covering the alley behind the house.

"Why after nine o'clock in the morning?" Lydia asked.

"What?" Billy asked as he turned to look through a back window at a car that had just driven by.

"Why does he choose to hit this place after nine?"

Vernor looked at her. "It's rather obvious, isn't it? Most honest people are at work this time of day."

"The house has a burglar alarm," Lydia said.

"What?" Vernor said, turning to look at her.

"The sticker on the window next to the door. It belongs to an alarm company."

Vernor looked out the window. "That don't mean a damn thing. People put those stickers on their windows even when they don't have an alarm."

"Uh, huh," Lydia mumbled, skepticism in her voice.

Vernor turned to Lydia. "I know what you're thinking. How would our suspect know if it's real or not unless he's already been inside the house?"

"The suspect doesn't actually have to be the one who knows there's no alarm in the house," Lydia said.

"The informant!" Vernor said, suddenly realizing what Lydia was driving at. "My goddamn informant told him. He's probably been inside the house."

Lydia nodded. "Does he have a legitimate job? Your informant? Like someone who goes door to door. A salesman or maybe even a repairman?"

"Are you kidding me? The guy doesn't work."

"Where does he get his money to live on?"

"How the hell should I know!" Vernor was becoming exasperated.

"What kind of hold do you have on him?"

Vernor shook his head. "He's scared to death of me."

Lydia stared at him. "And why is that?"

"Sometime, the only thing that works with these people is to let them know you'll cut off their balls if they don't cooperate."

"And that works?"

"All the time."

"Even if the informant is a woman?"

"I don't have an informant who is…" Vernor stopped and looked at Lydia. He began laughing when he realized she was joking.

An hour later, Lydia noticed Vernor looking at his watch. "Are you thinking of giving up?"

Vernor shook his head. "I never give up. This guy's going to show."

"I have to pee."

"So do I. Do you see that empty plastic milk bottle in the corner? That's what we usually use."

Lydia looked in the direction he was pointing and saw the bottle with the small opening. She shrugged. "I guess I'm out of luck."

"Sorry."

"A pickle jar would have been better."

It was quiet for a moment in the van. Lydia tried to take her mind off her urge to go to the bathroom by letting her mind wander, but then Vernor abruptly broke into her thoughts.

"Who do you think killed your mother?"

Lydia shut her eyes tightly.

Vernor noticed. "Sorry."

Lydia looked at him for a minute before responding. "Just a few minutes ago, you said that *my mind* was like a race car."

"I guess I did," Vernor replied.

"I wish it did." She looked at Vernor. "I don't know who killed my mother. But the person responsible…that's an entirely different thing."

"Who would that be?"

Lydia didn't answer.

"But you know, don't you? Or at least, you have some idea of who it might be."

"Yes."

An hour later, a white Ford Econoline, a newer version of the one that Lydia and Vernor were in, pulled up in front of the house they were watching. The van had a sign on the side that indicated it was from Andy's TV Repair Service in Culver City. The sign was not painted on. It was a removeable magnetic stick-on.

The van backed up into the driveway. Two young men got out, both skinny, both wearing green T-shirts.

The driver went to the front door where he rang the doorbell while the other one went to the back of the truck where he removed a dolly and then wheeled it up onto the porch of the house. The man with the dolly looked casually out onto the street, shielding his partner who was bent over the door lock. Less than ten seconds later, the man had picked the lock and entered the house followed by the man with the dolly.

Vernor picked up the handheld radio and spoke to the officers covering the back. "We've got entry. Two male Caucasians wearing green tees with Andy's TV Service logo on the back. They do not look like they're armed."

The other unit acknowledged the call.

Vernor looked at Lydia. "We'll give them two minutes. I'll go in first. I don't think they're armed but have your gun ready."

"I can get to the door faster than you. Let me go in first."

"I don't care if you're fucking Wonder Woman. I'll go in first."

Two minutes later, Vernor looked at Lydia. "Are you ready?"

Lydia nodded.

Vernor picked up the handheld radio and said in a calm voice, "Let's go."

The uniform officers acknowledged the call.

Vernor might have been calm, but Lydia's heart was pounding so rapidly that she could hear it.

Vernor followed by Lydia burst into the living room with their guns drawn. The two men were in the act of removing a widescreen TV from the wall.

"LAPD," Vernor yelled. "Hands over your head! Now!"

The two men dropped the TV and stared at them in stunned silence.

Lydia saw the eyes of one of the men flicker. She thought it might have been her imagination because one of his eyes appeared to be looking in a different direction than the other. But she was wrong. The man was looking for a way out. He dropped his hands, turned, and took off running toward the hallway at the back of the room.

Lydia started to go after him but was stopped by Vernor who held out a hand.

"Handcuff this guy while I cover him," Vernor said. "The uniforms will get the other one."

Lydia did as she was told and expertly handcuffed the man.

A loud crash came from the back of the house, followed by angry voices and more crashing.

A minute later, the back-up team brought the other suspect into the room from the back. He was handcuffed and blood was streaming from his nose.

"What happened?" Vernor said.

"He ran into a door," one of the officers said. "A truly unfortunate accident."

Lydia sat in the back seat of the plainclothes car next to the prisoners while Vernor drove back to the station.

The suspect with the wandering eye leaned as far forward as the seatbelt would let him. "I know you. You're Vernor, aren't you?"

"It's Sergeant Vernor, asshole. And I know you too—and what you've been up to. So, sit back before I stop this car and have a few words with you."

The suspect looked at his friend. "Listen to him. He's going to have a few words with me. You know what that means, don't you? He'll beat the shit out of us."

"Shut up," Vernor said.

The man leaned forward again. "How come you haven't informed us of our rights?"

Lydia noticed that the man had a whiny voice. She repressed a desire to slap him across the face with the back of her hand.

"What rights are you talking about?" Vernor asked. "The right to free pizza?"

"Our Miranda rights, asshole. It's in the Constitution."

"Are you talking about that Supreme Court decision that tried to level the playing field for the habitually stupid?"

Silence for a moment.

The mouthy one turned to his buddy. "What did he say?"

"I think he just insulted us," the other one said in a quiet voice.

Lydia held a hand up to her mouth, trying to stifle a smile.

The mouthy one turned his attention back to Vernor. "Well, you're violating your own rules. You have to inform us of our rights."

Vernor stopped the car for a red light and turned in his seat. "We caught you breaking into a house that doesn't belong to you. We caught you removing a TV from the wall that doesn't belong to you. And on top of it, you were driving a stolen van with fucking stolen license plates. I don't need your fucking statement because I'm not going to question you. Therefore, I don't need to read your rights…asshole!"

CHAPTER TWENTY-ONE

IT WAS true that police officers didn't have to recite the Miranda Rights to arrestees if they had no intention of questioning them, but Lydia was taken aback when Vernor, without saying a word to her, took the quiet prisoner into an interview room and closed the door behind him.

Lydia stared at the closed door for a minute or two wondering what in hell was going on and then went back to check on the prisoner with the big mouth. He was handcuffed in a holding room with a large glass window used for temporary detention of prisoners and was protesting loudly that if they didn't get his attorney on the phone that goddamn minute he was going to sue every goddamned cop in the fucking place.

Lydia shut the door on the prisoner and walked over to the door of the interview room where Vernor had taken the other prisoner. She wondered what Vernor was doing in there.

"Officer Harte!"

She turned and saw Hardemann across the room motioning for her to join him in his office. She checked to make sure the mouthy prisoner had settled down before heading across the squad room toward Hardemann's office.

Hardemann was standing behind his desk and moving some papers around when Lydia entered his office.

He looked up. "Close the door and sit down."

Lydia did so.

After a moment, Hardemann also sat down. "I heard you were sick yesterday. Are you all right?"

"I'm fine."

Hardemann leaned back in the chair and stared at her for a moment. The expression on his face was unreadable.

"Did I do something wrong?" Lydia asked.

"Just a few moments ago, I saw the expression on your face when Vernor took the arrestee into the interview room and closed the door. It was obvious you felt hurt."

"I thought we had a good working relationship. I don't understand why he did that."

"Officer Harte, take a look out at the squad room."

Lydia, uncertain at what Hardemann wanted her to see, slowly and hesitantly stood up and looked through the plate glass window. It was busy in the squad room, detectives working at their desks, working on computers, moving around, and looking into file cabinets.

"What you see is a lot of busy work that is unproductive. We get a lot of new crime reports every day. There are a lot of people on the streets who are up to mischief. Yet…" He paused for a moment, looking out into the squad room, and then turned back to Lydia. "Do you have any idea how many arrests these men and women made last week…excluding the Homicide Unit?" Another pause. "I bet you can't even guess." He pounded his fist on the desk. "Well, I'll tell you, Officer Harte. The answer is eight! Think about it…eight arrests!"

Lydia wasn't sure where Hardemann was going with this.

"You and Billy made five of them," Hardemann continued. "And do you know how he did it?"

"By going out into the field?" Lydia offered.

"He does do that. Yes, he goes out into the field. But, did you ever think how he knows where to go?"

Lydia didn't answer. Now that she thought about it, it appeared that she and Billy had been lucky…being in the right place at the right time.

"He has informants," Hardemann continued. "He has lots of them, and he spends a lot of time developing them. He's always on the look-out for new ones, and he is very good at it. That's what he's doing in there with that boy. He's working him for information."

"But why did he exclude me from the interview?"

"Because his informants are his informants. He doesn't share them with anybody. He's afraid if he shares them with other detectives, they might end up alienating them."

"I think I understand," Lydia said in deep thought. She was thinking about the black binder Vernor was so secretive about. Was that where he kept information about his informants?

"Do you realize that if every team out there did what you and Billy did this week, this unit would have made over a hundred arrests this week?"

Lydia nodded.

"There's something else I need to tell you, Officer Harte. The reason why I asked you in here. Some unpleasant news about your assignment. The Captain got a call from Lieutenant Emma Marsh. She's the Women's Coordinator in the Chief's Office. She told Kemper to send you back to patrol."

Lydia was dismayed. "I thought I was taken out of patrol because of problems I had with some officers on P.M. Watch."

"That's true, but Lieutenant Marsh thinks you should not be deprived of the experience of working a patrol division just because some officers don't like you. She thinks you need some serious patrol experience before you move on to a detective assignment."

Lieutenant Emma Marsh was an overweight woman that dressed like a witch who decided she needed a new image but just couldn't get it right. Marsh had showed up one day when Lydia was in the Police Academy and took the seventeen women in the class out to the rock garden where she spoke about the trials and tribulations of women in law enforcement and what they could do about it. She told them that if any of them had a problem, all they needed to do was to call her and she would take care of it.

The result of her stark description of what life was like for women in the Department was that four women quit the Academy the next day without explanation.

Lydia wondered if there was anyone she could call if one of the problems she had in the Department was with Lieutenant Marsh.

"Do you have some concerns about going back to patrol, Officer Harte?" Hardemann said when he noticed Lydia grimacing.

"No, sir," Lydia said as she stood up. "But to be honest with you, I'm tired of being manipulated."

"You're not being manipulated, Lydia."

It was the first time Hardemann called her by her first name.

"Yes, sir."

"Do you want to talk about it?"

"No, sir." She paused for a moment. Hardemann was staring at her, expecting her to say more. "If it's all right with you, Lieutenant, I need to see the Watch Commander about my new work schedule."

Lydia walked out of the detective squad room, taking a last look at the closed door where Vernor was apparently trying to cultivate a new informant. A few minutes later, she was standing in front of Lieutenant Morton who was penciling in her new assignment.

"I have you working with Hagerty tomorrow night. Sorry for the mixup...being bounced around like this."

Lydia turned to go.

"I hear you did a good job in detectives."

"Thank you, sir." Lydia paused, looking up at the clock above the door.

"You look like you have something on your mind."

She turned to face Morton. "No, sir. I just thought of something I need to do before I go home."

When Lydia left the building and went out to her car, she found that all four tires on her car had been slashed. She went back into the station, past Lieutenant Morton who looked up, and into the area behind the front counter.

Boudrie was the only person manning the front desk, but he was zoned out and didn't turn to look when she came in.

Lydia looked at the three monitors covering the station, one from a camera at the front, two covering the parking lot in the rear. She could barely see her car on one of the screens.

"Are these being recorded?" Lydia asked Boudrie.

Boudrie turned toward her. "What?"

Lydia pointed to the three monitors. "Are they being recorded"

"Dunno."

"What's wrong, Harte?" Lieutenant Morton was standing in the doorway.

"Nothing, sir." She brushed past him and walked out of the station and called for a tow truck on her cell phone.

Sergeant Cooley joined her in the parking lot two minutes later. He looked at Lydia's car and said, "I'll get someone to take a report."

"It's not necessary, sir. I'll handle it." Lydia said with a tone of bitterness in her voice that left no doubt in Cooley's mind that she was thinking of fucking over whoever did this.

Cooley stared at her for a moment before speaking. "A report needs to be taken, Officer Harte. We can't let something like this go unnoticed."

Lydia turned away. "Yes, sir."

Lydia took a taxi to the Coroner's office in downtown Los Angeles. It was closed when she got there, so she had the driver turn around and take her home.

She paused for a moment when she stepped into her living room. It was eerily quiet. There was no street noise. No noise from the adjoining apartments. For some, reason, the absence of human activity made her feel sad.

Lydia had no living relatives. Sofia Benedetto was not really her grandma. Just her pretend grandma. Jonathan and Milo didn't count either. Milo was a creep and she sure as hell didn't trust Jonathan. Her former boyfriend was a liar and up to no good. Her best friend was a bisexual who was always trying to hit on her.

What fucking else could go wrong?

Maybe, she needed someone in her life, but that was not going to happen. Who would want a woman who had no womb, a woman who carried a fear in her that even if she tried to have sex, it would be painful?

She thought of Jenny Hamilton again, but it was not about sex

Lydia called her. "I need a favor."

"What kind of favor?"

"The kind you're good at. Hacking into computers."

"Who do you want me to hack into this time?"

Lydia had previously asked Jenny to get a copy of the files about the investigation into her mother's death from Robbery-Homicide and Intelligence, but Jenny couldn't get past the firewall they had set up.

"The Coroner's Office," Lydia said. "I want a copy of the post mortem on my mother."

"Okay." Jenny paused for a moment. "What's wrong, Lydia. You sound funny."

"I'm all right."

"Want me to come over?"

"Don't take this the wrong way, Jenny, but…"

"You want to be alone."

"Yes."

CHAPTER TWENTY-TWO

LYDIA ARRIVED at the Rivercreek Range in a rented SUV and found Jeremy Morgan waiting for her along with two other men who were law enforcement types. They stared at Lydia for a moment before their eyes wandered down her body and stopped when they saw the .357 Magnum on her service belt.

"Jane, this is Jules and Jim. Jules and Jim, this is Jane."

Lydia was about to correct Morgan on her first name when she realized he was using fictitious names.

Jules and Jim was the name of a classic French film.

They shook hands.

Lydia's attention was diverted when she saw three Hispanic men coming out of the mobile trailer, carrying coffee in paper cups. All three men wore holstered semi-automatics. All three were wearing shirts with the name of the Rivercreek Range on them. They too stared at Lydia as they walked past her toward the pistol ranges.

Morgan looked at the gun on Lydia's hip. "If that's your new gun, we'll have to sight it in."

"It's the same one I had last week," Lydia said.

"What kind of ammo did you bring with you?"

"I have 200 magnum rounds."

"It's going to be tough shooting that kind of ammo in the scenarios I have planned for today."

"I think I can handle it," Lydia said.

"Cocky, isn't she?" Jim said to Jules.

"What do you carry off duty?" Morgan asked.

"A Springfield XDS."

A Springfield XDS was a small .45 caliber semi-automatic. It was also one of the guns Lydia had taken from Jonathan's armory.

"Is it in your car?"

"Yes."

Morgan took her aside, away from the others. "How do you carry it?" he said quietly.

"In my purse."

Morgan looked away.

"What's wrong?"

"Have you ever tried to draw a gun from a purse? Even a small gun like the XDS?"

"Of course not."

Morgan looked down at her waist and then smiled.

Lydia was wearing a black, long sleeved, shirt made of spandex that was tucked in her black jeans. It showed off her athletic form, but it was so tight that it showed off a little too much.

"What's wrong?" Lydia asked, disturbed by the way Morgan was looking at her.

It turned out that his interest was more professional than personal.

"I never thought how difficult it might be for a woman to carry a concealed weapon…wearing the kinds of clothes you do." He thought for a moment, his eyes running down her legs to her trainers. He looked up at her. "Over the next few days I want you to think about what you usually wear when you go out for the evening and how you would carry a weapon without it being seen. If you don't have any clothes that could conceal a gun, then you need to buy some that will. The next time we meet, we can practice a few routines where you draw your off-duty weapon from wherever you're hiding it."

Morgan drove the three of them in a Jeep past the eight ranges to the far end of the lot. Lydia noticed that each of the ranges already had targets set up. The three Hispanics she had seen come out of the trailer had positioned themselves near three of the them.

When they had gotten out of the Jeep a hundred yards farther down the road, Morgan handed out safety glasses while telling them what they were about to do.

"If you look up the road, you'll see Jose, Jose, and Jose standing in front of three of my combat ranges. You will, on my command, one at a time, run as hard as you can toward my trailer with your gun in your hand, pointed at the ground, finger off the trigger. When one of my guys points to a range, you will turn and drop to one knee. The range will have three targets. They are white with a black bullseye about the size of a baseball in the center. You will fire one shot at each of those targets. Three targets, three shots. You will do this on three different ranges."

Lydia had no problem shooting this scenario. Even though she had to run over a hundred yards before she got to the first range, she had her breath under control and was able to hit all three targets all three times.

Jules and Jim had similar results. Despite the fact they were not in as good as shape as Lydia, they were able to keep their guns steady while firing.

When they were done with the exercise, Morgan had them gather around him. "Okay, we are going to do this again, except this time you will not stop and drop to your knee. When a Jose points to a range, you will keep running and fire a shot at each of the three targets. The purpose of this exercise is to learn how to shoot on the run. Do not stop running until you have fired at targets on all three ranges. And whatever you do, don't kill a Jose. Got it?"

They all nodded.

Lydia hit three of the targets on her run and discovered what Morgan had been talking about. It was easy to hold the .357 Magnum down when shooting from a stationary position, but it was difficult to do that while on the run. When she had finished the exercise, she looked at her right hand. The knuckle on her middle finger was bleeding and she felt a blister beginning to form on the heel of her hand.

"See what I mean," Morgan said as he put a band aid on Lydia's bleeding finger. "Now that you know what it's like to do this with a magnum round, I want you to switch to a .38 Special before you break your wrist." He turned to the others. "Now that you know how difficult it is to hit a target while on the run, what does that tell you?"

"Stop and take cover before you fire," Jim said in response.

"I agree that would be the best thing to do," Morgan said. "But that's not what this scenario is about. Someday, you might have to fire your weapon while on the run. We will continue to practice this type of drill for the next six weeks until you get it right." Morgan looked down at the far end of the property. "Get in the Jeep. I've got another exercise planned for you. Let's see how well you do with this one."

Morgan drove them nearly a quarter of a mile alongside the creek. He stopped the Jeep next to an eight-foot chain link fence. On the other side, was a mock-up of a village that looked like a Hollywood set. Alongside the creek was a structure that Lydia had never seen before. It was large and consisted of what appeared to be six massive wooden tables layered on top of each other with a space of about six feet between the two bottom tables and decreasingly smaller spaces between the higher platforms. A safety net was positioned on one side of the structure, and on the other side was a heavy beam hanging out about two feet from the top. A large rope hung from the beam.

"What is that?" Lydia asked.

Morgan looked at where she was pointing. "That's a mock-up of a village that LAPD and LASO use for SWAT training."

"I mean that thing with the rope hanging off it."

"That structure is called the Skyscraper. The Army and the Marines use something like that in recruit training. The Marines also use it for preparing teenagers who are in the delayed entry program. The object is to use your hands to swing yourself up to each of the platforms until you get to the top."

"What is the rope used for?"

"That's the way they come down." He looked at her. "Tell me you're not interested in trying it out?"

"No," Lydia said. "I was just curious. We used to climb a rope like that when I was in prep school. I'm really not interested in doing it again."

"Okay, listen up," Morgan said. "I'm just going to say this once. In this scenario, you will run up the road until one of my guys points out a range. You will enter that range, and…" Morgan stopped when he saw a hand raised. "Jules, do you have a question?"

"It's close to a half mile to the first range. I've never been in a foot pursuit that went that far."

"Actually, it's just a little over a quarter of a mile. I assumed all of you were capable of running that far when you signed up for the course, or I wouldn't have allowed you to be here."

"What are we supposed to do when we get there?" Jim asked.

"If you see a white target, fire. If you don't see any, move slowly into the range using all available cover until you find a white target. You may assume that any white target you see is a man with a gun who will shoot you if you don't shoot first. Make sure you keep your safety glasses on for this one."

Jules was the first to run the scenario. He took off running at a rate of speed that Lydia thought was not very fast. He passed three ranges before one of Morgan's men pointed to a range. Jules stopped and dropped to one knee.

Nothing happened.

He got up and began moving slowly in a crouch into the range until he disappeared. A second later, there was a burst of fire from what sounded like a machine gun. And then a single shot, and another machine gun burst of fire. A few seconds later, Jules came out of the range and walked over to the Jose while gesticulating wildly.

Morgan turned to Lydia and Jim. "That was fucking lame. When I tell you to run, people, I mean run! Jane, you're next."

"Did he just walk into an ambush?"

Morgan smiled. "He probably did. It's your turn. Be prepared for anything. Start running."

Lydia sprinted up the road toward the ranges and passed Jules who was walking slowly back towards Morgan.

"Watch out for the black target," he called out as she ran past.

Black target? thought Lydia. *Weren't we supposed to be shooting at white targets?*

She ran pass one Jose, then another. When she got to the third Jose, he pointed at the range opposite him. Lydia noticed he was holding what looked like a television remote in his hand.

Breathing hard, Lydia turned into the range and dropped to a knee behind a low concrete block wall.

She looked over the wall.

No white target. No black target. As a matter of fact, there were no targets at all. Just different kinds of objects she could use for cover; a mailbox that was pierced with bullet holes, a thick log, a precast concrete culvert, the bed of a pickup. It looked more like a junkyard than a combat range.

Lydia looked back at Jose, who was trying to suppress a smile. She rose and stepped slowly around the wall, keeping both hands on her gun, pointing it down at a forty-five-degree angle.

A target popped up to her left and she swung her gun around. It was a black target. She held her fire.

She paused for a few seconds before moving forward, keeping one eye on the black target. The ground in front of the target suddenly exploded, sending up a shower of dirt. Lydia dropped to her knee and aimed her gun at the target. She held her fire while the dirt rained down around her. Then it was quiet for a few moments.

Then another black target popped up, this one to her right. She turned toward it and another charge blew up. By the time she recovered and raised her gun, a white target was coming up to her left.

No time to take cover.

She fired at it and it went down. Seconds later another white target popped up. She fired at that one as well, and then another white target and another and another. Lydia kept firing until she ran out of ammo. She put her gun in her holster and turned to look at Jose.

He was watching her, amusement on his face. He pointed at the range. Lydia turned and saw another white target coming up.

Damn it!

She used a speedy loader to load her revolver and shot the target without crouching or taking cover. It fell. She waited for a few seconds. When no more targets appeared, she holstered her weapon and turned to Jose. "Any more tricks up your sleeve?"

There was another explosion behind her. She hunched down as she was showered with dirt.

"Tell me, Mr. Morgan, do you really expect a police officer would ever encounter a situation where someone is setting off explosions?" Lydia asked. "What you just put us through might be okay for training commandos, but we're city police officers."

They had finished for the day and were standing outside the trailer. It was just past the noon hour, and one of the ranges behind her was actively being used for target practice by members of a women's quilting guild.

"Come inside where I can hear you," Morgan said.

Once inside the office, Morgan led Lydia to a scarred metal desk where he sat down and turned on a computer.

Without looking up, he said, "There's fresh coffee over there if you want some."

Lydia didn't answer. She looked around the room. It was spartanly furnished, metal desks, a few chairs, and several filing cabinets. The walls were covered with posters of voluptuous models in camo carrying guns. Incongruously, a photograph of Pope John Paul II was on a far wall near a desk.

"Aha," Morgan said as he found what he was looking for on the computer. He sat back in his chair and looked up her. "To answer your question, Miss Harte, I don't expect that someone will be setting off explosives in a gunfight unless you get posted to the Middle East. But if you do get into a gunfight, the last thing you want is to be distracted by something unexpected. It could be anything; a car backfiring, some bystanders walking by, some asshole yelling at his wife, a car sliding through an intersection because it came up to too fast on a yellow light. In other words, anything that causes you to involuntarily turn, look, or jump. The purpose of the scenario I ran you through was to test your concentration and ability to focus on what you need to do to survive. From what I understand from Jose Number Three, you did pretty well with the first six targets, but then had to be reminded there was a seventh one."

Lydia said nothing in response.

"Can I ask you a personal question?"

Lydia shrugged.

"I typically ask my clients why they sign up for my course. They usually say they want to be more proficient with a firearm. They don't want to end up like those four officers who were killed in a gunfight in Newhall several years back. But you, you're different. You don't want to be a cop."

Lydia crossed her arms. "If that were true, I wouldn't be here."

"Maybe, I didn't state my case very well. I don't see you spending twenty to twenty-five years on the job."

"Maybe, you expect I'll go off, get married, and have babies?"

Morgan spread out his hands and looked down at his desk. When he looked up, his face was clouded with pain. "I'm sorry the way that came out. That was thoughtless of me."

Lydia stared at him for a moment and then said, "I'm here to learn how to shoot, Mr. Morgan. It doesn't matter how long I intend to stay on the job. I don't want to be taken by surprise again, and I sure as hell don't want to get shot again. That's the only reason why I'm here."

Morgan didn't know it, but that was the biggest lie that Lydia had told that week. She hoped she was convincing enough when she said it.

"Fair enough," Morgan replied. He swiveled the monitor around, so Lydia could see what was on it.

Lydia sat down and leaned across the desk for a closer look. It was a holster designed for women that didn't look like a holster. It was a blue flexible band about six-inches wide that had two pouches made of the same material. The pouch on the right side was designed to hold a small semi-automatic and one on the left could hold two magazines.

A series of pictures showed a model demonstrating how to wear the holster. One of the photos showed the model in a cashmere pullover. If she was wearing a gun, it couldn't be seen.

"It comes in different colors," Morgan said. "If you give me your address, I can have one shipped to you."

"Nice try, Mr. Morgan. I'll do the ordering, myself."

Morgan smiled. "Can I ask another question?"

Lydia shrugged. "You can ask."

"Are you seeing anyone?"

Lydia laughed thinking of Jenny. "Not at the moment." She felt her face turning red at the thought of Jenny.

"Would you like to go out for lunch?"

She looked down at her clothes. They were covered with dirt, and she needed a shower. "I have to work tonight."

"How about dinner tomorrow night—if you're not working, that is?"

Lydia stared at him for a moment. He was an attractive man with a wiry build, and she thought he might be fun to get to know. And he was different than anyone she had ever been out with. Her former fiancé, Jake Nilsson, was a nice guy who dressed well, but he was a bit pretentious at times, particularly when they were around other people. Jake seemed to have the need to prove himself as an expert on every topic that was brought up at the dinner table.

"I've just been reassigned to patrol." Lydia said after staring for a moment into Morgan's eyes. *How come I didn't notice how green his eyes were before, Lydia thought.* "I don't know what my schedule is like for the rest of the month. How about if I call you?"

"A brush-off if I ever heard one."

Lydia smiled. "It's not. I have your card. I'll call."

"Promise?"

"Promise has too broad a meaning. Can I ask *you* a personal question?"

"Shoot."

"How did you lose your leg?" Lydia instantly regretted asking the question when she saw the pained expression in his eyes. "I'm sorry. It's none of my business."

"I'll tell you what, Officer Harte. If you call me and we get together for dinner or lunch or whatever, we can compare boo boos."

CHAPTER TWENTY-THREE

LYDIA'S SHIFT on P.M. Watch didn't start off well. She said a quiet hello to the three women who were changing into their uniforms in the locker room. Two of them were veterans who looked at her with disinterest and grunted in response. The other one, who was still on probation and had been in the recruit class that graduated from the Police Academy six months before Lydia, greeted her with a chirpy 'hello'. Her last name was Evans but the guys who worked with her called her 'Mousey'. Lydia wasn't sure if she was called that because of her diminutive size or the trill in her voice.

Evans came over and asked Lydia about what it was like to work in detectives. Lydia answered as best she could without showing how pissed off she was about being bounced around the Division like an errant golf ball. She changed into her uniform and got out of the locker room as fast as she could.

The Crew was already seated in their usual place when Lydia entered the roll call room. One of them said something to the others, and they all glared at her with hateful eyes as she walked by.

When she got to her seat in the front row, she realized she had seen something back there that was not quite right. There were six people sitting in the back row. Somebody had replaced Searles.

Lydia got up from her seat and walked to the rear of the room as if she had forgotten something. On the way out the door, she glanced at the officers in the last row.

There *were* six of them. One was a stocky but pleasant-looking woman who wore her blonde hair in a pageboy. Lydia had never seen her before.

Lydia walked out into the hallway and stopped at a bulletin board that listed items for sale. No sooner had she gotten there when someone called out her name.

She turned to look.

It was Hagerty.

"Have you been in the roll call room yet?"

"Yes. Why?"

"Get your gear and come with me. The Lieutenant gave us permission to skip roll call."

Fifteen minutes later, Hagerty turned onto Gardiner Avenue where two police officers were manning a roadblock. One of the officers removed a barricade and waved them through.

In front of the Akheiser Storage Facility was a fire truck pumping water through a hose that snaked through a hole in the smashed front door. Most of the windows on the south side of the building had been knocked out, and the area around the windows had been blackened by smoke.

Two police officers stood guard on the sidewalk in front of the building. A television van with a camera on the roof was parked on the opposite side of the street.

Hagerty drove the police car into the driveway on the southside of the storage facility and into the back lot.

Lydia was amazed at the number of vehicles in the parking lot. A huge fire truck was parked near the ramp leading into the building and another pumper was at work, its hose running up onto the dock and into the warehouse. Three cars painted fire engine red and five plainclothes police cars were parked neatly in a row in the center of the lot. A television van was also in the lot, along with a local television news personality known for her humor who was watching the activity with a look of seriousness Lydia had never seen before.

Several roll-up doors on the south side of the building were open. A massive forklift came through one of the doors and dumped a load of charred wood onto the ground beneath the dock. With it came an acrid odor of burnt rubber. The firefighters working in and around the dock were wearing respirators.

From what Lydia could see, the fire had been confined to the southside of the building. A few minutes after they got there, Lieutenant Hardemann came out onto the dock, took off a respirator, and lit a cigarette. He took a puff, looked at the cigarette, threw it on the dock, and stepped on it. Hardemann was about to go back inside when he saw Hagerty and Lydia and waved them forward.

"Did Morton send you out here?" Hardemann shouted over the noise of the fire equipment.

"He did," Hagerty replied.

"Why?"

"He wanted to know if you needed any additional help."

"Well, the guys manning the barricades need to be relieved."

"He's sending other people who will be doing that. What happened here?"

Hardemann took out another cigarette and lit it. He appeared to notice Lydia for the first time. He quickly looked back at the building and then back at Lydia.

Lydia knew what he was thinking. She shouldn't be here. This was where she had been shot.

"We think Akheiser's in there somewhere," Hardemann said. "His wife told us he planned to stay the night in the warehouse. His office was destroyed by the fire. We found his shotgun in the rubble, so we expect to find his body in there as well."

"What happened to Vernor?" Hagerty asked.

"He's at the UCLA Medical Center with a concussion. He'll be all right."

"Billy was here?" Lydia said haltingly. "Here, when the fire broke out?"

"He was," Hardemann said. "He was watching the place from his car out on the street…without telling anyone about it, dammit! I talked to him in the hospital this morning. He told me he saw an eighteen-wheeler pull into the driveway of the warehouse. When he got out of the car to see what was going on, someone coldcocked him from behind. When he woke up, he was in the trunk of his car, handcuffed with his own handcuffs. He heard the fire engines coming and he began yelling. One of the bystanders heard him and told a police officer." Hardemann paused for a moment. "I understand Vernor brought you here a few days ago."

Lydia nodded.

"Why?"

"He wanted to talk to Mr. Akheiser about security."

"Wait a minute," Hagerty said. "If Billy thought somebody was going to hit this place, why didn't he ask for some help?"

"He did," Hardemann replied. "Special Operations Group was already committed. And we barely have enough manpower in patrol to cover the Division on a Friday night."

"What about the other team on the Burglary table?"

"I suggested that to Billy. He didn't want them involved."

"Jesus Christ! Who the fuck are we anyway? A police department or a bunch of fucking clowns? There are other people who would have been happy to help out."

Hardemann looked at his cigarette for a moment before speaking. "I know that now, Dick. In hindsight, that is exactly what we should have done."

"When I was here with Billy," Lydia said. "There was a large stack of TVs and other electronic equipment close to Mr. Akheiser's office."

Hardemann looked at her. "The stuff from Robert's Club?"

"Yes. Is it still there?"

"We had someone from Robert's come out and take a look. Most of it is gone. What's left was destroyed by fire."

A voice broke up their conversation.

"Lieutenant!"

One of the homicide investigators from Century Detectives was on the dock. He was wearing coveralls covered with soot.

"Yes, Owens."

"We found a body."

"Akheiser?"

"We don't know. It's badly burnt."

"I'll be right there."

Hagerty was in a foul mood. He wanted to look inside the warehouse, but the homicide investigators wouldn't let him.

"We had a chance to get them and we blew it," Hagerty said when they got into the car. "That makes number six. I wish Billy would have told me what he was planning to do."

"But you weren't working last night, were you?" Lydia asked.

"Doesn't matter. If I knew he was going to be out here, I would have been here with him. We would have caught the bastards."

Lydia didn't say anything. She picked up the mike to tell the dispatcher they were clear to take calls.

"What are you doing? Put the mike down!"

There was anger in his voice, and Lydia did as she was told. After a few minutes, Lydia noticed that Hagerty was not heading back to their patrol area.

"Where are we going?" she asked. "If you don't mind me asking," she added grumpily.

"Sorry for the attitude," Hagerty replied. "We're going to UCLA Medical Center to see Billy." He looked at Lydia. "So, I can tell him how badly he fucked up."

Billy Vernor was sitting on the edge of his bed eating dinner when Lydia and Hagerty walked into his private room at the Ronald Reagan UCLA Medical Center. He was not surprised when he saw Hagerty and Lydia.

"About goddamned time you got here," Vernor said as he put down his fork. He looked down at his hospital gown, saw that it had ridden up, and adjusted it to cover his knees.

A large patch of hair had been shaved from the top of Vernor's scalp and was covered by a thick bandage.

Vernor looked at his half-eaten supper. He pushed it away and reached for a small bowl of cherry-colored gelatin with a dab of cream on top. "The food's not half bad here," he said, "but I'm not hungry." He looked up at Hagerty. "Did you go to the warehouse? How's Akheiser?"

"They found a body in what was left of his office."

After several seconds of complete silence, Vernor said, "Sit down. Both of you. We need to talk."

Lydia looked around. There were no chairs in the room.

"Are you all right?" Hagerty asked.

"If you exclude having a fucking headache and being pissed off, I would guess so. How did Mrs. Akheiser take it?"

"We didn't see her."

Vernor nodded his head.

"What happened last night?" Hagerty asked.

Vernor stared at the cherry gelatin and didn't answer.

"Billy, are *you* all right?"

"I heard you," Vernor replied without looking up. "I got there last night just after 9:30. I knew Akheiser was inside with a shotgun, and he knew I would be covering him from the street."

"Did Hardemann know what you were doing?"

"No!" Vernor paused for moment to calm himself. "Shortly after ten, a semi with a trailer pulled into the driveway of the warehouse. I called Akheiser and asked if he was expecting anyone. He said no, so I got out to check it out. Then, bam! Lights out! I don't know how long I was out. I wake up. The first thing I hear is sirens, but I can't see anything. The fuckers put me in the trunk of my car and handcuffed me with my own handcuffs." He looked up at Hagerty and then at Lydia. "Do you know if they got any fingerprints? From the cuffs?"

Hagerty shook his head. "What can you tell us about the truck?"

"It was white. I think it was a Freightliner. Not sure about that. No markings on the trailer. The license plate light was out, so I couldn't get the number."

"Is there anything we can do for you?" Lydia asked.

Vernor smiled. "Of course, there is something you can do for me, Lydia. That's why I called Morton and asked him to let you come here."

"What do you need?" Hagerty asked.

"I want you two to find my car. My briefcase is in the back seat. There's a black binder in my briefcase. If it's not there, call me."

"And if it's there?" Hagerty asked.

"I want you to find a large envelope and put the binder in it. Make sure no one sees you doing it. Seal it. Give it to Lydia. Don't let anyone see you give it to Lydia."

Hagerty looked at Lydia and then back at Vernor. "Why Lydia? Don't you trust me?"

"I trust you, Hagerty. To do the right thing. Give it to Lydia. Her condo is more secure than your house."

"What do you want me to do with it?" Lydia asked.

"I need you to keep it for me. Hide it in your condo until I ask for it. Whatever, you do, don't look at it. And watch your back. Both of you."

"What was all that about?" Lydia asked Hagerty as they drove to the station.

"I expect that the black binder is where he keeps information about his network of informants." Hagerty looked sideways at Lydia. "Look, you haven't been around all that long. Have you heard the stories about Vernor?"

"What stories?"

"About what he does when one of his snitches crosses him." Hagerty looked at Lydia who was staring at him. "I guess not. Look, Vernor had an informant named Ronnie Jefferson who owned a string of pawn shops that handled stolen property. Jefferson was in a jam, so he gave Vernor vital information about a murder case. Vernor passed it to Homicide who used it to get a search warrant. The information that Jefferson gave Vernor led to an arrest. But it turned out that the defense attorney knew something was wrong with the source of the information and filed a motion to suppress evidence. The judge ruled that Vernor had to disclose the identity of his informant, so he could be interviewed. It was an important case. A murder for hire to kill a prosecutor. So, Vernor was forced to disclose the source of his information. When Jefferson was put on the stand, he denied he had ever given the information to Vernor. The judge granted the motion and threw out the case."

Hagerty glanced at Lydia who was listening intently. "Do you understand what happened…what I'm telling you?"

"I think I do. Why did this Jefferson guy lie to Vernor?'"

"Hell if I know. But I do know this. About five months after the case was kicked out of court, Vernor arrested a guy who was buddies with Jefferson. Vernor drove him by Jefferson's office and thanked him for the tipoff. He made sure the man he arrested saw him do that."

"I don't get it," Lydia said, shaking her head. "Why would Billy do something like that?"

"Because he wanted to make it look like Jefferson had betrayed the man he had just arrested. In other words, Vernor set Jefferson up. And Vernor knew his arrestee was a bad ass. He knew that when the guy got out of jail, he would be paying Jefferson a visit."

"So, what happened?"

"A few days later, the guy bailed out of jail. A few days after that, Jefferson disappeared. He left an expensive home in Palos Verdes and a wife and three kids. Poof! He was gone just like that. Nobody has ever reported seeing him again."

Hagerty looked at Lydia. "I expect that binder is a time bomb waiting to go off. Don't let anybody know you have it. Hide it and get it back to Vernor as soon as he is out of the hospital."

When Lydia got home that night, she placed the large envelope with Vernor's black binder on her desk. She got a glass of wine from the kitchen and came back to the desk. After a few moments, she turned the envelope over. Its flap was held together by a string wrapped around a small disc the size of a button. She was tempted to open it and look inside.

She thought about Billy Vernor and then about Richard Hagerty. When she joined the Police Department, she had no idea that men like that existed. They were doing a job most people were not capable of doing, and they did it for very little money. They were in sharp contrast to the six men, now five men and a woman, who sat in the last row during roll call. But she also remembered what Hagerty had said about Vernor setting someone up. Despite his dedication to police work, Vernor was not averse to dirty work by creating a situation that led to the disappearance of someone who betrayed him.

Lydia's final act before going to bed that night was to place the envelope with the black binder in it on top of the armoire in her bedroom. After checking to make sure it couldn't be seen by anyone entering the room, she got ready for bed.

CHAPTER TWENTY-FOUR

LYDIA WAS awakened by the soft 'ding ding' of the condo's intercom system. It was the doorman in the lobby who told her that a package had been delivered for her. She quickly dressed and went downstairs.

The package was a UPS envelope with an address label that indicated it was from Jenny.

Twenty minutes later, Lydia drove her rental SUV into the parking lot of the Beverly Café on Beverly Drive. It was Sunday morning and the inside of the Café was crowded, so she took a seat at a table on the sidewalk, making sure she was as far away as possible from other customers. She ordered a coffee and a light breakfast and stared at the envelope on the table in front of her for nearly a minute before opening it.

It was the Coroner's report on the death of her mother.

The first part of the report, the description of the body as it lay on the table sounded like a dry medical treatise It helped distance Lydia from the fact she was reading a medical examiner's report about her mother. But when the examiner began to report the trauma on the body in detail, the narrative became so devastating that Lydia's hands began trembling.

There were numerous bruises and lacerations on her mother's body, including the back, shoulders, breasts, abdomen, and thighs. The report indicated that the trauma could not have been caused by a single event such as a fall or a traffic accident. The examiner also found evidence of small metal particles in the lacerations on her mother's back and concluded that the trauma was caused by someone who whipped her severely with a braided metal cord prior to her death. There was a notation in pencil in the margin of the typewritten report that said, PROBABLE EVIDENCE OF TORTURE.

"Jesus Christ," Lydia muttered.

"What did you say?"

Lydia looked up. It was the waitress who had brought her breakfast.

"I'm sorry," Lydia said. "I was just talking to myself."

"Are you alright? Your hands are shaking."

"I'm fine. Thank you."

The waitress left, looking suspiciously back at Lydia before she went back into the cafe.

Much of what Lydia read in the rest of the report made her wonder about the relevance of the findings, such as the weight, size, and shape of the various organs as they were removed from the body. Lydia had no experience with post mortem reports and wondered why the medical examiner went into such detail.

But when the report began describing the observed internal injuries to the neck and the cervical spine, Lydia found she had to read it several times before she could break through the medical jargon and understand what it was saying. The examiner concluded that the cause of death was asphyxiation that was further caused by a catastrophic failure of the cervical spine and the spinal cord. The examiner further concluded that these injuries occurred before the trauma caused by the traffic accident.

"In other words," Lydia said quietly, "she was dead before she went over the cliff." She looked up and saw that an elderly couple seated next to her table were staring at her.

Lydia stuffed the report back into the envelope and went inside the café to pay her bill.

The first thing Lydia did when she got home was to call the number she had for Intelligence Division and leave a message for Sergeant Maldonado to call her. When she put the phone down, she noticed her hands were still trembling. She put on her work-out clothes and drove the SUV out to UCLA where she parked and walked to Drake Stadium.

It was Sunday and the track was being used by a dozen students, some of them student athletes, but none of whom Lydia recognized from her days on the track team. She ran wind sprints for nearly thirty minutes, pausing several times to catch her breath. When she was done, she began a long-distance run around the track. When she had finished nineteen laps, she ran the final one as if she was running 440 meters in competition and passed a football player who was doing wind sprints.

When Lydia got home, she checked her messages. There were none. She looked at her hands. They were no longer trembling. The anxiety she felt when she had read her mother's post mortem report was gone.

She called Jenny who immediately answered. Jenny was on her way out and asked her to make it quick.

"Can you tell me what happened when you tried to get into Intelligence Division's file?"

"I got nothing, Lydia." Jenny's voice sounded stressed.

"What's wrong, Jenny? Is everything okay?"

"It's not. I'm on my way to meet Rod and try to talk some sense into him."

Rod was Jenny's boyfriend, one who had proposed to Jenny in the past, and then called it off, only to propose again.

"What happened?"

"He found out."

"About what?"

"Well…you know. You had firsthand experience."

"Oh, my God! How did he find out?"

"Someone told him."

"I'm sorry, Jenny. I truly am. You got more important things to do. I'll call you tomorrow."

"Lydia, please don't hang up. You just might be the only friend I have right now. Let me sit down for a minute."

Lydia heard a sharp sound on the phone as if it were dropped on a wooden table. A minute later, Jenny was back on the phone. "Sorry about that. What did you want?" Her voice sounded slurred.

"Are you drinking?"

"I am."

"You're not going to drive out to the Palisades after you've been drinking, are you?"

"Come on, Lydia. You drive all the time after you've been drinking."

But, Lydia thought, *I don't drink a whole bottle of wine at a time.*

"Do you know what, Lydia?" Jenny continued. "Why should I worry about one guy? There are three or four billion men on this planet, and there is enough dick out there to build a fucking bridge to the moon."

Notwithstanding the fact that Jenny's estimate of the number of men on the planet was way off, Jenny's comment about all the available men in the world made Lydia feel uneasy.

"So, I can make time to talk to my only friend in the world," Jenny continued. "What do you want Lydia? Did you get the Coroner's file?"

"I did, Jenny. Thank you. I owe you dinner for that one. I want to know what you found out when you tried to get into Intelligence Division's website."

"I drew a complete blank, Lydia."

"I know you said that, Jenny, but how far did you get?"

"I got into the Division's master index. That was the easy part. There were a lot of sub-files with names on them. Every time I tried to get into one of them, my search was shut down, and I had to start all over again."

"Did you ever see a file with Maldonado's name on it?"

"I did. Every detective in the Division has a file. I tried to get into Maldonado's and drew a blank. I spent some time trying to break through his password but had to stop when someone began trying to worm their way into my computer to find out who I was."

"Were you able to stop that from happening?"

"I shut it down before they did."

"What about using another computer?"

"Like at an Internet café?"

"Yes."

"I can try."

"Thanks."

"No, thank you. Talking to you has made me feel better."

"I'm so glad, Jenny. What are you going to do about Rod?"

"Fuck Rod. I'm going out to a sports bar and see if I can lure some hunk into my apartment. What I need is more alcohol and a good fuck to set things straight."

Later that afternoon, Lydia's phone began ringing. She rushed to the phone, thinking it might be Maldonado returning her call, but it wasn't. It was from Billy Vernor. He had been released from the hospital.

"Have you put my notebook in a safe place?"

"I have."

"Did you look at it?"

"Of course, I looked at it. I saw Hagerty put it in a large envelope."

"Don't be so disingenuous, Lydia. Did you look inside the binder?"

"Oh, now we're using big words, Billy. No, I didn't look inside. I did what you told me to."

"Good."

"I hope you're not coming to work tomorrow."

"The doctor put me off-duty for five days. I could use the time off. I've got a few things I need to clean up."

"Work things?"

Vernor ignored the question. "Thanks for helping out, Lydia. Whatever you do, don't open the binder."

Before Lydia could reply, Vernor hung up. She put the phone down and wondered if there was a hidden meaning when he spoke about the binder. He mentioned it twice, first asking if she looked inside, then telling her not to look inside. Was he really suggesting she look at it without saying so?

But why would he do that?

Lydia stayed in her apartment for the rest of the day hoping that Maldonado would return her call. The only other call she got was from Jonathan Benedict later that afternoon. When she saw who the caller was, she didn't pick up the phone. The call went to voicemail.

Jonathan's voice sounded pleasant like always. He wanted to talk to her about the gun she took. He needed to know the serial number. He then concluded the call by saying that Victoria had suggested they get together this week for dinner and for her to call back as soon as possible.

Lydia didn't return his call. She went to bed that night, wondering if Jonathan called because he found out that more than one gun was missing.

CHAPTER TWENTY-FIVE

LYDIA GOT up early Monday morning, dressed in a tight-fitting work-out shirt and shorts and went to Drake Stadium at UCLA where she repeated the same routine she did the previous day. There were at least two dozen student athletes using the track, most of them women.

When she got home, she showered, dressed in a pullover sweater and jeans, and then called Intelligence and asked to speak with Sergeant Maldonado.

"Hello, Lydia," Maldonado said in a cheerful voice when he got on the phone. "How can I help you?"

"Did you get my message yesterday?"

"No, I didn't."

There was a degree of hesitation in Maldonado's voice that caused Lydia to believe he wasn't telling the truth.

"Well, I called and left a message. I need some information about my mother's death." She paused for a second. "It *was* murder, wasn't it?"

A few seconds passed before Maldonado answered. "We consider the circumstances to be questionable."

"What do you mean by questionable?"

"Look, Lydia, I've told you this before. The investigation is confidential because of your mother's connection with Jonathan Benedict." After a long pause, Maldonado continued, "Can I ask you a question?"

"Why should I answer your question when you won't answer mine?"

"Because it's in your best interest to tell me what you know about Jonathan Benedict."

"Somehow," Lydia said, "I believe you know more about Jonathan Benedict than I do."

"But you have inside information, Lydia. Information that can help us."

"I won't be your snitch, Sergeant Maldonado, and it's not because I like Jonathan Benedict. As a matter of fact, I detest him. I don't like being around him. For me to cooperate with you means I've got to spend more time with him than I care to, and I won't do that."

"You were seen entering his estate last week, Lydia. What were you doing there?"

Lydia didn't want him to know she went there to borrow a gun. But if he knew she had been there, did he also know what they had discussed in the library? She didn't think that was possible considering the difficulty of getting into the place, so she lied. "I went to check on Sofia."

"Sofia wasn't there."

"That's right. I didn't know that until I got there."

"Who was there?"

"Why are you asking me that when you already know the answer?" Lydia said, trying to contain her fury. "You already knew Sofia Benedetto wasn't there. So, you have to know who else was there."

Another long pause before Lydia continued in a calm voice. "Jonathan and his girlfriend Victoria were there. So was Milo. Carlos Aldana was manning the front gate. I didn't see anyone else in the house. The staff had already left for the evening."

"What did you talk about?"

"I asked about Sofia. I was told she was out. Visiting friends. I was invited to go to dinner with them. I declined. That was it."

There was another long pause on the telephone.

"Tell me something, Sergeant Maldonado," Lydia said. "Have you ever worked homicide?"

"I'm a detective."

"I know you are a detective. Have you been to the Department's homicide school at the Police Academy?"

"I work Intelligence, Lydia."

"You still haven't answered my question. Have you ever worked homicide? And don't lie to me. I know you have."

"Why are you so persistent about this?"

"Because I know my mother was murdered, Sergeant Maldonado. She was dead before that car went off the cliff. All I want to know is what you're doing about it?"

Another long silence before Maldonado answered. "Where are you getting your information, Lydia?"

"It doesn't matter where I got my information."

"Have you tapped into our records system?"

"I haven't, Sergeant Maldonado. All I want is some answers."

"I told you before. You need to help us. Get close to your father and find out what he's doing. You're a police officer now. Act like one."

"So are you, Sergeant Maldonado, but you don't act like one any more than I do. And stop calling me by my first name, dammit. I don't know you that well."

Lydia hung up.

Later, when Lydia thought about her conversation with Maldonado, she wondered if she did the right thing, talking to him that way. She always had a pleasant relationship with the detective, and he seemed like he was a kind person who was truly interested in her well-being. Maybe, all his kindness was a front. Maybe, what he was trying to do was to develop her into an informant. If that was his intention, Lydia was determined she wasn't going to let that happen.

Lydia drove to the rental car agency and dropped off the SUV. One of the agency's employees drove her to the tire shop to pick up her car. While she was waiting at the counter for an employee to bring her car around, she noticed that a television in the waiting area near a coffee service was showing police activity at the entrance of an apartment complex.

She wandered into the waiting area to get a better look at the television screen. The sound wasn't on, and she couldn't find the remote. The screen switched to a pleasant-looking female reporter standing on the sidewalk.

Lydia stepped closer to the TV to read the words that were scrolling across the bottom of the screen. It read, OFF-DUTY LAPD OFFICER GUNNED DOWN IN AMBUSH. She watched for a while, hoping to find out where the shooting occurred.

"Are you Lydia Harte?"

Lydia turned to find an employee of the tire shop standing behind her, holding her car keys.

"We have your car ready. It's parked out front."

"Thank you. Would you happen to know where that shooting took place?" she asked, pointing at the television.

"Somewhere out in the Valley. A cop was coming home from work last night and somebody ambushed him."

Lydia took the keys and began walking toward the door.

"Miss Harte."

She turned to look at the employee.

"If I were you, I'd watch my back. Those flat tires were no accident. Somebody used an ice pick on them."

Lydia's next stop was Tactical Gun & Ammo on Olympic Boulevard where she had previously ordered a .357 Magnum. The gun was not in yet, but she didn't go there for the gun. She wanted to find out if they carried any concealable holsters designed for women.

A young woman wearing a white T-shirt and jeans came out of the back office when she saw Lydia at the counter. She was wearing a holster containing a .45 caliber 1911 pistol. Her T-shirt had the name 'TINA' embroidered on it.

When Lydia explained what she was looking for, the woman asked what kind of gun she was carrying.

"A .45 caliber Springfield semi-automatic."

Tina arched her eyes. "That doesn't help much. What model? A small one? The XDS .45 ACP perhaps?"

"That's the one."

"The holster for that gun is made of neoprene and has no padding, so you'll need to wear an undershirt. Even then, I've had complaints from women about chafing."

Before Lydia left the store, she bought two belly band holsters, one in white, one in black. She also ordered two magazines for the Springfield XDS and two boxes of ammo.

Tina gave her one last warning before she left. "You need to practice drawing with that holster. Make sure the gun never passes over any part of your body. I've heard of two cases where women have shot themselves in the ass while pulling a gun out of that holster. You're looking at one of them."

CHAPTER TWENTY-SIX

WHEN LYDIA arrived at the station, she went straight to the locker room without checking the assignment sheet posted next to the Watch Commander's Office. She was surprised to find that not one of the four female officers in the locker room had heard about the shooting. They were busy chattering away about some show they had just seen on television that afternoon. They also didn't notice that Lydia was wearing an unusual looking holster holding a small Springfield .45 and two loaded magazines when she took off her pullover.

The mood in the roll call room was somber. The Crew was down to four officers today, none of whom noticed Lydia enter the room. They were huddled in the back row speaking in hushed tones. Her stepbrother Milo in uniform was with them.

She stopped halfway down the aisle and looked around for Hagerty. He wasn't in his normal place. The third man on their car, Kenny Ferris, was sitting where Hagerty normally sat. He saw her and nodded for her to take a seat beside him. She did so.

Lydia looked around. The room was unusually quiet. She leaned closer to Ferris.

"Don't tell me it was one of ours who got shot last night."

"You haven't heard?"

Lydia shook her head.

"It was Mike Stoddard. He was ambushed last night outside his apartment."

Lydia recognized the name. Stoddard was a member of the Crew. She looked toward the back of the room. The four officers in the back row were still in a huddle. Milo was now standing up, looking down at them.

She turned back to Ferris. "Do they know who did it?"

"No."

Lieutenant Morton entered the roll call room followed by a sergeant by the name of Joanna Watson. Morton sat down at the desk, opened his notebook, and stared at it as if seeing it for the first time. Watson sat next to him, sighed, and leaned back in her chair.

Finally, Morton looked up. "I guess you all heard what happened early this morning to Mike Stoddard. Captain Kemper will be down in a minute to talk about it."

The roll call room was silent.

A few minutes later, Captain Kemper walked into the room and stood in front of the raised platform. He looked around for a few seconds and nodded to some officers before he began speaking.

"I suppose all of you know by now that Officer Michael Stoddard was killed in an ambush early this morning around 12:55 a.m. just outside his apartment in Van Nuys. We have no suspects in custody. We have no witnesses, and we have no idea where he went after he left work. His death is being investigated by Robbery-Homicide. Lieutenant Grayson asked me to ask if any of you were with him at any time yesterday after he left work."

A few seconds passed with no one saying anything.

"Come on, people. Did any of you see him after work? Did he say where he was going?"

"He and I went out for a drink last night after work," a voice said from the back row. "At Mickey's Place on Pico."

Lydia turned around. It was one of the officers in the back row.

"Was anyone else with you, Jackson?"

"No, sir. Just him and me."

"What time was it when you last saw him?"

"He left the bar early. About 12:20. He had court scheduled this morning."

"Did he say where he was going?"

"I assumed he was heading home."

Kemper looked down and started scratching his eyebrow with his middle finger. Lydia thought he looked tired...or frustrated. He had probably been up all night.

Then someone in the back spoke up. "Sir, do we know when his funeral will be?"

"Good question. We're not sure when his funeral will be. But I want all of you there at the church service and at the gravesite when he is buried. In uniform, as a group, and in formation. The only excuse for not attending is if you have been subpoenaed to court. Does anybody have any questions?"

"Was he married?" asked an officer seated just behind Lydia.

"He was divorced. He and his ex-wife had two children," replied one of the officers in the back row.

Kemper looked around. "Any other questions?" He waited a full minute before continuing. "Okay then. Officer Jackson, I need you to report to my office to make a formal statement. There are two detectives there from Robbery-Homicide who will want to talk to you. If there are any of you who can shed light on what happened last night, you need to tell Lieutenant Morton, so he can relay it to Robbery-Homicide."

Lydia Harte in her short career had not worked with many police officers, but Kenny Ferris was the most unusual police officer she ever worked with. He was a skinny man whose dark complexion was made darker by a heavy beard that needed shaving twice a day.

The first impression Lydia had of him was that he looked shifty because he had a habit of looking out of the corner of his eye when speaking to her that was unsettling. But he did talk, and when he talked, his speech was clipped and to the point.

He was one of those officers who wore his pants and gun belt so low on his hips it seemed as if the whole thing might slide off at any moment. His weapon of choice was also a Smith and Wesson .357 Magnum, but unlike the one Lydia carried, his had a four-inch barrel.

Lydia found him to be a competent police officer, not in the same league as Dick Hagerty, but one who went out every day and did his job efficiently and quietly without complaining. The difference between him and Hagerty, Lydia thought, was that Ferris lacked imagination.

But Ferris surprised Lydia by his ability to anticipate a potentially unpleasant situation when they received a call to go to the station at 7:31 p.m.

"Is your gun loaded with magnum rounds?" Ferris asked.

Lydia looked at him.

Looking at her out of the corner of his eye, he said, "Magnum rounds. Full metal jackets. Is your gun loaded with them?"

"Yes. Why?"

"Have any .38 Specials at the station?"

"I have six in my pocket." Lydia was curious as to why he was asking.

"Load your gun with them and dump the jackets when we get to the station."

"Now?"

"Yes, now."

"Why?"

"Because when we get to the station, they're going to ask you to turn over your gun. They're going to run ballistics on it, and you don't want to be caught having Magnum ammo in it."

What Ferris said failed to immediately register with Lydia. "Why would they do that?"

"My guess would be that they already found out that Stoddard was universally disliked. They might think one of us might have killed him. By now, they might even know the caliber of the bullet that killed him. They are going to examine our guns, and we don't need to get caught carrying the wrong kind of ammo."

Ferris was right. When they reported to Lieutenant Morton, he told them to go to the roll call room. Two detectives from Robbery-Homicide and a civilian employee from the Forensic Lab were seated at the table on the raised platform. A small stainless-steel trolley was parked in front of the platform.

There were four other officers from P.M. Watch spread out across the roll call room. They were busy writing. They didn't look up when Lydia and Ferris entered.

One of the detectives, a man with a florid face wearing a suit a size too small for his bulging waist stood up and introduced himself as Sergeant Nick Ryan.

"Officers Ferris and Harte. Please, remove your weapons and place them on the stainless-steel tray in front of you."

"Are you going to confiscate them?" Ferris asked. "Because the weapon I'm carrying is my personal weapon and not the Department's."

Lydia was surprised by the defiance in Ferris' voice. She also noticed he was not looking at Ryan out of the corner of his eye but was staring directly at him.

Ryan sighed and blew air out of the side of his mouth. "Look here, Ferris. All we're trying to do is eliminate our officers from the investigation into the murder of Officer Stoddard. One of the papers says it has a reliable informant who told them that it was a police officer from this station that killed him, so that's why we're going through the fucking motion. Now, if you refuse to do what I ask, you will be disciplined for failing to obey an order of a supervisor, and I will take your fucking gun away from you whether you like it or not. If you really decide not to turn over your gun for examination, I'd suggest you call someone from the Union who can properly advise you."

Ferris smiled. "Sergeant, I wish you had explained it to me that way in the first place." He removed his revolver from the holster and opened the cylinder.

"Leave the ammo in the gun," Ryan said.

"Yes, sir. When will I get my gun back?"

"As soon as Mr. Jamison test fires your gun and examines it. In the meantime, I want you to pick up one of the forms on the table behind you. Read the instructions and answer each of the questions on the attached 15.7."

Lydia removed her revolver from its holster and placed it on the metal tray. She grabbed one of the forms and sat down. The form consisted of several questions asking her to state where she had been last night between the hours of 11:00 p.m. and 2:00 a.m., the names and addresses of people who were with her, and if she had received or made any phone calls during that time period.

She wrote that she was in her condo the entire time, she was alone, and she neither received nor made any phone calls. She signed it and handed it to Sergeant Ryan who looked at it and then stared at her as if she was lying.

Their guns were returned to them within thirty minutes. Jamison, the civilian employee who did the tests, whispered something in Ryan's ear.

Ryan looked at Ferris. "Officer Ferris. Is there any reason why the bullets in your gun have no fingerprints on them?"

Lydia looked in surprise at Ferris.

"I may have had gloves on when I loaded it."

The other detective leaned over and whispered something in Ryan's ear. Ryan chuckled and looked at Ferris. "You're done here. Thank you for your help."

Once they were in the car and Lydia cleared them for calls, she turned to Ferris. "Why did you wipe your bullets? And don't give me any nonsense about loading your gun with gloves."

"I don't know, Harte. Just as a precaution, I guess."

"A precaution against what?"

Ferris didn't answer.

"You do know about gunshot residue, don't you?" Lydia said. "They can find gunshot residue on you if you've fired a gun."

"Not if you shower and burn your clothes."

She stared at him for a moment.

"You're thinking I might have killed Stoddard, aren't you," Ferris continued.

"I was thinking no such thing!" Lydia responded.

"Do you know what, Harte? I wish I had. The guy was a bastard, and I resent being told I have to go to his fucking funeral. I won't do it. Last night, I was in Santa Barbara with my girlfriend, and I can prove it." He looked sideways at her in that sneaky way of his. "What about you? Can you prove what you were doing last night?"

"Afraid not," Lydia said, shaking her head.

The phone rang in Lydia's apartment a few minutes after she got home.

It was Billy Vernor.

"Do you still have my black notebook?"

"I do."

"The first thing tomorrow morning, I want you to get it out of your apartment and put it in a safe place."

"Billy, what's going on?"

"Lydia, chances are in the next few days, your apartment is going to be searched. I need you to take my notebook out of your apartment and put it in a safe place."

"Billy, I..." Lydia paused for a moment. "Why do I need to do that?"

"Because, Lydia, there were only three officers on night watch who had no alibi for when Stoddard got killed. You're one of them. And you're the only one who carries a .357 Magnum. Do you know what that means?"

Lydia paused before answering. "Stoddard was shot with a .357 Magnum?"

Vernor's silence answered her question.

CHAPTER TWENTY-SEVEN

EARLY TUESDAY morning, Lydia removed the large folder containing Vernor's black notebook from the top of the armoire in her bedroom and took it to the kitchen where she laid it on the counter. She made coffee and then stared at the folder a long while, wondering where she could hide it.

Then it dawned on her!

What in the hell was she doing just standing there?

It was 6:30 a.m. If they were going to search her apartment as Vernor suspected, they might arrive at any minute. She turned off the coffee pot, grabbed her car keys and the binder, and headed out the door.

She stopped in the hallway and remembered that the guns she had taken from Jonathan's arsenal were in her bedroom closet. She went back inside her apartment, got them, and then took them down to her car where she locked them in the trunk.

Twenty minutes later, Lydia was seated in the Beverly Café at a table well away from the other customers. She ordered coffee and a cinnamon roll. After the waitress left, she pushed the plate and utensils away and laid the folder containing Vernor's black binder in front of her.

Should she open it?

Why not?

The contents of the black binder were separated into seven sections by dividers, the first six tabs marked with initials, the last one marked 'MISC'. The first tab was marked 'ASF'. She opened it and found a burglary report for the Akheiser Storage Facility that was dated November 23, 2005, over three months ago.

She read the report. Nearly $500,000 of electronics were stolen, all big-ticket items, each valued at $2,000 or more.

But what surprised Lydia was what was attached to the report. There were three P.M. Watch assignment sheets for three consecutive days, the day before the theft, the night of the theft, and the day after the theft. Vernor had highlighted some of the names with a yellow marker. Lydia recognized most of them. They were the names of the officers who called themselves the Wrecking Crew

Lydia turned to the next index tab. Another burglary report, this one from Michaels' Big Box Warehouse. Items stolen included high-end kitchen appliances such as refrigerators, stoves, dishwashers, and microwaves, most of them costing $2,000 or more.

Whoever stolen the appliances would have to know how to use a forklift to move them out of the warehouse. They also had to have a large truck to move the goods. And they also had to know enough about alarm systems to be able to disconnect the burglar alarms.

Attached to the Michaels' burglary report were three watch assignment sheets with the same names highlighted in yellow. On this set of assignment sheets, Vernor had also highlighted the name of Sergeant Cooley, the assistant watch commander.

By the time, Lydia finished reviewing the third report involving a burglary of another warehouse she saw the pattern.

The burglaries occurred on a Friday or Saturday night, the busiest nights for P. M. Watch in Century Division. The names marked in yellow were members of the Wrecking Crew, and the assignment sheets showed that most of them, if not all of them, worked the night before and the night after the burglaries. Only two of them worked the night of the burglaries. She checked the next three sections in the notebook. They showed the same pattern; burglaries occurring on either a Friday or Saturday night and only two members of the Wrecking Crew working the night of the burglaries.

Lydia sat back for a few moments trying to understand the significance of what she had just seen. It was obvious when she thought about it. Billy Vernor had reached the conclusion that the suspects pulling off the burglaries were LAPD officers.

The big question was why Billy didn't do something about it.

She opened the section of the binder labeled MISC. It also contained burglary reports. There were twenty-one of them, involving burglaries of small businesses, most of them jewelry shops or stores that carried small electronic items. Lydia quickly scanned through them.

Every one of the reports were completed by officers who belonged to the Wrecking Crew. Over half of them had portions of the narrative part of the report highlighted in yellow. The items that were yellow-marked noted that the alarm systems had been disabled by the "perpetrator(s)".

One of the reports had a note scribbled in pencil, "Check to see how officers got the call."

Lydia guessed what Vernor was driving at. If the officers got the call based on a call from an alarm company, why was the alarm disabled when the officers got there? Did burglars work that fast? Maybe on a Friday or Saturday night when the call load was heavy and police response times were ragged.

Pasted to the back of the binder was a handwritten note. "Per Lieutenant Morton, Cooley completes P. M. Watch assignments every deployment period. He's the only sergeant who likes doing it."

Lydia sat at her table for a good thirty minutes, staring at the notebook, drinking coffee until her stomach started rebelling. At one point, the waitress came over and asked if she was all right. Lydia said she was and would be leaving soon.

The implication of the burglary reports coupled with the assignment sheets was that Vernor suspected a group of renegade officers were committing the burglaries.

Had he told anyone about it?

If not, why not?

But now, she had two immediate problems she needed to take care of. The binder and the guns she took out of Jonathan's vault! She had to hide them.

Lydia picked up her telephone and called the office at her condo and got hold of the property manager, Elma Weaver.

Elma was surprised to hear from her. "How can I help you, Miss Harte? You're so quiet. We hardly know you're around."

"Are the Connors still in New Zealand."

"Yes. Why? Do you need to get in touch with them?"

"I wonder if I can borrow their garage space. I have a girlfriend visiting from Chicago, and I could use the extra space for two weeks."

"I can do better than that. You're entitled to two spaces and you're only using one. Let me find one for you and call you back. When you get in, I'll have a second card key ready for you."

"Thank you." Lydia got ready to hang up.

"Are you still with the police?"

"I am. Do you have a problem?"

"Not really. Two police officers came by early this morning and asked for a copy of our video recordings for the past three days. I wondered if you knew what that was about."

"I don't. Were they in uniform?"

"No. They said they were from downtown. I don't remember their names. They didn't seem all that upset when I told them I wouldn't release the recordings without a warrant. Our tenants and owners have their privacy rights, you know."

"Did they say they were going to get a warrant?"

"No, they did not. Do you have any idea what they were looking for?"

"I have no idea."

The next place Lydia stopped was a beauty shop where she tried on a blonde wig that curved around the sides of the face like an upside-down tulip. She liked the fact that it concealed part of her face, so she bought it. Next stop was a boutique in Beverly Glen where she bought a stylish gray hat that was Rodeo Drive's version of a newsboy cap.

She then stopped at a car rental agency where she wanted to rent a medium size car with front wheel drive. Most of the cars were gone from the lot and she had only two choices; a small subcompact about the size of a large dog and a Lincoln Continental. But there was also a Jeep Wrangler available that had four-wheel drive and was fitted for off-road use. Lydia chose the Jeep and was amazed when she reviewed the rental contract and saw a warning that the vehicle was not to be used off-road. She left the rental agency in her car, telling the rental agent she would be by later to pick up the Jeep.

She drove back to her condo, parked her car in its usual spot, went up to the lobby, and picked up the card key for the underground garage from

Elma Weaver who apologized for giving Lydia a space on a lower level than where she normally parked her car.

Lydia went out to the front lobby and ordered a taxi to take her to the car rental agency. She picked up the Jeep Wrangler, drove it a few blocks away where she stopped, put on the blonde wig, and covered it with the cap she had bought at the boutique on Rodeo Drive. She looked in the rearview mirror.

The wig looked okay. It matched her complexion even though she was a brunette. And she looked rather stylish in the newsboy hat. More importantly, she did not look like the Lydia she had so often seen in the full-length mirror in her bedroom. She looked different enough to fool anyone looking at her image through a low-resolution video camera. What she needed to make sure of that was a large pair of sunglasses.

After stopping at Walmart to buy sunglasses and a disposable prepaid cell phone, she drove back to the condo and parked the Wrangler in the space assigned to her by Elma Weaver. It took less than five minutes for Lydia to transfer the bag of guns and Billy's notebook from her car to the cargo space behind the rear seat of the Wrangler.

"Let me tell you a story, Lydia," Vernor said, "about what happens to people who discover something is rotten in Denmark."

Lydia had called Vernor using the disposable cell phone and told him to call her back from a public payphone. It turned out that Vernor had a disposable phone as well. He called her back a minute later.

"There was this former vice officer named Mickey Green who had been fired from the job because he killed someone in a DUI traffic accident. Green wanted his job back, so he had this idea he might regain favor with the Department if he told them what he knew about corruption in the Metro Central Vice Unit. So, he called the Chief's office and talked to the adjutant who set up a meeting with Green to take place in Echo Park. They sent out the captain from Internal Affairs to meet with Green. The only problem was that Green never showed up. As a matter of fact, he disappeared. Gone! Never seen again! Like a wisp of cigarette smoke."

"What the fuck are you talking about, Billy?"

"I'm telling you this because it's the reason why I never pushed this thing with the Crew. I told my boss about what I thought was going on, and he told me to call Internal Affairs. I did and guess what? Nothing happened. Nobody called me back to say one way or another whether anything was being done about it. I had to call back myself. And do you know what I was told? They told me there was nothing to it. They tailed the guys for a month, and nothing turned up.

"A few days after that, I drove into the garage at my apartment out in Valencia. Somebody was waiting for me in the dark. I saw someone hiding behind a pillar. I took cover and ordered him to come out with his hands up. The bastard ran off and I chased him down the street into an alley. He was carrying a gun, but he ran like a sissy. He jumped into a car that was waiting for him and took off."

"Did you call the police?"

"I called the Sheriff's at the Santa Clarita Valley Station. They told me it was probably a rapist who was operating in the area. Waiting in the dark for one of the girls who lived in the apartment to come home."

"So, Hardemann knows what happened and never did anything about it?"

"Michaelson was my boss back then. He was the one who suggested I contact Internal Affairs."

Lydia paused for a moment before asking the next question. "So, let me guess, Billy. You decided to handle this on your own, didn't you? Staking out that warehouse without telling anybody about it. What else are you up to?"

"What are you talking about, Lydia?"

"I'm talking about those guys that sit in the back row at roll call."

"You think that I…" Vernor left the sentence unfinished.

"I don't know what to think, Billy. How come you didn't ask me to go along with you on that stakeout at Akheiser's?"

"You were reassigned to patrol."

"I had Friday night off. I would have come with you."

"I know that, Lydia. But you had problems of your own. I heard about what happened to your car. I imagine you have some idea of who might have done that."

"I do" Lydia said. "Proving it is the hard part."

"There's always retaliation."

Lydia felt goosebumps on her arms. *Was he reading her mind or was he talking about himself?*

"Where did you hide my binder?" Vernor asked.

Lydia told him.

"I'll reimburse you for the car rental."

"No need to do that. How are you feeling? Your head, I mean."

"I'm alright. I'm following the doctor's advice and taking the rest of the week off. I have things that need looking into." He paused and when he spoke again his voice was soft. "Take care, Lydia. Watch your back. If you get interviewed again, don't let them buffalo you into saying something stupid. Keep your cool. You haven't done anything wrong."

After Billy hung up, Lydia thought long and hard about what he had said. *"I have things that need looking into."*

I bet you do, Lydia thought, *but so do I.*

Just as Lydia was getting ready to leave for work, the phone rang, and she let it go to voicemail. It was Jonathan Benedict asking her to call him.

Oh well! Need to talk to him sooner or later.

She picked it up.

It didn't take Jonathan long to get to the reason for the call.

"Lydia, I have a difficult question to ask."

"Okay."

"What gun did you take out of the vault?"

Oh, shit. He found out.

She sucked in a deep breath before answering "I took a Smith and Wesson .357 Magnum. You recommended the Model 66, but I took the Model 27. Do you need it back?"

"Did you notice if any guns were missing?"

"No. Why?"

"I think several guns are missing."

Lydia paused for a moment. "Jonathan, you don't think I took them, do you?"

"No, Lydia. Not at all. I had several people visiting who probably helped themselves. I got Aaron flying in on Saturday to go over my inventory."

Lydia had met Aaron Klein at Oceania Manor when her mother was still alive. He worked at Jonathan's gun manufacturing plant in South Carolina.

"That sounds like a good idea."

"How's the Magnum working out for you."

"It's fine."

"Not too hard to handle?"

Lydia remembered how she had to switch to a .38 Special cartridge while running drills at Jeremy Morgan's Rivercreek Range because of the difficulty of shooting a magnum round on the run.

"I've fired it several times. It hasn't been a problem. Thank you for loaning it to me."

"We don't see much of you. Busy with work?"

"Yes."

"That guy that got killed the other day? The cop? I heard he worked at Century Division. Did you know him?"

"He worked the same watch as me. I didn't know him."

"May I ask you a personal question?"

Lydia was slow to answer. "That depends."

"Well, maybe I shouldn't ask you outright about whether you like what you're doing. I just want you to know that if you really feel the need to do something different, I can find a place for you. With computers...doing what you've been trained to do."

"I know you can find a place for me Jonathan. I appreciate that. I really do. But I like what I'm doing."

"The offer stands, Lydia. Now or a year from now. Think it over."

"Thank you."

"Sofia's here with me. She wants to talk to you."

Damn, thought Lydia, *I have to get to work.*

Jonathan put her on the line.

"Hello, Lydia."

"Hello, grandma. I was just leaving for work."

"I won't keep you. We were supposed to meet for lunch. How about tomorrow at Beaulieu's Sur Mer."

"I have to work tomorrow night, grandma."

"Then, I'll come down to Westwood. We can meet for lunch at the German restaurant on Santa Monica Boulevard."

Lydia hesitated. "How about we do it later this week when I have a day off?"

"Hold on a minute, Lydia. I've got to check on something."

Sofia was gone for nearly a minute. When she returned to the phone, she was breathless. "I had to make sure he was gone. We really need to meet tomorrow, Lydia. I've got something to show you that belonged to your mother."

Chapter Twenty-Eight

IT WAS busy for a Tuesday night with lots of radio calls that Ferris put an end to by arresting a drunk driver who happened to be a Santa Monica City Councilman. The Councilman was released from custody before Ferris finished the arrest report.

"Might as well throw this one into the waste basket," Ferris said to Lydia as he got up from the report table and headed for the Watch Commander's office.

"Why do you say that?"

Ferris turned to look at Lydia. This time, it wasn't out of the corner of his eyes. He shook the arrest report as if it were on fire and he was trying to put it out. "Strange things happen when politicians get arrested. It's like the Twilight Zone. Arrest reports and blood alcohol tests disappear."

At end of watch, Lydia hurried to the women's locker room where she took off her uniform and changed clothes. Her cell phone rang.

It was Jenny. "I've got something for you. We've got to meet."

Lydia looked at her watch. "My God, Jenny. Can't it wait until tomorrow?"

"You'll want to see this. I broke into Maldonado's file, and you'll never guess what was in it."

Lydia met Jenny at a bar and grill called Donovan's on Wilshire near Westwood. Not surprisingly, the small parking lot was full, and she had to park her BMW on Clark Street around the corner. She was walking up the tree-lined street toward the bar when she thought she heard someone walking behind her. Subconsciously, she moved her right hand within reach of the holster on her back hip.

She turned and looked back down the street.

No one was there.

The street was mostly dark, the light from the street lamps filtering down through the trees created a half light on the sidewalk.

Lydia waited for at least thirty seconds, scanning the shadows around the houses. She saw nothing moving.

Five minutes later, Lydia entered the bar area of Donovan's. The place was crowded with people wearing the powder blue jerseys and T-shirts of UCLA. Tuesday night was an unusual night for a basketball game, but Lydia realized that the UCLA basketball team was in the playoffs for the PAC 12 Championship, and this crowd was obviously celebrating a win.

She found Jenny tucked in the far corner of the horseshoe bar next to a very large man who was facing the opposite direction and was animatedly talking to a very large woman who smelled as if she had fallen into a vat of perfume.

Lydia squeezed in between Jenny and the wall.

"Hell of a place for a secret meeting, Jenny."

Jenny turned toward Lydia, her breast rubbing against Lydia's right arm as she did so. Their faces were about a foot apart, and Lydia could smell sweet alcohol on Jenny's breath. Feeling uncomfortable, Lydia turned to face the area behind the well of the bar.

"What are you drinking, Lydia?"

Lydia looked at the drink in front of Jenny. "How long does it take to get a drink in this joint?"

"Too long."

"I'll have a chardonnay if we can get the bartender's attention."

"Good." Jenny stared at her for a moment, not saying anything.

Lydia slowly turned toward her, trying to avoid contact with Jenny's chest.

"What's wrong, Jenny?"

"What's that hard thing on your hip?"

Lydia smiled. "What do you think?"

"I almost forgot. You're a cop. Can I see *it*...sometime?" The emphasis on 'it'.

"See what?"

"Your gun."

"If you're a good girl."

Jenny laughed. "It's rather hard being a good girl. You should know that by now." She took a small envelope out of her purse and placed it in front of Lydia. "You're going to like this. But then again, maybe not."

"What's in it?"

"I got into the first layer of Maldonado's file. Open it."

Lydia opened the envelope and pulled out a single sheet of paper. She unfolded it. It contained a handwritten scrawl that said, "HELLO, OFFICER HARTE. CURIOSITY GOT THE BEST OF YOU? NICE TRY."

Lydia never did get her drink. She listened as Jenny explained how she tried to break into Maldonado's file. When she thought she had gotten into the file, it started to download and then unexpectedly shut down. She spent nearly three hours contending with whatever mechanism that was installed to locate unauthorized users. It was only after disabling the threat that she got Maldonado's message. Try as she might, she could not get past that message and into his file.

Lydia stuffed the sheet of paper into her pocket, thanked Jenny for her help, and forgot to ask her about what happened with her relationship with ex-boyfriend, Rod. A few minutes later, they left the bar.

The single sheet of paper that contained Maldonado's handwritten scrawl was the focus of Lydia's attention when she walked down the residential street where her car was parked, and it nearly got her killed.

She was staring at the paper in the half-light when a gunshot rang out from across the street.

The bullet buzzed over Lydia's head like an angry wasp.

Instinctively, Lydia ducked into a half-crouch.

Another gunshot!

The bullet was closer this time. Just inches above Lydia's head. She saw the flash of the gun. Whoever was shooting at her was using a parked car across the street as cover.

Lydia duckwalked to the front end of a car where she dropped to her knees. She was breathing so heavily it sounded like the roar of the ocean breaking on a beach.

A dog barked somewhere down the street, and a door slammed shut.

Lydia drew the Springfield XDS from her belly band holster and scooted to the rear of the car. She rose up slowly and looked across the street. There was no one in the area where she had seen the flash of gunfire. She waited, hearing nothing but street noises coming from Wilshire Boulevard.

Then suddenly, another shot, this time from behind a car about twenty yards farther down the street.

How in hell had he changed positions so fast?

A porch light from the house behind her came on.

Lydia peered into the darkness where she saw the flash of gunfire. She could see the silhouetted outline of a head looking in her direction over the trunk of the car and a glint of light reflecting off a gun.

She aimed her gun without being able to see the sights in the semi-darkness and fired three quick shots at the silhouette. But then a flash of fire and a loud blast erupted from behind a different car directly across the street. She heard the loud thwack as a bullet struck the side of the car she was using for cover.

Lydia fired three quick shots at the shooter directly across the street, emptying her small semi-automatic. She ejected the magazine of the XDS, stuffed it into the pocket of her jeans, and reloaded.

When she looked up, she saw a man running down the sidewalk on the other side of the street. She got to her feet and saw that the other man had joined him. They were running deeper into the neighborhood away from Wilshire Boulevard.

Lydia ran diagonally across the street without thinking about what she was going to do when she got there.

When she got to the sidewalk, she saw the two men running like hell about fifty yards ahead of her. She dropped to one knee and fired three rounds in their direction.

One of the men fell. He got back up and began running again. The two men, one of them limping, rounded the corner at the next street.

When Lydia got to the corner, she saw the men getting into a car parked at the curb. As soon as they jumped in, the car took off with its wheels spinning. She stepped into the street and dropped to one knee. This time, a nearby street lamp made it easy to line up the sights of her gun. She pulled the trigger and fired the remaining three shots at the car as it made a left turn.

Lydia stood up, trying to get her breathing under control. She could hear the tires of the car in the distance squealing as it made another turn.

She began thinking about her options. Should she call the station and report the shooting? She wasn't sure that was a good idea. The gun she had used was one of the ones she had taken from Jonathan's vault, and she didn't want to have to explain how she got it. She had plans for the guns she had taken and didn't want anyone knowing she had them.

Lydia made her decision. She couldn't go back to her car. Not right now. Instead, she walked down the short block to the next residential street and then north toward Wilshire.

Five minutes later, she was back in Donovan's. Jenny was gone and so were the fat guy and his girlfriend and at least half the UCLA fans. She ordered a glass of chardonnay. As she brought the glass up to take a sip, she noticed her hand was shaking so badly that the drink was spilling over the side.

Fifteen minutes later, Lydia walked out of the bar and looked down the street where her car was parked. It was quiet. Nobody was around. No evidence of police cars showing up on a "shots fired" call.

She could still smell burnt gunpowder when she got into her BMW.

When Lydia pulled into the underground garage at her apartment building, she already knew what she had to do. She walked down to the second level of the garage and stored the Springfield XDS in the cargo area of the Wrangler.

She stopped at her BMW and grabbed her gym bag. The next stop was the laundry room where she took off her clothes, put them in a washer, and set it to the heaviest wash cycle. She realized that her neoprene holster would also have gunshot residue on it from contact with the gun. After making sure the holster was washable, she tossed it into the washing machine.

Lydia ran the water in the wash basin until it got hot. She then scrubbed her face and hands with soap from her gym bag until she was sure the gunshot residue had been removed.

Finally, she dressed in her workout clothes and went up to her apartment where she took a shower in water as hot as she could stand it. Just before she slipped into bed, she looked at the clock.

It was 1:12 a.m. A lot had happened in the hour and a half since she left work.

CHAPTER TWENTY-NINE

LYDIA WASN'T sure how long it took her to come fully awake before she realized the doorbell was buzzing. She rolled out of bed and looked at the clock. It was 3:34 a.m.

What the hell! Nobody had ever called on her in the middle of the night! And how did they get past the security guard who was posted at the front door?

Lydia put a robe on, removed her nine-millimeter Beretta FS from the night stand, and checked to make sure a round was in the chamber. She padded out to the front room in her bare feet.

The peephole on the door to her apartment was covered with a piece of tape, and she hesitated before removing it. If someone was out there who wished to do her harm, they could fire several shots through the door.

She took the safety off the Beretta

Summoning up her courage, she tore off the tape from the peephole and looked out.

A young man wearing a hat was standing in the hallway.

"Who is it?"

"LAPD Homicide, Officer Harte. Can you let us in? We need to talk to you."

Lydia let the gun fall to her thigh. She set the chain and opened the door a crack. "Can I see your I.D.?"

The man held up his I.D. card. His name was John Hamilton and he was a Sergeant.

"Can you wait until I put my gun away?"

"Do you intend to shoot us?" There was humor in the voice.

"No."

"We're okay with the gun."

Lydia opened the door and saw there was a second man in the hallway. She recognized Sergeant Nick Ryan. He was the detective who ordered her and Kenny Ferris, to turn over their weapons for inspection the other night. He was wearing the same rumpled brown suit he wore the last time she saw him.

She stepped aside and invited them in by waving the gun toward the living room.

They stepped inside.

Sergeant Ryan looked at the gun in Lydia's hand and then back up to her face. "Officer Harte, we need you to get dressed and come to the station with us."

"What for?"

"We'll talk about it at the station."

"Okay," Lydia said. "Find a seat in the living room."

She turned to go back down the hallway and stopped. She thought she might be in serious trouble if someone could place her at the scene of the shooting near Donovan's and wondered whether she should call her attorney, Michael Honshino. But it was almost four in the morning, and she didn't have his home telephone number. But wait! Didn't he have an on-call service? She knew she had his card in her purse.

Lydia turned and stared at the two detectives for a moment. She needed to stall for time.

"Is something wrong, Officer Harte?" Ryan asked.

"The Peace Officer's Bill of Rights says I have the right to be interviewed at a reasonable time and reasonable place, doesn't it?"

Ryan shot a glance at Hamilton and then back to Lydia. "I don't think it applies to probationers."

"I think it does, Nick," Hamilton said. He paused for a moment. "I don't think we need to drag Officer Harte to the station to find out where she was two hours ago."

Lydia frowned. *Two hours ago?* Two hours ago would have been 1:30.

"I was in bed two hours ago," Lydia said, feeling relieved. They were not there because of what happened at Donovan's.

"Do you mind if we ask you a few questions about what you have been doing since you left work?" Ryan asked.

Lydia hesitated a moment and then said as casually as possible, "Of course, not. Let's go into the kitchen. I'll make some coffee."

A few minutes later, Lydia poured coffee for the two detectives. She was in the kitchen area, and the detectives were seated on stools at the bar facing her.

At one point, when she had dropped a spoon and bent down to pick it up, she realized how thin her night clothes were. She wore dark blue bottoms. That was not the problem, but the gray Henley shirt in waffled cotton showed a little more than she would have liked. Her nipples made button-like dents in the Henley.

After she served them coffee, she stood with her back against a counter, her arms folded across her chest.

Sergeant Hamilton pulled out a notebook, opened it, and flipped through a few pages. Sergeant Ryan kept his eyes fixed on Lydia even when he raised the cup to take a sip of coffee.

"Okay, now," Hamilton said, looking up from his notebook, pen in hand. "What time did you get off work. You worked a shift last night, didn't you?"

"We were relieved by morning watch a little early. Probably just before 11:30."

"What time did you leave the station?"

"I don't know for sure. Probably twenty minutes or so after we were relieved."

"And you carry a .357 Magnum on duty?"

"Yes."

"What do you carry off duty?"

Lydia wasn't sure how to answer. Hamilton looked up from his notebook when she hesitated. "I carry the Beretta I was holding when you came in."

"Do you mind if I look at it."

Lydia retrieved the gun, made sure the safety was on, and gave it to Hamilton. She leaned back against the counter and covered herself with the bathrobe after she noticed Ryan had spotted she was wearing nothing under the Henley.

"It's loaded," Lydia said.

Hamilton nodded. He was a big man, a couple of inches over six feet. He had a crewcut and looked ex-military. Unlike Ryan, Hamilton dressed well. He wore a light gray woolen sport coat, a blue tie with a funny look-ing tie tack, and charcoal slacks. Lydia noticed he didn't wear a wedding ring, but there was an indentation on his finger where one had once been.

Ryan was still staring at her. "Do you have any other .357 Magnum re-volvers other than the one you use for work?"

"No," Lydia lied. *There were two more in the bag in the Jeep Wrangler.*

"When was the last time you fired it?" Hamilton asked.

"The .357 Magnum?"

"Yes."

"Last Saturday at the range."

"Which range?"

"Rivercreek."

Hamilton looked up. "The one owned by Jeremy Morgan?"

"Yes."

"Are you taking Morgan's combat course?"

"Yes."

"Good girl."

Lydia didn't like anyone referring to her as a girl, but for some reason she didn't mind Hamilton saying it.

"Have you cleaned that gun?" Ryan asked.

"Yes," Lydia said. She paused for a moment while the two men stared at her expecting her to say more. "Can I say something?"

"Of course."

"That gun was turned over to ballistics for examination last night. I mean two nights ago. You were there, Sergeant Ryan. When I got it back..." Lydia paused, remembering something, becoming alarmed. "I might have to take back what I said earlier. I never checked to see if they cleaned the gun after it had been test-fired. As a matter of fact, I'm sure they didn't."

"Relax, Officer Harte," Hamilton said in an easy voice. "If your gun has been at the station since you left work, you have nothing to worry about."

"It's at the station. In my locker," Lydia said, thinking about what he could have possibly meant by that comment.

"Do we have your permission to open your locker and look at it?"

"Only if I'm allowed to be there when you do it."

"Of course."

Lydia nodded. "So, someone got shot this morning. After one?"

Hamilton didn't answer, but Lydia was certain he gave a barely perceptible nod. "When you left work, did you come straight home?"

Lydia realized they could find out what time she entered the garage by calling the manager. Even if Mrs. Weaver refused to tell them, they could get a search warrant. Lydia realized she had to tell them where she was between the time she left work and the time she got home. The only problem was that she didn't want to reveal who she was with.

"I went to Donovan's on Wilshire."

"Why did it take you so long before you answered that question?" Ryan asked.

"I didn't realize it took me that long."

"Did you have dinner there?" Hamilton said, casting a sidelong glance at Ryan.

"I went there to have a drink." Lydia had decided what her story was going to be. During the time she was there, she was tucked in a corner with Jenny, and the bartender never once looked in her direction. The only time he would remember her was when she came back for a drink after the attempted ambush.

"Did you meet anyone there?" Hamilton asked.

"No."

"Do you always drink alone?" Ryan asked.

"No. I was to meet someone there. He never showed up."

"And who was that?"

"I can't tell you."

"Why not?"

"He's married."

"And what if you were ordered to tell us?" Ryan persisted.

"I would if I talked to him, and he said it was okay." She was thinking she might be able to find someone she knew who would lie for her.

"Was there anyone in the bar who would recognize you?" Hamilton asked.

"The bartender."

"No one from your days at UCLA?"

Lydia shook her head.

"What time did you leave the bar?"

"I don't remember the exact time, but I got home a little after one. You can check downstairs in the office when it's open. They keep track of cars coming in and out of the garage. They have a video camera covering the entrance."

The two detectives looked at each other. Lydia knew what they were thinking. They were mentally computing the time it would take for Lydia to get to the bar, have a drink, and then drive home.

"So, you were in the bar for about an hour, more or less?" Ryan asked.

"Probably a lot less."

"How many drinks did you have?"

"Just one. I was waiting...hoping my friend would show up."

Ryan nudged Hamilton with an elbow. Hamilton nodded. He reached into his jacket pocket and pulled out a padded envelope. "Officer Harte, you have to understand we're not here to accuse you of a crime. All we want to do is to eliminate you as a suspect."

"A suspect of what? Murder?"

"How did you know someone's been murdered?" Ryan asked.

Hamilton looked at Ryan. "Are you serious, Nick? She knows we work Homicide." Hamilton turned his attention back to Lydia and showed her the package. "This is a gunshot residue collection kit. It is used to determine if someone has recently fired a gun. Have you ever heard of it?"

"I have," Lydia said. "I also know that using it to find out if someone has fired a gun is controversial. Even if gunshot residue is detected, that doesn't mean a person has fired a gun. The residue could come from touching a gun or coming into contact with someone who recently fired a gun."

"That's true," Hamilton said. "But we could clear you for sure if the test showed no gunshot residue on your hands."

Lydia wondered if she had scrubbed her hands thoroughly enough in the laundry room and in the shower to remove any trace of burnt gunpowder. But even if there was gunshot residue left on her hands, it could be explained away by saying she handled her .357 at work, and it hadn't been cleaned after it had been test fired by Jamison two nights ago.

She consented to the test and Hamilton took samples from both of her hands.

Hamilton turned to face Lydia when she escorted the two detectives to the door. "Thank you for your cooperation, Officer Harte. Sorry we had to bother you at this late hour, but we were told by our boss to check everyone who carries a .357 Magnum on P.M. Watch."

"Who got shot?"

Ryan answered. "Do you know Sergeant Cooley?"

Lydia thought for a moment. Sergeant Les Cooley was at roll call at the start of watch yesterday afternoon. "I know he's one of the sergeants on P.M. Watch. But I don't know him personally."

"He was ambushed this morning just after one o'clock when he left a bar in Venice."

Lydia did not know Sergeant Les Cooley very well. Of the three sergeants on P.M. Watch, he was the least accessible. She never saw him while on patrol and never had the occasion to talk to him except for the one time he came out to the parking lot to inspect her car after someone had flattened the tires. But Cooley was also one of the people whose name had received special attention in Vernor's black binder.

After Hamilton and Ryan left her apartment, Lydia went back to the kitchen and poured herself a cup of coffee, thinking about the late-night visit by the two detectives.

Somebody had killed two police officers whose names had been marked in yellow in Vernor's binder. But, why had suspicion focused on her? Was it because she carried a .357 Magnum while on duty and someone had shot Stoddard and maybe Cooley with a .357?

She wondered if Homicide had gone out to Hagerty's house and checked out his gun. He had been off the past two nights. She would call him in the morning and find out.

It wasn't until she took a sip of coffee and the bitterness assaulted her stomach when she realized what time it was. She poured the coffee into the sink, turned off the kitchen lights, and went back to bed.

CHAPTER THIRTY

LYDIA WOKE up with the sense that something was seriously wrong. She had slept soundly, but the first thought that jarred her mind was that something terrible had happened to her last night. And then she realized what it was.

Two men had shot at her and she had returned fire.

She lay on her back looking up at the ceiling for a moment before realizing it was going to be a busy day and she needed to get out of bed.

The first thing she did was to call Hagerty at home. After answering a few pointed questions by Hagerty's wife about who she was, the woman's voice warmed up rapidly and said she would get Richard.

"Have you heard about Cooley?" Lydia asked when she had Hagerty on the phone.

"I have."

Detecting a bit of hesitancy in Hagerty's voice, she said, "And?"

"And what?"

"Did you have a problem with him?"

"I didn't, but the Department did. He was bounced out of a narcotics unit and sent to a disciplinary board because of misuse of operating funds. He beat the rap and has been playing the part of the good boy ever since."

"Was there any connection between Cooley and Stoddard?"

There was a long pause on the phone, and for a moment, Lydia thought Hagerty had put it down.

"I'm not sure if they really knew each other very well."

"I'm talking about the fact that two people from our Division got killed on two consecutive nights."

Another long pause on the phone before Hagerty answered. "Could be a coincidence. I've never saw them talking to one another."

"Did you know that two nights ago they had everybody come into the station and write up a report about what they had been doing the morning Stoddard was killed? They took my gun and Ferris' gun to the lab and test fired them. There were only three of us on the watch who carried a .357."

"They'll probably ask for mine when I get to work tonight."

"Maybe so. Did you get interviewed by Robbery-Homicide?"

"No?" Another pause, then with alarm in his voice, "My God, Lydia, did they interview you?"

Lydia told him about the visit by Ryan and Hamilton in the early morning hours. When she finished, Hagerty asked her to go over what they had asked, and she did. Just before she finished, she mentioned the gunshot residue test.

"They had you do that test? In your apartment?"

"Yes."

"Why did you consent to be interviewed like that in the middle of the night? You have the right to be interviewed at a reasonable time and place. You also have a right to representation. Didn't anyone ever tell you that?"

"They said they wanted to eliminate me as a suspect."

"And you fell for that?"

"I have nothing to hide," Lydia said, realizing that was not strictly true. Nothing big to hide, just a little gun battle in which she shot one of her assailants in the leg.

"Listen, Lydia," Hagerty continued. "I know Hamilton. He's a good man and a good detective. And Ryan, he may look like a bum, but he's been around a long time, and he knows what he's doing. Their boss didn't send them to your home to eliminate you as a suspect. They were sent there because they believed it's possible you might have killed Cooley and Stoddard."

It was Lydia's turn to be quiet for a moment or two.

"But why would I kill them?"

"Maybe, somebody fingered you as a suspect. There are some people in the Division who think you killed Searles."

"So, what do I do now?"

"Nothing, right now. If they interview you again, insist on having someone represent you. If you don't have an attorney, I'd see about getting one as soon as possible. If you're interviewed again and can't get a hold of anyone, call me. I'll come down and represent you."

It was only after breakfast that Lydia remembered the message from Maldonado that Jenny had given her at Donovan's. Absentmindedly, she went back to the bedroom and looked for it in her purse. It wasn't there.

What did she do with it?

She thought back to when Jenny gave her the message. They were in Donovan's. Did she put it in her purse? But she didn't have a purse with her when she went into the bar.

Then she remembered. She took the slip of paper with her when she left the bar and had it in her hand when the first shot was fired. She dropped it when she drew the Springfield XDS.

That piece of paper was evidence that might tie Lydia to the scene of the shooting. That and the empty cartridge casings that probably had her fingerprints on them.

Lydia got ready to go out. She put the Beretta FS into its clip-on holster and attached it to her belt under her pullover, noticing how big and clunky the gun was in comparison to the little Springfield XDS.

Lydia tried to find a parking spot at least two blocks away from the place where someone tried to ambush her earlier that morning. The only problem was that the street was clear of cars because of a no parking sign indicating it was street sweeping day. She found a pay parking lot on Wilshire two blocks east of Donovan's.

She decided to approach the scene of the shooting from the opposite direction she had taken earlier that morning, so she wound her way through the neighborhood until she came to the connector street where she had fired three rounds at the retreating car.

Lydia walked slowly, looking for cartridge casings in the street. A streetsweeper had come through, its wet marks still visible. There were no cartridge casings in the street. They had probably been swept up.

She turned the corner onto Clark Street. The neighborhood consisted of older homes with manicured lawns and shade trees lining either side of the street. No one was around. The only car on the street was a Chevy Monza that had been ticketed.

Lydia walked slowly, looking around, hoping that no one would see her, hoping that if they did, they would assume she was just out for a walk. When she was nearing Wilshire Boulevard, she saw a little boy sitting cross-legged on a sidewalk leading to a small house. His attention was focused on the sidewalk.

When she got closer, she saw what the boy was doing. He was playing with a set of matchbox cars and had set up what appeared to be a slalom made with small brass cylinders. Lydia stopped when she realized what those little brass cylinders were. They were cartridge casings and there were five of them.

Lydia paused for a moment, wondering how she might be able to recover the casings, when a young woman appeared at the screen door of the house, looked out at the small boy, and then went back inside. There was no chance at recovering the casings without making her presence known, so she moved on until she found the message from Jenny that she had dropped earlier that morning. It was torn into shreds. She bent down to pick them up. They were saturated with a slimy substance. A dog must have ripped it apart. She stuffed the pieces of paper into her pocket and wiped her hand on her jeans.

A glint of light in the verge caught her eye. It was a cartridge casing nearly hidden by thick Bermuda grass. Making sure no one was watching, she bent down and picked it up. Stuffing it into her pocket, she continued walking toward Wilshire, crossed to the other side of Clark Street and walked in the other direction.

That was when she saw the man and the little dog.

He was a little way down the street, bent over as if looking for something he had lost. He was old, very old, with a neatly trimmed beard. Lydia thought he might have been a homeless person from the way he was dressed, but on closer inspection, she noticed that his clothes were clean. He wore a gray Fedora, a woolen sport coat over a knitted sweater, and woolen slacks that was neatly pressed.

As Lydia approached the man, she noticed he was looking at something shiny in his hand. His dog, a terrier of some type, saw Lydia and began whining.

The old man looked up at her.

"Somebody dropped this," he said, holding out a cartridge casing.

"What is it?" Lydia asked.

"A cartridge casing. Looks like .40 caliber. I also found a few .45s a few yards down the street."

Lydia felt her pulse racing.

"I can use the .45s," he continued. "I reload ammo for practice."

"Where do you practice shooting around here?" Lydia asked.

"It looks like somebody got some practice in the neighborhood last night." He looked at the house nearest him. "A bit unusual. The gangs haven't come out this far yet."

The little dog jumped out to extend his leash and started sniffing at Lydia's trainers.

"Where do you practice?" the old man asked suddenly.

Lydia looked up from the dog.

"You're carrying a gun on your right hip under your jersey," the old man continued. "I can see the outline."

"I don't practice often enough," Lydia said, suddenly alarmed.

"You should. I practice twice a week with some guys from my Detachment." When he saw the puzzled look on Lydia's face, he continued. "The Marine Corps League. I retired from the Marines right after Korea. The League is one way I stay in touch with my comrades."

Lydia didn't know how to respond. Here was a man who could place her on this street if anybody came around asking questions. She wanted to get out of there as soon as possible.

"Do you live in the area?" the old man asked.

"No. I'm looking for another place to work. I tried some restaurants on Wilshire, but they're not hiring."

"Well, good luck, Missy. I have to be movin' along."

He walked past her, mumbling to himself, still examining the cartridge casings in his hand.

One minute later, Lydia found the first drop of blood on the sidewalk. It was at the far end of Clark Street where she had seen one of the men fall to the ground. She went back to her car.

Lydia sat in her car for a few minutes thinking about what to do next. She was worried someone had gotten a good look at her while trying to find the piece of paper Jenny had given her. The only person who did was the

Marine veteran, and he knew she carried a gun. The other problem was the possibility of fingerprints being found on the cartridges. Any worries about that were dispelled by the fact they were picked up and handled by the little boy and the old man. But still, she was bothered by the uncertainty of it all.

She picked up her throwaway phone and called Vernor.

He answered. "Yes?"

"Is there any way you can find out if a shots-fired call came out last night near Wilshire and Clark?"

Lydia thought she could hear Vernor thinking on the phone before he answered.

"I can. Call you right back."

"Wait. Can you also check to see if anyone checked into a hospital early this morning with a gunshot wound to the leg?"

"That would be more difficult. Might have to wait until I get back to work."

"Okay."

"Are you working tonight?"

"Yes. Why?"

"Take a look at the rotator before you go to roll call. You might find something in there about the shooting."

The rotator was the clipboard that was kept in the Watch Commander's office and contained reports of recent crimes in the Division. It was used by the Watch Commander to brief officers before they hit the streets.

"I will," Lydia replied.

"Is my binder safe?"

"Very."

Lydia heard Vernor take a deep breath.

"Did you hear about Cooley?" Vernor asked.

"Yes." Lydia paused before continuing. "I was interviewed this morning."

"By who?"

"Ryan and some guy named Hamilton."

Another long pause on the phone.

"I didn't do it," Lydia said, sarcastically. "Would you happen to know anything about it?"

"Watch your back," Vernor said as he hung up.

CHAPTER THIRTY-ONE

LYDIA ARRIVED at Schroeder's Deutsche Hofbraumarkt five minutes before Sofia Benedetto was scheduled to show up. She had been here once before. Her mother and Jonathan took her to the restaurant after she had won two events in a track meet at UCLA.

The restaurant was elegant and decorated in Old World style with smoky, dark wood paneling and a fireplace that was always burning brightly even though the temperature outside might be hovering around 100 degrees. The hostess led Lydia to a table in the back corner of the restaurant. She ordered iced tea.

A few minutes later, a waiter, clad in a white shirt with bowtie and immaculate white apron came over and told her she would have to move to accommodate Mrs. Benedetto. Lydia got up with her glass of tea and followed the waiter to the front of the restaurant where he stopped at an entrance to a small room and gestured for her to enter.

Lydia had never seen the room before because the door had always been closed when she had been there previously. The room was small but classically decorated; its walls were paneled in mellow oak and contained at least a dozen niches displaying tiny marble statutes. Several paintings showing medieval town squares were hung on the walls.

Sofia Benedetto was seated in a wheelchair at the small but intimate table. She smiled when she saw Lydia, but Lydia didn't smile back.

The old woman's appearance was shockingly gaunt. Her cheeks were hollow, and her white hair, normally luxuriant, was cut short and plastered in tight little curls that seemed glued to her head.

An attendant, a woman in her late forties, dressed in black scrubs, stood at Sofia's side.

"Sit down, Lydia dear, and don't look at me that way."

"Good morning, grandma."

Sofia held out a hand and Lydia took it, treating it as if she was picking up a newborn kitten.

"Don't be shocked," Sofia said. "I'm not dead yet. I only look dead."

Lydia sat down. "Are you all right?" Lydia said, taking a quick glance at the attendant.

"I'm fine. I've just had a few falls lately. Jonathan insists I take Miss Grouch with me when I go out."

Lydia noticed that the attendant smiled.

Sofia turned and looked up at the attendant. "Alice, you may go now. Remember what I told you? Anything you want on the menu is on the house."

"Yes, ma'am. Do you need anything else?"

"Yes. I need to be left alone with my granddaughter."

The woman left the room, and the waiter came in with menus.

"Did I tell you we were ready for menus?" Sofia asked.

"No, Mrs. Benedetto."

"Then get the fuck out of here."

Lydia was surprised at the tone of Sofia's voice. She had never heard Sofia Benedetto use profanity before.

Surprisingly, the waiter smiled. He slammed the menus on the table, looked at Sofia, and said, "Fuck you too, madam." He turned to leave the room.

"Now that's more like it, Jamie boy. Next time don't treat me like some fucking prima donna."

"Yes, your holiness. I'll remember that the next time I piss in your soup."

Jamie shut the door behind him.

Lydia stared in stunned silence at Sofia.

"Don't look so shocked, Lydia. I've known that boy since he's been in the witness protection program."

Lydia leaned forward. "What witness protection program?"

"It's not the kind you're thinking of, Lydia dear. He's being protected from the Feds. They want him…badly."

"Who's protecting him?"

"Jonathan."

"What did he do?"

"My son, Jonathan? He's done lots of things. Mostly bad."

"I'm talking about the waiter."

"Jamie?" Sofia looked thoughtful for a moment. "He killed the wrong person."

"And Jonathan hides him?"

"No. He hides himself."

"Does Jonathan own this restaurant?"

"Jonathan owns lots of things. Or he thinks he does." Sofia leaned forward. "Come closer."

Later, Lydia would find out that Sofia, for some reason, deliberately evaded the question about who owned the restaurant.

"He never has enough, Lydia," Sofia whispered in a thick voice. "He wanted what your mother had, and he couldn't get it. Now he wants you!"

Lydia drew back in her chair and stared at the old woman, amazed at the radical transformation in her demeanor. She had heard of what Sofia had done in the past and how ruthless she had been in dealing with her business interests before she turned them over to Jonathan, but Lydia had never seen Sofia look and act so menacing as when she spoke those words.

Sofia was now smiling. "Shocked you, didn't I?"

Lydia didn't know what to say.

The old lady bent over and picked up her purse. She looked inside and took out a small address book.

Lydia recognized it. It had once belonged to her mother.

Sofia slid the book across the table. "Do I need to tell you what this is?"

Lydia picked up the address book and opened it.

"I hid it from the cops," Sofia continued. "Actually, that's a lie. I hid it from Jonathan."

"Why?"

"I wanted to save it for you. That's a lie too. I hid it because I was trying to save an old friend of your mother's. I think that's who Vivienne was going to see when she drove off that road. Her name is Vera Bradley, and her address is in that book. You might want to talk to her. She lives off Mulholland Drive, not far from the so-called *accident*."

The way Sofia emphasized the word 'accident' caused Lydia to look up from the address book. She leaned forward and whispered, "You believe my mother was murdered, don't you?"

Sofia looked away.

"Come on, grandma. Tell me what you think happened."

Sofia turned toward her. "I wish you wouldn't call me grandma. It makes me feel old."

"You are old, Sofia. You just don't know it yet. Why are you ducking my question?"

"I am not a duck, so I can't duck your question."

Lydia sighed and tried again. "I asked what you thought happened to my mother, and you never answered my question."

Sofia took a handkerchief out of her purse and dabbed one corner of her eye. When she looked up again, Lydia thought Sofia Benedetto looked like she was a hundred years old.

"She was worth a lot of money, Lydia. Some say it was close to eight hundred million dollars. She owned a small shipping company."

"I already know that, grandma."

Sofia leaned forward. "But what you really need to know, Lydia, is who benefits by your mother's death."

After pondering a moment about what Sofia meant when she used the word 'benefit', Lydia said, "I get my mother's estate when I reach twenty-six."

"Darling girl, you really need to think about this. What happens if you don't reach twenty-six?"

"I'm young…in good health."

"Seems to me you got shot a while back. You're a police officer, Lydia. It's dangerous work. At least one LAPD officer gets killed every year. You need to think about quitting before it happens to you. Or find a job where you can't get hurt." Sofia paused. "So, I am going to ask you an important question, Lydia, and I want you to think about this before you answer. Who do you think benefits by *your* death?"

"I don't understand what you're driving at."

"You heard me, Lydia. Who do you think benefits by your death?"

"I don't know. I haven't seen the trust document. I don't have a copy."

"Why don't you? You're the beneficiary. You're entitled to a copy."

"Nobody ever gave me a copy."

"Then you need to contact your mother's attorney and get a copy."

"I thought the last trust was done by Jonathan's attorney."

"It was, but your mother's attorney has a copy.

Lydia had never seen the trust document Sofia was talking about, and she didn't know the name of the attorney who had drafted it. But she did know the name of her mother's attorney. He was Eric Milburn from Santa Monica, and he had been her mother's attorney for years.

Two years before her death, Vivienne told Lydia that she was going to have the trust redone by Jonathan's attorney, but not to worry about it. It was her habit to have the trust reviewed every four years anyway. Lydia would remain the primary beneficiary in the event of Vivienne's death. She was currently receiving $10,000 a month from the trust and would continue to receive that amount until she reached twenty-six years of age.

But there was one thing that Lydia knew was not covered by the trust and that was her condo. Vivienne bought the condo for Lydia's use while she attended UCLA, and she had made sure that title to the condo was in both their names as joint tenants. When Vivienne died, Lydia became sole owner of the condo.

When Lydia got home, she called Eric Milburn's office and made an appointment to see him. She then sat down and began looking though her mother's address book. The person she was looking for was her mother's old friend, Vera Bradley, and she found it in the book. She lived on Bel Air Crest Road, not far from where Lydia's mother had died.

Lydia dialed the number for Bradley and got a recording stating the number had been disconnected. She then called directory assistance and asked if they had a new number for Vera Bradley.

There wasn't one.

CHAPTER THIRTY-TWO

LIEUTENANT MORTON entered the roll call room along with Sergeant Joanna Watson. They quietly took a seat at the table on the raised platform and were followed shortly by Captain Kemper who looked as if he had been up most of the night.

Kemper stopped in front of the platform and turned to face the officers. One hand was in his pocket, nervously playing with loose change.

"Most of you know by now of the death of Sergeant Les Cooley who was ambushed shortly after 1:00 a.m. this morning when he was getting into his car in Pacific Division. This is serious business, people, and we need your help. If any of you were with him after work last night, you need to talk to Robbery-Homicide."

Kemper paused for a moment, looking around the room. "Everyone who worked the shift last night needs to write up a 15.7 indicating where and what time you last saw Les Cooley, and to record all of your activities from the time you left the station to 2:00 a.m. this morning."

"Does that mean Robbery-Homicide thinks one of us had something to do with killing Les?" someone asked.

"That means," Kemper said evenly, "you do what I just told you."

"What can you tell us about the shooting?"

"There's not much to tell."

"Any witnesses? Any suspects?"

Lydia noticed Kemper's eyes involuntarily flicker toward her for just a moment.

"None."

"Where was he drinking?" an officer with a German accent asked.

Lydia recognized the voice. It was Klaus Holzer, a naturalized citizen who was born in Bavaria and a member of the Crew.

"Who said he was drinking?" Kemper asked.

"Why else would he be out and about at one in the morning?"

Lydia felt her stomach tightening at a thought that was ridiculous but might be true. *Was Cooley the person she shot early this morning?* She knew one of her shots hit one of her assailants, but she was sure it had been in the leg.

"Is it true that some of our officers were singled out for an interview by Robbery-Homicide early this morning?"

Lydia knew that voice. It was Hagerty. She resisted the urge to turn and look at him.

"I have no knowledge of that," Kemper replied.

Again, the involuntary eye movement toward Lydia, but it was caught before their eyes met.

He was lying and Lydia knew it.

"Were those officers who were interviewed this morning considered suspects?" Hagerty persisted "And if so, why?"

"Again, Officer Hagerty, I have no knowledge of any officer being interviewed this morning. Apparently, you do, but I don't." Kemper looked around. "Any questions? No? We need your help on this one, people. Thank you for your time."

Lydia was loading a shotgun alongside the patrol car when Hagerty approached her. She looked up at him.

"I need to have a word with you."

Lydia inserted the shotgun into the rack and then turned to face Hagerty.

"Now or later?"

"I read your 15.7. You need to know they will go to Donovan's to find out if anybody saw you there. They will also ask if the restaurant has CCTV. If it does, they will check the recordings to see if you were actually there."

Lydia thought for a moment. She didn't consider the fact that Donovan's might have a CCTV system.

"What's wrong?" Hagerty asked.

"I didn't tell them the whole truth about meeting a friend at the bar. I told them he didn't show up."

"Did you meet someone there."

"Yes, an old friend from UCLA."

"Why did you lie?"

Lydia didn't answer. She was wondering if she should tell Hagerty about how she was ambushed. She decided it was not a good idea.

"Do you know there's some nasty things being circulated about you by some of the assholes in the back row? Hagerty continued. "They're saying you're a lesbian."

Lydia looked away for a moment and shook her head.

"I'm telling you that, Lydia, just so you know."

She looked up at Hagerty. "Thank you."

"There's something else you need to know. If Homicide thinks you might be a suspect, they might put a tail on you, and you won't even know it because they're damned good. They'll have four different cars following you, and you'll be lucky if you spot the same car twice in your rearview mirror."

At 9:13 p.m., they got a call to take a stolen vehicle report at McCormick's Diner on Olympic. Hagerty pulled the car into the parking lot of the restaurant. There were two police cars already there, parked side by side in the shadows at the back of the lot.

"What in the hell," Hagerty muttered under his breath.

"Who is it?"

"Don't know."

Hagerty parked the car under the lights near the entrance to the restaurant.

Lydia got out of the car and looked back at the two police cars.

"We got company," Hagerty said. "And I don't like it."

Three uniformed police officers had emerged from the cars and began walking toward them. They stopped about thirty yards away in the half-light.

Lydia heard a soft click behind her. Hagerty had unfastened the snap on his holster.

"What do you want?" Hagerty called out.

"We want to speak to Harte."

Lydia recognized the German accent. It was Holzer.

"Send her over here."

"Like hell, I will. Come out in the fucking light where I can see you."

"We just want to talk. We can do it in one of the cars."

Hagerty turned to look at Lydia and said in a low voice. "Do you want to talk to them?"

"Not really." She paused for a moment. "Let's see what they're up to."

"Are you sure?" he whispered back.

Lydia nodded. She noticed that Hagerty had a hand on his gun.

Hagerty turned his attention to the three men. "She'll talk to you, but it has to be in the restaurant."

"Out here!"

"Inside, you fucking kraut! Where I can see you."

The three men huddled for a brief conversation.

Hagerty, keeping his eyes on the men, touched Lydia on the shoulder. "They're afraid, Lydia. I can smell it."

The three men began walking toward them. Clay Jackson and Ronnie Haines were with Holzer. One member of the Wrecking Crew was missing. John Forrester wasn't with them. He also didn't answer when his name was called during roll call.

Holzer stopped in front of Hagerty. He was a good head shorter than Hagerty and had to look up at him.

"We need to talk to her alone."

Hagerty looked at Lydia. She nodded.

"Fine," Hagerty said. "You can do it in the restaurant. I'll watch from outside."

Holzer held out a hand inviting Lydia to enter the restaurant.

The restaurant was reminiscent of a 50's diner, decorated in white and accented by red and chrome trim. The dining room in the rear was full of customers, but the front part of the restaurant facing the street was largely empty and consisted of six booths and a long counter with backless stools.

The waitress offered them a seat in a booth close to the entrance, but Holzer pointed to an unoccupied booth at the far end of the aisle.

Clay Jackson and Ronnie Haines took seats facing the doorway with their backs to the wall.

Lydia sat down facing them. Holzer tried to sit next to her, but she shook her head and pointed to the seat on the opposite side of the table.

Holzer squeezed into the bench where the two others were seated.

"What's the matter, Harte?" asked Jackson. "Don't like to sit next to men?"

Lydia started to say something, but Holzer nudged him forcefully. "Knock off the shit, Jackson. Have you forgotten why we're here?"

Holzer's eyes flickered, urging Jackson to look out the window. Jackson didn't see the gesture, but Lydia did.

Hagerty was on the sidewalk, not more than ten feet on the other side of the window, glaring at them, a cigarette hanging off the corner of his mouth.

The waitress took their orders, coffee for the three men, decaf for Lydia, and walked away.

The three men stared at her for a few moments, expecting her to say something, but she didn't.

Lydia stood up. "Well, I guess I'll leave since you brought me here to show off your impersonation of storefront dummies"

Holzer held out a hand and said in a soft purring voice, "Please sit down, Harte. We're a little uncertain about how you'd react to our proposition."

Lydia regarded him a moment and then slowly sat down. Holzer had to be the ugliest person she had ever seen, bulging eyes, pockmarked face.

Jackson leaned forward. "Are you wearing a wire?"

"You got to be kidding me," Lydia said. "Why do you think I'm wearing a wire?"

"Your shirt. You got something under it."

Lydia looked away in disbelief.

"It's a bullet proof vest, Clay," Holzer said.

"Yeah, but it's sticks out a little bit."

Lydia looked down at the table and put her fingertips to her forehead. *Fucking unbelievable!*

"No shit, Clay," Holzer said. "She has tits in case you haven't seen any in a long while. What does that tell you about how far her vest sticks out?"

Lydia looked up. "Can we quit fucking around and tell me what you want?"

Holzer nodded. He looked at the others for a moment. Jackson was glaring at her. Haines was looking down at the table, mumbling something unintelligible.

"Look," Holzer said. "We came to make a deal. And we have some disagreement about whether we should even be talking to you. But the fact of the matter is you got to lay off us." He paused for a moment when he saw the expression of disbelief on Lydia's face. "In return, we'll tell you something you need to know."

"How do you know what I...?" Lydia looked out the window. Hagerty's back was turned to them, and he was looking down the street. She looked at each of them in return. "What do you mean lay off of us?"

"It means," Holzer said slowly, "that you stop this vendetta you're on."

"What vendetta?"

"I'm talking about what you did with Stoddard and Cooley," Haines said.

Lydia sat in stunned silence. These jokers thought she killed Stoddard and Cooley, and they were scared of what she might do in the future. She decided to take advantage of it. She leaned forward and locked eyes with Holzer. "Okay. I think I understand what you want. If I promise not to bother you, what can I expect in return?"

"You need to promise first," Jackson said.

"Jesus Christ, Clay. This is not some kid's game we're playing here," Holzer hissed. He turned back to Lydia and whispered, "It's about what happened the night you got shot and killed Searles."

"I didn't kill Searles," Lydia shouted. She turned to see if anyone in the diner heard her.

Two men in UPS uniforms sitting at the counter were staring at her. Lydia turned back to Holzer and then remembered that Lieutenant Grayson from the Officer-Involved-Shooting Team had ordered her not to discuss what had happened in Akheiser's warehouse.

It was too late for that now.

"Don't you understand," Lydia said in a quiet voice. "I didn't shoot Searles. My bullet went high. It struck the door frame."

"Okay," Holzer said, his voice thick with sarcasm. "So, you didn't shoot Searles. But would you like to know how you ended up there?"

"Where?"

"In the warehouse."

Lydia stared at him for a moment before responding. *What in hell was he getting at?*

"It was an alarm call," she finally said.

"Yeah, it was an alarm call, alright, but there was no burglary. You were set up to take a fall."

"Take a fall?" Lydia asked.

"By your brother, Milo," Haines said. "He wanted you dead."

"What?"

"You heard me. Milo wanted you dead!"

"How do you know that?"

"Because one night at Code Seven he talked about that scene in the movie where Gere kills his partner while on duty."

"Yeah," Jackson added. "It was from *Internal Affairs*."

"We were sitting around," Haines said. "And Milo said that he thought what Gere did was all wrong. He claimed that Gere would have been caught because any dummy homicide cop would eventually find out the guy died because he was strangled."

"And then Milo asked, how would you go about doing something like that so you wouldn't get caught." Holzer said. "We thought he was joking. But Searles told us that Milo approached him a few days later and asked if he would help get rid of you."

Lydia bit her lip. "Milo?"

"Yes, Milo," Holzer said. "Searles told us that Milo wanted you off the force and asked if he could help."

Lydia looked down, her eyes dancing in confusion.

"So, the night Searles got assigned to you, he called Milo and told him that he was going to work with you and asked if he had any ideas. You know, about getting rid of you."

"But we didn't know he wanted to kill you," Haines eagerly added.

"We thought he wanted you off the force. That you didn't belong. Searles said they were going to set you up to take a fall for misconduct."

Lydia looked up. "And how were they going to do that?"

Holzer shrugged. "He never told us."

"How did you know what Milo told Searles? Were any of you with Searles when he made the phone call?"

"Searles told us what Milo said right after he got off the fucking phone."

"But," Haines interjected, "We never thought Milo was going to kill you. We had no idea he was planning to do that. At least, not then. We would have never let that happen if we knew."

Lydia looked down at her coffee. She started to reach for the cup but set her hand down in her lap when she saw how badly it was trembling.

"So, do we have an agreement?" Holzer asked.

Lydia looked up. "What?"

"Do we have an agreement?"

"I need to think about it."

"But I thought we had an agreement! We would've never told you about how Milo set you up if you hadn't agreed."

"I'm sorry," Lydia said. "We have an agreement. I just needed to think about it for a minute."

"And you promise to lay off us?"

Damn, Lydia thought, *these jokers are running scared.*

"I promise."

"No more ambushes?" Jackson asked. "Like with Cooley the other night."

What the fuck were they thinking? That she killed Cooley? How in hell did these bozos think she could have gotten to Pacific Division in time to kill Cooley after they ambushed her? And how would she have known where he was drinking?

"No more ambushes," Lydia agreed. She got up and looked down at them with undisguised contempt. "I assume that also applies to you."

"It does," Holzer said. "You leave us alone, we leave you alone."

Lydia shrugged. "Actually, I don't think I need to worry too much about that. How many shots did you guys fire at me last night? Not one of them even came close to me. And what did you hit? A car, for God's sake! You killed a fucking car!"

Holzer took a quick glance at Haines who was sitting next to him. Haines' face turned red, while Jackson stared at his hands, looking as if he didn't want to be there.

"I noticed that Forrester called in sick last night," Lydia said, grinning. "Tell him if I had just a little more light on my sights, I would have nailed him in the ass instead of the fucking leg."

Lydia turned her back on them and left the restaurant.

The two men in UPS uniforms stared at her as she walked past.

"So, what did they want?" Hagerty asked after he had driven the car out onto the street.

"They wanted me to stop killing them."

Hagerty began laughing so hard he started wheezing.

"It's not funny," Lydia said.

"Sorry," Hagerty said when he regained control of himself. He pulled the car to the curb and turned sideways to look at her, wonder in his eyes. "And you promised?"

"I did."

"They really are a bunch of dumb shits, aren't they?"

Lydia didn't respond. She was looking down at her hands in her lap.

"Did they give you anything in return?" Hagerty asked.

Lydia looked up. "Yes, they did."

"Are you going to tell me?"

After a moment of silence, Lydia said, "I'm not sure that would be a good idea."

"Okay."

Lydia turned to look at him. "They think I killed Cooley. If they had really thought about it, they would have realized there was no way I would've known where he was."

"How's that?"

Lydia decided to tell Hagerty what had happened after she left Donovan's. When she had finished, Hagerty was quiet for a moment. He took out a cigarette and lit it. "I take it that you didn't tell Ryan and Hamilton you were ambushed when they came around to talk to you?"

"I didn't."

"And the gunshot residue test. Did you pass it?"

"Yes. I cleaned up pretty good."

"Why didn't you tell them?"

"It was the gun I used. They would have wanted to check it out, and I didn't want them to do that."

"Why not?"

"I got it from my stepfather. It has what you might call a questionable provenance."

"Okay, I got that. Did you get rid of it?"

"Temporarily."

"You hit one of them?"

"I believe so."

"And that's why Forrester didn't show up for roll call?"

"Yes."

Later that night after she finished showering, Lydia walked into her bedroom and looked at her naked body in the mirror. The scar from the bullet and the surgery was barely visible in the half-light.

Milo you sonovabitch, you did *this to me!*

She looked up into her eyes. There was a different person looking out at her, someone she didn't recognize. She never remembered her eyes looking that cold before.

CHAPTER THIRTY-THREE

LYDIA ALWAYS felt guilty when she didn't take the time for a morning work-out at UCLA, but she had several things that needed to be done before she reported for the P.M. shift at Century Division. The first was to pay a visit to her mother's old friend, Vera Bradley.

Lydia didn't know much about Vera Bradley except that she had gone to college with her mother at Claremont. She had met Vera when Lydia's mother took her to watch Lydia run the 440 and 440 hurdles at Drake Stadium. They had gone out to dinner afterwards on at least two of those occasions, and Lydia had found Vera to be a very pleasant and friendly woman.

Vera Bradley lived in Bel Air, an exclusive community in the hills just north of Westwood where million-dollar homes with million-dollar views precariously lined the top of sharp ridges. Lydia entered Bel Air at the West Gate where several hundred homes were scattered over rolling hills. Most of them had swimming pools, all of them were surrounded by lush vegetation. A few blocks further north, the gentle slopes gave way to rugged hills that did not prevent the wealthy and adventuresome from scouring out the rocky ground to build a home on land that would have normally been accessible only by helicopter.

Lydia could afford to live in Bel Air if she wanted to when she reached twenty-six, but the farther up she went into the hills, the more she wondered why anybody in their right mind would want to buy a home in a community that used thousands of gallons of water to transform barren hills into an oasis of wealth.

She found the address she was looking for on Bel Air Crest Road. The house that belonged to Vera Bradley sat secluded amidst overgrown landscaping on a half-acre shelf overlooking the 405 Freeway. It was a simple ranch-styled home that probably would have cost a little under $400,000 in the southern part of Century Division but would fetch several millions in Bel Air.

Lydia turned into the drive and parked in front of the house.

The doorbell was answered by a crusty old woman wearing a full-length bathrobe frayed at the cuffs. When Lydia asked if she could speak to Vera Bradley, the woman said she didn't live there anymore and slammed the door shut.

Lydia took out her badge and rang the doorbell again.

The woman opened the door. "Go away! I told you she doesn't live here. What's wrong with you."

Lydia held up the badge. "Police business. I need to find her. Do you know where she moved?"

The woman stared at the badge for a moment and then looked at Lydia. "She's dead. You should already know that. It was in the papers. I don't know where they buried her, and I don't care." She slammed the door shut, harder this time.

Lydia rang the doorbell again, but this time no one answered. She walked to the car and looked back at the house. For a second, she thought she saw a curtain move in one of the windows, but she wasn't sure.

She got into her car and began driving further up the hill. When she stopped at Mulholland Drive, she looked in her rearview mirror and saw a white panel van coming up behind her. She turned right on Mulholland and then looked in her rearview mirror again.

The van turned left.

It was not difficult to find the place where her mother had died. Lydia knew where the nearest address was, and the photos given to her by Prentiss clearly depicted the turnout where her mother's car was pushed off the road. The only difference in the site was that a guardrail had been installed at the edge of the turnout. She had to look at the photos again to make sure she had the right spot.

Lydia got out of her car and walked over to the guardrail. The slope was very steep, almost at a forty-five-degree angle. Traces of the tire tracks were still visible, two ugly gashes in the hillside. The car had gone down the hill a good distance, its travel unimpeded by the chaparral that thrived on the slope. If the car had plunged another fifty yards beyond where it finally stopped, it would have landed in the backyard of the house below.

Absentmindedly, Lydia took out her burner phone and dialed Vernor's number.

Vernor quickly answered. "Yes."

"Vera Bradley. Have you heard of the name?"

"Sounds familiar. Who is she?"

"She was my mother's best friend. Do you have any way of finding out how she died?"

"When did this happened?"

"Probably three years ago."

Lydia heard a vehicle drive past behind her, but she didn't turn to look. "Do you know her date of birth?"

"No. She was in her fifties. Lived on Bel Air Crest Road."

"Got it!" Vernor hung up.

Lydia turned to go back to her car and saw that a white panel truck had driven past and was rounding a bend to the east. She redialed Vernor's number.

"What now?"

"I'm being followed."

"By who?"

"I don't know for sure. Probably someone from downtown."

"You better hope it's somebody from downtown."

"Why."

"It might be the same people who killed your mother."

CHAPTER THIRTY-FOUR

ERIC MILBURN was a senior partner in a law office located on the top floor of an Art Deco office building on Ocean Avenue in Santa Monica. He had a corner office with curved glass windows that overlooked Ocean Avenue directly below and the crude and tacky pier to the southwest that for some bizarre reason attracted out-of-town visitors.

Milburn greeted Lydia warmly and led her into his office. He seated her on a small couch next to a coffee table and sat down in an easy chair across from her.

The first thing Lydia noticed on the coffee table was a colorful figurine about ten inches tall of a decrepit knight on horseback, the horse being led by an overweight squire. She had not seen it when she had been in his office before and wondered what its significance was.

Milburn noticed she was staring at it and smiled. "Don Quixote," he said. "Have you read it?"

Lydia shook her head.

"A fool being led by another fool," he said. "I keep it there to remind myself not to become overly confident."

Milburn was an overweight man with an earnest face and a baritone voice. He had been Vivienne's lawyer ever since Lydia's father had died. Lydia had met him on several occasions and liked him. His soothing and comforting voice projected a certain kind of trustworthiness that was rare in the attorneys that Lydia had encountered on previous occasions.

When Milburn noticed Lydia was staring at him, he became serious. "I am at a loss to understand why you never got a copy of the trust. You should have been mailed a copy. Angie will have a bound copy for you in a moment."

"Thank you," Lydia said in a quiet voice.

"I hope you have been getting your monthly checks on time. If the trustee has been negligent, I can take care of that problem for you."

"I don't have a problem with the checks, Mr. Milburn, but I do have some questions about the trust. Why did my mom use another attorney instead of you?"

Milburn leaned back in his chair. "I was not happy she used another attorney, Miss Harte. And it was not because I lost the business." Milburn stood up and looked out at the pier. "You have to understand that I know Jonathan Benedict's attorney all too well." He looked back at her. "I have reservations about him...the attorney I mean."

"What kind of reservations?"

"I have to be careful what I say, Miss Harte. Don't want to slander another person in the profession. As far as I know, Jonathan's lawyer is a fine lawyer. It's just that I seem to have an inner compass that doesn't let me stray away from certain moral principles. I always put my client's best interests first. My goal when I draft a trust is make sure that it reflects the desires of my client and not what the beneficiary wants."

Lydia thought that Milburn was being overly cautious. He was trying to convey a message to her that had a subtext she didn't completely understand.

"So, what are you trying to tell me?" Lydia finally asked.

"I'm telling you that I advised your mother not to sign the trust document."

"You reviewed the trust before she signed it?"

"I did. She was sitting on that very sofa when I gave her that advice. I felt so strongly about it that I put it in writing."

"What was wrong with it?"

"Jonathan wanted to be named co-beneficiary. I asked your mother if that was what she wanted. At first, she didn't answer. You knew your mother better than I did, Miss Harte. She was in love with Jonathan and wanted to please him. But then after prodding from a friend she brought along, she finally said she wanted you to be the only beneficiary."

"What friend are you talking about?" Lydia interrupted.

"I think her name was Bradley."

"Vera Bradley?"

"That sounds about right." Milburn noticed the sudden look of alarm on Lydia's face. "Is something wrong?"

"No. So, what happened?"

"Your mother asked me for help. She wanted you to be the primary beneficiary, but she didn't want to do anything that would cause a problem between her and Jonathan. I suggested she could name her husband as an alternate beneficiary. Your mother liked that idea and that was what she took to the other attorney. From what I heard, Jonathan was not very happy about it, but after considerable thought, he agreed to the change."

Lydia stared at the figurine on the coffee table. "What does alternate beneficiary mean?" she said slowly, already having an idea of what it meant.

"Well, to put it bluntly, Miss Harte, if you die before you reach twenty-six, Jonathan Benedict becomes the beneficiary."

When Lydia spoke again, her voice was in a husky whisper. "In other words, it becomes a motive for murder."

"Pardon me, what did you say?"

Lydia bit her lip and looked toward the window. "But, I'm still the beneficiary?"

"Yes."

"Without any conditions?"

"Well, no. You don't get the assets in the trust until you reach twenty-six."

If I survive that long, Lydia thought.

"It's all in the trust document, Miss Harte," Milburn continued. "When you get home, read it. If you have any questions, give me a call."

Lydia stood up. "Thank you."

"Did you ever marry that fellow? Jake Nilsson?"

"I did not," Lydia said. "Why do you ask?"

"Jonathan wanted him to be the president of the board of directors of the Western Pacific Shipping Company. I personally didn't think he was qualified, and I advised your mother not to allow it." When Milburn saw the look of alarm on Lydia's face, he quickly added, "I'm sorry I offended you, Miss Harte. If you're still going out with Mr. Nilsson, I wouldn't want you to think I think the less of him."

"So, what happened? Is he the president of the board of directors?"

"He's not. The bank handling the trust hired an experienced business-man to do that. I can get his name for you."

"Mr. Milburn, that won't be necessary. I have another question. Would it be a conflict of interest for you to be my attorney?"

"It wouldn't, Miss Harte. I would be delighted to be your attorney. What do you want me to do?"

"Well, the first thing would be to get permission for me to attend the board meetings of the shipping company. The second thing is to look after my interests in the trust."

"I would be glad to do that. Can you wait until my secretary draws up a retainer agreement? If you need to go, I can have it mailed you."

"I can wait."

Lydia waited in the break room of the law office while the retainer agreement was being drafted. The trust document, bound in leather dyed a dark red, lay on a table in front of her.

She poured herself a cup of coffee and went to the window overlooking Ocean Avenue and the beach. Her eyes followed an old VW bus painted like a tie-died shirt as it proceeded north on Ocean. When it disappeared from view, she spotted a white panel truck parked on the other side of the street about two hundred feet to the north. A man in a white T shirt was leaning with his back against the front of the van and looking in the direction of the building occupied by the law offices of Mr. Milburn.

Lydia's mind was racing with confusion when she reported for work at Century Division. Billy Vernor had called and told her that Vera Bradley had been found by her maid on the deck of her house. She had been shot to death. Bradley's body had been found on the same day that Lydia's mother died.

Lydia was assigned to work with Hagerty that evening. The first few hours were busy. They took a stolen vehicle report at the Pacific Mall and handled a family dispute call with an abusive husband and equally abusive wife that led to the arrest of the husband when he picked up a lamp and threw it at his wife when she called him 'dickless'.

But then the radio died down and it got quiet. Hagerty drove silently through a residential neighborhood for a half hour without any conversation between the two of them. Lydia had been staring at the glove box of the car for some time when she realized Hagerty had stopped the car and was looking at her.

"What's wrong?" Lydia asked.

"You're not going to find him in that glovebox."

"Huh."

"You've been staring at that glove box for nearly an hour. We've got a burglar on the loose in this neighborhood, and he's definitely not in there."

"Sorry." Lydia looked out the window.

"What's wrong?"

Lydia didn't look at him.

"Can I help?"

"No. It's just something I've got to deal with."

"Don't mean to pry, but I will. Family problems?"

"You could say that." Lydia looked at him. "I'll be all right. I'll try to pay attention to what's going on."

Hagerty stared ahead, watching two teenagers on the sidewalk who had suddenly decided to change direction when they saw the police car. "I don't want to get into your personal life, Lydia. But you need to know that Morgan called me today and asked about you."

"Who?"

"Jeremy Morgan. The owner of the range at Rivercreek. He wondered if you were okay. Said you were supposed to call him but didn't."

"I forgot all about it. What did you tell him?"

"That you were busy."

Lydia nodded. That was true.

"He's a good guy, Lydia. Has his head on straight."

"I'll call him tomorrow."

"Good."

When Lydia got home that night after work, she forgot all about Jeremy Morgan. She began thinking about Jonathan Benedict and that little creep Milo and what they might be doing tomorrow night. She looked at her watch. It was after midnight, already Friday morning.

Friday night was poker night at Oceania Manor, and the game usually went past midnight. Jonathan always had five or six of his cronies over for dinner and a game, and they came with bodyguards who mostly stayed outside.

Lydia poured herself a glass of wine and went out onto the balcony. It was nice outside, a free breeze coming down from Beverly Hills. The golf course was dark and quiet. The lights from Century City shone brightly, but the Santa Monica Mountains in the distance were dark and gloomy. Somewhere out there, past the mountains, up the coast lay a feudal-like mansion harboring a man or men who murdered her mother and who wanted her dead.

She went back inside, a plan formulating in her mind like boiling water. She went to her den and picked up the Thomas Map Book for Los Angeles County and found what she was looking for; a detailed map of the area around Oceania Manor. It didn't show the fire roads scouring the hills behind the estate, so Lydia went to her computer and turned on a mapping application. When she switched to satellite view, she found the entrance to the closest fire road behind the mansion was just off Vermillion Canyon Road.

When Lydia went to bed at 3:00 a.m. that morning, she dared not look at her reflection in the mirror. She was afraid of what she might see there.

CHAPTER THIRTY-FIVE

THE NAUTICAL Surplus Store in San Pedro was an excellent place to find anything a skipper of a sea-going vessel needed in a rush. It was also a place where a person planning a night time raid could buy the supplies they needed.

Lydia called the store as soon as it opened. They had what she needed; heavy duty rope about two inches thick, the same kind of rope she had seen hanging off the stacked platforms at the police training facility next to Rivercreek Range. She ordered forty feet and asked that it be shipped to her condo as soon as possible. Later, she realized she made a mistake by charging the rope to her credit card. If someone decided to look at her financial records, they might start asking questions about why she needed forty feet of nautical rope.

At 7:30 a.m., Lydia went down to the lobby of her building with a cup of coffee in her hand. The security officer, a man named Pedersen, was outside smoking a cigarette. She went out and asked if she could borrow a cigarette.

Pedersen looked at her in surprise. "I didn't know you smoked."

"Just started."

"Then you should quit." Pedersen pulled out a pack of cigarettes, shook one loose, and offered it to Lydia. "Sorry, Miss. I sometimes forget where I'm working."

Lydia took the cigarette. "Where did you work before you started here?"

"I was a correctional officer for twenty-five years."

"Really?"

"Really. That's why I like it here. A better class of people to deal with, don't you think? Do you want me to light that cigarette for you?"

"I just realized I have to make a phone call, Mr. Pedersen," Lydia said as she turned to go back inside. "Thank you for the cigarette."

Lydia had seen what she was looking for. Across the street was a high rise and alongside it was a driveway leading to a parking lot in the rear. A light blue car was parked halfway up the drive. When she had stepped outside to talk to Pedersen, the man behind the wheel rapidly scooted down.

The first call Lydia made when she got back to her apartment was the hard one. What she had in mind would take a lot of time and a lot of convincing.

She used her throw-away phone to make the call.

Billy Vernor answered immediately. "Trouble?"

"It's getting hot outside," Lydia said.

Vernor paused before speaking. "Is there anything I can do to help?"

"I'm talking about you. You can't keep on doing what you're doing."

For a moment, Lydia thought that Vernor had hung up. When he spoke again, his voice was barely above a whisper. "What are you talking about?"

"I'm talking about hunting at night. It's illegal."

"I don't hunt at night."

"Listen to me," Lydia said. "I need the weapon you're using. And I don't mean the one you carry at work."

"What are you talking about?"

"Dammit, Billy, I know what you have been doing, so cut out the crap!"

Lydia could hear Vernor breathing heavily. She knew it would be a tough sell trying to convince him to turn over the gun he had used to kill Stoddard and Cooley.

"Are you wearing a wire?" Vernor answered after a long pause.

"Are you fucking kidding me?" Lydia yelled into the phone. She held her hand up to her mouth, realizing her voice could carry into the next apartment. "I'm trying to help you." Her voice much softer now. "If you give me that weapon, I can make damn sure it's found in the hands of somebody who deserves to be sent to hell. I'm assuming the one you use at night isn't the one you take to work with you."

Vernor took a long time before answering, "It isn't," he said hesitantly.

"I need it."

"It's too dangerous for you to have it. If they find you with it, you'll go down for murder…or at least, accessory to murder."

"I won't have it with me for more than an hour."

"You're being followed, dammit."

"I can shake the tail."

"A lot of people in prison thought they could shake a tail."

"I can shake the tail!" Lydia repeated emphatically.

Another long pause on the phone. They talked some more. When Vernor finally hung up, Lydia was pretty sure he would do what she asked.

The second call was a lot more fun. She went down to the lobby and sat on a sofa where she could see the plainclothes car parked in the drive across the street. The man's head was clearly visible above the steering wheel.

Lydia dialed 911 and in a whispered voice said, "I'm in the liquor store at Olympic and Forrest. Two men are robbing the store."

"Where are you, Ma'am?"

"On the floor." Lydia paused and then said breathlessly, "My God, he sees me," and then hung up.

She picked up a gardening magazine from an end table and began casually leafing through it while keeping her eye on the car across the street. The address she had given to the police dispatcher was not more than four blocks away from her condo building. For a moment, she wondered whether she would get the response she hoped for. A few seconds later, she got what she wanted.

The man in the car suddenly jerked upright. He started the car and began rapidly driving down the driveway. He made a left turn at an unsafe speed directly in front of oncoming traffic on Olympic and sped off down the street.

"I wonder what the hell he was doing over there," a voice said behind Lydia.

Lydia jumped up and turned around. The voice belonged to Pedersen. He had been standing five feet behind her, and she wondered whether he had heard what she said over the phone.

"Sorry, I startled you, Miss Harte," Pederson said. "I've been watching that guy for a good part of the day. I went over to find out what the hell he's up to. Turns out he's a cop. I think he was on stakeout. Looks like he got what he came for."

Lydia nodded her head and started for the elevator, feeling satisfied that Pedersen didn't hear her make the call.

The roar of an automobile engine out on the street caused Lydia to pause and look back. A black Mustang raced past the building in the same direction as the plainclothes car that had been parked across the street. Seconds later, a backfiring white van chugged along after the Mustang.

They were on their way to a robbery in progress call.

The first place Lydia stopped after making sure she wasn't being followed was Tactical Gun & Ammo. A small room off to the left contained police supplies and equipment. She found a rack of black police tactical uniforms and looked through them. None of them were her size. She tried on a pair of black gloves. They fit nicely. She grabbed a black baseball cap off a rack and went into the main store.

The woman named Tina was waiting for her at the counter. "Your gun is in."

"What?"

"The gun you ordered...the .357 Magnum. You did order a .357, didn't you?"

Tina turned and walked into a back room, leaving Lydia quietly swearing to herself. She had forgotten about the gun she ordered.

Tina came out of the back room and laid a walnut gun case on the counter. She opened it and showed Lydia the gun. Lydia picked it up and examined it. It was a beautiful weapon, a Model 27, nice and heavy, in a perfectly blued finish.

For a moment, Lydia wondered why she would still need it. After tonight, she would have to decide whether she should remain on the job. She decided to go ahead with the purchase. No telling who might be coming after her in the future. She also bought five boxes of ammo for the new gun and a box of .45 ACPs for one of the guns she had taken from Jonathan's vault.

Lydia's next stop was a hardware store where she bought a heavy-duty bolt cutter and a three-cell mag light. She then stopped in a sporting goods store where she looked through athletic clothing for women until she found what she wanted; a black hooded jersey with matching pants and black trainers. The jersey and warm-up pants were nylon and waterproof and had a sheen to them, but they were the only workout clothing in the store that didn't have a manufacturer's logo on them. She also bought a small backpack.

She then stopped at the tire shop where she ordered a set of tires and wheels for the Jeep Wrangler. The clerk told her that the wheels she wanted would be special order and they could expect delivery in two days.

Lydia thought about it for a moment. She needed a place to store the Jeep Wrangler after she had finished with it as well as a place to change the tires. A solution came to mind. The nearest storage facility with space big enough to store the Jeep Wrangler was two miles from her condo. Thirty minutes later, she rented a garage to store the Jeep.

When she arrived at her condo building, she drove her car down to the second garage level and stored the work-out clothing, the cap and gloves, mag light, and the bolt cutter she had just bought in the back of the Jeep Wrangler.

Before she went to her apartment, Lydia stopped at the lobby to pick up the box containing the rope from the Nautical Surplus Store. It was heavy. Pedersen saw her struggling with it and got a dolly out of a storage room. He helped load the box on the dolly.

On her way to the elevator, she looked out the lobby window. The plainclothes car was back in its usual space. She wondered what the surveillance crew thought when they discovered she had been away. Would they have guessed she was the one who made the robbery-in-progress call? She didn't have time to worry about it.

Once in her apartment, Lydia opened the box and pulled out the rope. She went out onto the balcony, looked down, and tried to estimate the distance to the ground. At the bottom, she noticed there was a row of bushes about three feet high that ran along the base of the building. The only way they might cause a problem was if they had thorns on them.

The balconies on the rear of the building were staggered and not every unit had one. There were no balconies on the two floors directly below Lydia's condo, but there were rather large windows. She was confident she could place the rope to the side of her balcony so that it wouldn't dangle in front of the windows.

At 2:00 p.m., Lydia called the station and talked to a sergeant on the Day Watch. She reported she was sick and needed to take a sick day. When the sergeant asked what was wrong, Lydia said she had food poisoning and was vomiting.

She spent the rest of the afternoon reviewing her plans for that evening, making sure she had thought of everything that could go possibly wrong. Of all the contingencies she thought of and planned for, it never occurred to her that one of her problems might be Sofia Benedetto.

CHAPTER THIRTY-SIX

AT 9:15 that evening, Lydia looked over the railing of her balcony. A light was on in the unit directly below, but none was on in the unit on the first floor. She checked the other balconies on her floor and the ones staggered on the floors below her. No one was outside enjoying the evening. She had counted on that. Most of the people in the building were retirees and were either winding down for the night or already in bed.

She fastened one end of the rope to the bottom rail of the wrought iron railing where it was attached to the building and tugged on it to make sure it was secure enough to hold her weight. When she was satisfied it would hold, she carefully lowered the rope, making sure it didn't drop in front of any windows.

There was more than enough rope. At least five feet of it coiled up on the bushes below.

Lydia looked at her watch. It was getting late. It would take at least an hour to get to Oceania Manor, and she had to first meet with Vernor. She changed quickly into a royal blue track suit and then called the station. Sergeant Joanna Watson answered the phone. Lydia told her that she was feeling better and asked her to check the line-up to see if she was scheduled to work tomorrow. Watson verified that she was. Lydia already knew she was scheduled to work with Hagerty, but she wanted to go on record as calling the station from her condo late in the evening.

Five minutes later, Lydia, wearing her blonde wig and cap, drove out onto the street in the Jeep Wrangler. One block later, she pulled over to the curb and looked in her rearview mirror. The surveillance unit that was parked across the street from her building did not follow.

Billy Vernor had asked Lydia to meet him at the Park & Ride lot on Skirball Center Drive just east of the 405 Interstate. Lydia got there at 9:47 p.m. and found only two cars parked in the lot. The area was strangely isolated even though the 405 was not more than fifty yards to the west with heavy traffic flowing northbound. The nearest houses were high up on the hill to the east. Somewhere up there was where her mother's friend, Vera Bradley, lived before she was murdered.

Lydia got out of the Jeep Wrangler and looked around. No one was around. There were no sidewalks in the area. It was an ideal place for a rendezvous.

But where was Vernor?

She waited a few minutes and began to get antsy. If Vernor didn't come, she would have to alter her plans. That was no problem. She didn't need his gun. There was a .45 Springfield 1911 in the bag of guns that would do nicely, and she had bought a box of .45 ACPs from Tactical Gun and Ammo in case she needed them. The cartridges also fit the smaller model Springfield XDS.

Lydia got back in the Wrangler and decided this was as good a place as any to change into the black workout clothing she had bought earlier that day. She took off the cap and blonde wig and tossed them into a plastic garbage bag she had brought along just for that purpose. She had to slide sideways in her seat to remove her royal blue sweat pants. Just as she was removing her bottoms, the passenger door opened, and the interior light came on.

Lydia grabbed for her gun.

"Take it easy there, pardner," a voice boomed. "If I knew you would be that excited to see me, I'd come sooner."

It was Billy Vernor.

"Shut the goddam door and let me finish dressing, asshole."

Vernor laughed and shut the door.

A minute later, Lydia, now fully dressed in black, reached across the passenger seat and opened the door for Vernor. He was carrying a cloth shopping bag with a heavy object in it.

He got in and stared at her in amusement. "Jesus, Lydia, what are you doing dressed up like that?"

"Where were you? I didn't see a car drive up."

"Never mind where I was. What are you planning to do?"

"Did you bring your gun?"

Vernor held up the cloth bag he had brought with him. "Do you always answer a question with another question?"

"I learned it from you."

Vernor chuckled. "All right. I was up in the scrub making sure you were alone."

"You don't trust me?"

Vernor looked at her. "You wanted me to bring *the* gun. Are you crazy? Of, course, I didn't trust you. But when I saw you take off that fucking wig, I knew you were up to no good and weren't here to set me up."

Lydia smiled grimly. "I guess I would have done the same thing if I were in your shoes."

Vernor turned and looked at the back seat. "Where do you want me to stow the gun?"

"Is it clean?"

"If you mean, are there any fingerprints on the gun, well it's clean. If you mean if it's traceable to me, it isn't."

Lydia nodded. "Sit the bag on the floor."

"I hope you don't plan on driving very far with it. If you get stopped, you're going to go down for murder."

"I won't get stopped." She looked at Vernor. "Do you want your binder? It's in the back."

"Can you get rid of it for me?"

"Yes."

"What are you planning on doing, Lydia? They put surveillance on those assholes in the Crew. They're hoping whoever's picking them off will make another stab at it."

"It doesn't involve them, Billy."

"What doesn't involve them?"

"It."

"Wiseass."

"So, I've been told."

"Can I help?"

"I have to do this alone."

Vernor stared at her a long minute.

Finally, Lydia broke the silence. "Are you planning on getting out of my Jeep sometime tonight?"

"I have this funny feeling, Lydia," Vernor said slowly, "that I may not ever see you again."

Lydia stared at him for a moment and then put both hands on the steering wheel. She leaned forward and rested her forehead on the back of her hands. She did not want him to see the tears in her eyes.

"Are you all right, Lydia?"

"I've got to be going, Billy. Please leave."

"Can't wait to read the fucking papers tomorrow, Lydia." Vernor said, shaking his head. He opened the car door. "Give me a minute before you start up. Good luck."

Vernor quietly slid out of the car and shut the door.

Lydia sat in the Jeep for a full five minutes. Finally, she started the car and drove north on Skirball Center Drive.

When she stopped in the left turn lane at the intersection with Mulholland Drive, she could not help but look toward the east. Not more than two miles from here, her mother had died.

Lydia wasn't aware how long she had been stopped at the red light when she heard a driver honking a car horn behind her. The light had turned green. She looked in the rearview mirror.

It was a police car. Not an LAPD unit from Century Division, but one that belonged to the California Highway Patrol.

She waved a hand in apology and made a left turn. The police car followed. When she turned left onto the 405 on ramp going south, the Highway Patrol car continued west on Mulholland.

CHAPTER THIRTY-SEVEN

LYDIA KEPT the Jeep at the speed limit driving up the coast on California Highway 1, not wanting to attract attention. About a half mile south of Oceania Manor, she turned east on Vermillion Canyon Road. When she arrived at the entrance to the fire road, she pulled over to the side of the road opposite the gate. The iron bar that stood for a gate had been pulled back. There was no need for the bolt cutter she had purchased.

But another problem came to mind. What if some couple was using the fire road for a tryst?

Up ahead, the headlights of a car approached from around a bend. A sleek Mercedes drove by, and Lydia saw the white face of an elderly lady behind the wheel who stared suspiciously at her.

Lydia waited for a minute and then turned onto the fire road. She drove across the bumpy terrain for a few hundred yards until she came to a shallow creek lined by scrub oak. After she crossed the creek, she stopped and backed her car off the road so that it would be partially hidden by the trees.

She got out of the Jeep and opened the back hatch. She removed the Springfield XDS and loaded it with fresh ammo. She put the gun in the belly band holster, strapped it around her waist, and adjusted it so that the gun rested comfortably on the back of her right hip. She then loaded the Springfield 1911 and placed it in the backpack.

Most of the other guns she had taken from Jonathan's vault were already in the backpack. She planned to return them except for the .357 Magnum she borrowed from Jonathan, which she decided to keep for the time being. If the .357 Magnum was found in the house by the police, it could be traced back to her, courtesy of the ballistics test run by LAPD, and it would be difficult explaining how she returned the gun without being seen by the surveillance crew from Intelligence.

She put on her new black leather gloves, slung the backpack over her back, and set off in a light jog up the fire road. She carried the .357 Magnum that Vernor had given her in her right hand and the mag flashlight in the left.

Getting to the twenty or so acres occupied by Jonathan's medieval manor took some effort. It involved climbing halfway up a steep fire road, sliding down a hill studded with loose dirt, rocks, and chaparral, crossing a deep creek bed with little water in it, and then entering the property under the fence by duck-walking through a culvert that held a half foot of stagnant water over a layer of slime. Lydia knew where the cameras from the CCTV were aimed, and she knew that not one of them covered the culvert.

The first thing Lydia did once she was on the property was to check the garden shed at the back of the property, and sure enough, she found a large trapdoor in the floor of the shed. When she pulled it open, she saw a ladder leading down to a tunnel that headed in the direction of the house.

She went back outside and followed the creek until she reached a vantage point where she could see the circular drive in front of the house. Nearly every room in the house was lit up. Five black sedans were parked in the drive, gleaming brightly under the battery of lights illuminating the front of the house. Four bodyguards were hanging around one of the cars, smoking cigarettes and speaking in low voices.

The lights were also on in the gatehouse near the entrance to the estate. Lydia knew from experience that Carlos wouldn't be in the gatehouse tonight even though he was working. He would be watching the card game from a stool in the corner of the library/office where he could keep an eye on everyone.

It grew cool as Lydia waited. The wind shifted and a light breeze of sea-scented air began blowing in from the ocean. Just as Lydia began to shiver, Jonathan's guests began emerging from the house and going to their cars. Lydia couldn't make out their faces, but there was one face she did recognize.

It was Jonathan Benedict. He came out onto the porch and began talking to one of the men who appeared to be waiting for him.

The other men slowly got into their cars, warily looking back at the two men standing on the porch.

Jonathan waved them off with an angry motion of his hand.

When the cars left, Lydia could hear loud but indistinguishable voices. Jonathan and the man who remained behind were arguing about something. When the man turned and his face fell under the light, Lydia saw who he was.

It was Jake Nilsson, her former fiancé.

A minute later, Lydia saw Jonathan push Jake back rather violently. Jake reacted by pulling a gun out from under his coat. He pointed it at Jonathan.

Then another man, a big man, came out of the house and hit Jake with his fist, knocking him flat on his back. It was Carlos. He picked up Jake's gun, pointed it at Jake's head, and looked at Jonathan for guidance.

Jonathan said something to him.

Carlos shrugged, put the gun in his belt, and helped Jake into his car.

After Jake had driven off, Jonathan went back into the house and Carlos walked down to the gatehouse.

The lights on the circular drive were turned off, and one by one, the lights in the house were turned off—all except for one room that Lydia would soon be visiting.

CHAPTER THIRTY-EIGHT

THE ONLY problem Lydia encountered in the tunnel was pushing her way through the cobwebs. She hated spiders, but she hated the creepy feeling of having a cobweb gliding uninvited over her face even more. It felt like unclean spirits were caressing her face as she made her way through the moldy darkness.

She arrived at the underground entrance to the vault, feeling greatly relieved. Lydia had no problem working the combination to the door, but when she opened the heavy door, she was surprised to see the lights were on. Jonathan probably took his guests on a tour of the vault that evening and had forgotten to turn them off.

Pausing to make sure no one was coming back, Lydia entered the vault. She planned to return most of the guns she had taken but had no idea of the exact locations where they belonged. There were plenty of open spaces at the bottom of each of the cabinets, so she decided to place the guns in the display cases where she thought they belonged.

After she was done, Lydia headed out of the vault, carrying the Springfield 1911 in the left hand and Vernor's .357 in her right.

Seven and six, she thought. If she couldn't get the job done using thirteen rounds, she needed to spend more time at Rivercreek Range. Plus, she had the loaded Springfield XDS in the belly holster as a back-up.

The massive wood-paneled library in Jonathan's house was used for just about everything but a reading room. A large stonework fireplace occupied the northern wall of the room, and in the corner not far away was an oversized desk that was used by Jonathan during the day to look after his empire.

In the evening, the library was used as a gathering place for cocktails before going out to dinner, as was the case the night when Lydia came to borrow a gun. Milo, the weirdo with the large head, frequently preferred to sleep there instead of his bedroom. He would bring a blanket and pillow down from his bedroom and sleep on one of the several comfortable couches.

Every Friday night, the sofas were pushed back to the walls and a large circular Persian rug purchased cheaply from a fire sale was laid down to protect the expensive tapestry-like carpet manufactured in Italy. A large and extravagant poker table with a felt top was brought in and set in the center of the rug, and eight soft leather chairs were neatly spaced around the table. A freshly stocked drinks cabinet was opened and a table with gourmet-quality snack food set out. The fireplace, which was rarely used, was lit for the night and was now burning itself out.

The first sign of what went on in the library just a half hour ago was the heavy smell of cigar smoke and spilled liquor that assaulted Lydia's nose when she entered the hallway leading to the library.

She paused to listen at the door. From what she could gather, only Jonathan and Milo were in the library.

Milo was speaking in a voice that was near hysterical. "You should have killed him!"

"Here? In front of my house? With surveillance on us? You truly are one dumb son of a bitch, Milo."

"Carlos would have disposed of him."

"And where would we have gotten another fucking warehouse and a trucking company to go with it?"

"We got contacts."

"You're not thinking, Milo. Nilsson's sitting on a million dollars of goods that belong to us."

"So, what do we do?"

"We scare the shit out of him."

Lydia stepped into the room with the .357 Magnum in her right hand and the Springfield 1911 in her left.

Jonathan was holding a small tumbler filled with an amber-colored liquor in his paw and was resting his backside against the front edge of his desk. Milo was seated in a sofa facing him.

"Are we having problems in Camelot, Jonathan?" Lydia asked.

Jonathan straightened up.

Milo sprung up from the sofa as if a spring had broken. "What the fuck! How did she get in here?"

Jonathan was now smiling. "It's obvious Milo. She came through the tunnel. She's covered with spider shit."

Milo's head swiveled toward Jonathan. "What tunnel?"

Jonathan didn't answer. "Why are you here, Lydia? Dressed like a fucking Israeli commando? Or have I lost track of time and it's Halloween already?"

"I want to know why you killed my mother," Lydia said, pointing the .357 in his direction.

Jonathan began sliding sideways toward the edge of his desk.

"Stay right where you are, Jonathan!" Lydia shouted.

"Take it easy, Lydia. That gun might go off."

"You're damn right, it might go off! Don't move!"

Jonathan put his drink on the desk and halfheartedly raised his hands. "It was an accident, Lydia. She had been drinking, and she drove her car off a damn cliff. I didn't kill her."

"How do you know she had been drinking?"

"She always drank when she went out with friends. I saw her drink a Manhattan before she left the house. She was going to see a friend, and they always had a bottle or two of wine."

"You're a fucking liar, Jonathan! She wasn't drinking that night."

"How do you know? You were in school."

"Because I read the autopsy report, goddammit!" Lydia screamed. She brought her voice down to a whisper. "My mother hadn't been drinking, Jonathan. There wasn't a trace of alcohol or drugs in her body."

Jonathan shrugged. "Lydia, can you put that gun down so we can talk this thing through? I never killed your mother. I was here with some friends the night it happened."

Lydia noticed that Milo had quietly moved to a position behind an ornate lamp on an end table. She pointed the .357 in his direction.

"Milo, step away from that goddamn lamp and put your hands where I can see them."

Milo sidestepped away from the end table like a clumsy marionette.

Jonathan had now backed up to the far corner of the desk where he kept a gun.

Lydia aimed the .357 Magnum at the center of Jonathan's body. "Jonathan, I swear to God if you don't come back out of there, I'll put a fucking bullet in your gut."

Jonathan didn't move.

Lydia aimed the gun at the right side of his head and fired.

The bullet flew past Jonathan's right ear and hit a framed photograph on the wall behind him.

Jonathan ducked instinctively and kept his head down for a moment before rising slowly.

"Jesus Christ, Lydia, that was close!"

"It was intended to be close. Now, get your ass out in front of the desk where I can see you! And you, Milo, stay right where you are!"

Lydia suddenly realized she wasn't doing what Jeremy Morgan taught about using available cover. The poker table had a base of solid wood. She began moving toward it.

"Lydia, what do you want me to say?"

"I want you to admit you killed her, Jonathan. For her money. For her shipping company. And that you sent Milo to kill me."

"Then what?"

"I'm going to kill you."

"She's not going to kill us, Dad," Milo said. "She's left all kinds of trace evidence in this room. They'll know she was here."

"Of course, they'll know she's been here," Jonathan said. "Use your fucking head, Milo. She was here last week."

Once Lydia had moved closer to the card table, she realized she had Jonathan and Milo lined up perfectly. One shot to drop Milo, then move the gun a little to the right to nail Jonathan.

"Lydia, what can I do to make this right? What if I promise to leave you alone?"

"Admit you killed my mother."

"He didn't kill your mother, Lydia. I did!"

The voice didn't come from Jonathan or Milo. Lydia looked toward the doorway and realized she had been played. Jonathan had been stalling for time.

Carlos was standing in the hallway, using the door frame as a brace for a semi-automatic pistol. All Lydia could see of him was the right side of his face, his hand on the gun, and the bottom of his right leg.

"Drop the guns, Lydia."

Lydia began slowly dropping down to her knees.

Carlos waved the gun up and down. "What the fuck are you doing, Lydia. Drop the guns."

"I'm going to lay them on the carpet, Carlos," Lydia replied. She laid the guns on the rug and stayed down on her knees.

Carlos stepped out from behind the cover of the door frame. He watched her for a moment and then said, "Push them away from you."

Lydia followed his instructions.

He smiled at Lydia, his gun now held carelessly in his hand. "What do you want me to do with her, Jonathan?"

"Take her out to the desert and bury her with the others."

Carlos shook his head. "Pity, a waste of fine meat like that."

"Let me kill her," Milos said. He was rummaging through the drawer of the end table next to him.

Jonathan stepped away from the desk. "Carlos, get her out of here before this fool gets blood on my carpet."

Carlos turned towards Lydia. "On your feet, pussycat."

Lydia didn't move. "Fuck you, Carlos!"

"I'll say this, Jonathan," Carlos said. "She knows how to growl. A bullet in her gut didn't slow her down none." Turning his attention back to Lydia, he said. "Now, get up, pussycat, nice and slow."

Lydia leaned forward and put her left hand on the floor to push herself up. She groaned and put her hand behind her back as if she had suffered a sprain.

"Maybe, she's not so fucking tough after all," Milo said. He had a semi-automatic pistol in his hand and was pointing it at Lydia.

Carlos held up his left hand. "Put the gun down, Milo. Let me handle this."

"Do what he says, Milo!" Jonathan said.

Milo lowered the gun and muttered, "Jesus Christ."

Carlos turned his attention back to Lydia. "Get up on your feet, Lydia. We're going to have a little fun for old times' sake, and then we're going for a little ride."

"I can't get up," Lydia said weakly. "I hurt my back." Her right hand was now on the gun in the belly band holster.

Carlos stepped forward, reached down, and pulled Lydia to her feet by her jersey. He smiled. "For old times' sake." He leaned forward intending to kiss her.

Lydia pulled the Springfield XDS out of the holster, planted it in Carlos' belly, and pulled the trigger.

The muffled blast rocked the room.

Carlos was knocked backwards and fell heavily to the floor.

Lydia turned to her right and dropped to one knee.

Milo, a panicked look on his face, raised his gun.

Lydia fired one shot.

Milo went down, a bloody hole where his nose had been.

Lydia dropped the Springfield XDS, picked up the .357 Magnum, and stood up.

Jonathan had taken a few steps forward and stopped when he saw the gun pointing at him.

"Don't move, Jonathan," Lydia said. Her attention was diverted by a sucking noise coming from the floor to her left. She turned to look. Carlos was on his back, clutching his belly, gasping for air.

"You killed them," Jonathan said.

"I don't think Carlos is dead yet," Lydia said.

Carlos raised his head, staring at her with glazed eyes.

"Goodbye, pussycat," Lydia said as she swung the Magnum toward Carlos.

She pulled the trigger.

The bullet hit Carlos in the middle of the chest. His body spasmed and he flattened out on the floor.

Lydia turned her attention to Jonathan and began walking toward him.

Jonathan raised his hands and began backing up. "Don't, Lydia! Please!"

Lydia stopped and looked down at Milo. She couldn't resist. She aimed the gun at his groin and pulled the trigger. She looked up at Jonathan.

"Too bad he wasn't alive when I did that, Jonathan. He would have known what it was like to lose your ability to create life."

Jonathan continued backing up. "Lydia, what do you want, for God's sake? I'll give you anything."

"I know what you did with my mother's trust, Jonathan. I know why you tried to have me killed. But why did you have to kill her? She loved you."

"It was because she found out about the prostitutes."

This didn't come from Jonathan.

It came from Sofia Benedetto who was standing in the doorway.

Someone, Lydia hadn't counted on.

CHAPTER THIRTY-NINE

LYDIA WAS so startled by Sofia's appearance that she swung the gun in her direction. She had been so focused on planning her final confrontation with Jonathan and Milo that she had forgotten all about Sofia Benedetto being in the house.

"You better keep your eye on Jonathan," Sofia said. "He's moving toward his desk. That's where he keeps his rubbers and his gun."

Lydia turned the Magnum back on Jonathan.

He stopped moving, raising his hands slightly.

"Tell her about the whores, Jonathan. She needs to know what you did."

Lydia looked back at Sofia. She was amazed at the change in the old lady since she had seen her a few days ago. Her face was chalky white, and she was unsteady on her feet, her body trembling. She was holding onto the door frame for support.

"He runs whores out of his topless bars, Lydia. He brought them home when your mother wasn't around. Your mother told me she thought Jonathan was cheating on her. But she never knew for sure until she came home early one day and caught him screwing one of them on his desk."

"Sofia, shut up!" Jonathan screamed. He started moving forward.

Lydia waved the gun at him and he stopped.

"She packed her suitcases and left," Sofia continued. "He called her and tried to reason with her, but your mother said that was it. She was leaving him. But Jonathan knew she would cut him out of the trust. So, he and Carlos killed her."

"Mom, will you shut up? Please!"

"I don't think I will, Jonathan. I've warned you this day would come. You don't kill people who love you."

Sofia began groaning.

The old woman was still leaning against the door frame for support but was now bent over, holding her stomach. She looked up slowly and pointed a shaking hand at Lydia. "I have to go to the bathroom, Lydia. Watch him!"

Jonathan had backed up so far that he was now at the far corner of the desk.

Lydia aimed the gun at his chest. "I'm telling you for the last time, Jonathan. Don't move or I'll blow your head off."

What Jonathan did next caught Lydia off guard. He dropped to the floor and scuttled like a cockroach behind the desk.

Lydia moved forward and dropped to one knee behind the end table next to Milo's body. A second later, she heard the squeak of a desk drawer being opened. She aimed the Magnum at a spot just above the desk where she expected to see Jonathan to appear after he armed himself.

But what Jonathan did next surprised the hell out of Lydia. He raised the gun from behind the desk without showing his face and pointed it in the direction where he had last seen Lydia. He blindly fired three quick shots at where he thought she was.

The bullets flew past Lydia, not one of them coming close to her. Lydia didn't move. She kept her eyes focused on the sights of her gun and the area above the desk.

And then it was quiet. The only sound Lydia heard was her own heavy breathing.

A minute later, Jonathan's big head began slowly rising from behind the desk.

Lydia didn't need to move the gun to set her sights on him.

She squeezed the trigger and Jonathan went down with a bullet in the forehead. A moment later, Lydia heard groaning, but it didn't come from Jonathan. She stood up and looked behind her.

Sofia was sitting on the floor, her back against the wall, her hand clasping a bloody patch just below her left shoulder.

Lydia dropped the gun and rushed toward her. She knelt beside her.

Sofia's eyes met hers. "Lydia," she said, "he might not be dead."

"I've got to call an ambulance."

"No," Sofia said with so much effort she grimaced. "A phone. Get me Jonathan's cell phone. It's on his desk. What did you do with his gun? Make sure he's dead."

Lydia got up. Before picking up the phone, she looked behind the desk. The .357 Magnum had done its job. If there was going to be a funeral service for Jonathan, it would be closed casket.

When she turned to go back to Sofia, Lydia was surprised to see the old woman was on her feet, holding herself steady with one hand on the wall. Lydia rushed toward her and tried to take hold of her, but Sofia pushed her away.

"Give me the cell phone and get out of here!" Her voice was surprisingly strong.

"But you need my help."

"I need the phone, Lydia. I'll call for an ambulance."

Lydia gave it to her.

"And give me your gun."

"Why?"

"I need it."

"I'm not giving you my gun."

"Get out of here. I need to call 911. You can't be here when they come."

Lydia nodded. "I'm not giving you the gun."

Sofia was looking around the room and laughing quietly.

"What's so funny, grandma?"

"You," Sofia said, looking over the carnage. "All of this"—she waved her hand around the room—"didn't come from your mother, Lydia. She was too gentle. This had to come from your father's side." Sofia grabbed Lydia by the arm. "You need to go. I need to call for help before I bleed to death."

Lydia looked into her eyes one last time.

Sofia held up a hand. "And stay away from Jake Nilsson. They were fighting tonight."

"Over what?" Lydia said, remembering the argument Jonathan had with Jake on the front porch.

"Over merchandise they stole from somewhere. Jake stores it for them until they can sell it."

"Electronic equipment, like televisions?"

"Yes. Now get out, so I can take care of things."

Lydia left the three guns she had brought with her on the poker table in the library. Just before she left the room, she saw Sofia had used a walker to get to the fireplace where she picked up a box containing matches. Lydia paused for a moment wondering what she was up to, but then quickly decided she had to get out of there.

Lydia duckwalked through the slimy water in the culvert and was climbing up the steep slope behind Jonathan's property when she heard a muffled gunshot coming from the house. She looked back.

There was a flickering orange light in one of the library windows. Something was on fire.

Once Lydia was heading south on Pacific Coast Highway, she began looking for the paramedics responding to Oceania Manor. She hoped Sofia would have called for help, but maybe she didn't. Lydia remembered hearing a gunshot coming from inside the house. Maybe Sofia didn't make the call because she was dead.

Lydia was thinking about stopping and calling 911 when two fire trucks went by, screaming up the highway toward Oceania Manor, followed by an emergency medical services unit.

Sofia had made the call.

CHAPTER FORTY

THERE WAS no activity around Jake's warehouse when Lydia drove by except for a security officer who stood outside the guard shack smoking a cigarette. Three trucks were backed up to the docks and several roll-up doors were open, but no one was working in or around the dock. Fluorescent lighting flooded the interior of the warehouse, but the attached wooden structure that was the office was dark and silent.

The street behind the warehouse was also quiet. An abandoned factory with a huge parking lot under dim lighting lay like a sleeping hulk on the opposite side of the street. The area directly behind the warehouse was dark and had a narrow road that ran across its length. It was an ideal place to cut through the chain link fence because there was no traffic on the street.

But there was one problem. Lydia's Jeep would look suspicious sitting by itself in a commercial area. A police officer with the instincts of Hagerty or Ferris would stop and check it out. She solved the problem by parking her Jeep a block away in a residential neighborhood.

Getting into the lot occupied by the warehouse was the easy part. She cut a small hole at the bottom of the chain link fence with the bolt cutter and crawled through. Getting into the warehouse was not so easy. She tried both back doors. They were locked. She went around the east side of the building where the fueling area was located. Next to the fueling area was a flight of wooden stairs leading up to the office. She tried the office door. It was locked. She continued her way past the fueling pumps and stopped near the front corner of the office building.

The security officer at the front gate was now inside the guard shack and appeared to be reading something.

The only way Lydia could get into the warehouse was to move out into the open. She moved as quickly as she could past the front of the office and up the stairs onto the dock while keeping an eye on the guard shack. She went inside the warehouse through the first open door.

Stacks of goods on pallets were lined up on the concrete floor all the way down to the far end. Lydia walked in that direction, passing forklifts and fire extinguishers standing like sentinels next to each rollup door.

Halfway down, she found crates of goods stacked on top of each other that looked like the ones she saw in Akheiser's warehouse. The stencils on the crates had been crudely blanked out with black paint from a spray can. She took a close-up picture of one of them with her cell phone and then backed up and took another picture. Exploring a passageway on the side of the crates, she found one stencil that had not been marked out. It read, ROBERT'S CLUB AND WAREHOUSE. She took a picture of the stenciled image with her cell phone.

On her way out of the warehouse, she saw a door with a sign marked OFFICE. The door was unlocked. She went inside. The office was dimly lit, the only light coming through large plate glass windows and from a bank of CCTV monitors against the wall. The office contained a half dozen metal desks spaced evenly in two rows across a cheap linoleum floor. A small partitioned office with glass windows overlooked the front lot.

Lydia went to check out the bank of monitors. There were a dozen screens showing various angles around the facility.

She groaned when she realized that she had walked through the field of at least three of the cameras. If the images were being recorded, Jake would have no problem identifying who she was.

It occurred to Lydia that there might be CCTV monitors in the guard shack. She looked out the window. The guard had his head down. It looked as if he were nodding off.

Lydia looked around the office, hoping to find something she could use to destroy the CCTV system but found nothing large enough. An idea came to mind when she remembered that the fuel station was right next to the office. She found a huge bucket in a closet and went outside.

The pumps were turned off. She located the master switch, but it was secured by padlock. She retrieved the bolt cutter she had left lying at the chain link fence and cut the lock. When she turned the master switch to the fueling pumps on, a bigger problem occurred.

Fluorescent lights came on and lit up the entire area around the pumps.

Lydia looked toward the guard house. The security guard had not moved.

A fast check of the pumps revealed most were for diesel fuel. Only one had gasoline. She filled the bucket with gasoline and turned off the master switch and the lights with it.

One bucket would have to do. She could not risk having the lights come on again. She went into the office and poured gasoline on the bank of television screens and the linoleum floor.

Another problem. How to light the gasoline without turning herself into a human torch?

She looked through the desks until she found a book of matches. Once she was out on the landing, she took cover against the wall and tossed a match into the office.

A big *whoosh* as the office blew up in a ball of flame.

Lydia was about to leave when she thought of another idea to make damn sure there was a big enough fire to destroy the entire office. She removed the gas nozzle, set it to flow, and then laid it on the concrete.

She then turned on the master switch. The lights came on and gasoline started flowing. She paused, hoping the gasoline would flow toward the office, but it didn't. The concrete apron was level and the gasoline began forming a large puddle. She looked up at the office windows.

The fire had taken hold.

A few minutes later, she was in her Jeep and driving toward the warehouse.

The office was now fully ablaze.

Once Lydia had parked the Jeep in the garage she had rented, she turned on the lights and pulled down the roll-up door. She took off her cap and dirty sweat suit and stuffed them into the plastic bag. She put on clean underwear and royal-blue sweat clothes with matching cap and trainers.

She checked the Jeep to make sure she didn't miss anything. When the new wheels and tires came in, she would have to pick them up and install them herself. She didn't want to explain to the guys in the tire shop why she was changing tires that were brand new. The Wrangler would also need a drive through a carwash to make sure the undercarriage was clean before she returned it to the rental office. Once she was certain she had done everything she needed to do, she left the garage and locked it.

It was just past 4:00 a.m. when she broke out onto the street into a fast jog. It took her less than fifteen minutes to get to the golf course behind her condo. Stopping at a restroom on the ninth green, she scrubbed her hands and face for at least five minutes. She knew she could not remove all traces of gunshot residue from her body, but it would make things more difficult for any follow-up investigators if she went to the range and sighted in her new .357 Magnum before reporting to work.

It was an easy run through the golf course and its sprinklers, and it was still dark when she arrived at the rear of her condo. It had been several years since Lydia had climbed a rope in high school. The only difference was that the rope hanging from her balcony was twice the length as the rope in her high school gym.

Lydia began climbing and got up to the first floor just slightly to the right of the window. The blinds were drawn. She continued up. When she pulled herself up to the second floor, she was shocked to see a man in the window in the half light, smoking a cigarette, looking out at the golf course with unseeing eyes.

The man didn't see her, or at least, Lydia didn't think he did. His eyes never wavered.

Lydia moved quickly and quietly until she drew level with the floor of her balcony. She pulled herself over the railing and onto the balcony. She untied the rope from the railing and let it fall into the bushes below. It would be safe there for a day or two, but she would have to figure out a way to get rid of it without anyone seeing her.

Seconds later, Lydia was in her apartment, dialing a number on her throwaway phone. Vernor answered with a sleepy groan. "What?"

"It's me."

A pause, then, "Are you all right?"

"I've sent you some pictures and an address. You better get there fast. The place is on fire."

She hung up and went into the bathroom to take a shower.

Lydia was naked when she walked into her bedroom. When she walked toward the dresser where she kept her pajamas, she got a glimpse of herself in the full-length mirror. She stopped and looked at her image. It seemed as if a stranger, another person, another being with lost humanity, was staring back at her.

Her raven hair fell wet and stringy to her shoulders. She saw a face that was wildly beautiful but bore the look of a feral woman who had just fought her way through a jungle. Her body, lithe and trim, had once been perfect but was ruined by an ugly red scar where a bullet had ended her ability to do what women are uniquely qualified for.

Lydia felt no emotion at seeing this stranger in the mirror. She went to bed without putting on her pajamas and fell asleep not thinking of what she had done that night.

CHAPTER FORTY-ONE

IT WAS beginning to get light when Vernor arrived at the scene of the warehouse fire. The side street on the eastern perimeter of the lot had two television vans parked next to the chain link fence. News cameramen were on the sidewalk, their cameras pointing in the direction of the warehouse complex. A police helicopter circled overhead, trying to keep two news copters at bay.

The street in front of the warehouse was blocked off at both ends with uniform officers manning the barricades. Vernor showed his identification and was waved through.

He stopped his car just past the empty guard shack and surveyed the scene. There were no lights on in the parking lot or in the warehouse. Several large light towers powered by noisy gasoline generators had been erected to illuminate the area where firefighters were working. There were at least six pieces of fire equipment on the lot. Two large hoses ran from a fire hydrant on the street through a hole cut into the chain link fence toward the warehouse.

Vernor noticed that only a small part of the eastern end of the warehouse had been consumed by fire. Most of the rollup doors were open, but the firefighters were concentrating on the area that had been burned. Vernor saw a large forklift bring a heap of smoking debris out of the warehouse and dump it on the concrete in front of the dock where a firefighter poured a stream of water on it.

A smaller structure to the left of the warehouse had collapsed and all that was left of it was smoking rubble. To the left of the debris, Vernor could see several firefighters working around some fueling pumps with a hose.

Vernor parked his car away from the pandemonium and stopped a firefighter who was hurrying out to the street. "Who's the boss?"

"He's by the docks."

"What happened here?"

"A fire," the man said over his shoulder as he walked away.

Vernor found the Battalion Fire Chief standing on dock, watching the forklift operator dump another load of debris off the dock.

Vernor held out his badge and called up to him. "What happened here?"

The Chief looked at his badge. "You'll want to talk to the arson investigators. They're by the fueling area."

"Is there anybody here in charge of the warehouse?"

"What?"

"I want to know if there's a warehouse manager on the scene."

"He's talking to the arson investigators."

"Is it safe for me to go inside and look around?"

"Listen, buddy, I'm fucking busy here."

"Well, that's just too fucking bad, Chief. I've got a job to do, too. Just answer my fucking question and I'll leave you to it."

The Chief stared at Vernor for a moment. "What was the question?"

"Is it safe for me to go in and look around?"

"As long as you don't go near the area where we're working."

"Thanks."

Vernor managed to pull the warehouse manager away from the two arson investigators and from the overpowering smell of gasoline. The manager was a small man with a thin mustache, the kind worn by actors who played detectives in the movies back in the 1930's. He was startled when Vernor displayed his badge.

"What do you want?" the manager asked, apprehension in his voice.

Vernor noticed the man had a nervous tic that caused his eyes to rapidly blink.

"Well, first of all, why are you so damn nervous?" Vernor asked.

The man looked around. "It's…it's the gasoline. They haven't got it contained."

Vernor looked at the pumps. The firefighters were flushing out the area around the pumps. There was no evidence the fire had originated in that area.

"What happened here?"

"Someone set the office on fire and then turned on the gas pump. We're lucky the fire didn't spread."

Vernor looked at the smoking rubble. "That was the office?"

"Yes."

"What do you do here?"

"I'm the warehouse manager."

"So, you know what's stored in the warehouse?"

The man looked away for a second. "I suppose so."

"What does that mean?"

"I work days. I don't always know what goes on at night."

"What is your name?" Vernor noticed the little mustache on the man's lip started twitching in sync with his blinking eyes. All he needed to transform himself into a vaudeville act was to start tap dancing.

"Clemens…Sid Clemens."

"Who owns this place?"

"Jake Nilsson. He's the senior partner."

"Is he here?"

"No."

"Where does he live?"

"I don't know."

"Do you have a phone number for him?"

"I tried calling him. He doesn't answer. He's probably at his girlfriend's house."

"And I suppose you don't know where she lives?"

"Look, Sergeant, I could get the information you want if I could get into the fucking office, but that rubble over there is what's left of it. Someone torched it pretty good."

Vernor looked at the remains of the office. He wondered how Lydia discovered the warehouse was storing stolen merchandise and why she decided to light it up.

"How do you know it was torched?" Vernor asked Clemens.

"Because that's what those arson people said. Somebody turned on the power and then opened a nozzle on one of the gas pumps. It's a wonder the fire didn't spread."

Damn, Vernor thought. *Lydia must have been really pissed to do something like this. How did she get in here without anyone seeing her?*

Vernor looked at the guard shack. "Did the security officer see who did it?"

"I don't know. The firefighters said he wasn't here when they arrived."

"Did the firefighters find any bodies on the premises?"

"I don't think so. Look, if you're thinking the security guard died in the fire, you're wrong. I called his wife. She said he came home early. He said something about quitting."

"Have you talked to him about what happened here?"

"He wouldn't come to the phone."

Vernor looked around the lot. "Does this place have any more trucks other than those three in the lot?"

"Yes."

"How come they're not here?"

"They're in the harbor being loaded. We have two shipments that came in yesterday from Japan and South Korea."

"Okay, Sid, let's take a walk. I need a guided tour of the warehouse."

"Okay." Again, apprehension in his voice.

"I do have your permission to look inside, don't I?"

"Yes."

"And you have authority to let me see what's in there, right?"

"I guess so…well, yes."

"Why the hesitation?"

"It would be nice if the boss were here."

"Why do you need the boss?"

"I don't."

"So, what's the problem?"

"There is no problem. I'll show you the warehouse."

Vernor and Clemens entered the warehouse through one of the rollup doors a few doors down from where the fire had started. A sharp odor saturated the air. When Vernor asked Clemens what it was, he replied that it probably came from furniture that caught fire. It had been manufactured in China and was made of composite material that was probably toxic.

Vernor looked back to see if the firefighters inside the warehouse were wearing respirators. The firefighters working inside the warehouse had them on.

He turned his attention in the opposite direction. The main aisle that ran the length of the warehouse was at least one hundred yards long and was lined with crates and pallets of goods stacked on top of each other, some of them reaching as high as the ceiling.

"This place would have been something to see if it lit up," Clemens said. "I told the boss time and time again, we need to install a fire sprinkler system in here."

"It doesn't have a sprinkler system?"

"Uh, uh. Exactly what are you looking for?"

Vernor pulled out his disposable cell phone and looked for the photos Lydia had sent him. He showed Clemens a picture of the crate holding goods stolen out of Akheiser's warehouse.

The man's face turned pale. "Jesus!"

"You know where these crates are stored?"

Clemens looked up at Vernor. "Listen, boss, I had nothing to do with that shipment."

"Show me!"

"You have to believe me. I had nothing to do with it. I knew something was not right when I saw that shit. That stuff showed up in the middle of the night. I asked the dispatcher about it. He told me Jake said it was a delivery for a special client and not to worry about it."

"Jake?"

"Jake Nilsson. The senior partner."

"Who brought it here?"

"I don't know."

"How can I find out?"

"The dispatcher might know."

"Is he here?"

"No. I tried calling him too. He doesn't answer."

"Do you keep records of deliveries?"

"We do. But they were in the office."

"And the office has burned down."

"Yes."

"Okay, Sid, you did good. Now show me where this merchandise is."

Clemens started walking down the aisle.

"And do something about those twitching eyes of yours. It's making me nervous," Vernor muttered under his breath.

"What did you say?"

"Nothing of importance."

CHAPTER FORTY-TWO

LYDIA HAD set the alarm for 11:30 a.m. She woke up feeling refreshed even though she didn't have more than five hours of sleep. She rolled out of bed and padded to the bathroom, stopping to look at her image in the mirror.

There was a different young lady there now, her face and naked body warmly colored by diffused light coming from a bedside lamp, no reminder of the havoc she had inflicted on her enemies earlier that morning.

Lydia started to move away toward the bathroom but stopped and turned toward the mirror again. When she first looked in the mirror, she didn't notice the scar from the operation on her bullet wound. But it was there, just below her bellybutton, four inches long, a tiny white slit almost invisible.

She looked up at the mirror image of her face. She found herself smiling. Her hair fell naturally across her shoulders as if she had just brushed it and had not just come out of bed. She liked what she saw and went into the bathroom.

After drinking a cup of tea and eating a piece of toast, Lydia turned on the television news. The feature story was about a warehouse fire in Culver City. She watched with interest and then turned it off, not wanting to hear about another fire on an estate near Pepperdine University.

The nearest private shooting range was not far from Lydia's condo, and during the short drive, she could not tell whether she was still being followed.

It took Lydia just seventeen shots to sight in her new gun, the last three rounds hitting the bullseye at fifty feet. She cleaned the gun and headed back to her apartment, stopping on the way for a proper breakfast at a café that she knew did not have a television set glaring soundlessly at its patrons.

Not a single member of the Crew was in the back row of the roll call room when Lydia entered. Hagerty looked up when he saw her pass by and called her name. He waved her to come closer. "Are you all right?"

The question startled Lydia. Had he been talking to Vernor about what had happened earlier this morning?

"You called in sick, yesterday. Are you okay?"

"Just an upset stomach," Lydia said, feeling relieved. "Something I ate."

Hagerty nodded.

Lydia took a seat in the front row.

Roll call did not go well. Three members of the Crew who were scheduled to work did not show up for work, and it took more than a few minutes for Lieutenant Morton to readjust the work schedule.

The phone rang while he was doing it. The assistant watch commander, Sergeant Joanna Watson, picked it up. She said a few words in the receiver, listened, and then hung up. She looked down at Lydia. "The Captain says your presence is requested in the detective squad room."

Lydia stared at her for a moment before she got up from her seat and started for the back door.

Hagerty sat up straight as she passed and mouthed the words, "What's going on?"

Lydia shrugged.

Lydia found Billy Vernor waiting for her in the hallway just outside the detective squad room. He grabbed her arm and said, "Why did you set that damn place on fire?"

"Let go of my arm, Billy."

Vernor let go of her arm. "You might have burned all of the stolen property. We would have no case without the evidence."

"I guess I let my emotions get away from me, Billy. I get a little upset when people lie to me."

"Who?"

"Who what?"

"Who lied to you?"

"Everybody. The owner of that goddamn warehouse in particular!"

Vernor looked down the hall. "God, Lydia, I'd hate to think what you would have done if he really pissed you off."

"What's going on, Billy? Why does the Captain want to see me?"

"First things first. Did you get rid of the gun?"

"I did…and I made it looked like someone else used it."

"Now, how in hell did you do that?"

"You don't want to know. What does the Captain want with me?"

"We have a suspect in custody. The skipper wants to talk to you about him."

All eyes were on Lydia when she entered the detective squad room. Vernor led her toward the Lieutenant's office where Hardemann and Captain Kemper were waiting. Both men rose when she entered the office.

Vernor shut the door.

Hardemann spoke first. "Officer Harte, do you know a man named Jacob Nilsson."

Lydia feigned surprise. "I know a Jake Nilsson."

"How do you know him?" Kemper asked.

"He used to be my fiancé." She paused and then said, "Why are you asking about my personal life?"

"You're here to answer questions, Officer Harte. How long ago was this?"

"Was what?"

"When he was no longer your fiancé."

Lydia relaxed. Something was up, and it involved Jake. She guessed they were probably looking for him in connection with what was found in the warehouse.

"I broke it off with him about six months ago," Lydia replied.

Kemper stared at her with his arms folded.

Lydia looked at Hardemann. "What's going on, Lieutenant?"

"We'll tell you in a minute. But first, we need you to answer some questions about your current relationship with Nilsson."

"There is no current relationship."

"Why did you break up with him?" Kemper asked.

Lydia turned away from the question. "I had just been shot. I was in the hospital. I just didn't feel right about getting married after what happened."

"Can you explain?" Kemper asked.

"It's personal, Captain," Lydia said, looking at the floor.

"I need you to answer my question, Officer Harte."

Lydia felt heat rising in her face. She looked up at Kemper and shouted. "It's personal, Captain!"

"Jake Nilsson has been arrested, Officer Harte. And for reasons I can't tell you right now, we need to know why you broke up with him."

Lydia looked away. Through the plate glass window, she could see the detectives in the squad room watching them.

She turned to Kemper, her face flushed with anger. "All right! If you really want to know, Captain. I got shot in the stomach! I don't have a uterus. I can't have babies! I don't even know if I can have sex anymore." Lydia looked down, tears in her eyes. "I was depressed," she said, "and I didn't want to see him. I didn't want to see anyone! I felt like jumping out of the fucking window!"

Lydia flinched when she felt Vernor's arm gently touch her shoulder.

Kemper glanced at Hardemann who was looking at Lydia with pain in his eyes. He turned back to Lydia. "I'm sorry, Officer Harte, Kemper said. "I hadn't realized."

"Lydia, please sit down for a moment," Hardemann said. "We have something important to ask of you. I would really like for you to take a breather before we do."

"I don't need to sit down," Lydia said, her voice calmer now. "What's going on?"

Hardemann looked at Vernor. "Sergeant Vernor, could you get Officer Harte a cup of coffee."

"I don't need a cup of coffee," Lydia said. "If I did, I wouldn't send Billy out to get it. I want to know what's going on."

After a moment, Hardemann asked, "Do you know what Nilsson does for a living?"

Lydia found it surprisingly easy to lie. "Of course, I do. He's an attorney."

"How do you know that?" Kemper asked.

"He told me. I saw his office. He took me there once."

"Where was this?"

"In Santa Monica. On Main."

"Did he ever tell you that he owned and operated a warehouse and trucking company?" Hardemann asked.

Lydia shook her head. "Did he?" She was beginning to enjoy this. She found it surprisingly easy to lie.

"He did. A part of it burned down this morning. Sergeant Vernor was called to the scene and discovered there was potentially a million dollars of stolen merchandise in the warehouse. Some of it was from Akheiser's storage facility. When we asked Nilsson how it got there, he said he didn't know. When Sergeant Vernor told him that one of his employees was willing to testify he saw him supervising the unloading, Nilsson responded by saying he wanted to talk to you." Hardemann held out a hand toward the door. "We would like for you to talk to him and find out what he wants."

CHAPTER FORTY-THREE

VERNOR STOPPED Lydia when she was halfway across the detective squad room.

"Sorry about all that."

Lydia's mind didn't process what he said. "What?"

"I didn't know."

"Didn't know what?" Lydia asked.

"About what happened to you."

She shrugged and looked across the squad room where there was a large holding cell with large plate glass windows. She thought Nilsson might be in there.

He wasn't.

The room was occupied by two men who Lydia had never seen before. They were seated on a bench and handcuffed to a metal bar running along the bottom of the bench. They were wearing work clothes.

"One of them is the driver of the tractor trailer that hauled the stuff out of Akheiser's," Vernor said. "The other one is his helper. They told me that Nilsson was with them when they hit the warehouse."

"If you got a statement from them, why do you want me to talk to Nilsson?"

"Because Nilsson wants to make a deal. He says he can supply names."

"Like Jonathan Benedict's for example?"

Vernor looked back at the Lieutenant's office. "Jesus Christ, Lydia. Be careful what you say. If Hardemann heard what you said, you'd have a hard time explaining how you knew Benedict was involved in this mess."

"Listen Billy. I'm not the dummy you think I am. I met Jake through Jonathan. They were friends."

"Well, be damn careful what you say. If Nilsson tries to play on your sympathies, get out of the room as fast as you can. This interview is supposed to be about a deal he wants to make. Don't let him manipulate you."

Jake Nilsson appeared to be studying the crude carvings that were etched into the wooden interview table when Lydia entered the interview room. He looked up. His frown turned into a half smile when he saw Lydia.

"Lydia!" He tried to stand up, but his movement was restricted by a handcuff attached to his right hand and a ring on the table leg. "I knew they would find you."

Lydia shut the door behind her and turned toward him. "Sit down, Jake."

Jake sat down slowly. "How have you been, Lydia? God, you look great. That uniform! Wow!"

Lydia crossed her arms and glared at him. "It isn't the first time you saw me in uniform, Jake."

"I haven't seen you for a long time, Lydia. Can't I just be happy seeing you again?"

"What kind of trouble have you gotten into, Jake? They tell me you run a fucking warehouse and a trucking company. I thought you were a lawyer."

"I am, Lydia."

"Then why did you lie to me?"

"What are you talking about? I never lied to you."

Lydia looked at him in undisguised contempt. "You never told me you were partners with the Benedicts in a trucking company."

Nilsson stared at her for a minute. "Listen, Lydia, I...I just didn't want..." He looked away without finishing the sentence.

"You didn't want me to know how tight you were with Jonathan, isn't that right, Jake? You ask me to marry you, and you kept secrets from me. How does that work in a relationship?"

Nilsson looked back at her. "I'm sorry, Lydia."

Lydia remembered the reason she was talking to this bastard and got to the point. "What do you want, Jake? They said you wanted to talk to me."

"I want to make a deal, Lydia, but I don't trust them. I trust you."

"I have no authority to make a deal, Jake. Neither does the detective who arrested you. Only the D.A.s office can do that."

"Can you be my go between?"

"What in hell does that mean, Jake?"

"Talk to them about what I have to offer."

"What do you have to offer?"

"I can give your bosses what they want. I can give them enough information to put Jonathan and his organization in jail for a long time."

Lydia had to bite her lip. Jonathan was not going to jail...*ever*. She had already taken care of that.

"What organization are you talking about, Jake?"

"You have to talk to them, Lydia. I have a lot of information they can use."

"Damn it, Jake! What kind of information do you have?"

Jake looked away. He stared at a blank wall for a moment. He suddenly turned back to face her. "Some of your cops were involved."

Lydia was silent for a minute before she responded. "Involved with what, Jake?"

Jake looked at her with hope in his eyes. "I can't say. Not until we make a deal."

"Okay Jake. What kind of deal are you talking about?"

"I want out of here."

"That's not going to happen, Jake. I know of at least one man who was murdered while you and your buddies were looting a warehouse."

"I had nothing to do with that, Lydia."

Lydia shook her head in disbelief. "You don't understand, Jake. You were involved in a murder. You're going to jail for a long, long time."

"Talk to them Lydia. See what you can do. Tell them that I can give them enough information to put a whole lot of people in jail."

"Did he say who was involved?" Kemper asked Lydia. They were in Hardemann's office.

"He did not. All he said was that cops were involved."

Vernor entered the room. "Leslie Maddox, herself, is coming down."

Leslie Maddox was the Assistant District Attorney in charge of criminal filings. The detectives usually referred to her as the 'princess' because of her high regard for her own importance.

"Did Nilsson ask for an attorney?" Hardemann asked Lydia.

"He is an attorney."

"I hate to tell you this Lydia," Vernor said. "He has been disbarred."

"I guess I'm not surprised."

"Some guys in Narcotics set him up," Vernor continued. "They had some drinks with him after Nilsson had beat them in court defending a major violator on a narcotics charge. They led him down a garden path that ended up with him in jail, and Nilsson didn't see it coming. They started joking about him being the attorney for a narcotics ring and asked if he could get them some dope. The fool took them seriously and said he could get them all the dope they wanted. They nailed his ass when he actually produced several grams of low-grade heroin."

"When was this?"

"About five years ago."

Lydia bit her lip. "He served time?"

"About one year."

Lydia looked down at her shoes and shook her head.

"Do you have any problems talking to him again?" Hardemann asked.

Lydia looked up. "I don't. But I haven't told you everything. He wants to meet with me outside."

"What the hell?" Kemper asked. "He wants us to let him go free before he talks?"

"No. He just wants to meet with me outside in the parking lot. He thinks the interview room is bugged."

Kemper looked at Hardemann. "I think he might be planning to escape. I say we don't do this. Anything he has to say to Harte has to be in the interview room."

"He won't escape, Captain," Vernor said. "If you give me a couple of men like Hagerty, I promise you he won't escape."

"If what he says about some police officers being involved in this mess is true, Captain, we need to find out what he knows," Hardemann said.

"Are you suggesting we do this?"

"I'm not suggesting it, Captain. I'm saying we have to do this."

CHAPTER FORTY-FOUR

"JAKE, YOU'RE walking too fast," Lydia said. "Where in hell do you think you're going?"

They were walking in the aisle between two rows of plainclothes cars behind the detective squad room. Nilsson was walking a little too fast toward the street.

Lydia stopped. "Jake, if you're thinking about running, you better stop and look up at the roof behind me."

Nilsson stopped and slowly turned.

A police officer was on the roof above the detective squad room aiming a rifle at him. Nilsson turned and looked toward the street. A police officer carrying a shotgun emerged from behind a plainclothes car.

Nilsson turned to face Lydia. "Fuck, Lydia. I wasn't going to run. I wanted to get out of that filthy room."

"How far do you think you would have gotten if you tried, Jake? That guy on the roof would not hesitate to shoot you."

"I know the law, Lydia. There is no way a cop would shoot a fleeing prisoner wearing handcuffs."

"You might know the law, Jake. But you don't know the man up there on the roof. They call him Gunsmoke, and it isn't because he reminds people of James Arness. And you sure as hell don't know me either. I'd have those handcuffs off your body long before the Coroner got here."

Nilsson stared at her for a moment. "Okay, okay. Can you at least take the handcuffs off?"

"No, Jake. We'll talk right here…with you in handcuffs."

"In the middle of the lot? Out here in the fucking sun?"

"It wasn't my idea, Jake. You're the one who asked to meet me outside. Now, tell me who else is involved in the warehouse burglaries."

Nilsson sighed and leaned against the back of one of the police cars. "There were six of them," he said. He looked up at Hagerty on the roof of the police station. He sighed again and said, "They called themselves the 'Wrecking Crew' or something like that."

"Names, please."

"I don't know all of them. The boss was a Kraut named Holzer. A sergeant was involved, name of Cooley. There was Searles, Stoddard, and Forrester. I don't remember the others. They told me you killed Searles. Milo was also involved."

"Do the names Jackson and Haines sound familiar?"

"Yeah. That's them."

"Tell me how they did it."

"It's a long story."

"I got all day. Let's start with what happened at Akheiser's."

"Look, Lydia. I had nothing to do with killing that man. I'm pretty sure Holzer did it."

"How do you know Holzer did it?"

"I was on the loading dock when I heard the shot. When I went in to see what was going on, Holzer came out of Akheiser's office holding a shotgun. Later, I saw the body in there. Holzer set the place on fire to cover the evidence."

"Tell me how it worked."

"What?"

"What was your game plan for breaking into warehouses? You must have had a game plan."

"Well, these guys...they would scout out places to hit and find out which ones had the best stuff. Once they decided on a place, they would schedule a break-in on a Friday or Saturday night...when all the other cops were busy chasing their tail all over town. Two or three of them would take the night off. They would do the actual break-in. The others who were working a shift that night would cover for them in case an alarm went off. But that never usually happened. One of them—I think it was Haines—worked for a burglar alarm company. He knew how to disable an alarm."

"How were you involved?"

"I brought in the truck and a crew to haul off the merchandise. I would store it in my warehouse until Milo found a buyer."

"You mentioned the others would cover for the break-in. What do you mean by that?"

"Well, just in case the alarm couldn't be disabled. If a radio call came out about a burglary alarm going off, they would take the call to keep other cops from showing up."

"What was the plan if some other police officers showed up and saw what they were doing?"

"I don't know if they had a plan for that."

Lydia looked away for a moment in disbelief. When she turned to look back at Nilsson, her eyes were burning with anger. "You really are a fool, Jake! They would have to kill the officers. Either that or go to jail."

"They'd never do anything like that. I know them."

"Didn't you just tell me Holzer killed Mr. Akheiser?"

Jake's mouth began moving like a goldfish trying to escape from an aquarium.

They were silent for a minute or two. Lydia looked back at the station. Hagerty was still on the roof, relaxed, rifle cradled in his arms. Billy Vernor was standing in the shadows of the porch at the back door watching them. It was getting hot, and she wanted to get this over with and get back inside the air-conditioned building.

Lydia turned to Nilsson. "So, I understand from what you said that Milo would find a buyer for the stolen goods."

"Yes."

"Who bought them?"

"I don't know."

"What did you get out of this?"

"Not nearly enough for the risk I was taking. Ten percent. I thought I should get twenty or more. I had been talking to Jonathan about it."

And you nearly got your ass killed last night doing it, Lydia thought.

"Who coldcocked Billy Vernor?"

"Who's Billy Vernor?"

"The detective you guys locked up in the trunk of his car."

Nilsson started laughing. "That was Milo...and I think maybe Haines was there too. They saw him staked out on the place. Milo coldcocked him. He wanted to put a bullet in his head, but a couple of old farts rounded the corner walking a dog. They put him in the trunk of the car and got out of there."

"How do you know that?"

"We had a drink later—after we moved the merchandise. Milo was laughing about it."

"So, how did all of this start?"

"I already told you. One of the guys scouted out the place."

"I mean who came up with the idea to burglarize warehouses in the first place?"

"It was Milo's idea."

"So, let me get this straight. Milo approaches Holzer and his buddies and says I got a great idea. Let's start burglarizing warehouses together. Jesus Christ, Jake! That's a load of bullshit!"

"No. No. It wasn't like that at all. These guys—the cops—were strictly small timers. They would get a burglary call, say a jewelry store or department store or liquor store, and they would steal some of the merchandise. Strictly, small stuff. Milo saw what they were doing and said why?…why the small stuff? If you're going to do something serious enough to put you in prison, why not do something big? It was his idea to hit warehouses. It took some working out on how to do it without getting caught. Milo was good at that. In the end, they all agreed to do it as a team."

"There's something I don't understand, Jake. You got six police officers involved in this along with a sergeant. There's you and your people, there's Milo, and who knows who else. How much money was Holzer and his bunch getting out of this?"

"Milo was paying them $500 apiece. For each job."

Lydia whistled.

"What's wrong?"

"That's small potatoes for murdering someone. And so is your ten percent."

"I didn't murder anyone. That was Holzer, not me."

"Tell me something, Jake. What law school did you go to? Didn't they teach you about the felony murder rule? Don't you know that you can be charged and convicted of murder if you participate in a felony and your accomplice kills someone?"

Nilsson looked at the ground and muttered, "Oh shit!"

"Oh shit is right, Jake. I don't know what kind of deal you expect to get, Jake, but you're definitely going to serve some time."

Lydia was greeted by Billy Vernor when she walked into the detective squad room with Nilsson in tow.

"Well?" he asked.

"Jake is willing to talk, provided he gets ten years or less."

Vernor looked at Nilsson. "Good luck with that, partner." He looked at Lydia. "Take him into the interview room. The Princess is waiting for him."

Lydia had a sly smile, waiting for Vernor to respond.

"What's so funny, Harte?"

"Your comment about luck, Billy. You are extremely lucky to be standing here today. Milo was the one who decked you outside Akheiser's. The only reason he didn't kill you was that someone's dog needed to take a piss. I'll tell you about it later."

Hardemann and Assistant District Attorney Maddox were waiting in the interview room when Lydia and Nilsson entered. It was the first time Lydia had ever seen the woman everyone called the Princess. But it was not the first time Lydia had seen a woman whose makeup made her look more grotesque than she already was. Maddox was a big woman, like a rugby player who had gone to seed, with a massive amount of fiery red hair exploding from her head like a lava flow.

Hardemann sat on the same side of the table as Maddox but as far away as possible without being obvious.

Lydia busied herself handcuffing Nilsson to the ring on the table leg. When she finished, she looked at Hardemann, being careful not to let her eyes wander to the creature sitting next to him. "Mr. Nilsson is ready to talk to you, Lieutenant. When he gets done, you'll be needing Sergeant Vernor to start drawing up search warrants."

Hardemann nodded and smiled.

As Lydia left the room, she heard Maddox asking Hardemann who she was.

Hardemann's reply surprised Lydia.

"Her name is Lydia Harte. She's promising to be one of our best and brightest."

Later that night, Lydia was in the detective squad room writing up a robbery report when she heard loud voices coming from down the hall. Seconds later, she saw Vernor enter the squad room, accompanied by Captain Kemper and Lieutenant Hardemann. They were followed by two detectives from the Homicide Unit who had two prisoners in custody.

Lydia was not surprised when she saw who they were. Klaus Holzer and Ronnie Haines were in handcuffs, looking glum with downcast eyes.

Holzer looked nervously around the squad room. He saw Hagerty first and then Lydia. He muttered the word "bitch" just before Vernor pushed him into the interview room.

Hagerty looked at Lydia and said. "It just occurred to me that the word 'bitch' is misogynistic. There's no counterpart for men."

Lydia smiled, surprised that Hagerty had used the word 'misogynistic'.

"You know what that word means?" Hagerty asked.

"Of course, I do. I went to university, you know." She paused for a second and then said. "There is a term like bitch for men, you know."

Hagerty raised his eyebrows. "Oh?"

"Asshole," Lydia said.

Vernor came out of one of the interview rooms just as Lydia and Hagerty were getting ready to leave the detective squad room.

"We got three of them," Vernor told them. "Clay Jackson is still on the loose, but we'll find him before the night's over. Haines wants to make a deal. Says he'll testify he saw Holzer kill Akheiser if we cut him some slack on jail time."

"But you already got a deal with Nilsson," Lydia said.

"We do, but Haines doesn't know that, and we want to keep him talking as much as possible before he finds out."

"Where's Forrester?" Hagerty asked.

"In the hospital," Vernor said. "With a gunshot wound in his leg." He looked at Lydia and smiled. "Forrester told Kemper you shot him. Kemper asked him to explain, and Forrester suddenly clammed up and wouldn't say anything else. They recovered the bullet from his leg, so they might be asking you to turn your guns over for testing."

"No problem," Lydia said. "It wasn't my gun that shot him."

Hagerty looked puzzled at first and then smiled. "I don't think that came out the way you intended, Lydia."

Lydia frowned. He was right. The implication was that she used someone else's gun to shoot Forrester.

Hagerty shrugged. "I guess it was just a poor choice of words."

"It was a poor choice of words," Lydia agreed.

CHAPTER FORTY-FIVE

LYDIA WAS awakened by a call on Sunday morning.

"Did you forget where you were supposed to be yesterday morning?"

It took a moment for the fog to clear.

"Is this Jeremy?"

"It is."

"I'm sorry for not calling, Jeremy. I was busy."

"I can arrange something for today, if you want."

Lydia looked at her watch. "I can be there in an hour." She paused for a few seconds. She had a lot to do today. There was the rope to be retrieved that she had dropped in the bushes below her window. It had to be disposed of before someone found it, and she had to shake off surveillance before she could anything about that.

"What's wrong," Jeremy asked, sensing her hesitation.

Lydia put a hand to her forehead. "Listen, I've got a lot to do today. I can't make it today. I'll be there next week."

"Did I do something to offend you? I can get a little out of line sometimes."

"No, No. I'm just busy today."

"Okay, call me when you're not busy."

Morgan hung up before Lydia could answer.

Around noon, Lydia received another phone call. She hurriedly picked it up, hoping it was Morgan calling her back.

"Yes."

"Officer Harte, this is Lieutenant Hardemann. I need you to come to the station right now."

"What's going on?"

"I'll tell you when you get here. I'll be in the Captain's office."

"Do you want me to bring my guns in for testing?"

Shit, she thought, *why did I say something so stupid as that?*

That question stopped Hardemann for a moment. "I don't know why you would ask a question like that, Officer Harte. Get in here as fast as you can."

Lydia was totally surprised when she saw who was in the Captain's conference room. Hardemann and Kemper were there, but so was Sergeant Hector Maldonado from Intelligence and Sergeants Nick Ryan and John Hamilton from Robbery-Homicide.

There were also two people she had never seen before; a man and a woman, both wearing casual clothing, the man wearing a gun and badge on his belt that Lydia didn't recognize, the woman wearing a compact shoulder holster over a white blouse.

Hardemann got up from his seat at the conference table. "Come in, Officer Harte."

Lydia paused and looked around. "Am I going to need my attorney?"

"You're not going to need an attorney. These two detectives are from the Sheriff's Homicide Unit. They want to ask you a few questions."

Lydia saw that Maldonado was smiling. He nodded his head slightly. That was encouraging. Lydia took a seat at the head of the table. The officers from LAPD were on her left with Hardemann the closest to her. The woman and man from the Sheriff's office were seated on her right, the woman seated the closest to Lydia.

The detectives introduced themselves. The woman who looked in her early thirties said she was Lieutenant Shepherd from the Sheriff's Homicide Unit and her partner was Sergeant Simeon.

Shepherd asked the first question. "Are you aware of the deaths of Jonathan and Milo Benedict," she paused while looking at a notepad in front of her, "and Sofia Benedetto and Carlos Aldana?"

"I was."

"How did you become aware of them?"

Lydia blinked her eyes for a few seconds not fully comprehending what was asked of her. Her attention was focused on Shepherd's eyes, which were a translucent light blue color she had never seen before.

Lydia shook her head, trying to clear the distraction. "Excuse me. But, do I know you?"

Shepherd paused. "I don't think so."

"What did you ask me?"

"How did you learn about the deaths of the Benedicts?"

"It was on the news. On television."

"How come you didn't contact us?"

"Contact you?" Lydia cocked her head. She looked at Shepherd's face. She was stunningly beautiful, pale skin with not a crease in it, golden hair with waves that curved around the sides of her face.

"I heard about the fire. I heard nothing about a homicide investigation. Why should I call?"

"Fair enough," Shepherd looked at her notes again. "Did you go out there to see what happened?"

"No."

"Why not?"

"I had to report to work. I would have never made it back in time for roll call."

"Jonathan Benedict was your father. Is that right?"

"He was my stepfather."

"Understood. He adopted you, right?" Before Lydia had a chance to answer, Shepherd added. "We have information you thought he killed your mother."

Lydia didn't respond. *Was that meant to be a question?*

"Is that true?" Shepherd persisted.

Lydia looked at Hardemann for a second who nodded at her. She turned her attention back to Shepherd. "That's true."

"Do you have any proof he killed your mother?"

You're damn right, I do, Lydia thought. *But I'm not going to tell you.*

"No."

"When did you last see Jonathan?"

Lydia thought for a moment or two about whether she should admit driving up to Oceania Manor two weeks ago to see Jonathan about borrowing a gun but then remembered Maldonado knew she had been there.

"I drove up to see him about two weeks ago."

"Why did you pause when I asked you that question?"

"I was trying to remember the exact date."

"So, you drove up to Oceania Manor about a week ago. Is that right?"

"No. It was two weeks ago."

"Okay. Why did you go there?"

Lydia thought about lying but didn't. "To borrow a gun. I needed a gun for work."

"Excuse me. I thought your Department provided you with a weapon."

"They do. But I wanted a .357 Magnum. I knew Jonathan had several guns like that in his vault. He agreed to loan me one until I could buy one of my own."

"You had no problem going to Jonathan's house even though you thought he killed your mother?"

Lydia shrugged. "I wasn't afraid of him, and I needed the gun."

"We have phone records that show he called you several times in the past week."

Was that a question? How in hell did this woman make lieutenant? Lydia began to think that Shepherd got through promotional exams by dazzling the interviewers with her extraordinary beauty.

"Excuse me, Lieutenant, was that a question?" Lydia asked in a calm voice, trying not to sound confrontational.

"Of course, it was. Well, did he? Did he call you several times during the past week?"

"Yes."

"What did he want?"

"He wanted to meet me for lunch."

"And?"

And what? Lydia thought.

"Did you meet him for lunch?" Shepherd added when Lydia didn't answer.

"No."

"Did he say what he wanted to talk to you about?"

"No."

"So, the last time you saw Jonathan was about two weeks ago."

Lydia leaned across the table. "Listen, Lieutenant. I mean no disrespect, but I already answered that question and the answer is still the same."

"You understand why I have to ask these questions, don't you, Officer Harte? This *is* a murder investigation after all." Shepherd looked at her notes again and frowned. She looked up. "I find it rather curious that you haven't asked why we're involved with this case."

"I don't understand."

"Well, we are homicide investigators, and you haven't asked us a single question about why we're involved."

"I'm not sure what you're driving at, Lieutenant. You seem to be implying that my failure to answer a question means that I already know this is a murder case. When I took a seat at this table, Lieutenant, it was with the understanding that homicide detectives investigate murders, so why should I ask a question I already know the answer to?"

Out of the corner of her eye, Lydia saw Hardemann shifting in his seat. She heard Kemper chuckling.

Lieutenant Shepherd looked at them, clearly annoyed. She quickly turned her attention back to Lydia.

"Did you know that Jonathan Benedict was involved with organized crime?"

"I have heard something like that," Lydia replied. She glanced at Maldonado who was smiling.

"What have you heard?"

"That he was involved with organized crime."

"Nothing else?"

"Nothing else."

"When you learned about the deaths of Jonathan Benedict and his family, did you reach any conclusions?"

"Yes."

"And what were they?"

"That they died in a fire."

Shepherd looked down at her notes. After a moment she scratched her head and looked up at Lydia.

"Did you work a shift last Friday evening?"

"I was off."

Can you account for your whereabouts on Friday night and early Saturday morning?"

"I can. I was at home."

"You never left your house that night?"

"I live in a condo, and I never left my condo that night or during the early morning hours. I was sick."

"So, is it fair to say that you were not at Jonathan Benedict's house on the night of the 13th and the morning of the 14th?"

"Wait a goddamn minute," Hardemann said, rising from his chair and glaring at Shepherd. "You told me that Officer Harte was not a suspect in this case, but you are treating her like she is."

"I'm trying to exclude her as a suspect, Lieutenant. You ought to know that."

"You told me that all you wanted to find out was what Officer Harte knew about the Benedicts. You had us bring her here under false pretenses, and I resent it."

"I did no such thing."

"I'm going to insist you give her the Miranda warning."

"She's not in custody, Lieutenant Hardemann. I don't have to give her the Miranda warning if she's not in custody."

Ryan held a hand up. "I think I have a solution to this problem."

"What are you talking about?" Hardemann snapped.

Ryan stood up and looked at Shepherd "Lieutenant Shepherd, can I talk with you and your partner in private for a minute out in the hall?"

Shepherd looked at her partner who nodded.

They left the room.

"What the fuck is going on here?" Captain Kemper asked Hardemann.

Hardemann shrugged. "I haven't a clue."

"I do," Lydia said.

They looked at her and Hardemann nodded for her to go ahead.

"A surveillance team has been covering me for the past few days. I was wondering who they were, and I think I just found out. I believe those guys from Robbery-Homicide are going to verify that I never left my condo Friday night."

Kemper tapped Hardemann on the shoulder. "Did you know about this?"

"Surveillance? No. But I knew that Robbery-Homicide was looking at her as a potential suspect in the murders of Cooley and Stoddard. They told me they got an anonymous tip."

"Jesus Christ," Kemper muttered as he put his hand to his forehead. "Does anybody trust anybody in this Department?"

Lydia stared at Kemper for a moment and then looked past him. Sergeant Maldonado from Intelligence was looking down at a notebook in front of him and was quietly laughing.

A few minutes later, Shepherd came back into the room with her partner and Ryan and Hamilton from Robbery-Homicide. Shepherd sat down and looked at Lydia. "I think we can move on now."

"Wait, a minute," Kemper said. "Can you tell us what you discussed in the hallway?"

Shepherd shrugged. "Sergeant Ryan convinced me that Officer Harte was telling the truth about where she was Friday night."

Kemper stared at Ryan for a moment. "What the fuck! You guys had her under surveillance and you never told me about it!"

Ryan nodded sheepishly.

It was quiet in the room for a good minute before Shepherd spoke again. "Can we continue the interview?"

Kemper nodded. "As long as you stop treating Officer Harte like a suspect, Lieutenant Shepherd. If you want to find out what she knows about Jonathan Benedict and the other people who died in that fire, be my guest. But let me warn you. No more accusatory questions."

"I can live with that." Shepherd smiled charmingly and then turned to Lydia. "Officer Harte, do you know why you were under surveillance?"

"Wait a goddamn minute, Lieutenant," Kemper said as he rose to his feet. "This interview is over. Go back up to Malibu and tell your boss to send someone down here who knows what the fuck they're doing."

Shepherd also rose to her feet. "Listen, Captain, I'm conducting a homicide investigation here. I have a right to ask questions."

"No, you don't," Kemper said angrily. "You're on a fishing expedition. Get out of my fucking station and get back to your fucking beauty salon." He turned to Ryan and Hamilton. "You two! In my office now! I want to know what's going on."

Lydia was about to go to the locker room and change into her uniform when Hardemann stopped her in the hallway.

"I'm sorry about that. What Shepherd did was uncalled for. Are you all right?"

"I am."

"You handled yourself very well."

"Thank you."
"Are you working tonight?"
"Yes."
"Take the night off. I'll arrange it with Morton."
"Thank you, sir."

Chapter Forty-Six

LYDIA LEFT the station feeling relieved. Shepherd had picked up information from someone that Lydia thought Jonathan killed her mother but then inexplicably ended that thread of inquiry when Lydia admitted it. Lydia had not been trained as an investigator, but she knew that Shepherd should have asked why she believed Jonathan killed her mother. If Shepherd had done so, she would have opened a whole new avenue of questioning that might have explored some areas Lydia would not want to discuss.

She had learned several things she didn't know. She learned that it was Robbery-Homicide who had been tailing her. More importantly, she learned she not only had the support of Lieutenant Hardemann, but Captain Kemper as well. She was feeling good, so good that when she got into her car, she pulled the cell phone out of her purse and called Jeremy Morgan.

"What are you doing tonight?" she asked when he answered.

Before going to her apartment, Lydia stopped in the lobby and looked across the street. The surveillance unit usually parked there was gone. She went outside and walked down to the sidewalk, thinking about going to the back of the condo and retrieving the rope. When she turned and saw Pedersen, the hotel security guard, watching her from inside the lobby, she decided against it. She could not risk going behind the building without him wondering why. She went back inside and headed for the elevators.

"Something wrong, Miss Harte?" Pedersen asked pleasantly.

"I was thinking about taking a walk," Lydia replied.

He smiled at Lydia as she walked past him to the elevators.

"That undercover across the street is gone," Pedersen called after her.

"What?"

"You know. That undercover cop we talked about a few days ago. He's gone."

"Oh."

"They must have got what they wanted."

"I imagine so," Lydia said as she got on the elevator.

When she got back inside her apartment, she went out to the balcony and looked down at the bushes where she dropped the rope. She couldn't see it.

Alarmed, she went into her bedroom and put on her jogging clothes. Minutes later, she was out the front door of the condo and headed east at a leisurely pace. A minute later, she found the entrance to the small park that led out onto the golf course.

When she arrived at the rear of her condo building, she looked up to make sure no one was on any of the balconies. Satisfied no one was watching, she jogged up the incline to the bushes where she dropped the rope.

It wasn't there.

That night, Lydia met Jeremy Morgan at a small boutique restaurant called Ricardo's in Santa Clarita. She had dressed casually, wearing a black long-sleeved mock turtleneck and black jeans. Jeremy was wearing pressed khaki shorts and a blue long-sleeved, dress shirt with a button-down collar.

People watched them as they walked into the small restaurant, first looking at Lydia, and then Jeremy, and then Jeremy's artificial leg before looking away.

It was a pleasant evening and a pleasant dinner, the two of them getting to know each other. When they were halfway through the second bottle of wine, Lydia asked Jeremy where he lived. He stared at her for a moment in a way that made Lydia think she had given him the wrong impression.

After a moment, he answered. "I live on a small ranch at the back of a canyon off Francisco Canyon Drive. It's not far from Rivercreek."

Lydia was instantly interested. "Do you have horses?"

"I have three horses. Do you like horses?"

"Yes. I used to ride when my mother sent me to a school up north." Lydia stopped abruptly, her face getting warm.

"Is anything wrong?"

"No, I was just thinking about how much fun it was." One of the reasons she had so much fun riding horses was that she went riding with her track coach at the Napa Valley Preparatory School. They would ride out through wine-scented air in the vineyards until they found a secluded place where they would hurriedly undress and fuck like rabbits in the grass. The memory not only caused her embarrassment about the way she lived her life back then but was painful as well. She wondered if she could ever have normal sex again.

Lydia noticed that Jeremy was staring curiously at her. She shrugged off the memory and said, "Tell me about your ranch."

He shrugged back. "It's not much. Just a small cabin really, sitting on thirty or so acres. It's at the far end of a canyon that has no name. It's next to a year-round stream that comes down out of the Sierra Pelona. The only neighbors are a few deer and a mountain lion that likes to visit on occasion to see what I'm doing. It was built by an actor from the silent film days who wanted a place where he could get away from Los Angeles."

Lydia was quiet for a moment, thinking.

Jeremy smiled pleasantly at her.

She held up her empty wine glass.

Jeremy picked up the wine bottle and looked at it. Nothing was left. "Shall I order another bottle?"

Lydia smiled. "Do you have any at your ranch?"

"Not as good as this."

Lydia looked around for the waiter. "Can we order a bottle to go?"

That night, all of Lydia's fears about her ability to enjoy a normal sex life were erased forever in Jeremy Morgan's bedroom.

CHAPTER FORTY-SEVEN

ON HER way to UCLA's Drake Stadium on Monday morning, Lydia was stopped by Sergeant Hector Maldonado from Intelligence who pulled alongside her and waved her into a drugstore parking lot. Somehow, she was not surprised by his visit. She was expecting it after what she had learned that morning from her attorney, Eric Milburn.

But she was surprised by the first question Maldonado asked once they had gotten out of their cars.

"How do you feel about what happened up at Oceania Manor?" Maldonado asked.

Lydia shrugged. "I'll miss my grandmother."

"But not Jonathan and Milo?"

Lydia said nothing.

"Will you stay on the job now that your problems have been solved?"

"I don't know what problems you're talking about."

"Well, I know you were trying to find out who killed your mother, and that's why you joined LAPD. Now that Jonathan is gone, I would not have expected you to stay on the job."

When Lydia didn't respond. Maldonado continued, "I have something important to tell you. Maybe, we should get a cup of coffee."

"Maybe, you should tell me what you want so I can go for a run and get to work on time."

Maldonado nodded. "Very well." He lit a cigarette and looked up the sky. "I suppose you heard about what you inherited?"

"What are you talking about?" Lydia asked, knowing exactly what he was talking about.

Maldonado had always treated Lydia as if he were her friend, but now he was deadly serious. "Let's not play games, Officer Harte. You are Sophie Benedetto's sole heir. She gave you everything. You own a German restaurant, Oceania Manor…or rather what's left of it…and several brokerage accounts worth more money than I could ever dream of."

"So, what's the problem?" Lydia asked. "I came by it legitimately."

"Of course, you did. The problem is what Jonathan Benedict owned. None of it came to him legitimately."

Eric Milburn had told her the shocking news earlier that morning. All of Jonathan's estate was to pass by will to Milo. But Milo was dead. Under California law regarding intestate succession, Jonathan's estate with few exceptions would pass to his relatives, the first in line being his children. Jonathan's only natural child was Milo, but Lydia was adopted by Jonathan at her mother's insistence. Lydia would get Jonathan's estate… and the headaches associated with it.

"So," Maldonado said, as he crushed out his unfinished cigarette and pulled a small notebook from his coat pocket. He leaned against the hood of Lydia's silver BMW, opened the notebook, and read from it. "His estate includes a seventy-five percent partnership interest in a warehouse and trucking company in Culver City." Maldonado stopped and looked at Lydia. "Strangely enough, someone set that warehouse on fire the same night Oceania burned down."

When Lydia didn't respond, he smiled, and continued reading. "He also owned an automotive conversion facility in Culver City, a weapons manufacturing plant on the East Coast, assorted strip joints in California, several assorted adult book stores, and a small casino just across the California border." He looked up at Lydia. "You are his only living relative. Milo was his sole heir. Milo's dead, so by California law you get everything Jonathan owned."

Lydia managed to keep a blank expression on her face.

Maldonado frowned. "You're not surprised?"

"No, I'm not surprised." Lydia said. "And getting rid of it won't be a problem. I'll have my attorney handle it."

Maldonado smiled. "I don't know how to tell you this, Officer Harte, but it is your problem." He looked away. "You know as well as I do that

Jonathan has ties to organized crime. A good part of the property he owns does not belong to him. He's the front man for some very unsavory people. They will be contacting you to get it back."

"Okay," Lydia said uncertainly. "I already have more money than I'll ever spend. I don't need any more. I'll have my attorney deal with getting rid of Jonathan's estate. I don't need the headaches."

"I know you have money, but that's not the point. I need your help. The Department needs your help. I think I know who Jonathan's partners are, but I need to know more about them. You can help me by dealing directly with these people—without your attorney."

"I need to think about it."

"Have you ever considered the fact that Jonathan wasn't acting alone when he tried to gain control of your mother's shipping company? That he might be doing that on behalf of someone else. That your mother caught on to what he was doing and paid for it. You think your part in this ended when he died, but believe me when I tell you, it didn't. There are people out there who are just as responsible for your mother's death as Jonathan."

"Wait a minute," Lydia said "What are you talking about? What exactly did my mother find out?"

"She found out why Jonathan tried to get control of that shipping company?"

"And why was that?"

"Access to foreign markets. They needed the shipping company for their operations."

"And how do you know that?"

"She told me."

Lydia didn't catch the significance of what he was saying. "Who told you?"

"Your mother."

"My mother was talking to you?"

"She was my…" Maldonado paused.

"Informant?" Lydia said, her eyebrows raised.

"I guess you could say that."

Lydia stared at Maldonado, dumbfounded.

"So, will you help us?"

Lydia shook her head in disbelief and then walked away from Maldonado, thinking about what he said. She went into the drugstore and bought a bottle of water. She paused before paying for it.

What in the hell was going on? Had she, like her mother, been working for Maldonado but didn't know it? Was she all along being manipulated by Maldonado to help him bring down Jonathan Benedict?

"Can I help you miss? Is anything wrong?"

It was the teenager girl at the register who had a concerned look on her face. Lydia realized she had no idea how long she had been standing in the center aisle of the drugstore in deep thought.

"I'm all right," Lydia said. She paid for her bottle of water and left the drugstore.

When she came back outside, Maldonado was still standing next to her car. He had a lit cigarette in his hand.

"So, what do you think?" Maldonado asked.

"I think, maybe I should just forget it," Lydia said. "I need to go on from here. I got things to do." She found herself thinking about Jeremy Morgan and his ranch.

"And let those thugs get away with what they did to your mom?"

"Pardon me, Sergeant Maldonado. I have to go and you're standing in my way."

"Can I show you something?"

"You've shown me enough already."

"No, this is something different. Come around to the back of my car. I want to show you something."

Maldonado went to the back of his car and opened the trunk.

Lydia didn't move. She stood alongside her car, watching him carefully.

"I am your friend, Lydia," Maldonado said. "I want you to know that. Come over here and look at what I have in my trunk."

Lydia walked slowly toward Maldonado, her eyes fixed on him, aware that he was now calling her by her first name. She stopped next to him, watching him carefully.

"Look inside," Maldonado said. He was smiling.

Lydia looked inside the trunk. The rope she had used to get into her apartment the night she killed Jonathan and Milo Benedict lay coiled inside the trunk.

CHAPTER FORTY-EIGHT

LYDIA WAS devastated at what she saw in the trunk.

"What am I supposed to be seeing?" Lydia asked, trying to act as if she was not interested.

"The rope."

Lydia shrugged. "What about it?"

"I found it behind the building where you live, Lydia. Beneath your window. It was loosely coiled. I'd say about thirty feet or more. Long enough to reach your balcony."

When Lydia didn't answer, he continued. "You're an athlete, aren't you? You'd have no problem climbing up a rope like this."

Lydia turned her back on him and walked toward her car where she opened the passenger door. She began looking in her purse for the business card of Michael Honshino, the attorney she hired when she was about to be questioned about the night she got shot.

Just as she was about to call Honshino, Maldonado laid a gentle hand on her arm to keep her from speed-dialing the attorney's number.

"You won't need an attorney," Maldonado said.

"I think I do."

"I showed you the rope, Lydia, because I want you to know I'm your friend. Two hours from now, it will be in a trash dump and no one will ever know where I found it."

Lydia didn't finish her journey to Drake Stadium. Instead, she went back to her condo, opened a bottle of white wine, and poured herself a glass. She positioned a chair close to the balcony window and sat down. She was about to take a sip of wine when she realized she had to go to work that afternoon. She went out onto the balcony and poured the wine out.

She went back inside and sat down.

Work!

She had to go to work tonight. Maybe, she should just go in and turn in her badge.

Screw Maldonado!

She was not going to be manipulated into doing something she didn't want to do. So what if he knew about the rope? They would have a hard time proving that it belonged to her. What's more they would have a hard time trying to prove that she killed Jonathan and Milo.

They didn't know about the Jeep, did they? But if they got her credit card information, they would know she rented a vehicle, and they would ask her questions about it. If they followed up with the rental agency, they would find out she rented a Jeep, and she would have a tough time explaining why she rented it.

Then there was the rope.

Shit!

The rope? She remembered she used a credit card to pay for it. They would have no trouble tracking down where she bought it. And whoever sold it to her might be able to identify her.

Could she trust Maldonado to get rid of it?

The more she thought about it, the angrier she got. She didn't like being manipulated, even if she got what she wanted while being manipulated. She realized that being manipulated was a strong word for what had happened. She did what she needed to do when she joined LAPD—to find out who killed her mother and why. And she took care of the problem in her own way. But she had to admit that on her journey to discover the truth, she was being closely watched by Maldonado who saw her as an answer to solving some of his own problems.

She looked in her purse until she found his card. She called his number and he answered quickly.

"Lydia?"

"Call me Officer Harte, Sergeant Maldonado. Better yet, call me Miss Harte, because I'm turning in my badge today."

"But…"

"I quit, Maldonado, so you can take that rope and shove it up your ass."

Hagerty was walking toward the roll call room when he saw Lydia coming down the hall with her badge and I.D. in one hand and her gun belt with the Department-issued Beretta in the other. He stopped in the middle of the hallway, stunned when he realized what Lydia was going to do.

He stepped in front of her.

Lydia stopped. "What do you want?"

"I need to talk to you."

"About what?"

Hagerty didn't answer. He grabbed her by the shoulders and looked down at her startled face.

"Let go of me!"

"What in hell are you doing, Lydia? Get your ass back in the locker room and get dressed for work."

Lydia looked away, trying to control her anger at being manhandled.

Hagerty didn't take his hands away. Instead, he looked left and right and saw an open door to the janitorial services room. He pushed her inside, turned on the lights, and shut the door. He turned to face her.

Lydia crossed her arms and looked at the floor like a child about to be scolded.

"Answer me this, Lydia. What in hell do you think you're doing?"

She looked up at him. "I'm quitting, Hagerty. What the fuck does it look like?"

"Well, fuck me!"

Lydia stared at him for a moment, trying to think of a response that wasn't funny, but ended up saying nothing.

"So, what are you going to do after you quit? You got a degree in computer engineering. Great! So, you go to work for a big computer company or someplace like that, and you sit on your ass all day in front of a computer with a bunch of nerds staring at your tits because you're the only person in the room who's got them."

Lydia was now staring at the floor.

"Oh, I forgot! You're rich! You can do anything you want. Go on vacation anywhere in the world. Places like the south of France, Monaco, Greece, Venice, hook up with the rich and famous. But you would get tired of that in a hurry, Lydia, because the people you would meet in places like that have nothing but air in their fucking heads to keep them afloat."

Lydia looked up at him. "There are a lot of things I could do."

"Like what?"

"Try out for the Olympics."

"Fine, then go ahead and do that. Go out there and run your ass off and be a star for a few years. And then when you get old and wobbly, you'll sit around in a mansion somewhere looking at your trophies and thinking about your glory days."

Lydia didn't say anything in response.

"You need this job, Lydia. I don't have the money you have, but I love this job. But you need it more than I do. If you quit, you will piss your life away and have nothing to show for it."

Lydia looked up at him. "You're wrong, Hagerty," she said in a soft voice. "I've got problems you haven't dreamed of. I've got to get out of here."

"Ride with me, tonight and let's talk. Maybe, I can help."

"I don't need help."

"Okay, you don't need help. But I'm not going to let you walk out of here without you telling me what's going on. Ride with me. Just one more time. If you want to turn in your badge tonight, fine. Turn it in after the shift is over. But I need to know what's going on."

Lydia agreed to do just one more shift before quitting. She felt like she owed it to Hagerty who, along with Billy Vernor, tried to keep her out of trouble while working one of the most difficult jobs in the world.

When they got out of roll call and were heading for their assigned police car, Hagerty suddenly stopped and said, "Has Ferris let you drive yet?"

"No."

"You drive tonight. You think you can handle that?"

"I know how to drive."

"But you have never driven a police car, have you?"

"Come on, Hagerty. They put us behind the wheel of a police car at the Academy practicing traffic stops. We also went through a three-day pursuit driving course at the track on Terminal Island." She paused for a moment. "Why do you want me to drive?"

"Because I need to sit and listen to what you have to say without any distractions."

It was Monday night, one of the quietest nights of the week in Century Division, and they received no radio calls during the first two hours of the shift. Lydia told Hagerty about the deaths of Jonathan and Sofia and how she would inherit everything they owned. She then told him about the meeting she had earlier in the day with Maldonado and what he had told her about the problems facing her because of what she was inheriting. When Lydia told Hagerty that she refused to cooperate with Maldonado, he told her to pull the car over to the curb.

"Wait here."

Hagerty got out of the car. He took a cell phone out of his pocket and made a call.

Lydia rolled down a window to hear what he was saying, but the call was quick. When Hagerty got back into the police car, Lydia confronted him.

"What was that all about?"

"I had a talk with Morton. Told him I need to be off the air for an hour."

"Why?"

"I told him my probationer needs counselling." Hagerty smiled when he saw the look on Lydia's face. "Just kidding. Told him I had a stomach problem I needed to take care of."

Fifteen minutes later, they were sitting in the back corner of a coffee shop where they could talk without anyone overhearing.

"So," Hagerty asked, "why don't you want to work with Maldonado?"

Lydia thought for a moment before she answered. "Because, he's been manipulating me."

"How has he been manipulating you?"

Lydia thought long and hard before answering. She sure as hell didn't want to tell Hagerty about how Maldonado found the rope.

"He's been sucking up to me, because he thinks I can help him in his investigation into the mob."

"What's wrong with that? That's his job."

Lydia didn't respond,

"You need his help, Lydia," Hagerty continued. "What are you going to do when these people approach you?"

"I'll let my attorney handle it."

Hagerty looked away for a moment. "Lydia, you don't know what you're getting into. If you sell or give away those assets to the mob or even deal with them on your own, the Department might file criminal charges against you."

"For what?"

"For dealing with organized crime. For money laundering. For anything they can fucking dream of."

"I don't see how anyone could charge me with a crime if all I want to do is to get rid of Jonathan's property."

"Do you realize who these people are?"

"I don't know who they are. As a matter of fact, I don't give a shit who they are."

"They kill people, Lydia. It's what they do. If they have a problem, they kill whoever's causing it."

Lydia didn't respond.

"Look what happened to the Benedicts. They pissed someone off big time. They're dead because they fucked up."

Lydia nodded. Hagerty was right about that but wrong about who they had pissed off. She stared at the table for a long time.

Hagerty watched Lydia, hoping to get some type of acknowledgement from her that what he was saying was the truth. After five minutes, he leaned toward her.

"Look, Lydia. I sure as hell don't know if tonight is your last night on the job. But there is one thing I want you to know. If you ever need me to help you, whether you're on the job or not, call me. Will you promise me that?"

Lydia looked up at him. "I promise," she said in a quiet voice. "If I need your help, I'll call you."

Chapter Forty-Nine

THE REST of the night went by quickly. They took a stolen vehicle report from a popular singer whose Ferrari was taken from a valeted parking lot, they handled a family dispute where the wife got the best of her husband by hitting him over the head with a golf club, and they arrested a drunk who was annoying moviegoers in Westwood.

It was near the end of watch, and Lydia was slowly heading toward the station when she noticed that something caught Hagerty's eye just as she came to a stop for a red light at Olympic Boulevard.

Lydia followed Hagerty's eyes off to the left where a royal blue Corvette was parked facing eastbound on Olympic waiting for the light to change. It took Lydia a few seconds longer than Hagerty to process what she was seeing.

"Why did he stop when he has the green?" Lydia asked.

"He stopped when he saw us and then quickly looked away," Hagerty said as he tightened his seatbelt.

Lydia watched the man in the half-light behind the wheel of the car. He looked young, maybe in his early twenties, pale white skin.

The light turned green for Lydia.

"Don't move. Let's watch what he does," Hagerty said.

They were in the left turn lane and a driver behind them started blowing his horn when the light had changed. Hagerty reached over and turned on the police car's emergency lights.

The man behind the wheel of the Corvette turned his head sharply toward them. Seconds later, he punched the accelerator and the Corvette took off, wheels screaming, across the intersection against the light which had just turned red.

"Let's go get him," Hagerty said in a soft voice that he likely used when talking to his children at bedtime.

Lydia turned on the siren, looked to make sure traffic was clear on her right, and then turned the car eastbound on Olympic.

The Corvette was directly ahead of her, rapidly picking up speed.

Lydia felt a surge of adrenaline course through her veins. She was amazed at the calmness in Hagerty's voice as he spoke into the mike.

"Five-Adam-99 is in pursuit of a possible stolen vehicle. Eastbound on Olympic, approaching Randolph." Hagerty leaned over to Lydia. "You concentrate on driving. Let me worry about everything else."

"He's getting away from us," Lydia yelled. She felt her heart beating almost as fast as if she had just finished a 440 with hurdles.

"Concentrate on your driving," Hagerty said. "Nothing else! You drive. I broadcast. Concentrate on your driving and we'll catch him."

Lydia did what she was told. She tried to ignore the noise of the siren, the roar of the car's engine, the rushing by of brake lights of cars pulling to the side of the road. She tuned out what Hagerty was saying over the radio and the calm, measured response of the dispatcher and concentrated on her driving. She now felt calm inside, but it felt as if the goosebumps on her arms were on fire.

The brake lights of the Corvette quickly came on and the car made a quick left turn.

Hagerty was right about catching up with the Corvette. Lydia drove faster into the corner and was now forty yards behind the Corvette. For a moment, she realized she didn't even know what street she was on.

But she remembered Hagerty's instructions.

Concentrate on the driving and let me worry about everything else.

They were now on a long residential street with cars parked on both sides.

The Corvette came to an intersection without slowing down and bounced off a shallow drainage channel, setting up a shower of sparks that looked like a skyrocket had burst on the ground.

Lydia involuntarily slowed her car when she saw the Vette bottoming out.

Hagerty yelled at her. "Get back on the gas!"

She did so. The car bounced violently over the drainage channel, and a rooster tail of sparks from the rear of the car lit up the interior.

Ahead, the Vette made a right turn.

Lydia followed.

The Vette made another quick left turn onto another residential street and Lydia again followed at high speed, the wheels of the police car screaming as she oversteered into the turn. She was now twenty yards behind the Vette.

Then a silly thought crossed her mind.

He's so slow he should pull over and apply for a house number. Where had she heard that before?

Then she remembered. One of her coaches from UCLA had said that while watching a long-distance runner from USC. That same thought applied to the driver of the Corvette who did not know how to take a car into a corner without scrubbing off a lot of speed.

Hagerty suddenly yelled out, "Brakes!"

Lydia saw what he saw before he did. Up ahead, a car was backing out of a driveway onto the street.

The Vette slammed into the rear of the car and spun it sideways.

Lydia hit the brakes and slid to a stop a few feet behind the Corvette.

The driver of the Corvette was out of the car and running south toward the driveway of the nearest house.

Forgetting about the suspect, Lydia jumped out of the police car and ran toward the car that had been hit.

It was a small Toyota.

Lydia looked in the window on the passenger side and saw a teenage girl behind the wheel. She was conscious but was holding her head with both hands and looking down.

Lydia ran around the car to the driver's side and opened the door. "Are you all right?"

"Somebody hit me," the girl mumbled.

Her head was bleeding.

"Don't move," Lydia said. "I'll get an ambulance."

Lydia stood up and looked around. Hagerty was nowhere to be seen. She could hear dogs barking off to the south.

A woman came out of the nearest house and Lydia yelled at her to call an ambulance. The woman stood there, frozen.

Lydia noted the house number, got in her car, and backed up to the end of the street where she could see the street name. She rolled down her window and listened. Dogs were barking to the southeast of her.

She again picked up her mike. "Five-Adam-99. Officers need assistance. My partner is in foot pursuit of a hit and run felony suspect in the neighborhood south of Blair and Lyon. Request an ambulance for an injured driver."

Lydia began driving south on Lyon. She had no problem tracking Hagerty's foot pursuit by the barking of the dogs. When she got to the point where the barking was directly to her left, she drove down to the next street and stopped her car in the intersection.

Six houses to the east, Lydia saw a dark figure run out of a driveway, cross the street, and enter the driveway of the next house over. Seconds later, she saw the tall figure of Hagerty running across the street chasing the suspect.

Lydia drove down two more streets and turned left hoping to intercept the suspect as he emerged from the next row of houses. She got out of the car and listened. A dog was barking behind the house nearest her, but abruptly stopped. Then all was quiet.

She looked down the street.

No suspect. No Hagerty.

Where in hell had they gone?

Lydia grabbed her flashlight and ran down the driveway of the house where she heard the dog. A chain link fence with a padlocked gate did not present a problem for her. She lofted herself over the gate and into the backyard.

She looked around. The houses in this area were World War II starter homes with little or no landscaping. Bare chain link fences separated each backyard.

In the distance was the rising sound of a siren, an ambulance from the sound of it.

Lydia felt something soft touch the back of her hand. A big wooly dog had come alongside her and was licking her hand.

"Where did they go, boy?" Lydia asked.
About four houses to the east, a backyard light came on.
Seconds later, she heard Hagerty yelling.
"Put that gun down, boy, now!"
Lydia began running toward the light.

The Final Chapter

WHEN HAGERTY saw the suspect bail out of the Corvette, he jumped out of the police car and ran after him. The suspect first ran east past the Toyota and then turned south into the driveway of the nearest house. Hagerty went after him, confident that Lydia would check on the condition of the driver of the car that had been hit.

The suspect ran through an open gate into the backyard. Hagerty went after him and entered the backyard just as the boy, using his hands, lofted himself over a chain link fence into the next yard. Hagerty followed and chased the suspect south through the backyard and onto the next street.

When the suspect ran out into the street under the illumination of a street lamp, Hagerty could see that the suspect he was chasing was small. He was likely a teenager…maybe even a girl.

The suspect ran into the driveway of the house across the street and crashed through a gate made of split redwood so hard that it fell off its hinges.

Hagerty followed.

Three blocks and five backyards later, Hagerty lofted himself over another fence into a back yard that was suddenly lit up by security lights mounted on the eave of the house.

The suspect had stopped and was on his knees in the grass. He was facing Hagerty and breathing heavily.

It was a boy, maybe sixteen-years of age, his eyes on fire with distress.

He rose to his feet and pointed a revolver at Hagerty.

His gun hand was trembling.

"Go away. I don't want to shoot you." the boy said, his voice shaky with fear and exhaustion.

"Put the gun down," Hagerty said calmly. His right hand was paused not more than six inches away from the grip of his .357 Magnum.

"Go away!"

"It's over, boy. Put the gun down."

"I will shoot you if you don't go away." The boy's voice was high-pitched. He sounded hysterical.

"Put that gun down, boy, now!" Hagerty repeated, this time in a louder voice.

The boy raised the gun and pointed it at Hagerty's chest. "Leave me alone." He shut his eyes and began pulling the trigger.

The chain link fences between Lydia and the backyard where the suspect had surprised Hagerty were four feet high. The hurdles that Lydia ran in NCAA competition were just short of three feet. The taller height of the chain link fence didn't enter Lydia's mind when she began running.

She leapt over the first fence with ease, landed in the soft grass, and sprinted toward the next fence.

There were three more fences to go before she reached the backyard where Hagerty was in a stand-off with the suspect.

Lydia set up a pattern, running as fast as she could, ignoring the extra weight of the police utility belt and body armor, gauging the height of each of the fences, and cleanly vaulting over each of them in turn.

The boy didn't see Lydia coming, but Hagerty did. He caught a blur of motion out of the corner of his eye. At first, he thought it was some large animal that had lofted itself over the fence. He was relieved when he saw it was Lydia.

Lydia without hesitation quickly closed the gap before the boy realized she was there. She lowered her head and hit the boy like a defensive line-man blindsiding a quarterback. They both fell to the ground with Lydia on top of him. The boy turned underneath her, trying to bring his gun up to shoot her.

Lydia smacked the boy across the side of his face with her flashlight. "Lie still, you little bastard!"

Hagerty ran forward and kicked the gun out of the boy's hand.

Lydia put a knee into the boy's back and pushed his face into the grass with her right hand and held it there. She looked up at Hagerty. "Are you all right?"

"Damn straight. Are *you* all right?"

A big smile broke out on her face, the backyard light shining on her face. "God, that was fun."

"He would have shot me if you hadn't come over the fence like that," Hagerty said.

"But he didn't," Lydia said. She heard a helicopter approaching from a distance. "Come on, Hagerty. Just don't stand there. Tell me if this wasn't one of the most exciting moments in your life."

"It was, Lydia, but you need to let that boy get his face out of the grass before you smother him to death."

Before heading to the station with their prisoner, they stopped to make sure the girl in the car that had been hit by the Corvette was receiving medical attention and that a traffic unit was on the way to take a traffic accident report.

The Corvette turned out to be stolen and so was the gun the kid had pointed at Hagerty. The boy had just robbed a liquor store. That meant extra reports and overtime.

Four hours later, Hagerty stopped Lydia as they were heading for their cars in the parking lot behind the station.

"Didn't you forget something?"

Lydia stared at him for a moment. "What?"

"You forgot to turn in your badge and I.D."

Lydia smiled. "So, I did."

Lydia noticed she had a message on her cell phone before she went to bed that night. She opened it.

There was no text. Just a picture taken during daylight hours.

It was a picture of a coiled rope laid out on the dirt.

It was burning.

Lydia went to bed and slept well that night, secure in the feeling that she had friends in the Department. She dreamt about Jeremy Morgan. It was the first time she had dreamt about a man in a long time.

Author's Bio

Ted Kozak is a proud veteran of the United States Marine Corps. He served for nearly twenty-six years with the Los Angeles Police Department where he once had a tour of duty as the Commanding Officer of the 77th Street Detective Division. On retiring from the Department, he worked for ten years as an attorney in California and another ten years in Kentucky. He lives in rural Kentucky with his wife and two dogs.

This is his sixth novel. He is the author of Charlie Wolf's Revenge, Charlie Wolf's Justice, The Messiah's Spy, Alex and Christina—Saving Lumenaria, and Teresa—The Snake Witch

Lydia Harte has a supporting role in *Charlie Wolf's Justice* as the leader of Apache Platoon making a forcible entry into a building occupied by armed felony suspects.

The author can be contacted at ted12kozak@gmail.com.

www.ingramcontent.com/pod-product-compliance
Lightning Source LLC
Chambersburg PA
CBHW030646020726
47493CB00006B/1894